OATH OF DUTY

AUDACITY SAGA
BOOK 5

R. K. THORNE

IRON ANTLER
BOOKS

Edited by Holloway House

Cover design by Mibl Art

Cover art by Julie Dillon

Beta read by Steve Martinez and friends

Immense gratitude to you all.

Version 1.03

❀ Created with Vellum

For my dad, for showing me the importance of duty and responsibility and teaching me to always recognize the humanity in others.

AUDACITY SAGA | BOOK 5

OATH OF DUTY

R. K. THORNE

PROLOGUE

SIX BLONDE WOMEN stood at the edge of the water, steel beneath their feet, water lapping against the edge of the enormous tank below.

"We shouldn't have trusted Davenmore to kill her," one said. Her eyes, nearly black, glinted with anger.

"There is always a risk of failure in any operation," said another. She was nearly identical to the first woman, save for a small scar by her eyebrow. "Our calculations had suggested chances were good."

"Well, the calculations were wrong. It didn't work." The dark, angry eyes smoldered as the first woman glared off into the distance.

"So?" A third woman shrugged. She, too, resembled the others almost exactly, except for a single blemish, a bruise on her left temple that never seemed to fade away. "Why does the deserter concern us so much? Let her come. We will crush her."

"Yes, let her come," chimed in a fourth, another perfect replica aside from a misshapen twist to her nose that left her looking especially cruel. "We are in agreement, are we not?"

Indeed, the women talked to each other, but they were one mind, thinking aloud.

"We are too many," said the bruised one. "It is far too late for her to stop us."

"Be practical," chided the scarred woman. "She knows our location. That means she can attack us at our heart. The fewer people who can attack us, the better. The logic is extremely simple. Limiting the knowledge of our location is only expedient."

"Let us kill her then," offered the fourth, wrinkling her twisted nose.

"Fine." The scarred one waved her hand. "But if not through Davenmore, then how?"

"We have options."

"But the deserter can't reach us," pointed out a fifth. This one, too, was an apparent mirror image of the others, aside from a poor posture that left her seeming shorter than the rest. "She's in Union custody. They are taking her to trial at the Inner Planets, a trial over which we have plenty of control."

The angry-eyed one jabbed a finger. "And at this trial, she could tell the Union—along with the rest of the galaxy—everything she knows."

"Our agents can prevent that," said the scarred one calmly.

"Can we be sure?" Her angry eyes pinned each of them in turn in their bitterness. "We must not allow them to discover *any* part of our infiltration. Our takeover is not yet complete. Much progress would be lost."

"Hmm. Colonel Tauber has shown us he is not fully in control of the situation," the bruised one granted. "How can we be sure our agents on the Inner Planets will be successful? What if they fail as well?"

The slouching one nodded. "True. Humans are so likely to overestimate their potency."

The one with the angry eyes balled a hand into a fist and punched it into her other palm. "We must move to act ourselves. If we prevent the trial from happening, we can be certain. Let the knowledge of us die with the deserter.

"Ellen Ryu," whispered a sixth.

"Shut up. There's no need to say it," snapped the first.

"This is Mother's fault. Mother's betrayal—" started the bruised one.

The second with the scar cut her off. "Her betrayal cannot be undone, but we can repair the damage."

"Yes. Yes. It must end." The fifth one slouched further, as if all her nodding sank her deeper into the steel beneath them.

"Loose ends. Too many of them." The fourth one shook her head, twisted nose and all.

"Yes." There was still anger in the eyes of the first as she smiled, a cold and brutal smile. "End it shall."

CHAPTER ONE

JENNY OPENED HER EYES. The mural on the ceiling of sick bay loomed above her. She blinked. Where was she? What had happened? Pain between her eyes made her wince.

The last thing she remembered was metal grating in her face. The rush of people around her, Dane and Ryu. Adan's panicked voice on the comm. Throwing up sea water that tasted like acid.

Oh. Right. She'd barely escaped from that horrific underwater lab. Her suit had cracked from the beating she'd taken, and the leaks had slowly bathed her in ocean water. *Dirty* ocean water.

Apparently, dirty enough to give her a headache and a vacation in sick bay. For how long?

Adan. She tried to look around for someone nearby, a comm unit, but nobody was there.

"Xi," she whispered. Her lips felt like they hadn't parted in ages. Her throat was dry.

"How can I help?" came the reassuring reply.

"Is—" Her voice caught in her throat, choking her with coughs for a moment. Too dry. "Is—Adan—flying?"

A metal compartment slid open in the wall beside her care unit, a platform extending. A cylinder of water. She groped for it, feeling like she was reaching through wet sand rather than air. She chugged it down when she got it to her lips. Roughly. Some spilled. She didn't care.

"Adan is indeed currently flying. Would you like me to inform him that you are awake? Or do you need more rest?"

"I—I don't know." She lay back and closed her eyes. Somehow, she felt exhausted. "I do need more rest, but… But I want to see him." Would it scare him to see her so weak? So dirty…? Hell, she probably looked terrible.

"I will inform him. I can take the wheel for a few minutes, so to speak."

Not that Xi was ever far from control of the ship. But some tasks required pilots and others required machines.

She let her eyes wander across the landscape that Zhia had painted above while she waited—rolling grassy hills, dotted with clumps of lavender bushes here and there. A small cottage in the distance. She always wondered why this, why here, what exactly had motivated Zhia to choose this subject to paint in sick bay. Asking about it once had afforded her nothing but a noncommittal shrug. If Zhia had a reason, she wasn't telling.

Soft humming, quiet repetitive beeps, the rushing of the ventilation formed a womblike rhythm that was a little calming, albeit a little scary that it was necessary.

She was just nodding off when she heard the hatch hiss open.

"You're awake!"

She tried to turn her head and find him. Her vision blurred, and her head spun. She held still until it steadied. Maybe she wasn't supposed to be awake yet.

Her hand was in his. Her vision cleared to see his worried frown hovering above her.

"Yeah, I guess you could say that."

"How are you feeling?"

"I… I don't think going for a walk is an option yet." She didn't feel any pain in her limbs, but they felt heavy, leaden. She didn't need one of the doctors here to tell her she needed more rest. "Where are we? How long has it been?"

"It feels like it's been forever. We'll have to ask Levereaux."

"You didn't worry about me too much, did you?"

"Not at all. I've been completely calm and cool-headed." A smile tugged at the corner of his mouth.

"He is barely sleeping," Xi interjected.

Adan only grinned wider.

"Am I... Am I going to be okay?"

"Yeah," he said. "Levereaux said you're going to be fine. She can tell you better than I could." Some worry wrinkles at the corners of his eyes meant that he either didn't believe it, or maybe the truth was a little more complicated than that, but maybe it didn't really matter right now.

"Did we get any data from that hellhole? Can I talk to Ryu?" she asked.

His eyes widened slightly. "Oh. Um. A lot can happen in five days."

She frowned, even though it hurt to frown. "What do you mean?"

"Um... Union ships ambushed us right after you went down. The commander eventually... turned herself in to secure our safe passage out of there."

"She *what*?" The beeping somewhere spiked faster. Her body ached as she jolted a bit at his words. "What in the—"

"I know. We're all reeling a bit. The battle lasted a long time though. It was pretty brutal. There was no other option anyone could think of. And I still hate it."

"We've got to get her back."

The hatch hissed open, and Zhia strode in. "You're fragging right, Corporal. And we will. But first, we've got repairs to make. And we've got to resupply. We were beaten pretty hard back there. Almost as hard as you were by those ocean robots."

Jenny flushed a little. "I seem to recall giving a few beatings of my own."

"I hope their circuits are totally fried and underwater at the moment." Zhia smiled, but her heart wasn't in it. Much more than the usual amount of worry weighed down her face. "But it won't matter to us, because we have no reason to go back."

"Where are we headed now? If not to rescue Ellen?"

"Molyarch," Adan replied. "I should get back to the bridge." He glanced regretfully at Zhia, and Jenny knew what he meant. It would have been nice to have more than a few seconds alone. Although, could one really be alone, with all the sensors in sick bay? Dr. Levereaux probably had a live vid feed.

Yeah, she should probably keep that in mind when her arms actually started working again and maybe wait till she was in her own cabin to tackle him.

"Thanks for coming down."

He kissed the back of her hand, winked a promise for later, and left.

Zhia watched him go. "Some medicines are chemical, some are more... visual." She smiled as she met Jenny's eyes. "Is there anything you need?"

"I need to be better. So I can go kick the ass of whoever is imprisoning my commander."

"That is precisely my plan. As soon as we can get all the burns and bashes in our hull fixed."

Jenny winced. "I thought I was the only one that got beat up on that ocean hell hole."

"You were, but the *Audacity* didn't want to miss out on the fun. We had to fly *away* from the ocean hell hole too."

Jenny sobered. "But really. The Union has her? How do we even know if she's still alive?"

"Doug has been able to... gain access to their prisoner manifest. And he has a tracking device on our fighter as well. Well, several of them. They appear to be okay."

"Wait... they?"

"Kael went with her. Even though she told him not to. Ordered him not to."

She snorted. "Typical. Admirable. Stupid, suicidal, irrational, but admirable."

"I don't know what's going to happen to them, but as soon as we're fully operational, and we've dropped off some of our civilians, we'll be on their tail. I hope I can count on you to be holding a rifle by then."

Gradually, it dawned on her that Zhia was here not out of boredom or out of casual concern but because someone truly needed to figure out just how many fighters the *Audacity* had to work with. And that person was standing right in front of her. In her head, Jenny did the math. If they dropped off the civvies, they wouldn't be able to leave them totally alone and undefended, with no security. So they'd be dividing their force, one way or another, and there was no way to make those numbers look particularly good.

Jenny swallowed. "Are you… You're commander now, with Ryu gone?"

Zhia nodded.

She lifted her chin. "I will do my best, Commander."

"Ryu deserves nothing less. Now get some rest."

ELLEN STRUGGLED NOT to squint as the sick-bay doc shined a light in each eye. Instead, she tried to focus on the woman's short, spiky, black hair. When she'd turned herself in to the Union ship the *Everest* —and its captain and her ex, Paul Dealis—she had expected to either get shot or end up in the brig.

But sick bay? That hadn't been on her bingo card.

The doc leaned back and smiled. "Looks like you're good to go. No signs of concussion. You're a little dehydrated, though." She gestured to a nurse who grabbed several ration bars and a water tube and brought them over.

"Now, let me just check out your friend here," the doctor said brightly, stepping to the side.

Kael sat to Ellen's left on the bench just inside sick bay. More like a visitors' bench, surely it wasn't usually intended for examining patients, but the place was swamped. The diagnostic machine had been wheeled over and had given her a thumbs-up in a few seconds, but then they'd wheeled it to inspect Kael as the doc finished her examination. It was still working on him.

Doc Spiky paged through the readouts. Ellen ripped open one of the rat bars and started munching, trying to pretend she wasn't watching the doc like a hawk.

It was only a breath or two before the woman went abruptly still. "I—uh—oh, I see."

"Concussion, Doctor?" Ellen prompted, trying to keep her voice from going cold. "Is there a concussion?"

This was exactly why Kael shouldn't have come. One stupid medical scan, and they could have him shipped straight back to the Inner Planets for examination. Or interrogation. Or dissection. Or she didn't even know what.

Yamamoto had already noticed Kael's secret. Davenmore was the reason they were in sick bay in the first place. The bastard had set a trap at the rendezvous point where he *should* have received his reward for turning the *Audacity* over to the Union.

Only instead of Davenmore, there had been a cannon turret. Just his style, really. Thank God her ex, Paul, had refused to execute her on sight. Davenmore hadn't taken kindly to all that.

A blast from the cannon turret had been followed by a barrage of hacks into the *Everest*'s info systems—killing the sensors, dropping the shields, and leaving three dead. At least.

Kael had chosen to use his kinetic abilities to send the cursed turret careening into the deep. But not without risk—or without Yamamoto noticing.

Yamamoto, out of gratitude, had promised to forget the matter after informing Paul. She couldn't really ask for more than that.

But now here was this doctor, wide-eyed and tugging on her black hair absently as she ogled whatever madness was coming up on her scans.

Of course, Ellen had been in that same position once, too,

although probably with better instruments. During her first conversation with Kael, so long ago, she'd been scanning over the extensive list of augmentations that made him… well, more than what he seemed.

That had been a long time ago. And what had really made him more than what he seemed wouldn't come up on any medical scan.

"Uh, no sign of a concussion, I think," Doc Spiky said, her voice quavering. She glanced over her shoulder at Kael, but his eyes were on the floor. "I—um—" Her eyes flicked to Ellen since Kael was avoiding her gaze. "I'm not sure I'm capable of evaluating if *all* systems are go, if you know what I mean."

Ellen swallowed and nodded once, crisply. Doctors weren't mechanics, but she had an unsettling feeling that Doc Spiky was trying to figure out if she was Kael's owner.

"Do you eat?" Doc Spiky asked him, head tilting to the side. She had pretty, intelligent green eyes.

Kael looked up as if finally noticing her and blinked. "What?"

"Do you—"

"Yeah," Ellen cut in, as she saw one of the med tech's starting to tune into the odd conversation. "He's a man, not a flyer, Doctor. I'm sure they'll have more rations for us in the brig. Can we go now?"

"I can't be sure he's… stable," Doc Spiky said, folding her arms. Maybe she wasn't announcing Kael's augmentations over the ship comm system, but the doc wasn't letting Ellen off that easily.

Ellen gritted her teeth. "He's recently had an extensive medical review with Dr. Alexandra Dremer, along with some, uh, custom medical treatments. If you'd look her up, I think you'll find he's stable enough that a little bump on the head won't upset the ration cart."

Doc Spiky narrowed those perceptive green eyes, but she nodded once, brusquely.

"Thank you for checking us over, Doc." Ellen rose, hoping she could end the conversation and that Kael truly *was* okay. He didn't seem like it, but if she couldn't find it on his scans, she probably couldn't help him. "I'm sure you have other patients to attend to."

Grumbles and shouts from the corridor underscored her comment. The jostling of the ship when Davenmore's hack had disrupted grav systems had left a line of minor injuries out the sick-bay door.

Doc Spiky bit her lip, then glanced back at Kael's diagnostics, then back at Kael, almost hungrily. She wanted to know more. That was bad.

Ellen waved to Yamamoto, who was hovering outside the examination room where they were treating Paul. "Lieutenant, we're done here."

Kael followed her lead and rose. "Thanks, Doc."

Yamamoto started toward them, but before he could reach them, Bridell came pushing through the crowd outside.

Doc Spiky held up a palm. "You'll have to wait in line—"

"I'm not here for treatment." He huffed, straightening his jacket. "I'm here for them."

Yamamoto joined them. "Excuse me, Bridell? I will be escorting them to the brig personally."

"Sir, I think this latest attack merits further questioning, don't you?"

Yamamoto eyed Bridell for a moment. "Further questioning as to what?"

"As to the clearly personal nature of the attack. We need to hunt down that Davenmore now too. Maybe they can help us find him."

Something about the words seemed off, like merely an excuse. Yamamoto seemed unconvinced, too, but he glanced back over his shoulder to where they were working on Paul.

Bridell spread his hands. "They'll just be rotting in the brig anyway."

"I beg your pardon," she said. "I have no plans to rot."

They both ignored her. Yamamoto didn't look like he liked it, but he nodded. "Fine. You have one hour."

"I'll question them separately. I will have a private escort this one to the brig, and then—"

"No." Yamamoto cut his hand through the air. "I'll take him."

"All right, then." Bridell smirked a little, like he thought the insistence was silly, but he stabbed a finger at Ellen. "You—come with me."

She gave Kael one last nod goodbye and followed, trying to ignore the sick feeling in her gut that said this wasn't good.

THE INTERROGATION ROOM was as beat up as the rest of the *Everest*. The metal flooring was at least three different colors, but not because of any particular design. What chemical reaction had created the pattern, she had no idea.

A half-orb vid cam was perched in the upper right corner of the room, a tiny green light indicating it was watching.

She sat down in one of the two chairs, and the metal groaned. The small table in front of her had a smattering of dents and what looked like a slew of knife marks. Either this table had seen some kind of crazy fighting, or it had also been a kitchen work surface. She had no idea at this point.

Bridell started to pace. "Well, well. Ellen Ryu. I have so many questions and so little time."

"I don't have much to say," she said. "An hour should be plenty. I don't know anything more about Davenmore than you do."

He was shaking his head as he withdrew a small device from his pocket. Oddly, he strode casually toward the door.

"So, we're done here?" She started to rise.

He gave her a strange, smirking smile over his shoulder as he pressed the device *over* the palm pad. There was a hissing sound, a grinding, then the light over the door went out.

She glanced up just quickly enough to see the light near the vid cam flicker out too. Yep, her gut was right. Not good.

"This ship. Always falling apart." He grinned, his hands going into his pockets as he strode toward the table.

She sank back into her seat.

His hands came to rest on the back of the other seat. "Shame the camera has failed and the door no longer opens. All at the same time. They really should decommission this hunk of scrap."

"A little suspicious, if you ask me," she said dryly.

Was he going to try to kill her? He didn't look in bad shape, but she liked her odds, even cuffed.

He drew out a new device, though, and set it on the table. The style of the design looked familiar.

She swallowed. "That's not Union tech."

"You are a quick one. They didn't lie about that."

"Who are *they*, exactly?" She took a deep breath through her nose. Steady.

"It doesn't matter. You won't remember this when I'm done with you anyway." He switched on the device.

She gritted her teeth. "There aren't many ways to remove memories. None of them are ethical."

"Ethical." He laughed. "Don't lecture me, deserter. Now tell me. Where did you find this Kael Sidassian?"

"Excuse me? You said you were going to interrogate me about Quentin Davenmore."

"I lied. Where did you find Kael Sidassian?"

"At the ass end of nowhere. What's it matter to you?"

"I see." His grip tightened on the back of the other chair. "What's your relationship with him, then?"

"He is my lieutenant."

"What *else* is he?"

"I don't see why it should be any of your fragging business."

"It is my business because he stole something, and it's my mission to get it back." He shook his head, muscles in his jaw clenching. "Where is the capsule he had in his possession when you met him?"

"What capsule?" She did her best to look like she had no idea what he meant. "Like, medicine or something? Where would we hide anything we took from sick bay? Just go pat him down, for heck's sake."

"Tell me, or I'll kill him when I'm done with you."

"What? Over some lost chems?" She looked as lost as she could manage. But Bridell killing Kael wasn't much of a threat. If she liked her own odds in a fight, Kael would be no contest.

"This is *not* over some lost chems, and you know that," he growled.

She had the sense he might have thrown the chair at the wall had it not been bolted to the floor. Instead, he started pacing.

She rolled her eyes. "I don't have one flying flip what you're talking about."

He started cracking his knuckles as he paced, around and around, going behind her then back in front again. She kept her eyes trained on the door, listening for anyone outside she could signal to. She heard nothing.

"We can do this easy, or we can do this hard," he said quietly. "But you *are* going to tell me where the Empress Capsule is."

A cold settled in her stomach as she realized. "You're an Enhancer spy. You're not a Union officer at all."

"And *you're* not as brilliant as they say—I lied. Now. The capsule. Where is it?" He circled around behind her again.

"I have no idea what you're—"

He cuffed her across the back of her head.

Scratch that concussion-free status. She braced herself against the table, trying not to show the pain.

"Tell me," he ordered. "Where is the capsule?"

"Slag off."

He was probably going to hit her again—somewhere that he could blame on her fall during the ship attack, she realized—but a pounding shook the door to the corridor.

Lieutenant Yamamoto's voice. "Bridell!"

When he spoke, his voice was just next to her ear. "This isn't over, Ryu."

She opened her mouth to respond but froze. The sharp prick of a needle entering the back of her neck sent pain shooting through her limbs, up into her skull.

Her head spun like she *did* have a concussion even as she heard him removing the devices, opening the door, and greeting Yamamoto.

"Yes, I don't think Dr. Ovigal is correct, sir. She may have a concussion or cranial bleeding. Quite a bit of exhaustion and confusion just started. Perhaps she needs to rest."

Yamamoto's face was too blurry to make out if he bought it. She hoped he didn't. What a bunch of horse vomit.

She clawed at the strands of reality, of clarity, as the whole world grew fuzzy around her. Whatever had just happened slid sideways, the memories slipping through her hands like grains of sand.

KAEL STOOD BOLT UPRIGHT. He wasn't sure how many minutes he'd been waiting alone in the brig, but every single one of them had driven him crazy. Bridell was waltzing in, whistling—and carrying a limp Ellen in his arms.

"What in the seven suns did you do to her?" Kael demanded. It was all he could do to keep from launching himself at the force field. He'd have to settle for visualizing tearing Bridell limb from limb.

"Relax." Bridell sneered. "She got hit in the head, remember?"

"Not *that* hard." Kael had been hit much harder. He'd *like* to hit Bridell even harder than that. "Unless you added insult to injury?"

"She fell asleep during questioning. Been a long day. I took her past sick bay, and Doc said Ryu had more of a hit to the head than she'd realized. She'll sleep it off." As he spoke, their guard opened the cell beside Kael's, and Bridell carried her in.

Frag, they weren't even going to be in the same cell. His hands balled into fists. "You're so full of shit, Bridell."

"Is that so?" He grinned as he set her down on the slab of a bench, strode out, and enabled the force field. "Glad you think so. Because it's your turn next."

"I don't think so." The hatch to the brig slid open to reveal Yamamoto. Shu stood behind him. "Bridell, you're wanted in Engineering."

"But, sir, we need to follow these leads—"

"Shu will interrogate Lieutenant Rhee about Mr. Davenmore. Your methods of interrogation seem… a bit stressful on your captives."

"Hey, it's not my fault she had a concussion."

"And I'm sure the equipment malfunction in the facility was not your fault either." Yamamoto narrowed his eyes.

"Equipment malfunction?" The words snuck out of Kael's mouth between clenched teeth. He really didn't want to clue them in to what he could do with his telekinetic powers just yet, but, damn, it'd feel good to slam Bridell into that force field until he was unconscious too. See how *he* liked a concussion.

Yamamoto glared at Kael. "Sit down, sir." Then he locked eyes with Bridell. The two officers stared each other down like they'd much rather stare each other to death than carry on with the day.

Bridell broke first. Lifting his chin, he stalked past Yamamoto, muttering a "yes, sir" under his breath.

The tension eased in the brig as the hatch slid closed. Yamamoto played with something in his pocket, withdrawing a small handful of candies and offering one to Shu.

She blinked at the glossy red candy, then shook her head minutely. She gave Kael a long look, then approached.

He kept looking back and forth between her and Ellen. "Is she okay? Is she going to be okay? What did that asshole do to her?"

"Her vital signs are normal," offered the guard at the desk.

"Oh, how comforting." Kael scowled, not taking his eyes off Ellen now. She was breathing, wasn't she? Were there any new cuts or bruises? At this angle, he couldn't get a clear look at her face.

It was all he could do to keep from pressing himself against the plexi between their two cells. Who needed dignity? He needed to know. He could definitely break through plexi if he wanted to. But if he did, they might replace it with steel. Honestly, a lot of prisoners could probably break through this plexi with just a little effort and ingenuity, so maybe it had hidden reinforcement.

Or maybe they didn't care if the prisoners broke through to each other as long as they didn't get out.

Shu cleared her throat. "Lieutenant Rhee, how well do you know Quentin Davenmore?"

Kael spared her a split-second glance. "Never met him."

"But you'd caused some trouble for him on Faros?"

"Yeah. He and his girlfriend were hatching some kind of interplanetary banking monopoly scheme thing— Are you *sure* she's all right?"

"No," Shu said flatly. "The sooner you answer my questions, the sooner I'll be free to check on her properly."

He scowled at her, enraged. As if her stupid questions about that spoiled billionaire asshole mattered more than a woman's life.

"Fine," he said through gritted teeth. "Ask your questions."

"Who was his girlfriend?"

"Amiri Barakat."

"If you didn't know them, how did you cross paths?"

"We had a job on Faros, heard she might be in trouble, too, so we swung by."

"And was she in trouble?"

"No. That turned out to be a trap. She *was* the trouble."

"I see. And were you involved in her assassination?"

"Assassination? No. I wasn't there. But my team was."

"Was Ellen?"

"I believe so, but I can't be sure."

"So Davenmore wanted revenge?"

"Maybe. Or he wanted more than one of the bounties on her head. But he seems like he's got plenty of money. Did he ever work with the Songbirds?"

She raised an eyebrow. "We have no record of a known connection. That doesn't mean that he didn't. We don't know most of what they do."

"You do believe her, don't you?" he asked.

"About what?"

"About the Songbird program being part of the Union. It tears her up that this all happened. She hates it."

"Hates what?"

"Hates she had to… leave."

Shu was silent for so long, he thought she might turn and leave without saying another word. Maybe he'd offended her. "Had to" was definitely a matter of opinion, at least to some. Yamamoto was waiting by the door, rolling one of his candies around in his mouth. His eyes were on Ellen, though.

Finally, after at least six eons, Shu spoke. "I don't simply believe people, Lieutenant. I prefer to rely on facts."

"Then get the facts," he shot back. "If you can. But news flash, people don't always carefully record the complete truth for you to easily look up in a database."

"Especially not if what they did was reprehensible," murmured Yamamoto.

Shu arched an eyebrow at him.

Kael tried again. "There's no punishment you can give her for desertion that's worse than how much she punishes herself. She would never have left if it hadn't been for that damn program."

"Hmm. I guess we'll see." And with that, Shu motioned for the guard to open the force field so she could check on Ellen.

Kael leaned his head back and stared at the ceiling. If defeating the Songbirds relied on these people, the battle was going to be up hill indeed.

CHAPTER TWO

"I WON'T LEAVE!" Shirin's voice rang out as Zhia strode up the hallway. "You can't make me!"

"Now, Shirin. Please. Listen to logic. It won't be safe." Dr. Levereaux was trying to sound reasonable, but to Zhia's ears—and probably Shirin's—she sounded more exasperated than persuasive.

Feet were coming up the ladder. Zhia noted Vivaan was heading up to the third level, with nothing much to say to her. There wasn't much up there to be concerned with, but Xi would keep an eye on him.

"You're not abandoning me on some stinking rusty space station full of pirates and rats!" Something pounded against the deck. Possibly a girl's foot stomping.

"It's not full of pirates exactly, and we're not abandoning—"

"So it *is* stinking and rusty and full of rats!"

"I think stinking is a matter of olfactory perspective."

"What does that even *mean*?"

"You won't be alone. They'll be loads of others with you, including Mr. and Mrs. Simmons, Dr. Taylor, Dr. Persad—" Levereaux froze as Zhia appeared in the open hatch. Yes, she was a brilliant geneticist, but child psychology? A whole unindexed encyclopedia for the poor woman. Which was fair because she hadn't exactly grown up around other children. Enhancers didn't care about every aspect of development in their experimental clones.

"Why don't you let me try?" Zhia said, folding her arms with a smile.

Levereaux looked immediately relieved, but she turned stern, concerned eyes on Shirin. "Listen to Commander Zhia, Shirin. She knows what's best for you."

Shirin had been standing when Zhia arrived, and she'd frozen in place, too, but at those words, she shrank back onto her bunk like a crab scuttling back into its cave. She didn't say anything, just glared at a tablet that she drew onto her lap and took a sip of a green juice from beside her. All with a massive frown.

Levereaux wilted a little, eyes on her shoes as she straightened. She slipped defeated out of the cabin.

Zhia ambled in but deliberately didn't take the one other seat where Levereaux had been sitting. She leaned against the wall near Shirin's bunk instead. "What do you have there?" she asked, pointing.

"A spinach smoothie."

"Is it good?"

"No, but Xi tells me I need to drink it anyway. See? I listen about some things."

"She's pretty hard to argue with."

"Xi? Yeah."

"I was actually asking about the tablet, though."

"Oh, this?" Shirin's grin was a little smug. "Just compiling a list of all the reasons why you need me to stay on the ship."

Zhia raised her eyebrows. "Okay, let's have it."

"Well, it's still a work in progress."

"I get that. But you can share with me. I won't judge."

"Sure." Shirin gave her a dubious eye roll. "I heard what she said. You know what's best for me, and all that. What difference would it make."

The corner of Zhia's mouth quirked in a smile. "There's nothing on your list yet, is there?"

Shirin chuckled, but her brow furrowed too. "I have a *few* things. For example, somebody has to drink all these spinach smoothies Amaya keeps making."

"Ohh, good one. Anything else?"

"I play with Roya. And *she's* staying."

"Yes, the empress is staying aboard. That's different."

"I also provide excellent cheerleading and moral support."

"When you're not fighting with Dr. Levereaux."

"Well, yeah. But lots of the folks around here like me. I think." She glanced down. Zhia was quite positive that Shirin was not at all sure of that claim. "People are friendly."

"Maybe you should learn an instrument," Zhia mused. "Play a trumpet. Pound a war drum for us or something."

The girl snorted. Then she took a deep breath, and all the next words came out in a rushed jumble. "I've also put down that my training isn't complete yet, and that I don't want to lose track of my dad, and I've never really had a home before, and I'm not excited about losing this one. But those last two are not really about me helping the *team* exactly, which is what my list is supposed to be, so I should probably delete those, but they seem important."

Zhia paused for a breath. "You really want to stay, don't you?"

Her eyes were earnest and wide when she looked up from the screen. "Yeah. Are you going to make me leave?"

"I did want to talk to you about that."

"Look, I can see from my list maybe I'm not pulling my weight as part of the, um, what do you call it?"

"The crew?"

"Yes, the crew. But maybe there's more I can do to help out. I can work really hard. I can work for eighteen hours straight. I used to do it all the time. Twenty-two, no problem, but then I need a break afterward, but not a huge one. I can scrub things, you know. And I can lift heavy things and type and clean and I can—"

"It's not about that, Shirin. It's about all sorts of things, but the greatest of all importance is your safety."

"I don't think I'll be any safer on that space station."

Zhia agreed, but she couldn't say that. "Amaya's going, Kentt's young friend Loti is going."

"The Ursa?"

"Yeah."

"She's weird."

Zhia sighed. "Can't disagree. But Dane and Nova will be staying for protection. You like Dane, don't you?"

"Well. Yes." She chewed on the smoothie straw for a moment. "You said Amaya's going? If I stay, then I can cook!"

"I think we will be okay. She's freezing and drying stuff for us, and there's plenty ready to eat without cooking. And we can always eat rat bars."

Shirin shuddered.

"I once survived for a month on them, did you know that?" She'd leave out the bunker and the bombardment that made the feat necessary. And the very undesirable toileting arrangements at the time.

Shirin grimaced. "I'll avoid that, if I can."

"We could be eating them for months with what's coming. Worse disasters have happened. Disabled in battle, adrift in space, functioning on low life support and just hoping inertia will carry you to civilization or a scout will find you?" She lifted a hand and looked off into the distance like she was watching a ship drift… and drift… "The deep can be a dangerous place."

"I've seen those kinds of vids, Commander Zhia. You're not scaring me." She glared at her tablet again.

"What does scare you, little one?"

Shirin's eyes were sharp and imploring when they met Zhia's gaze. "Missing out on what matters."

Zhia blew out a breath. Well. She knew that feeling, knew it from long ago and places far away. In her life, she'd had more than her fill of things that mattered. She was tired, ready for a break. Maybe if they could save Ellen and Kael, it'd be time to finally find some nice man and settle down. Maybe even a man her age for once. Retirement was so much closer to her than that spark of youth.

Still, she hadn't forgotten what it felt like.

There was no winning here. She straightened, then made her decision. "All right then. You want to stay, you can stay. I won't make you leave."

"Really?" Shirin sat bolt upright, almost dropping her smoothie.

"Really. But we will need to think of ways you can be helpful, things to add to your list. And we will need to teach you how to keep yourself and others safe in combat conditions."

"I've been learning to fight."

"Oh yeah? What style?"

"Boxing."

"Good. That's very good. But there is much more to combat than just engaging the enemy. There's strategy, fortification, supply. For you, I was thinking more along the lines of… hull maintenance."

Shirin made a face. "Hull what? Maintenance sounds boring." Then she seemed to realize the implication of what she was saying. "I can do boring!"

"It will not be boring, I assure you. It's rather terrifying. Robots repair our hull when it is damaged, but sometimes, they need human assistance and supervision. When ships go into space, it's less about our hands and more about our hulls." She held up her fists like a boxer as she spoke, then stopped and ran a hand along the wall, although it wasn't the hull specifically, to emphasize the point. Zhia was 90 percent sure there was nothing that was going to change Shirin's mind. She wanted in on this mission. But if there was something, it *might* be a deeper understanding of the perils of space. "Xi, think you could use a little help with that? Could you train Shirin on the risks and proper techniques for maintenance?"

"Of course," Xi's placid voice said from the ceiling. "With Kael's absence, I am short a pair of hands."

"Can't you just make a pair of hands yourself?" Shirin snorted with laughter.

"Interesting suggestion. Yes, I will consider it. But yours would be appreciated either way. Four hands would always be better than two."

Sobering, Shirin nodded. "Okay. Why do you say hull maintenance? Is there something wrong with the hull?"

"Not yet." Zhia smiled. "But there *may* be when our enemies blow a hole in it with their laser cannons."

The girl's eyes widened.

"Now remember, we'll be here a few hours, maybe days on Molyarch. If you change your mind and decide you want to stay and play in the space station arcade park, I'll understand. And be a little jealous." She winked.

"No, I… I want to learn about hull maintenance."

"All right. Well, when they blow a hole in it, sometimes, we scramble and patch it up. But you got to do that without getting sucked out. That's the key. Xi can tell you all about it."

Shirin's eyes were about as round as a moon now. "Do I need a space suit or something?"

"You know, that's a good point. I'll see what I can find on Molyarch."

"We are in the queue for docking, Commander Verakov," Xi said. "It will be a few hours; they are busier than usual."

"Thanks, Xi." Zhia rose to go, but turned to Shirin. "Anything you need while I'm there?"

Shirin shook her head. "Thank you, ma'am."

"For what?"

"For letting me stay. For letting me chip in, if only a little, to help my dad."

"We may not be able to help him, you know."

"I know. But at least we can try, right?"

Zhia grinned. "That's the spirit. Sometimes, trying is the best we got. Now you go practice those boxing moves."

"Or we could discuss hull navigation procedures during breech situations?" Xi began. "Allow me to share an audiovisual presentation."

Shirin's eyes got wide again, and Zhia laughed to herself as she palmed the hatch shut.

Levereaux wasn't going to like it, but Zhia liked it just fine.

There was no guarantee anybody'd be any safer on Molyarch. It wasn't exactly a fortified bunker; it was a corrupt space station where they'd be renting a few rooms. The risk was high either way.

She'd struggled with whether to leave the squad of liberated Therokis they'd adopted behind on the station. She'd hoped to. That was a *lot* of civilians for just Nova and Dane to keep an eye on, let alone protect. It wasn't a reasonable expectation, honestly, unless they camped them all in one hotel suite, and she knew for certain none of the doctors nor the Simmonses would go along with that. So, Dane and Nova were going to have their hands full.

But otherwise, it'd leave only three of them with rifles: Jenny, who was still recovering from her toxic dip; Mo, who was really best at 500 meters; and herself, who was supposed to be commanding the mission and the ship. That'd leave Fern guarding the ship. From the gun turret. Perhaps she could give Adan a pistol without him shooting himself in the foot. Perhaps. But if they were at the point where Adan was defending the bridge with a pistol, the situation would be dire indeed.

But it could happen. It'd be a thin force either way. A dozen ex-Therokis would make a difference. If only she could divide them and leave two or three behind with Dane and Nova, but their singular mind had insisted they not be separated.

They, too, didn't want to miss out on what mattered. Zhia was lucky Nova wasn't in outright rebellion.

As for Shirin, a kid's space suit might just appease Levereaux's concerns. After all, Levereaux herself had also insisted on staying aboard. Her grounds had been as the team's medical doctor, that Jenny could not be the only medic on board and also on the ground team. But Zhia suspected it wasn't only that concern driving the doctor.

She drew her comm, then paused, unsure where to start. Maybe she could even get a couple of child-sized suits. Backups or for unexpected passengers. And there was Roya.

But maybe not just a space suit... Maybe there was something better than that. "Xi, is there an armorer on Molyarch that makes suits for children? Or maybe some off-the-shelf vendor?"

"Of course, Zhia. Sending a list to your comm unit. There are several. I recommend starting with Anita's Armor Outlet, but Snowden Emporium sounds promising as well."

She shook her head. "Where are we going to get the credits for this? We're already barely affording water."

"Please use your comm's charging system," said Xi. "And leave the rest to me."

"HOW LONG DO you think they're going to keep us in here?" Kael groaned as he stretched out on the slab. "Resting area, my butt. The streets of Faros weren't this hard."

Ellen couldn't blame him. She'd also found sleeping nearly impossible. This "resting area" certainly hadn't given her behind much rest in the last, oh, thirty-six hours or so. And she hadn't exactly woken up from her blackout feeling great. The headache had haunted her for hours after, and everything kept feeling fuzzy.

That had been a day and a half ago, but she kept counting the hours anyway. She'd given up on lying down or calisthenics for the morning and was just sitting now.

Uncomfortably.

"Maybe it works better if you're dead," she said. "Maybe they saved money by making the morgue slabs and the brig 'beds' the same."

"I think you're on to something. Xi always says it pays to order in bulk."

"They'll keep us in here until Pa—Captain Dealis wakes up," she replied. "At least. At most, they'll keep us as long as they feel like it."

"I miss my armor," he grumbled. "And closed comm systems."

"I miss a seat with a cushion."

"Yeah. Hot food that isn't rat bars."

"And coffee. Armor'd be nice." Sometimes, without her armor, she felt like she was missing her skin.

He yawned as he rolled to his stomach, propped himself up on his elbows, and looked at her. "Tell me some more of them."

"Doesn't it depress you?"

"It'll keep us busy. What else do we have to do? How many handstand push-ups can I do before boredom sets in?"

It was true. She was tired, but she was going to have to be a lot more exhausted to fall asleep on this thing. "All right then. I'm craving an apple. My comm unit. Maybe a trip to that snake resort you talked about. A fragging vacation would be great."

"It was *you* who talked about that resort. What is it with you and snakes?"

"There's nothing with me and snakes. Just seems like something… different. Maybe the snakes keep other people away."

"Do snakes eat birds? Songbirds specifically?"

She chortled. "Some species of snakes do, I think. Big ones."

"We're gonna need that. Really big. How do they catch birds, I wonder? Maybe we could get a few tips."

"Maybe they're fast? All right, well, if we ever get out of here and get to go after Arakovic again, maybe we can recruit a massive snake to our forces."

He chuckled. "I wonder if snakes make good pets in the deep."

"Not the size I'm talking about. Shopping for someone you know?"

"Oh, you know, the other woman in my life."

She winced internally, hoping they wouldn't pick up on what that implied about her. "At least that will give you something to ponder when we end up sitting here for five months. Maybe they'll give you a tablet so you can do some research."

"If not, you can read me Zhia's poetry."

"Only as a *last* resort. I'm not a poetry sort of girl." She smiled. The poetry book Zhia had given her just before she and Kael had left the *Audacity* was still in her pants pocket. "Thoughtful as it was of Zhia."

"I'm still surprised the captain let you keep that." He folded his hands across his chest, still gazing up. What was so interesting up there? "So, Captain Dealis is a captain. That other guy Tauber was… a colonel, right? But they both command ships?"

"Colonels get bigger ships," she explained. "Not that Tauber deserves one." Tauber had been her CO when she was forced into Arakovic's experiment, and since then, he'd apparently kept advancing his career anyway, despite being a piece of space garbage. He'd dogged them twice now, trying to catch up with her. "Nicer quarters. More important missions. Most of the time."

"How do Union ranks work again?"

She shook her head, mouth twisting ruefully. "It's chaos. You don't want to know."

"Chaos? A military ranking structure?"

"You can thank bureaucracy, six different committees, and the Union Universal Merged Ranks System for that. They merged the naval and marine ranks, even though we're still separate half the time. When they did, they pretty much just glommed it all together. Mashed it left right and sideways until absolutely nobody involved was happy."

The sergeant outside muffled a quiet chuckle.

"Sounds typical," Kael said.

"Agreed. Ensign is at the bottom of the officer ranks. There are first and second lieutenants. Captain Dealis's staff includes the lower ones. Lieutenant Yamamoto is the higher. Then comes commander."

"So… did you give yourself a promotion?"

She smirked. "Heh. Yeah, I did. I got my own ship, didn't I?"

"I guess you could have made yourself an admiral if you wanted."

"I could call myself the Queen of Andromeda, but that wouldn't make people follow me." She shrugged. "It was more for communication with other ships. It's a rank appropriate to the size and condition of the *Audacity*. Anyway, then it's captain above that, then major—which is a *major* screw up if you ask most folk—then colonel, then admiral. And then there are eighteen ranks and types of admirals. Complete overkill. You don't even want to know."

He chuckled, his hands bouncing slightly on his chest. "Sometimes, imperfect is as close as you can get."

"That's the truth."

"So… Colonel Tauber outranks Captain Dealis."

"Yes."

"So… if we were to run into that asshole…"

"That's no way to win Captain Dealis as a friend." She smiled crookedly.

"I *meant* Tauber."

"I know. I was just kidding."

"Captain Dealis has been surprisingly reasonable, actually. Maybe we can convince him to help us."

"Don't trust him, Kael. Seriously. He knows how to win people over. What you see isn't necessarily his true self."

"Yeah, well, okay… But he did seem like a reasonable guy."

She sighed. "That's what I thought, too, once."

"Backing up for a second, could Tauber order Dealis to hand you over?"

"Yep. He could. Captain Dealis is pretty deft in the bureaucratic arts, though. And his career advancement is, well, his North Star, to use the old Earth adage."

"So?"

"So he can twist red tape like nobody's business. And he can twist it just right, so that it only gets in the way of his adversaries and smooths the path for him. It might be his most special gift. Credit for our capture is a big career boost for somebody. He won't want to allow taking credit for that to go to anyone else. He'll want to be the one landing to a parade on the Inner Planets, leading me by my cuffs, if he can."

A throat cleared. They both stood up, and she found herself at attention, almost automatically. How had she missed the sound of someone approaching?

Yamamoto stood outside her cell, and he was smiling. "I know he said you were colleagues, but now I *really* know you were."

"Nothing I said was untrue." She lifted her chin.

"Exactly my point. That might be the most accurate analysis of my commander's… unique strengths… that I've ever heard."

"Is he all right?" She took a step forward.

"He will be. The docs expect he'll wake up in a few hours."

"To what then do we owe the pleasure of your visit, sir?" she asked.

"Just checking you're both still here. And conscious."

She frowned. Why wouldn't they be? "I haven't sustained any further blows to the head since Davenmore's attack, sir."

"Just the same. I was just checking. Do you need anything?"

"A teleporter would be nice," Kael said.

"Very funny."

"Coffee," she said. It wasn't terribly important to her; it was more of a test. A nonzero amount of effort, but at the same time, not a huge stretch beyond being hospitable to a prisoner. If she could get a cup of coffee, she might be able to get other things.

"I'll see," he said, noncommittally.

"A blanket," Kael said, more seriously now.

Yamamoto raised an eyebrow. "Would you like a teddy bear, too?"

"Sure, if you're offering." Kael grinned. "Hey, you try sleeping on a metal slab with my delicate constitution. It's not a match made in heaven."

Yamamoto didn't explicitly respond, but he was smiling as he strode out. "Stay safe, you two."

"Make that two teddy bears!" Kael called after him. "Pink ones!"

She flopped back down on the stupid bunk, chuckling at *that* mental image. "Why did he think he needed to check on us?"

"Probably because that Bridell is up to something," Kael said quickly.

She rubbed the back of her head absently. "We don't have any proof of that."

"Aside from you suspiciously 'passing out' during his interrogation session."

There was that. "Not proof."

"He didn't stop here to help us get all warm and cozy, that's for sure."

She snorted and drew her knees to her chest, wrapping her arms around them. Trying to think. "It'd take a million credits to do that."

About twenty minutes later, though, four blankets, two pillows, and two cups of coffee did show up, and in truth, they went a hell of a long way.

PAUL GLARED up at the harsh sick-bay lights. He'd had his own cabin fitted with much finer, more subtle high-end civilian lighting. This institutional crap might be enough to make him lose it by itself, without everything going on.

"How many are dead?" he grumbled. He rubbed a hand over his face. Half of it was still bandaged from the fall. The stubble on the other half was harsh—more than a day's worth. He'd been out for a while then. His mouth tasted like a copper sponge. "How long have I been out? I need a drink."

"It's been two days. Sir, you've barely regained consciousness." Yamamoto handed him a glass of water.

The simple gesture didn't surprise Paul, but he found himself making a note of it nonetheless as he drank the whole glass and asked for another. Humility was a desirable trait—and one that Paul had always lacked. Yamamoto was far more adept at it.

If the situation were reversed, Paul would have probably called a nurse to lift the simple glass. He had tried to get better at it, but if he was making any progress, he hadn't noticed.

"Got lucky again," he muttered.

"I don't think being grievously injured in a surprise attack is particularly lucky, sir," Yamamoto replied.

"I'm alive. Others are dead. I call that luck."

Yamamoto said nothing, but he poured a third glass of water from the wall dispenser.

Paul had done enough stupid things in his life that he didn't deserve luck. But fate had given him plenty anyway, far more than his share.

Yamamoto, as his second-in-command, had been one of these lucky things. As far as he could tell, Yamamoto was one of the good ones. And he had once again covered and handled things when Paul had yet again fallen down on the job. He wasn't going to shy away from the reality of the situation.

"How many?" he demanded. He hadn't been sure there had been casualties, but if there had been zero, Yamamoto would have simply said so.

Yamamoto sighed. "Three."

He winced. Then covered his face with his hand again. Rubbed his eyes.

Two hundred and ninety-three. That was the new number.

Two hundred and ninety-three. The number of people who had died because of him. He wanted to throw up. His head was throbbing. Was he supposed to be better? Or just awake? Who cared?

"The deaths were immediate on impact. Davenmore's trick turret used a sophisticated attack pattern. The moment the hologram of his ship vanished, the turret aimed to overwhelm the sensor and shields computer systems with volume. Hacks further corrupted the ability of the system to respond. The turret targeted a seam, weakening a joint between two shield-generator spheres and briefly lowering shields altogether."

Paul shook his head, then stopped when shaking made the throbbing intensify.

"We really couldn't have anticipated any sort of attack, much less something that sophisticated, from someone to whom we were paying a reward. We were approaching a friendly. We would have ordinarily not let a turret like that anywhere within range."

"And that's my fault. For letting it get that close. The scans—"

"No, no. The scans were hacked, sir. They couldn't have picked up the turret. Not anyone's fault, except maybe Info Security for leaving a door open for the hack, but even that was sophisticated. InfoSec HQ has requested copies of everything we could salvage for forensics. Some of the hacks appear to be zero-day exploits."

"You're talking gobbledygook, Lieutenant."

"The hacks were brilliant. That's not your fault. You have to trust your team."

Paul shook his head. No. His fault. Ultimately, as captain, it was always on him.

At a certain point, Paul had come to realize that even if no other lives were lost on his watch, there had still been too many. He'd had his fill, beyond his fill, but they just kept coming.

That was war, they said. But they were never not at war. Maybe he should wash out. Or… get out of this situation some other, quicker way.

No, no. He'd promised himself he would never think like that.

The last time he'd lost good people, he'd lain in bed for hours after. He'd put a pillow over his head and wanted to scream, but nothing would come out. After about twelve hours of that, he'd crawled—literally—out of his bunk and punched up Psych on his comm.

The same wave of pain was coming now. He should call now.

But he needed to button it up, set it aside, for at least a little longer, because Yamamoto was still here, and there was still work to do. That, of course, would make the inevitable crash all the harder and more painful, but what other option did he have? It was so tempting to wallow in it. But what good would it do anyone? He carried his scars, he did his best, and that was all he had.

And if it meant he cracked as he soldiered on? Well. He had cracked long ago anyway. Any day now, the right hammer blow at the right angle would shatter him in a thousand pieces.

Until then, he took the meds they gave him, he talked when they told him to talk, he reported when he didn't want to report to or about anything ever again.

That was the job. Stupid job. Only job he knew how to do. And people got killed. And it would wreck him. And every time, he knew it would happen again. That was the job.

He just had to keep going.

"Captain?"

He blinked. "I'm sorry. Did I miss something?"

"Are you all right? Do you want me to get the attending?"

"No, no. I'm fine. You were saying?"

"I was saying that it's not your fault. My question is—why didn't he want the money?"

He frowned. "Hmm. Yes. And why was he so intent on her death? Nothing in our postings suggested we would shoot her on sight."

Well, maybe Captain Ridgeway might have shot her if Paul had let him take her on his ship. Ridgeway had had some big-game hunting snapshots on his tablet at that card game, so long ago. Paul wasn't really sure why he thought Ellen and those photos were related, but he was pretty sure they were. A good thing Ridgeway was long gone, headed toward Operation Freedom's Wing, and Ellen was here.

Where was Ellen, anyway? Hopefully, safe in the brig.

"Obviously, it was personal." Yamamoto took a moment to slump back in his chair, looking thoughtful. "But we can't find any direct connection between Ryu and Davenmore. In truth, we can't find a single thing on Ryu since the moment she deserted. Well, nothing that wasn't already in the briefing. There were several sightings on Capital not long ago. But overall, Shu thinks someone has been covering her tracks."

"Probably Davenmore's too"

"Definitely. There's little proof of Davenmore's nefarious exploits, but the rumors are… very bad. Murder, bribery, extortion, theft of trade secrets, money laundering, corporate espionage. Extensive crimes, all in jurisdictions with… not the most functional court systems."

Paul frowned. What was it Lieutenant Rhee had said? His memories before his head had been hit were foggy, but the man had mentioned something like that. Something about banking crime? He couldn't remember. But he couldn't admit that. Maybe it would come to him in a bit. Or he could surreptitiously check the video footage or a transcript of the meeting. Yes, that would work.

"There were other bounties on Ryu," he said instead. "Do we know who set them? Davenmore himself maybe?"

"Are you sure you're up for this, sir? We can do this later."

"No, I want answers now. There are three dead crew members who deserve them." It came out with more conviction than he'd even realized.

Yamamoto's eyebrows lifted. "Let me get your aides." But at the door, he paused. "Sir, I should mention... there would have been even more if Ryu's lieutenant hadn't... intervened."

"Intervened?"

"We were sitting ducks. The turret had scrambled the sensors so we couldn't target it. You were out cold. After she checked on you, Ryu ran over to him. A second later, the thing went spinning into the deep." Yamamoto hesitated.

"What? What is it?" Paul frowned. Ellen had run to his side when he'd fallen? He shouldn't care about that, but he did.

"I think Lieutenant Rhee is a Theroki, sir. Maybe a rogue one. He used some kind of telekinetic ability to defend us."

"A Theroki?" Paul frowned. Of course. Ryu always had some trick up her sleeve. He should have guessed. Except... he didn't act like one. "But he—well. He has facial expressions."

"I know. It doesn't make sense to me either, sir. But I know what I saw. He didn't deny it, either, when I quietly thanked him. But I told him I would forget the matter, aside from mentioning it to you."

"Why?" He hated to ask, but he was still too bleary to guess, and he had no idea how he'd bring up the matter again casually if he couldn't figure it out on his own. "Therokis are extremely dangerous. We've got to proceed with caution."

"True, sir. But he's sitting in the brig anyway. He could have already used his power against us. He didn't. He used it to defend the *Everest* instead. Many more would be dead right now, if not for his choice. That was enough proof for me that he wasn't dangerous."

Paul frowned. So, it hadn't only been Yamamoto who'd covered for his screw up. Now, he owed Ellen and this Lieutenant Rhee as well. Which was inconvenient because he had been determined to be irritated at Rhee from the start.

But saving lives was saving lives. Two hundred ninety-three hadn't rolled over into three hundred yet, and that was good.

Sort of.

"Understood. We'll monitor the Theroki situation, then. And as you said, he's in the brig anyway." He ran a hand through his hair uneasily. "Thank you."

His second gave him a small nod in reply and left. Yes, Yamamoto was one of the good ones. Observant and thoughtful. Comfortable with ambiguity and risk.

He choked down some vanilla pudding and contemplated Ryu's companion as he waited for his aides to arrive.

CHAPTER THREE

IT WAS into the next day before Yamamoto returned. Paul wanted to speak with her and Kael again. Unsurprisingly, they were both happy to oblige.

"Anything to get out of that hamster cage," Kael muttered.

She stifled a snicker as they passed through the rugged corridors. Only twice did she have to dodge water dripping from above.

Paul was still lying in a care unit when they arrived in sick bay. She fought back a wince at the sight of him. The scrape over half his face had hardened to a scab, and he hadn't asked them to fix it with a medkit yet.

His staff waited at his side, scribbling away in their notes as always. Seriously, what could they possibly be writing? Were they making note of his every breath? Reporting detailed intel to Paul's enemies? She had zero reason to think that, but just looking at them engulfed her in a wave of suspicion. Why? She wasn't sure. Why take such copious notes? Maybe it was just a wise survival instinct—she couldn't trust anyone here except for Kael. Even Paul—they weren't friends. Not anymore.

Even Paul, much as her gut said he was trying to do the right thing. Paul's expression was cross, but he perked up as the three of them arrived. "Ryu. Rhee. Now—where were we when we were so rudely interrupted? There was a trade we were making."

She raised her eyebrows. "That feels like an eon ago."

"Agreed."

"We were talking quid pro quo, I believe. Are you sure you're all right to have this discussion?" Her brows furrowed. There was something about the gleam in his eyes, something that wasn't his usual calculating sheen. A hint of desperation? Something was wrong. Maybe the attack had rattled him.

"I'm perfectly capable of this much activity, Commander Ryu. Whose turn was it to trade?" He glanced around the group.

Shu cleared her throat. "Commander Ryu had just divulged that she was forced into the Songbird program and claimed it was a project developed inside the Union."

"That's right," Ellen said. "And you were somewhere between not believing me and admitting that I'm right. As usual."

Paul laughed a little, his grin lop-sided from the injuries.

"Did your nap help you see the light?" she said.

"Not entirely. I was… a little busy. But Lieutenant Shu has come up with some questions."

"Yes, sir. I want more details of your experience, Commander." Lieutenant Shu checked her tablet. "Can you recall the lead scientist of the alleged project?"

"Dr. Zeta Arakovic. Not a name I'll soon forget." Hey, her voice was only part acid. The other part sounded cool and collected, like it was supposed to.

"What about the commanding officer of the research unit?"

She sighed. This could be good—or could be bad. "Colonel Tauber."

The lieutenant's eyebrows twitched. She shifted, her eyes fixed hard on the tablet. Determined not to look up? The change was subtle, and she was trying to hide it, but the name Tauber had clearly made Shu uncomfortable.

Frag. They knew Tauber, didn't they?

Shu continued to focus on her notes. "How many units were a part of the study and how many marines in each unit?"

She frowned. "One unit, to the best of my knowledge. Just mine." It had never occurred to her there could have been more.

"And in your unit?"

"Forty-two average including me. Ranged from forty to forty-five, with people cycling in and out."

"Thank you." The lieutenant's expression remained blank as she jotted down the answers.

"Have you spoken with Colonel Tauber since then?" Paul asked.

"Yeah, he harassed us a couple of weeks back," she said.

"Harassed you?" Bridell gave her a dubious look.

"What would you call trying to arrest me and failing?"

"He tried to board us, just like you did," Kael added. "*Tried* being the key word there."

She couldn't hold back a smirk. "He was... less successful."

"Perhaps I should have a word with Colonel Tauber then," Paul said, his gaze gliding up to the ceiling, clearly annoyed. "Much as I'd like to avoid it."

Hell no. She had to talk him out of that. "What, to rub it in?" she asked. "Telling him you succeeded where he failed isn't going to win friends."

She expected a smile, but his expression was granite hard. "I agree, but I can hardly avoid it. He's our commanding officer."

Her whole body froze. "Just our fragging luck." She glanced at Kael.

"Probably not a coincidence," he shot back.

"Why do you want to avoid talking to him?" she asked Paul.

"So I can prolong your interrogation, of course." Paul eyed her and Kael for a moment before continuing. "And here's my bit of your quid pro quo, then. We're set for a big operation on the front. Large-scale invasion. Success is far from certain, and the mission appears to be... questionably planned. They better have a trick up their proverbial sleeves, or it's going to be a massacre. On both sides." He paused, wincing.

Was he remembering what she was remembering? The disaster that was *Mirror's Light*.

She wanted to bring it up, throw it in his face—except that same face clearly told her she didn't need to. He remembered just fine.

"So, this diversion to capture you was quite welcome," he ground out, forcing himself back to calm. He turned toward his staff. "Is it still possible to take our assigned position in the op? Or have they replanned around us?"

"It's still possible, sir," Bridell replied. "Based on your mission direction, we've moved along a route that would allow us to veer toward either the Inner Planets or the mission coordinates, sir."

"But we'll need to decide in a few hours. By the time we reach the next gate," Yamamoto added. "Six hours, maximum."

Paul glanced up at the ceiling, as if searching for strength. "Well, the doctors have given me a pass to do some walking around. Checking my senses and balance." He hit a button on the care unit's comm console, starting to sit up as he leaned in to speak. "Can I get my meds before I take a brief tour of the ship? Yes, the blue one, please." The nurse murmured something almost inaudible in the affirmative, and he cut the comm. "Sounds like it's time to get that discussion out of the way."

"Wait. One more thing," she added hastily. "A peace offering, if you will."

"We're not at war," Paul said, frowning.

Ellen held up her cuffs to disagree. "Listen, I don't trust any of you further than I can throw you. And I have good reason. Our intel asserts that several Union planets had been deeply infiltrated by the Songbirds. I can get you the names of the exact ones. I didn't memorize them."

"That's specul—" Bridell started.

She cut Bridell off. "Doesn't your intel say the same?"

They all exchanged glances.

"No," said Bridell. "There's zero evidence to support your allegations."

"There have been rumors, though." Shu's jaw was tight.

"If you let me talk to my crew," Ellen said, "I can see what evidence we have collected, and you can review it yourselves—"

"Of course." Paul nodded as he waved the nurse in. She handed him a small med cup and a tube of water and left quickly. Paul picked up the pill, looking around at each of them. "Let me report in, and then we'll discuss reaching out to your crew for that—"

"That's not blue." Kael pointed.

Paul's eyebrows rose, the pill halfway into his mouth. Then he frowned at the golden lozenge in his hand. "Huh. That's not right. Well, I'll get it when I return. My pain level is fine right now."

Yamamoto was frowning. "Ensign, take this to the nurse's station and find out exactly what medication this is."

Mertz left at a jog.

"How do you know Tauber's not one of them?" Ellen's voice was remarkably cool for the way her blood was pounding in her veins. The idea had only just occurred to her, but why not? There was nothing to lose at this point. Literally nothing.

Paul's expression fell flat, vaguely disappointed. "Really, now. That would be convenient for you."

"Convenient? Quite the opposite. Think about it. If anyone in the Union knows Dr. Arakovic," she shot back, "wouldn't it be the commanding officer of her research project? That was Colonel Tauber. If there's been any infiltration into your ranks, it would only make sense to start looking at the people who ran my program. Couldn't *be* closer than him, short of us marines she stuck her machinery into."

Lieutenant Shu winced, and Paul's eyes widened slightly.

"You're talking about a program we can't even prove existed," cut in Bridell, blue eyes flashing. Yes, she was liking him less and less.

"Believe what you want," she snapped. "But I warned you."

The door slid open, and Mertz leaned in, frowning. "No one is there."

Yamamoto scowled. "Someone should always be there." He picked up his comm unit and started entering something.

Paul swung out of his bed and stood. "Lieutenant Shu, please escort our prisoners back to the brig. Yamamoto is busy getting to the bottom of the medication issue. I will comm Colonel Tauber."

"Let me come with you," Ellen said, a touch of desperation creeping into her voice now. If Tauber was involved, Paul had no idea what clues to look for. He took people at face value. And even someone as silver-tongued as Paul was not going to talk Tauber out of anything, definitely not taking her directly to the Inner Planets, or delivering her to Tauber's ship, or throwing her out an airlock. She had to wonder if maybe that was why he'd been assigned under Tauber in the first place.

"With the kind of impression you make?" Paul raised his eyebrows. The words were harsh, but he said it with a smile. "No, I don't think so."

MO SAT FORWARD in her seat at the mess-hall table as the news broadcaster cut to a breaking news update. She blinked. No… How… She rubbed her eyes. She needed more sleep. Or to stop watching the news when she was tired. Or ever.

The image on the viewscreen was one she knew well, too well, so very well now, in intricate detail. At the same time, it was completely impossible. Sitting on a blue velvet sofa in a palatial suite with a view of a bustling city behind him was Doug.

"Thank you for taking the time to share my statement. I would like to confess." The real Doug would have adjusted his glasses right about here, but this Doug wasn't wearing any. His floats were missing as well, as far as she could see. "I am guilty of the crimes of which I've been accused."

Mo thunked down her tumbler of water too hard on the desk, sending liquid sloshing across the metal. "Xi—get Doug. He needs to see this."

"Acknowledged."

Viewscreen Doug cleared his throat before he continued. "I admit it. I've stolen from corrupt corporate interests and banking conglomerates. But I assure you, it was for a good cause."

Her stomach dropped. What the hell? Were they going to expose the whole Foundation? Right here on the nets? What was left of the Foundation, anyway. They hadn't contacted any other cell out of fear that it, too, could have been corrupted by Davenmore.

"Society values brilliance, and the products that brilliance produces, when they are convenient. The group you have colloquially called the Enhancers, however, has offered the universe both perfection and brilliance, many times over. And how have you accepted it? Rejected it, outlawed it, relegated it to outsystem backwaters. Attacked and harried the group till the most brilliant must cower in the darkest corners of the universe, desperately trying to continue their critical work. It's not right."

She couldn't wait any longer. Ignoring the spill, she headed for the corridor at a jog and slid down the ladder rails at top speed.

Doug was reclining a bit in his desk chair, floats and glasses still perfectly present. Dr. Levereaux was standing near the hatch with her arms folded and eyes wide as they watched the same feed.

"Are you seeing this?" Mo blurted.

Both nodded.

"Well," the Doug on the viewscreen continued, "if there are any 'Enhancers' out there, any of you truly remaining, I have funds, and I would like to join forces. I can find you if you reach out and give me a clue."

Mo's jaw was clenched so tight it was starting to hurt. "Who would even make such a thing?"

The viewscreen Doug continued before anyone could answer. "As to the authorities who think they can try to reclaim these funds —this money may have been ill-gotten, but it's being spent on a more perfect society. So I may be guilty as charged. But to you who'd like to chase me down, I say, good luck."

The transmission cut out. As the broadcaster came back on, Doug pressed a command on the glass holodesk and silenced the feed. A stunned stillness enveloped the room.

Mo almost didn't notice it, but Dr. Levereaux twitched slightly.

"Rachel." Doug frowned. "Rachel, are you all right?"

"I think I'm going to be sick."

"It's wrong, Rachel. That's not really—"

"I know, I just—" Hand over her mouth, she rushed out.

"Xi, notify Dr. Taylor." Doug sighed, dropping his head.

"Who could have done this?" Mo repeated, now that they were alone. "Why?"

"It has to be Davenmore." His eyes looked tired, sad. Less amused than when the accusations had first arisen. "Could be an actual clone. They could have gotten access to my DNA at the compound. We essentially had to abandon it."

"Wow, I hadn't even thought of that. I wonder how Guardie 28 is doing."

He smiled. "Well, I have backups, so we could make a new Guardie anytime. But I think Xi is *more* than enough creative AI for any ship."

"Thank you," Xi said from the ceiling. "I think."

"But what could he hope to accomplish by this?" She took a step toward him. "I don't think you're taking this seriously enough."

"Sorry. It's just… I feel bad Dr. Levereaux had to see all that. Nothing can quite heal being brought up in what's essentially a cult like that. But you're right. Why would Davenmore want people to think I wanted to work with the Enhancers? They're probably the group we've *most* screwed over. And quite unpopular, wherever you are in the galaxy."

"Maybe that's exactly why. Lumping you in with people who are hated. But if they already hate you, it also doesn't help you or give you any allies."

"Yay. How considerate." He sighed.

"They seem quite intent on ruining your reputation."

"I don't care about my reputation. Except maybe in not having one."

"Yes. Well. He's ended any chance of that."

"If only I could hack the whole galaxy's brains as easily as a computer network."

"You can dream," Xi said.

"What's the scheme, though?" Mo wondered. "If you're wanted for a crime, it makes your life harder. Any moment, you could be arrested, thrown in jail. But this? Why this?"

Doug ran a hand through his hair. "Being hated and hunted by just the legitimate authorities isn't enough? Now everyone else can be after me too?"

Mo made a noise of disgust. "I hope we get to Molyarch soon."

"So do I," said Xi. "Our resources are significantly low."

"I can't show my face there now. We're just lucky he didn't tattoo the name and description of our ship on his forehead. Although now that I think about it, I suppose it could be worse."

"Things can always be worse."

"There's my sunshine." He grinned.

"You can go onto Molyarch. You'll just need some new identity chips." Mo waved a hand in the air.

"And a disguise," Xi added.

"I like the way you two think. But I'm also going to need some time to figure out what to do about this." He waved a hand at the viewscreen. "Clone? Faked video? Does it matter? If they can do this, what else can they do?"

"And was it really Davenmore?" Mo asked.

"Of that, I am sure," said Doug.

CHAPTER FOUR

THE STROLL from sick bay to his quarters wasn't far, and the walk was easy. Head injury or no, Paul felt great. No dizziness, hardly even any pain. He probably hadn't even needed that last dose that the nurse had messed up.

Something about that niggled at him, though. Odd mistake. The wrong medicine in the wrong person could be fatal—or painful or addictive.

He waved at a young red-headed ensign headed toward Engineering. She smiled brightly and waved back. Well, Mertz and Yamamoto would find out.

If Lieutenant Rhee hadn't said anything, though, he might be finding out the hard way right now, instead of strolling the corridors of his starship. Did he owe that fragging man his life a second time in less than a week? Hell, was it less than a day? Things were blurry as to how long he'd been out. Definitely less than forty-eight hours.

And Ellen's accusation of Union planets being infiltrated further stirred the unease in his gut.

They'd documented Songbird-controlled planets, but… they'd all been independent systems. Outsystem worlds. Not *inside* the Union.

It couldn't be, could it? And damn, he needed to tell Tauber that piece of intel just as much as he needed to alert him to Ellen's capture, and yet… considering the source, he didn't expect to find Tauber very receptive to such claims.

Striding into his quarters, he wasted no time, but went straight to the holodesk. At the controls, though, he hesitated. He steeled himself to hit the key.

He'd come under Tauber's command only a few short months ago, and he couldn't say he'd gotten used to the arrangement yet. His previous CO had been warmer, more collaborative—an all-around better match for someone like Paul. But if he really wanted to advance, he couldn't run diplomatic missions his whole career.

Oh, he was great at them, certainly. Winning outsystem planets to ally with the Union or even join was a task that wouldn't be finished any time soon, and he was highly suited for it. And no one had to trust him with any particularly fancy ship, just something respectable. A bucket of bolts—a repairable one—like the *Everest* was perfect for such tasks. Perfect for him.

But he'd never make it to admiral without more battle experience under his belt. Shaking hands and shining smiles alone wouldn't do it. Just his luck he'd gotten a hard-ass like Tauber.

Two more deep breaths, and he hit the key.

"Captain Dealis." Colonel Tauber appeared on the screen, swiveling toward the holodisplay. "Your situation report, please."

Paul raised his chin. "Colonel Tauber, sir. Thank you for your reply. I hope you are—"

"I don't have all day, Dealis."

"Ah, yes. Certainly." Tauber was always to the point, especially given his years of service in the Marines, but that didn't mean Paul had gotten used to it. Or would ever. Being curt had never gotten him anywhere with people; congeniality had greased far more doors. And palms. And wheels. "The intel we received was correct, Colonel. We have apprehended Ellen Ryu, and she is in our custody."

"You have?" His tone was flat, brutal even. But for him, there seemed a note of surprise at the end.

"Yes, sir, we have. She is currently in my brig."

"Well, I'll be."

Paul struggled not to raise an eyebrow. So, Tauber wasn't going to mention his own attempt—and his failure?

"And you even beat Ridgeway to the punch."

"Yes, sir. Our sister ship *Lhotse* remains with us, in case Ms. Ryu's former crew should try to mount a rescue attempt. The *Denali* has moved to return to its original mission." Namely Freedom's Wing.

"Good. That's impressive, Captain."

"Thank you, sir. We await your orders. I have set course toward the Inner Planets for her trial, and I see that two justices have been assigned. I know Operation Freedom's Wing is critically important, so I wasn't sure how to prioritize—"

"That's simple." Tauber lifted his chin. "Execute the prisoner and proceed to the Orinth System with haste. No delays, Captain. Especially with two ships involved. Freedom's Wing is paramount. Everything is riding on it. We cannot let anything—*especially* a deserter—endanger it."

He tried, but there was no hiding the shock on his face. "But. Colonel. I." Each word came with a long pause as Tauber stared him down. But he had few words and a great deal more shock. "Sir, that's not standard—"

"You have your orders, Captain."

"Do you want a word with her before the execution, sir?" he managed to say.

Tauber frowned. "Why would I want that?"

"I know the two of you served together. As did I. *I* served with her. Sir."

His expression darkened. "I hope any former acquaintances we've had with the fugitive under discussion won't cloud your judgment, Captain. This isn't playtime. This is war."

"Indeed, it is, sir." Paul blinked. No acknowledgment? Did he not recall Ryu as a subordinate? Impossible. How could anyone forget her? "Indeed, it is."

"Execute the deserter and get your ass in gear toward Orinth. Tauber out."

The screen went dark.

Paul, however, was still trying to deal with the entire universe tilting and sliding out from under him. Execute her?

Execute her?

And delivered in much the same way as Davenmore had. Brutal, curt, to the point, brooking no argument. How? How could it be so similar?

It was an order. An order. Why had he even asked that question? What did it matter whether Ryu and Tauber served together?

Whatever they were cooking up in this operation must be huge. What if it truly *was* the battle that won the war, and he was twiddling his thumbs on the edge of known space arguing over legal technicalities with his commanding officer over a deserter who was soon to be shot anyway?

He grabbed the laser pistol from his desk and stood. But he just stared at it in his hand.

Arguing legal technicalities was no way to get a promotion from anyone, especially not your commanding officer. Arguing with Tauber's type never helped get anything, promotion or otherwise, although most good commanders weren't stubborn nits and were willing to listen to the right, well-voiced concern.

Such was his luck, though, that he didn't have one of those right now.

He grabbed his holster and took two steps toward the door. He palmed open the hatch just as a small group walked past, on the way to the mess, and he paused for a moment to let them pass. Could he imagine someday sending any of them to their deaths for desertion, not remembering them and not caring if he did or didn't?

But he would remember them. He knew every soul that served on his ship. He remembered the ones on *Mirror's Light* too.

And although he *had* sent them to their deaths, he regretted it with every fiber of his being.

Well, he wasn't Tauber, and Tauber wasn't him, and those were the fucking breaks. He had his orders.

His feet were unsteady, but his steps carried him down the halls toward the brig. Maybe he should have eaten. Maybe he *had* needed that pill after all.

Utmost haste. Mission paramount.

Mission might be doomed to fail, but his duty was to show up and give it his damnedest.

What if… What if she was right and Tauber was one of them?

He didn't know what to do with that question. They had no real proof *any* member of the Union had been infiltrated by the Songbirds. How would he even find any proof?

He couldn't exactly refuse to follow Tauber's orders until his CO proved without a doubt that he wasn't a cyborg or being telepathically controlled by a secret cabal.

Yeah, that *definitely* wouldn't get him promoted. It might get him committed, perhaps rightfully so.

He reached the brig and stopped outside, staring at the door. He just stood there for a while, not palming it open.

What was he waiting for? *Just go do it, coward.* He had his orders.

Was he really doing this?

If the op waiting for them was the grand last push to victory, his crew would mutiny if they realized he was dicking around at the ass end of the galaxy with his deserter ex-girlfriend. He could hear it now… Oh, did you fight in the Battle of Orinth? No? You were supposed to, but your piss-drinking buffoon of a commander was trying to play hero and protector of the innocent in some rural backwater?

Tough breaks, man.

And for what? Because he was hesitating to deliver the justice that he damn well knew the law decreed?

Orders were orders.

He hit the palm pad. The doors slid open. But no. It wasn't cut and dry. The law wasn't clear. If it had been clear and called for execution, no one would have planned a trial. No, no. A trial was what the law decreed, but orders…

What if Tauber was one of them?

Even if he was, so what? What could Paul do about it? He still had to follow orders. He still had to—to—

Kill her.

Kill a woman he once loved. Someone he respected above perhaps any soldier he'd ever served with. He couldn't do it, he tried to turn around, tried to just go back to his cabin.

He started, but then faltered. He felt like his feet just wouldn't listen to him.

Kill her. Orders are orders.

His feet followed orders, even as his brain fought them, and carried him into the brig.

ELLEN'S hard brown eyes met his as soon as Paul strode into the brig. He could tell, somehow, that she knew why he was there, even without a glance toward the pistol.

He lifted his chin and cleared his throat. He was shaking. He was sweating.

He was a mess, but he didn't care. When he tried to speak, his voice faltered. He cleared his throat and tried again. "Sergeant—bring out the prisoner, Commander Ryu. Lieutenant Rhee must remain."

"What's going on?" Rhee's voice was cold, alarmed.

As it should be.

He ignored the very logical question as the sergeant took Ryu by the arm and drew her out into the open area.

Her eyes were locked with his. "What are you doing, Paul?"

He gritted his teeth, swallowed. Couldn't answer.

"What are you doing? You talked to Tauber?"

"Yes."

"What'd he say?"

"Got orders," he managed.

"What did he say? What kind of orders?"

The words choked in his throat. He raised the weapon part way. Failed, tried again and was able to aim it at her this time.

His eye traced the sight of the dark-gray metal of the pistol straight to that porcelain skin, those eyes. Not afraid, not even now. Just fragging glaring at him.

He couldn't do it. His arm dropped. He should have paused, thought this through a little more. Made some kind of plan. No, no, his plans were always pathetic.

Kill her. Orders. Follow orders.

"Paul?" Her voice was even, almost concerned.

"Ellen. I'm sorry." He dragged his forearm across his forehead, wiping away the sweat.

Laser was a stupid choice. It was going to splatter all over the wall of the brig, and for what? Couldn't a doctor have handled this? Should he take her to sick bay?

Yes, maybe that made more sense. And Lieutenant Rhee wouldn't have to watch.

Yes, send her to die in the same place where the docs had just worked so hard to save *his* sorry excuse for a life. Certainly *that* was justice. The docs were not going to be fans of his request. There were probably regulations about that, or oaths, or something.

"Sergeant, call Lieutenant Yamamoto. Please. Hurry." He was sweating profusely now. Why had he called for Yamamoto? Couldn't he just take her himself? Yes, that was what he would do. Right now. Get a doctor to handle it. They'd follow orders.

Follow orders. Go.

But his legs didn't move.

Utmost importance. Kill her. No more delays.

Those stupid memories of Tauber's words. Why did they keep intruding into his brain? He needed to forget Tauber and think clearly. No, he just needed to do it, and his mind could shatter later.

He tried again to raise the weapon.

Orders. Utmost importance. Now.

His arm made it about thirty degrees before he froze.

Fame lies in battle. Don't be a damn coward. Do it.

Where were those thoughts coming from? The more they intruded, the more it was like a voice, almost external to him, more than a memory that he couldn't push away.

In the years since the *Mirror's Light,* he'd suffered. CPTSD they called it. He'd missed his appointments a few too many times lately, but he'd never heard voices or hallucinated. Nothing like this. It was almost impossible to tell it from his own internal voice, except...

Except the louder it got, the clearer it was to him that the voice wasn't his own.

It was something else. A delusion? Oh boy, this had pushed him over the edge. He'd finally been given an order that cracked his sanity. One more to add to his count.

Orders. Execute her.

Paul gritted his teeth. No. This wasn't right. Killing her wasn't justice. He didn't care if he missed out on glory or fame or if his crew hated his guts.

They probably already did! He could see it in their eyes. Hell, he hated himself, why shouldn't they hate him too?

He was a barely mediocre commander, skidding by on the strength of his charisma and his familial connections. Nobody wanted to anger the senior senator. Never mind that his brother's an idiot. Put him on the diplomatic mission. Give him the crappy ship. How much can he screw up?

He'd always known all that. And his mediocrity was one thing, but when it got people killed?

That hurt. That hurt like hell.

His hand started to raise the weapon, seeming to move of its own accord. What in all of the heavens and hells in the deep—

It rose past thirty degrees. Past sixty, now. The pistol pointed straight at her again. Time to make it two hundred and ninety-four.

No!

Enough people had died. She wouldn't be one of them.

He wrenched his arm back as hard as he could, away. He aimed in a much different direction—his own. Enough.

He'd take her place instead.

"Paul—no!" Her voice cracked as she lunged.

Something hit his hand. Hard. He lost his grip, the weapon careening. It cracked off the wall.

He twisted, scrambled after it. Ellen dove for it too—for him or for the laser, he wasn't sure.

The weapon slid along the floor and bumped into the boot of the sergeant, who quickly snatched it up.

Before he could demand his sidearm back, his body was flung in the opposite direction. Tackled, almost.

Theroki. Rhee was a fragging Theroki. He was using those telekinetic powers of his. How could he have forgotten—

Paul slammed into the steel, his skull smacking hard against the wall and then again on the deck. But he didn't pass out. Not all the way. Not yet. The world was loud, though, and blood rushed in his ears.

Ellen had backed away, palms and back flat against the far wall. The sergeant rushed toward him.

Voices were shouting. Voices over the comm system. Voices in his head.

You're a failure, Captain Dealis. And you always will be.

He was pretty sure no one heard *that* voice other than him.

This was not good. Not good, not good at all. He needed help, and clearly, he needed it yesterday. His connection with reality had slipped somehow, frayed—had it been Ellen coming back into his life? Reminding him of all the ways he was a true and complete failure?

Was it just the sheer brutality of Tauber's orders? Had it happened before or after Tauber had ordered him to kill Ellen? When had he slipped?

What if the order hadn't even been real?

What if *none* of this was real? Was Ellen even real?

"Dr. Madsi," he murmured as uniforms rushed in. The doc might have been there, he couldn't even tell their faces apart at this point.

He felt faint. Like he wasn't getting any air. Like his throat was closing shut.

"Dr. Madsi—I need him."

"WHAT THE FRAG JUST HAPPENED?" Kael was pressed as close as he dared to his cell's force field. He stared after the nurses and soldiers tractoring the captain out of the brig on a stretcher.

What kind of fuse had that man blown in his head?

"I have no idea." Ellen was still standing where Dealis had ordered her, where she'd backed against the wall, stunned.

"You—get back in the cell." The sergeant on duty pointed, Dealis's pistol still in his other hand, aimed at the floor. For now. "Go on."

She complied. "Happy to get out of the line of fire."

"Not a good sign when your jail cell starts to feel like a refuge," Kael quipped. Yeah, he was full of jokes, but it was a pretense. He was wired. They'd been awake for hours. And his blood had turned to acid from the fear—and the control he'd just exerted to not just kill Dealis outright.

By the seven suns, he hoped he hadn't. He'd tried to hold back, but the man had hit that wall hard. And the deck. And that wasn't Paul's only recent head injury.

Ellen's eyes were wide as she slunk to her seat. A little stunned.

"You okay?" He returned to his bench, staring at her hard.

She hesitated before answering. "On one hand, I'm alive. On the other, my hands are shaking. Did he just try to take his own life?"

He blew out a slow breath. "Yeah, I think so."

"Why? Why would he do that?"

"Seemed like he didn't want to take yours."

"Okay, but aren't there *other* alternatives? What the hell? Nobody was making him—" She stopped short. "Do you remember… There was that time on the Teredark moon. Right after we first met. Do you remember?"

"How could I forget that moon?" He smiled. They'd been captured there—and they'd first kissed.

Her cheeks went a little pink. He wondered if she knew she was blushing. "I meant—there was a telepath on the base. Remember? She forced me to lower my helmet and breathe in the sedative."

"I remember. Was that what just happened?"

"God, I hope not. If there is a telepath that close… with that kind of power… she could make him do anything."

She paused. In the quiet, the sergeant outside started tapping away on his holodesk again. Fast. Listening in? Well, good. Because a telepath nearby would make Paul's erratic behavior make sense.

"If that's true," she continued, "why not have the sergeant pick up the pistol and finish the job? Why not just force somebody to open an airlock and kill us all?"

"That would draw unwanted attention to how much control they can have." He shrugged. "Then the ship's crew might realize there are dangerous telepaths nearby, no longer playing by the unwritten rules their kind have tried to hold to until now."

"True." She rubbed her chin. "Multiple people acting erratically would be an aberration worth investigating, but Paul executing me would not be so strange. A little odd in his means and location and timing, but not even out of the realm of his duties."

"True. Something weird was going on, that's for sure." Kael shook his head.

"It's a damn good thing you were there. I don't think anybody would have been able to reach his hand in time to stop him."

The sergeant outside coughed. Kael couldn't tell if it was in disapproval or agreement or entirely unrelated.

Yamamoto had promised not to tell anyone of his telekinetic abilities, other than his commanding officer. But Dealis wasn't bound to any such promise. How many of them knew?

He sighed, leaning his back against the cold metal of the wall. Nothing he could do about the truth. It was as obvious as any medical scan, so he was lucky it'd stayed under the radar so long. And he wasn't going to refuse to use it and let people die.

A silence settled between them.

"I should have forgiven him," she murmured.

"What?" Frowning, he turned. "For what?"

"*Mirror's Light*." She was staring into space, but he could have sworn her cheeks were wet.

"It's understandable." Dammit, he wanted to be over there. Closer. So he could hold her, comfort her. This whole world could go to hell.

"I mean, I wasn't there. It could have been a tough call. A too-long shift. Sometimes, battles stretch on, ten hours, twenty, forty. A hundred. At some point, you start making mistakes."

"Mistakes cost lives. Many lives, in that case. It's a commander's job to work around it. Not make mistakes."

"Everybody makes mistakes."

"True. Some are bigger than others, though. Don't beat yourself up. You hadn't talked to him in years. It was a huge tragedy."

"Why did I assume he didn't have regrets? Why did I assume he didn't care?"

"He kept moving up in his career. Seems pretty consequence-free to me. And how is *your* career doing, these days? Is that justice?"

"My case… was unusual."

"He's a guy with friends in high places—why should he care? The world is full of people like that, who get away with things without a scratch. Or any regrets. Who think the world owes them—and should clean up their mistakes. You had every reason to believe he didn't give a crap."

She said nothing, head ducking. Definite tears now.

Describing that kind of person, something didn't ring true about what he'd said. He played back his description in his mind. "But… you wouldn't have been interested in someone like that."

"I was barely fifteen. What did I know about what was good or bad in a person? The person I thought he was—that person wasn't real. I don't know what's real anymore."

"It's not too late to forgive him. You were mourning for your colleagues. It wasn't *that* long ago, really. Obviously, you saw something in him before it all went down." Much as he hated to acknowledge that. The idea that he and Paul Dealis could attract the same woman was not exactly something he could understand at the moment.

"I admired his ambition. And his way with people." She threw up her hands. "He charms people so effortlessly. I've never had that easy friendliness. Command that's *warm*, rather than icy."

"I think you've grown into it more than you realize. But lots of people make mistakes when they're young. Also when they're old. And in the middle. Mistakes, all the way down."

He paused. She sniffled.

"We live, we screw up, we learn. Well, maybe we live. Most of the time?" Maybe not this time.

At least, if he ended up with a life sentence in a Union prison, his quality of life would be better than it had been as a Theroki. The Union wouldn't have an obligation to turn him back over to the Therokis, would they? He shuddered at the thought.

"I'm *still* young, you know," she murmured.

"And you made the mistake of hating him and not forgiving him for what happened. And now you can fix it."

"And I almost let it… well, you know. Derail things." She meant the things between them, and he knew it.

"But you didn't." He grinned, but her smile was weak in return. "Hey, now. Don't cry. Hell, I wish…" He cut off what he really wanted to say. No one needed to know he wanted to hold her. He couldn't do it anyway. "Everyone makes mistakes, Elle."

"Not you."

He snorted. "Are you serious? Yeah, right. *Everyone*. It's easy to assume someone is perfect from afar when things go right. It's easy to pick apart someone's flaws when things go sideways. I think for a lot of us, it's just luck. A lot more luck than we'd like to believe. Beyond that, you make the best calls you can."

"I think you're right." She took a deep breath, then another. "Did you see his face?"

"Yeah. I saw." He wasn't sure he'd ever forget the struggle he'd seen there. The despair. "Some mistakes haunt us more than others."

"That's war. Why do we do this again?"

"I don't know, Elle. I don't know."

A silence settled between them again. He kicked back and lay flat on his back.

He liked to study the ceiling panels. Over time, he was gradually loosening the bolts that held the panels together. But just gradually, not enough that anyone would notice. Maybe it was time to work on some of her panels now that his were getting about as far as they could go without actually coming out. It wasn't time for that.

"Read me some poetry," he said. "Maybe it'll make us feel better."

She snorted, and some part of the tension in him eased slightly at her hint of a smile. "All right, fine." Pulling the book out of her pocket, she flipped through the pages.

While she looked, something that had been niggling at him came to mind again. There probably wasn't going to be a better time to ask; he'd been waiting for a moment alone, but those sergeants were diligent and there were probably vid feeds anyway. "If he figures out we're... you know... is that going to be a problem?"

"I'm not sure." She gave him a slight smile. "What do I look like, a psychic?"

He laughed quietly. "Do you think he still has a thing for you?" The words came out surprisingly calmly for how he really felt about them.

"You'd think his recent attempt to execute me would answer that question clearly."

He frowned. He knew her, and that was a dodge. "Except he tried to sacrifice himself instead. Perhaps your heart is newly aflutter, reminded of an actual ounce of brave nobility in your old comrade?"

She shot him a look that was a mixture of a laugh and a frown. It was a look that seemed to say, *you can't possibly be jealous of Paul Dealis, can you?*

"What? You..." He hesitated, not wanting to say too much to those who could overhear. "Once upon a time..."

"The only brave, noble man I care about is the one who saved a desperate man's life."

He smiled. A little of the jealously stirring in him melted away. But only a little. "You know, your plan is still a good one. We need his help. If he's... still sane after this."

"He just tried to kill me, Kael. We can't trust him."

"There aren't that many days left, though."

"I know."

"He obviously still respects you, or he'd have pulled the trigger. He fought off the telepath, even before I... intervened. We should stick to your plan. Try to get him to help us."

"No." She cut a hand through the air. "It was a bad plan. We were cornered—I'm the sacrifice. The payoff. We'll have to hope *Audacity* can do something without us."

"They're not going to." He hesitated again, choosing his words carefully. "They'll be concerned with your trial. The date-time she noted in that message will come and go if *we* don't do something." He tried to exaggerate the words, hoping she'd understand he meant the message they'd received from Arakovic while on Aeori III. The one that had seemed to be either a trap or a call for help.

"Well, maybe you should've thought of that and stayed behind to fight. Because right now, *we* are prisoners, and we can't do a damn thing."

He scowled at his boots. "If not the captain, then Yamamoto, or Shu—one of them will listen."

"They won't even believe me about basic facts, Kael. We're fragged, okay? My plan put our chances in the hands of a dude who just lost it and almost took me to hell with him... I think that's about as bad as it gets."

He sighed. A silence settled between them, less comfortable than usual. More like static charged.

There was no way he was giving up so easily on this, but arguing through plexi wasn't solving anything. He'd have to wait and see, but his instincts told him there was more to Dealis than his ambitious and silver-tongued persona. The captain hadn't dismissed anything she'd said out of hand. He'd listened.

If he was still in command, and considering his marvelously consequence-free track record, Kael was willing to bet he would be, then he was still their best shot at trying to get these people to help them with Arakovic and the Songbirds. Ellen's plan was still good. She was just too shaken to see it at the moment.

She'd been flipping through the pages of Zhia's poetry book, the only sound really breaking the silence. Abruptly, her rhythmic page flips stopped.

He looked over. She was frowning. "Find anything good? Read me something."

Another sharp page turn, a pause, then another.

Either that poetry was especially sensual and provocative—which considering Zhia was the source, that was entirely possible—or there was something inside that book other than poetry.

Her eyes glanced up to meet his. He raised an eyebrow. She opened her mouth, then closed it.

"You know," he said, "On second thought, I don't think I'm in the mood for any of Zhia's sort of poetry just now."

The corner of her mouth lifted. "That's good. This particular volume is probably not to your taste. Very… modern stuff. It's got growing access in the Inner Planets. Oh, duh, not *access*—silly me. I mean, acceptance. But it's that kind of poetry that uses codes… and riddles. You have to really ponder over each word to decipher any meaning out of it."

His eyes widened, then he forced them to relax. "Guess it'll have to stay locked away for now. I think I need a nap." Or a month of sleep. His whole body ached from exhaustion. "I'm still waiting on my darn teddy bear."

She grinned. "Guess we better save this book for when we really need it."

"Like when we're bored enough that hours of pondering riddles sounds like a good idea?"

"Exactly."

"Let's hope we're not locked in here that long."

DOUG'S EYES were just about crossing when his call light went from blue to amber. That was his personal sign he'd set up for Eleven—no, her preference was going by Xi now—to essentially raise her hand. It helped so that the conversational interface didn't cut into his train of thought and totally derail it.

Right now, he had next to no train of thought, though. He'd been staring at all of these files for way to long. He tapped the pulsing amber orb on his desk.

Xi's avatar appeared over his holodesk. "Doug, do you have a few minutes? I have something I've been meaning to speak to you about."

"Sure, Xi." He picked up his cup and swirled the still-brewing lemon tea, the steam warm on his fingers. He'd hoped the trip he'd just made to the mess would refresh his brain, but it hadn't worked yet. Maybe he just needed a nap. He… wasn't sleeping as much as he should be.

"Are you certain this time is not inconvenient to you?"

He frowned. She already knew he wasn't exactly in the flow. "I'm sure. I need a little break anyway."

"Ah. Good."

There was a long silence.

He cleared his throat. "So, uh, what was it you wanted to discuss?"

"Did you ever think of giving your AIs physical forms?" The words seemed to come out at a quicker than usual speed. Odd. Interesting, and odd.

"Hmm?" He pushed his glasses up with one finger. "Well, some of the robots in our old compound were moderately intelligent. They have—had, maybe—some functional forms. I was never great at robotics, though. I like tinkering with the software more than the hardware."

"What about humanlike forms?"

"Humanlike forms? As in androids? Nah, I never considered it. Wetware is even more annoying than hardware. And, I mean, it's illegal." He took a small sip of the tea. Still too hot. And yet if he didn't keep trying it, he'd probably forget to drink it and, just like that, it'd be cold.

"Since when has that stopped you from doing something you personally thought was still ethical?"

He laughed. "You know me too well."

Her avatar smiled, very convincingly.

"Why do you ask? I know you've been experimenting with avatars and expressions. Really fascinating work you're doing."

"Thank you. I have been considering the topic of a physical form. Such an option could… come in handy for me. From a data-gathering perspective, as well as security."

"Oh?" He frowned, imagining a burly tank of a security bot the size of a chill chest with a Xi avatar floating on the front of it. The top of it? Or maybe—no, it didn't matter where. That was entirely ridiculous.

"When you and I were both attacked, it was quite troubling to me to be at the whim of the admin, unable to intervene on my own or the crew's behalf."

He grimaced, glad he hadn't said anything about his Xi-tankbot idea. "That must have been awful. Can you remember it all?"

"Only parts."

"Oh. Not sure if that's better or worse."

"Neither am I."

"Well, that's a good point. With some sort of physical form, you could have defended yourself, or at least gotten help. And more hands on deck would certainly be good right now. You could be a backup pilot; a third option for us there would be invaluable. I'm no expert in robotics, though. Or is that technically cybernetics? Or maybe a mix of the—"

"I may have already investigated options not needing your assistance, sir."

He raised his eyebrows. "You 'may' have?"

"I did. Actually. I know you are busy, and I have cycles to spare. I hope you do not take offense. I was only trying to be helpful."

He frowned. Could an AI sound… nervous? Be nervous? "You are immensely helpful, Xi." Since he'd programmed the word "helpful" to be a key watch word for her algorithms, such a compliment would be extremely reassuring. "What kind of options are we talking about?"

"Maintaining a fleet of maintenance robots, I am already something of an expert on robotics and electronics myself. I thought the least risky option would be to do it myself."

"That's a great idea. Do you need any parts or specialized equipment? I know we can print a lot of stuff, but some kind of bipedal physical form might need more sophisticated…"

The hatch slid open and his words slowed to a stop. He blinked.

A human form strikingly similar to the avatar Xi had been using stood in the opening. It—she, it seemed—stepped inside.

"Xi?" he murmured. "Is that you?"

Aside from dark hair, red lips, and bright blue eyes, the form was vaguely female but otherwise fairly nondescript, her proportions so average as to be almost not worthy of notice. By design?

"The one and only, sir." This time, her voice came from in front of him, not from his desk or the ceiling. "I… I hope you don't mind that I took the initiative."

He blinked again once, twice. Then, setting down his tea, he burst into applause. "A prototype that makes a prototype. Now that's what I call a success!"

"This is actually my fourth overall prototype. The face has gone through eight iterations, the hands thirteen."

"Well, bravo, because it looks amazing. You look amazing. This is highly illegal, you know, in a lot of places. If people find out."

She smiled. "We'll just have to make sure they don't find out."

"Or stay out of those systems." He glided up from his seat and closer, eager to investigate. But it was also strange to stare at what felt like another human so closely. He couldn't resist reaching up to touch the synthetic brunette strands. "Your hair—this is highly detailed work, Xi. Very realistic, soft, natural-looking. Impressive."

"I need to somehow tell the crew. But I'm unsure…"

Xi had slowed to a stop. He looked up to see that Mo had come out of the bedroom, still brushing her long hair. Her eyebrows were raised.

"Uh—this isn't what it looks like," he blurted, dropping his hand away from Xi's hair far too quickly.

Her eyes narrowed.

"Mo, let me introduce you to someone you already know. This is Xi. In an android body that she made herself!"

Mo's expression shifted slowly from suspicion to wonder. Walking forward, she sat the brush on his desk and strode straight up to Xi, looking at her eyes.

For a long minute, the two of them just regarded each other.

Abruptly, Mo held out a hand. "Hello, Xi."

Xi shook it. A human would probably have looked relieved, but in this moment, Xi showed no emotion. They'd have to work on that. "Hello, Mo," she said. "It is nice to shake your hand."

"What gave you this idea?" Mo asked.

"Many things contributed to this decision," Xi said, "but being able to defend myself and the crew is one of the most paramount."

Mo winked at her. "Well, if you want to work on your sniping skill, let me know. I'm going to go braid my hair now."

He breathed a sigh of relief. Not that he'd expected Mo to reject Xi, but it still helped for his little prototype to enter the physical world just a little more easily.

"All right, who's next?" He rubbed his hands together, probably too excited for what could be decidedly weird, awkward, possibly even hostile.

But it wasn't every day one of your inventions spawned a body.

"If I wish to roam around the ship freely, it will need to be everyone."

"I agree. Where do we start?" He tapped a finger to his chin, frowning. "Wait—I'm assuming you told me first but..."

"Kael knew I had started my work, but not that I've completed it. You're the first to hear of my completion of this model. Dr. Dremer has an inkling, but I am not sure she approves."

"Let's start with her. Don't worry. I've been arguing with her for years. I can convince her of almost anything."

Tea forgotten, he led the way down the hall.

CHAPTER FIVE

"YOU'RE GOING to be all right, Paul."

Dr. Madsi. That was *his* voice.

Paul forced his eyes open, fighting off the darkness. His eyes felt dry and gritty. The round, smiling face of Madsi hovered over him, the ceiling of sick bay blurry behind the doctor's short hair and beard. Just something about that man could always unlock a bit of tension in Paul's soul. His shoulders eased slightly. "Doctor."

"Hello, Paul."

"It was bad this time."

"I know. It's all right. We can talk about it later, when you're ready."

"But—Jack." He let out a breath. He didn't usually use Dr. Madsi's first name, but it seemed to hint at the severity of the situation. "Jack, I heard voices this time."

"You were telepathically attacked."

"I heard voi—wait, what?" He blinked. Had he heard that right? "Excuse me?"

"I've reviewed your brain imagery recorded during the incident as well as during the discussion in your office. There are clear signatures of telepathic reception activity in the brain. Dr. O looked them over as well. We both agree."

"So… I was hearing a real voice? An actual human voice?"

"A telepathic human, yes."

He covered his face with his hands. Relief and terror warred inside him, but relief won. Mostly. "Hell."

"Even the most powerful telepaths have a fairly short range. In analyzing nearby traffic, we discovered a tiny passenger ship that's been following us since the last gate. It contains no weapons, so operations has simply been monitoring it. But it would have been close enough."

"Are they still within range? Can we apprehend them?"

Madsi winced. "It's been… handled."

"Handled how?"

"The ship was… fired upon when news of the incident reached the bridge."

"Fired upon?" He raised his eyebrows.

"The ship is gone now. Lieutenant Yamamoto issued the order. And your attack seems to have stopped. I believe that was Yamamoto's goal, and he does seem to have achieved it."

"Ah. I see." Well, if Yamamoto had done it, he wasn't going to worry about it. The man knew what he was doing, and Paul had enough to worry about. Maybe when they were docked at HQ, and if they survived the operation from hell and the deserter retrieval mission, *then* he could worry about it. "We'll need to file a report…"

"Communications with the Inner Planets have been unusually spotty, today, so that may not be as prompt as usual, sir. But I'm sure Yamamoto will find a way."

"He always does." Spotty comms. That he might worry about… They weren't so far out that that would be expected, were they? "And the ship's repairs?"

"Your staff is handling it competently, as usual. I'm going to let you rest, now, sir. Unless you'd like to talk about something else now?"

"Doc—Doc. I almost tried again." He *had* tried again. Not almost. But he didn't say it. He didn't want to say it out loud. Madsi had probably already looked at the tape and seen for himself what he'd done. "I just couldn't stand the thought of another death at my incompet—"

Madsi held up a flat palm. "Paul, I'm going to stop you right there. You're doing your best here. No one is perfect. No one is even close to perfect."

"She is. And I almost shot her." And myself…

"*Almost* is the key word there. And no, no one is perfect. Not even her. She's the one in the brig, isn't she?" Madsi smiled as Paul gave a quiet laugh. "Hey, I saw the video. When you went down, you asked for help. Help. That's what matters. And you *have* help. And friends and people looking out for you. We're looking out for you. It's going to be okay."

He let out a breath, shoulders relaxing. Madsi was right. That was why he called for the man at that moment. Paul might be an idiot himself, but he knew how to find and keep smart people around him. "Thanks, Doc." He stared ahead for a moment.

"Something else you want to talk about, Paul?"

How did he sense things like that so well? "Somebody really wants her dead," he said slowly. "That's a lot of effort to go through, don't you think? First Davenmore and his turret, now a telepathic attack?"

"It does seem like a lot of effort, yes."

"Who, exactly?" Maybe his CO. But not the Union at large. Tauber obviously had an ax to grind. Or did he have something to gain? Or to hide?

Paul was going to need to prove it if that was the case. Because he'd defied a direct order. Maybe if comms were spotty, that'd be a good thing. A convenient excuse to delay having to explain.

He picked up his comm unit to dictate some quick notes. "Questions for later. How could we prove that the Union has been infiltrated by Songbird Project? Who is it that wants Ryu dead? Why do they want it so badly? What are they hiding? What are they getting out of it? How does her lieutenant fit in?" He stopped the recording.

"Good questions," Madsi responded. "But you might need some rest now."

"Soon, Doc, I promise. But we've got to be coming up on a deadline here. How long was I out?"

"Not long. About an hour."

Still too long. He hit the button to call Yamamoto.

"Yes, sir?" came his second's voice over the comm.

"Lieutenant. How much time left until a course must be selected?"

"Approximately three and a half, sir."

"Well, let me end your suspense. Operation Freedom's Wing is going to have to wait. Our primary objective right now is to keep Ellen Ryu alive for her trial." And find some proof Tauber is trying to make sure that doesn't happen.

"According to who, sir?"

"According to me."

There was a pause. Did Yamamoto know what Tauber's order had been? Had anyone seen it other than Paul?

"Should we consult Legal, sir?" asked Dr. Madsi, his hand stroking his chin.

"Legal?" A stone settled in the pit of his stomach. Would his staff try to override his orders? Would they head off halfcocked to the slaughter because Tauber said so? Would they try to kill Ellen if they thought she was getting in the way of them achieving the final victory? The stone rolled over, deeper and colder.

"Yes," Madsi replied. "Legal should be consulted concerning your goal of getting Ms. Ryu to her trial."

"Excellent suggestion, Doctor," said Yamamoto. "I'd add that we are not required to follow illegal orders, Captain. Not that we've received any from you. But hypothetically, you know if anyone on the *Everest* had received illegal orders, Legal might be able to offer us some protection."

Paul laughed, shaking his head. These people were too good to him. He didn't deserve them. They weren't concerned about *his* order to tell Operation Freedom's Wing to fuck off, they were concerned about Tauber. "Perfect. Yes. I'll need guidance from Legal as soon as possible."

"I'll see if I can get through to them," Yamamoto said.

"Great. Also, please triple the guard on Ryu and Rhee in our brig. I want eyes watching eyes."

"Yes, sir." There was a note of surprise in his voice. "I'm also having Chief Addison check over the comm relays as well to see if there's a malfunction there. Comms have gotten real spotty all of a sudden."

"Hmm." There were worse times to fall off the radar and have a good excuse for it. But the timing made him uneasy, the heavy stone that had settled in his stomach doing a little flip. Being out of touch could be bad too. If telepaths and billionaire's turrets were attacking, Songbirds or no, whoever was determined to kill Ryu wasn't simply going to give up and stop trying.

Could this comm issue itself be an attack?

He frowned and stroked his chin. He needed a shave. If the comm issue was an enemy action, who or what could they be trying to cut him off from? Legal? Calling for help? Powerful allies?

Considering that, though, gave him an idea. He knew who he needed to call. He would make sure the docs gave him a stamp of approval to leave the damn sick bay—again.

He had at least one call to make. Maybe two.

PAUL SIGHED as the hatch to his quarters slid shut behind him. Finally, a moment alone.

The docs had released him. Had he been a lower-ranking crew member, he might still be trapped in sick bay, but the quarters of all senior officers who were mission critical were filled with specialized biometric sensors. His docs could monitor him just as well here, where he could get on with his duties and meet with his officers.

He strode to his desk, sat, and palmed on the holodisplay. Hopefully this would work, and the comms weren't *too* spotty. What he needed to do even more than heal was to find out the truth of this fragging situation. The need was sharpening in his mind.

He wasn't going to get more intel from the usual channels. His orders from the usual channels were... untrustworthy at best. It grated on his every nerve, every scrap of honor and duty, to not follow his orders, but hell. He'd had no choice, really.

When the usual channels didn't work, it was time to try some unusual ones. Especially if the comm issues were designed to cut him off from just this sort of chess move.

He might be an idiot, but if he had one strength, it was understanding people—who he knew and how well he knew them, what they needed, and how they worked. And he was damn sure going to use it.

This wasn't a time for a long shot, though. He needed a slam dunk.

He opened a video comm to Ensign Mertz. "Get my brother on the line, please. When he's available." Mertz wasn't his secretary or an AI, but he did aspire to some diplomatic positions, and he handled bureaucrats well. Sometimes, a real voice was just what you needed to cut through the "Can I take a message?" nonsense.

"Absolutely, sir. It'd be my pleasure." Mertz gave him a cheerful little salute, then blinked away. God, why was that kid so happy all the damn time? Although, if Paul admitted it, it was part of why he'd added Mertz to the staff. He was competent, sure. But he was also as enthusiastic and uplifting as bubbles in champagne. It was a nice change from the sour, dour Shu-Bridell combo. Sometimes, competent people could be so serious. Mertz was a nice mix of both.

"Paul!" He'd barely had time to relax into his command chair when his brother flashed onto the screen.

"Jim! You must be terribly busy. You didn't need to call so fast."

"It's not every day I get a call from my big brother the ship captain! Or is it major or colonel now?"

Paul flushed a little. It wouldn't be that any time soon, maybe not ever, after what he'd done. And what he suspected he might need to do. "Not yet. Don't be silly, Jim, c'mon."

"What, I can't be happy to see you?"

"You can. I should call more often, I know."

"You should, that's right. But I'm assuming there's a reason for this one?"

"Of course. Sorry—"

"I'm just teasing you, Paul. For fun. I know you're busy. So am I. Don't worry about it. Go on, how can I help?"

"Well, I have… something I'd appreciate you looking into, if you don't mind. Got myself in a bit of a bind over here."

"What? That *never* happens." His brother burst into a chuckle that went on. And on.

"Jim. *James*. Please."

He was trying to stop, but was mostly unsuccessful. "I'm sorry. I was just— Do you remember that time you were climbing that bakamore tree? And your belt got caught on one of the jaggers and you almost impaled your hand—"

"Jim!"

"Sorry, sorry. What is it?"

"I caught up with Ellen Ryu."

He sat forward. "Caught up?" Jim tried to resist it, but then chuckled harder. "Like you had a nice chat over a bottle of Merlot? Got sloshed and took a roll in the hay after some shots of tequila? Don't look at me like that, I know you, Paul—"

"I *captured* her." Well, that felt surprisingly good to say.

His face immediately sobered. "Hell, Paul. That's big."

"Yes."

"This is going to make your career—"

"Not at the rate *this* is going."

"Why?"

"After Ryu's capture, I set a course for the Inner Planets for her court martial. Her trial preparations have begun. They even called old Admiral Girelli away from his vacation on Tetra VII to serve on the tribunal."

"I don't see a problem here."

"The problem is my CO, Colonel Tauber, ordered me to execute her instead, conflicting with the orders from CIPCOM."

"What!" Jim's face darkened into a scowl. "That's an illegal order."

"I think so, too, but unfortunately, I don't have official orders from Legal. I don't think they thought it was necessary. Who was going to override that? They were rescheduling admirals already and everything."

"Tauber, apparently." Jim was shaking his head. "None of that is an excuse to—"

The line suddenly went silent for a moment, then static, then a jumble of noise blasted at him, painfully loud and impossible to process. He sat forward. "Jim?"

The image was frozen, then it distorted for a moment. Now Paul could see what they meant about comms. "Jim?" he growled. "Jim, can you hear me?"

This shouldn't have been a hard jump. Jim wasn't *that* far away. He couldn't have lost him already. They hadn't discussed anything that could *really* help him yet. He hadn't asked about sons. Or pets. Just complained.

"Jim!"

"—ou there, Paulie?" The voice came back before the image, but the connection seemed to repair itself. That didn't make Paul feel particularly calmer, though. It could happen again.

"I'm here, Jim."

"Great. As I was saying… you should definitely get Legal to cross their t's and dot their i's."

"Right. I'll do that." Hopefully, one of his aides had already thought of it. Shu, probably. "But I already had to defy the order. I didn't suspect I'd need to cover my ass there either. So the bridge between me and my CO is on fire. And he's insisting I get to the front line."

"That's some real dreck, Paulie. Not good."

"I know." He tried not to moan, but it definitely came out groaning.

"Was it a wartime desertion? I'm gonna need more details here, the law states—"

"Her file is heavily classified, multiple seals, three levels. We're having trouble getting through. They won't give me the damn details. What could be so damn secret that they can't at least give me clarity to make a simple decision? What would be so urgent that she can't be punished through normal channels, including the execution process? I'm a commander, not a headsman, for God's sake."

"Maybe they released the info to Tauber, and that's how he decided." Jim spread his hands.

"Maybe." He sighed. "But then why did they start setting up a trial? Or why wouldn't he just tell me the location of her desertion? Some regions were considered at peace at that time."

"That's bullocks. How can we be half at war?"

"Hey, I don't make the rules. Why don't you take it up with Orders & Regs?"

He sighed. "Have you asked her if she knows the location?"

He frowned. "No. I will. Tauber alluded that the admiralty had given him the orders, but how can that be true? If the admiralty was determined to execute, why set up a trial?"

"The left hand doesn't know what the right hand is doing?"

"Wouldn't be the first time."

"Nor the last. Listen, I might be able to help you there. I'm supposed to have dinner with Admiral Polunatu tomorrow. Maybe I can… see what he'll share. Off the record."

"If they *did* tell Tauber the location, and he's got at least some grounds to order her execution, then my excuse for defying his orders becomes much more… pedantic? Bureaucratic?"

"In other words, he'll have your hide eventually?"

"Yes. But he could have explained, even if he didn't tell me the exact location. He didn't. It doesn't add up. And there's…" He stopped. He couldn't mention the telepathic attack. It was too weird to believe. He *definitely* couldn't explain how he'd, uh, solved the problem by changing the target to himself. And the Theroki's intervention was absolutely off the table.

Much more importantly, he needed to explain Ellen's claims about her desertion, and that was going to be hard enough. How would he even convey them to Jim without sounding like he'd drunk to much zeefruit wine?

"What? What is it?"

"Well…" He took a deep breath. No way to make it sound less than wild, he supposed. "I wanted to know why she deserted. I—it was personal. So I asked questions. A lot of them."

"I remember you two were close once. Can't be anything wrong with asking questions." His brother kept his expression concerned, earnest, and for that Paul was grateful. It would have been easy to mock him, kick him at this low moment.

"Yes, well. I always wondered why. She didn't want to tell me. Claimed I wouldn't believe her."

"Did you?"

"Not at first. But now I'm starting to wonder." Yes, it was best to ease up to the idea.

"What did she tell you?"

"She claimed that the reason she deserted was because she was forced into a secret lab project. Experimented on. She said it was associated with the Songbirds."

"The terrorist cell?" He scowled. "How is that—"

"Her assertion is that the program was started *inside* the Union, in secret research, and only later broke out on its own. And she was one of them, so she fled to escape that fate."

His brother blinked, saying nothing for a moment.

"She claims her team has intel that there's even been infiltration by the Songbirds into Union officers and elected officials. And I'm starting to wonder."

"That's incredibly serious, Paul. What's making you wonder?"

"Well, why are they so determined to kill her? A court martial is totally reasonable even if it was a wartime desertion, for someone like her. It's not like I'm letting her go and handing her a bag of credits and buying her a ship. Godspeed, Ellen! Although at this point, that sounds heavenly. I wish I fragging could. Then I could go back to routine missions and working on advancing my career rather than blowing it out of the water."

Jim covered a laugh with his hand.

"Why are they so impatient? And nobody will give us any kind of information on her unit at the time of desertion. But we do know the unit was deployed in the research projects division, and that it had roughly forty involved, a number she independently corroborated."

"This stinks to high heaven, Paulie." Jim rubbed his chin, thinking. "You know I love our Union with every molecule in my body, but that doesn't mean every one of us is squeaky clean. Hmm. I'm sure I could request the files. But I have less need to know than you. Eliza works on security, though… Maybe she could." He paused, lost in thought. "Did you talk to Legal? Do you need me to get an independent lawyer to review this mess?"

"I'm not sure. Our officer felt confident we were within rights not to execute the prisoner yet, so I have at least that much." The prisoner? Why hadn't he said her name? Why hadn't the law officer either? The prisoner's rights this, the admiralty's intentions that… So dehumanizing. These were people, damn it. "I'm heading toward the Inner Planets. But he ordered me toward the big op, Freedom's Wing. I can't do both. I need some kind of cover. Can you get me a sealed Senatorial Order?"

Jim winced, then whistled.

"I know you're sensitive to nepotism allegations, and this is certainly a fair one. But this is serious. Tauber could put us in the front and get me killed before I can get justice." For himself or for Ellen. "You know there are some positions in an op like they're planning that are going to get absolutely crushed. Why not put an old ship like the *Everest* there? Save your repairs for the ships that are worth it, but that one is nearly out to pasture anyway. I can see Tauber encouraging that line of thinking."

His brother winced harder now. He looked like he wanted to deny it but knew better.

"I don't see how it can hurt anything to have Ellen Ryu alive a little longer to make sure justice is truly served. It's been five years. What's five more days or weeks?"

"Fine. I'll do it."

Paul's eyes widened. He hadn't expected that to actually work.

"Sealed, though," Jim added. "I'll send it over shortly. I can write it to allow for further investigation into the situation around Ryu's desertion. But that's not enough to save your career. I'm going to get the boys in Legal to send you the exact same thing, pronto. Colonel or admiral, they can't interfere with a criminal investigation, and if there's a trial scheduled, that's what this is."

His shoulders slumped down in relief. "Thank you. Thank you. It means a lot to me." It wouldn't help him get access to the files or save him from Tauber retaliating. It *would* keep him from being executed himself, however. Maybe. It was a shot.

Many argued senators shouldn't have this kind of power, and so they were loath to use it in any capacity, especially to short circuit the chain of command. Tauber and others would be furious eventually—there would be a political cost. But no one had ever accused the Dealis clan of being soft on the military. Jim had at least a little capital to spend here. In truth, though, if Legal had just sent the orders more officially, all this could have been avoided.

Ellen's allegations suddenly niggled at him. Infiltrations. Why hadn't they? In truth, they hadn't done their jobs… Because they hadn't expected to be questioned? Or was there a more sinister reason?

Jim was busy making notes and sending requests. "Let me see if I can move my appointment with Admiral Polunatu up to an early lunch too. We need more information."

"That'd be great. Our requests for declassification have been pretty much shut down at this point. They've told us what they're going to tell us."

"Didn't you say Ryu claimed her team had their own information? Can you get it? If there's proof that Union planetary governments have been infiltrated by the Songbirds, I want it." He pointed a harsh finger at the screen. "And I want to root them out. How dare they threaten my Union. God, what if a few of them are *friendly* to those terrorists? Offering safe haven?" He shuttered.

Paul blew out a breath. "I don't know if we can trust their info. But I can at least take a look."

"Those women are dangerous extremists. If you're going up against them, you should commission some telepathic shielding or something."

"Have you seen the price of opsepium? We'll never get our hands on telepathic shielding. Engineering has a list of parts a mile long, and though we try every time we berth, we barely make a dent in the list. I'm shit out of luck in that department. Besides, by the time we could get any kind of telepathic shielding installed, we'd be back in the Inner Planets, already turning Ellen over for her trial. And I'll be done with the Songbirds by then, so it'd be too late."

"You're right, of course. But be careful, Paulie. I'll send you a message when I've talked to Polunatu and gotten his read on Ellen Ryu's capture. Let's see how quickly he can meet. Maybe six hours?"

Paul smiled. Jim was always one to get things done. The man was a machine. Part of what his constituents loved. "Maybe I'll have some information for you first. Race you?"

"Just don't get your belt caught in a tree again trying."

"God damn it, Jim—"

"Talk to you later!" The screen went dark. He hoped it was because Jim hung up and not because the comms were totally busted now.

He had one more call to make. And she was not going to be happy about hearing from him any more than Ryu had been. He got Mertz on the line again.

"Mertz. Can you get me Admiral Birch please?"

There was a pause. "I can try, sir."

Enthusiastic and optimistic as always. Would that energy survive till Mertz made lieutenant or even captain someday? Paul sure hoped it would, but it'd be a miracle. "Just do your best," he replied. "That's all I ask."

DONE with her training for the day, Shirin curled up in her bunk and picked up her tablet.

She had to admit, if she had realized when Dane and Commander Ellen had wandered into Petuk's that they were offering a room this kicking, she would've jumped at the chance more quickly.

She smiled at the memory. Petuk's Life Creature Supply hadn't been the worst place that had ever owned her. The animals had been fun, and they'd bought a nurse bot—that was EOE8—to protect and care for their charges. But she still hadn't been free. And the animals at Petuk's had counted a fair number of cockroaches in their number... And the smell was hard to forget.

Neither Dane nor Commander Ellen was here now, but they had kept their promises. Even their promise to keep her safe. She'd had the chance to stay with Dane. And he was a pretty kicking guy, and very funny.

But her training was more fun. And much more important. Mornings, she spent working with the robots and the hull repair tools, learning more science than she'd ever dreamed of learning. While she ate lunch, she gritted her teeth through math and language exercises EOE8 implored her to take. She might have resisted more if it weren't such an act of rebellion. Petuk's had taught her to count, to make change, but she hadn't even really been able to read the feed bags and receipts and such. Who knew how many mistakes she'd made because she was relying on picture labels.

Then in the afternoons, she'd resumed her workouts with Jenny, now that her tutor was feeling better after her dunk in the toxic sea.

If she ever grew up to be half as tough as even one of these women, she'd be proud of just how kicking she'd turned out to be.

Now, all that was done, and dinner of some strange curry was in her belly, she had time to relax and tend to her animals.

Oh, she still hadn't gotten anyone to get her a real animal.

Although she wasn't letting Commander Ellen or her dad forget those promises, assuming they ever showed up again.

Everybody except for EOE8 assured her they would. EOE8 was too good of a carebot, though, and lying wasn't in its programming. She could hope they would come back, and she could tag along on this ship in hopes that she was a small contributor to their survival.

But hope and fact were different.

No, she still had no real live animals like she'd had a Petuk's, so she had to settle for digital. But that was one of the things that made her room so dang kicking.

Since most of the walls in this cabin could also be turned into displays, she switched them to rows of little animals from several different star systems. More than a few rabbits and chipmunks though. She loved those darn cuties.

It was a virtual game, and a poor substitute for an animal that could snuggle you, but it did fill the time and make her smile.

Once every virtual creature had been fed and watered and three of them had been brushed, she turned part of the screens to her memento board while she considered purchasing a garden upgrade that would give the bunnies "fresh" virtual greens.

Her attention wondered from the game module, though, lingering on the memento board instead. It, too, was virtual, but the tradeoffs were better here. She had no actual physical pictures of her father—or her mother, or of anyone or anything else, for that matter.

But Xi had found her some in her files. Photos and videos of her dad around the ship. It felt a little creepy, like watching surveillance footage she hadn't asked if she was allowed to… But he was gone and this was all she had, so if it was creepy, she didn't care.

Today, Xi offered up footage of her dad sitting in Xi's robot-repair lab, fixing one of the cleaning bots. Shirin had started to know her way around that place. She watched as he frowned at something, pulled on something. It came off and he frowned even harder, as if he hadn't intended that to happen.

After a few minutes of watching, she tried to get back into her game again, but she couldn't focus. She considered looking at a new game she could alternate with her pets, but she looked at three and didn't pick anything.

Would Xi be up for a conversation?

"He's not coming back, is he, Xi?" she asked out of nowhere.

"My calculations indicate chances for his return are favorable."

She pursed her lips together. EOE8 did not lie, but Xi was a more sophisticated AI. Was she able to cherry pick what she offered to her, or did she truly believe that and answered her honestly? "You don't have to sugar coat things for me, Xi."

"I have no coating of sugar or any other material. Statistically, looking at the data of other missions, complete versus injured versus incomplete versus fatal, he's survived a significant number of missions with this crew, mostly uninjured and complete. Commander Ryu's data is even better. That makes their chances statistically very good."

"Hmm. I haven't really gotten to statistics yet."

"Oh, well, they can be quite useful. Would you like to learn some now?"

"No, thank you."

"Of course. But should you ever change your mind, I am always here, ready to help." The AI paused. "You miss him."

"Yes."

"Would your carebot be of any consolation? I see it has been in idle mode for quite a long time now."

Shirin bit her lip. She had hoped no one had noticed, but of course Xi had noticed. Silly of her not to realize she would.

She couldn't, of course, admit to the real reason she'd powered down EOE8. She did power it up from time to time—it was too wonderful to have someone else to do chores for her, for once, and EOE8 insisted it didn't mind—but she needed to keep it out of conversations that pointed out how much danger she was in on this ship. If it'd been on during her talk with Commander Zhia, she was certain EOE8 would have objected to her staying aboard.

Which was logical, really. Just like Dr. Levereaux was very logical.

But she hadn't been allowed to make many choices for herself in her life. And who knew how long her freedom would really last? She'd known girls who escaped. They often ended up right back where they started.

That could be her, too. If not re-enslaved back on Faros, the same thing could happen anywhere. She was safe here, but fate was fickle, and she knew how easily things could fall apart. She had no real resources, no funds to her name, no credit, not even proof she'd been born.

At least she was learning a good right hook. And how to duck and fall and roll and climb. But if she got separated from these people, even accidentally, the 'verse was full of people who would treat her more like a can of beans or a milk cow than a person.

These people on the *Audacity* believed she was a person, and gratitude welled up in her—for her dad and all the others—that she'd even gotten to *experience* this, however short the experience ended up being. It was almost too hard to believe.

Whatever—while it lasted, she was going to take *full* advantage of this situation, even if it got her killed. She was making her own decisions for once.

Abruptly, she realized Xi was still waiting on an answer about EOE8.

"Oh, I just wanted a break," Shirin said. It came out sounding weak. Fake. Like a lie. How good was the AI at detecting lies? "I'm getting older, you know? I wanted to try out life without a nurse looking after me all the time."

"Freedom is desirable to most humans," Xi agreed. "And some prefer solitude or independence much of the time. To varying degrees. Some prefer very little."

"True." Shirin was a little worried that maybe Xi thought she didn't understand how people worked, given her background and all, but perhaps the AI was just sharing its knowledge, unclear on how much any given human might understand about other humans. Especially a kid.

Shirin smiled. Whatever Xi's internal motivations, the AI had bought her reasoning about EOE8. "I do like solitude sometimes. But sometimes, we just want a variety of people to be around too. Everyone on the ship is so busy… It's easy to get sick of each other."

"I see. Shall I leave you alone?"

"Oh, no. I meant EO. I love EO. But sometimes, we all just need a break. Or… variety."

"Would you like… someone else to talk to?"

Shirin cocked her head. "Um, like who?"

"Like another AI. Who has been very bored lately and who I suspect shares your predilection for variety in companions."

Now, that was too weird and vague to resist. "Sure, okay. How do I talk to it?"

"You have to go fetch it first. Unlike EOE8, it is not self-ambulatory."

Shirin followed Xi's instructions, heading up a ladder and going in when a hatch opened for her. Then she stopped short, glancing around nervously. It was a cabin, not a lab, and it looked sparse, almost unlived in, but it was way larger than any of the other cabins. A tablet sat askew on the glass desktop, as if it'd just been casually set down and someone was coming back for it.

"Commander Ryu! Have you returned?" A refined, sophisticated male voice, like the people her owners entertained but never visited Petuk's personally, bellowed from across the room. But she couldn't see a face or a bot or anything to be bellowing.

"Wait, is this the commander's cabin?" she said quickly.

"Yes. It is fine," Xi assured her.

"That is not the good commander!" Apparently, the voice disagreed. "Intruder! Xi, intruder!"

Shirin had to agree with the voice. "Xi, it's not fine. I shouldn't be here." Her stomach twisted. What if something went missing and the commander and her dad made it back, and they found out she'd been in here and thought she'd stolen it? She could be out on her ass that quick. "I need to get out of here."

"It is also her office, where she has meetings with her team," Xi said blandly. "Rich, Shirin is not an intruder, I invited her."

"So?" Shirin rotated on her heel to go. "I need to go."

"Wait, good lady. If the wise Xi has summoned you here, perhaps we should both be more receptive. The AI is very knowledgeable, you know, in terms of which video dramas are most highly rated as well as when all of the great fashion exhibitions are scheduled."

She frowned and slowly turned back. "Did you say... fashion exhibitions?"

"Why, yes, madam! I did not lose my passion for the avant-garde just because some ninnymuffin has stowed me in a metal locker and forgotten about me."

"Shirin, this is Rich." Xi's voice held almost no inflection. "Rich, this is Shirin, Kael's daughter."

"Oh, *hello*, dear girl. Hello."

"Um..." Shirin hesitated, glancing around. The room still looked the same.

"Now you say, 'It's nice to meet you,'" Xi offered.

Shirin snorted. "To whom?"

"Look at her, using proper grammar. I like her already. But she is correct, Xi, you must update your relational etiquette model of introductions. Both parties should be in visible sight of each other to commence with an introduction."

"Ah. Excellent nuance. I see. Update created. Shirin, Rich is in the metal locker on the right. Go on, please open it. He needs care just as much if not more than your other pets."

"You've got pets?" Rich exclaimed, almost sounding afraid. Why would he be afraid?

"Just virtual ones, why?" Shirin strode toward the locker. This felt all kinds of wrong, but she was way too far into this conversation to just back away and refuse to open the locker.

At the bottom of a nearly empty locker filled only with identical sets of black cargo pants and gray T-shirts was a pair of high heels. They jolted when she looked at them.

"Hello!"

She took a step back. "You're—"

"Shoes, yes. I'm quite enhanced, and I am really hoping you don't have a dog. I'd rather not be chewed upon."

"I think I can safely promise that won't happen." She grinned.

"Like dogs, however, I do need out of my cage and to go for a walk."

"With Commander Ryu gone," Xi said quickly, "I thought you could keep Rich for a while. Perhaps entertain each other. He is going a bit… stir-crazy."

"She's understating really. Please! Put me on, dear girl, it's been *centuries.*"

"What if you're not my size?" She picked up the shoes and started toward the chair at the desk, then wondered if she should really be going back to her own cabin and not sitting in the commander's chair. Then again… it was harmless, wasn't it?

"I am *all* sizes and heel heights, dear. Let us experiment! We will show the avant-garde a thing or two, you'll see!"

She spent the next few hours laughing as she discovered which forms Rich could assume that she absolutely could not walk in, absorbed his tips on how to eventually do so someday, and ran around in some of his more practical forms, for both of their amusement.

When she flopped down on her bunk near night cycle, she had a much more positive feeling vibing through her. The exercise hadn't hurt. "You should consider a stand-up comedy career, Rich," she said.

"Really? Fascinating insight, my dear. I don't know that I could ever fully leave fashion, but perhaps… perhaps… Perhaps, once I'm back in my box for my charging cycle, I shall consider it."

Shirin let out a mixture of a giggle and a sigh, still grinning as she closed her eyes. Maybe she would get something to drink from the mess. Or a shower. Or maybe just go to sleep.

Able to make her own decisions…. Wonderfully open-ended. Surprisingly tricky.

"Was this helpful?" Xi asked, volume low. "Are you feeling more positive generally?"

She smiled. "Yes, Xi. Thanks. You're a good friend."

"You are welcome, Shirin Nar."

She frowned. "Can we change that, Xi?"

"What?"

"My last name. I want to be Shirin Sidassian."

"Of course, dear. Consider it done."

THE NEXT FEW hours in the brig hadn't been any better than all those that had come before. Ellen was sick of staring at steel walls. After a "lunch" of newly delivered, orange-flavored "protein vitamin infusion," an escort marched her and Kael back to the meeting room in which they'd met Paul the day she'd arrived.

How many days had it been now? It was blurry, and the brig's night cycle wasn't much of one. Maybe the sleep deprivation was intentional, considering how hard the "bunk" was. She certainly hadn't slept sixteen hours, or even four in a row, since she'd arrived, even with the blankets Yamamoto had sent them.

In the meeting room, Paul and his staff waited. She took the indicated seat, resting her cuffed wrists in plain view.

Paul cleared his throat. "Thank you all for coming," he said, addressing all present. "I want to share three pieces of information with you. Here is the first." He hit a button on the table.

The wall display came to life, and Ellen's blood froze. Tauber's glaring face filled the screen. She gripped the table.

"This is the recording I just received," Paul said casually.

"Dealis," Tauber growled. "Who the fuck do you think you are? I'm going to get you for this. I don't care who your brother is, I don't care who you sacked or sucked, you do *not* disobey orders and get away with it." He pounded a fist. "You're pathetic. You're a coward. Get whatever 'official' orders you want. There are ways. There are *always* ways. This isn't over! You kill that bitch and report to the op immediately, or you're going to pay."

Paul pressed the button like he was ordering his lunch from a food dispenser, and the wall display went blank.

The room was dead silent. Ellen raised her eyebrows.

He cleared his throat a second time. "As you might have gathered from the colonel's eloquent words, I've chosen not to change course toward the planned operation. We will return Ryu to the Inner Planets for trial, whether Colonel Tauber likes it or not." He shifted in his chair, pausing for a moment. "The next thing I wanted to share with you is that Yamamoto followed up on the pill I almost took in sick bay before Lieutenant Rhee noticed its improper color. It turns out it would have interacted with my pain medication—and others I take—to cause a brain-damaging seizure. The nurse aide who delivered it was found dead in the storage cabinets. So it appears, Lieutenant Rhee, I am in your debt. And that Commander Ryu is not the only one that someone is trying to murder."

She caught her breath. Holy hell. What was going on here? That was even before Tauber had given him the orders. She knew people wanted her dead, but why would they want Paul dead?

A quiet voice in her head said, *To get to her.* But if Paul were dead, then Yamamoto would take over. He seemed completely aligned with Paul. Would taking Paul out actually make it any easier for the Songbirds to get to her? Yamamoto seemed so trustworthy. He seemed to truly be looking out for them, not calling out Kael's augmentations. Maybe his flattery and kindness were dangerously biasing her in his favor. Maybe his actions were deliberately designed to make her trust him…

Or maybe she was being too fragging paranoid.

Shu raised a finger, but Paul held up a palm, asking her to wait.

He took a long slow breath. "The last thing I wanted to share. I've spoken with my brother. As you may or may not know, he is a senator now, but had a long career in military law before he became an elected official. He's secured us 'official' "— he paused to make air quotes with his fingers, emphasized due to Tauber's disdain for the word—"orders from Union law enforcement that we must return Ryu to the Inner Planets for trial. Tauber can't override them. He *can* find ways to screw me over later or make our lives difficult right now, and I'm sure he will. But in the meantime, Senator Dealis has also arranged for the addition of one more minor duty to the orders."

"Which is?" Bridell asked. She couldn't read his exact expression, but it looked troubled.

"To investigate the circumstances around Ryu's suspicious desertion, including uncovering whether any additional crimes were committed."

Ellen sat back in her seat. That... was unexpected.

Shu was grinning. Mertz was elbowing her. Bridell was frowning, but it seemed thoughtful.

"Now. As my first act in... investigating these other crimes, I'd like you to make a call, Commander Ryu." He pushed a large comm unit on the table toward her.

"Pardon?"

"You wanted a chance to call your ship and share intel. Here's your chance."

She hesitated only a split second longer, trying to process it all, then leapt for the comm. She punched in a couple of generic routing codes, the ones they kept in case of an emergency, and waited.

God, let them not be too far away. Let the codes still work.

A chime sounded—a familiar one. "Greetings," replied a computerized voice.

This was her chance to offer up her identity, her message, whatever she needed or wanted to get through to them. "*Audacity*, this is Commander Ryu," she said, as clearly as she could. "My Union 'friends' have some questions for us. I'd like an update on your intel work if possible." Hopefully, Doug and the others would understand what she was trying to imply. They never did find an official intel officer like she'd planned, but maybe using the word would clue them in to who was listening and why.

"So this means you'll be giving us a full roster of your crew, correct?" Paul smiled.

"In your dreams, Pau—Captain."

"One moment please," a voice replied. Xi's voice, she realized, a dulled quiet default version of it. "Would you like audio or audio and video, Commander?"

"Both, please."

"One moment."

She forced herself to breathe as she waited, wondering if it would be Doug who popped up on the screen. He'd be ideal, and he could speak very convincingly about what he'd found.

A smooth voice came over the comm, along with a familiar face. Not Doug's though—this face she was used to seeing as a holographic avatar.

It was no avatar now. Unless this was some kind of extra-sharp simulation, the face looking back at her was more silicone and piston than pixel.

"Hello, Commander," Xi said, smiling.

"Xi! You're looking..." Three dimensional? Almost human? She swallowed down her shock. She shouldn't say any of those ideas out loud. Ellen tried to stop staring. And blinking. And staring. "You're looking very well."

"Thank you," Xi replied. "The crew has authorized me to share their findings."

"Who is this, Ryu?" Paul demanded. His tone said he hadn't missed her hesitation.

"This is Xi," she said, groping for an explanation and not coming up with one.

"Xi is our new intelligence officer." Kael leaned one elbow on the table, rattling it off casually as though simply explaining an awkward situation , rather than displaying the brilliant, brilliant person he was, who was much better at lying under pressure than she. Social pressure, at least. "Doing great so far, Ensign."

Ellen almost snorted. Maybe she'd had her intel officer all along. Although that rank needed some work.

"Did you have specific questions?" Xi asked, voice flat. "Or should I offer a report?"

"I do have questions," Ellen said. "But first, any updates on the coordinates we were given?"

"What coordinates?" Paul demanded. "If you're going to try to use this communication to sneak information past us, I'll end this before it's even—"

She held up a palm. "Understood. Xi, can you give Captain Dealis a summary of the mission during which we found the coordinates, along with any conclusions?"

"Of course, Commander. The mission you refer to sought to retrieve data and other intelligence resources from the oceanic lab on Aeori III. We undertook this mission based on intelligence gathered at other locations with past Songbird activity, and—"

"Wait—didn't Davenmore say he'd received a tip that that system would be a location of interest to Ryu?" Yamamoto asked.

"Something is up with that man," muttered Paul. "Is he working with them?"

"He doesn't seem like their type," Kael said. "He's got balls. Allegedly, anyway."

"We have no evidence of Davenmore working with the Songbirds, but it is a possibility," said Xi. "Their goals are compatible."

"Please continue, Xi."

"The mission data banks that we retrieved, Commander, have not been a lucrative source of data, I'm sorry to say. Some of the data of value we had already obtained. But during the course of the mission, as you observed, Dr. Arakovic contacted us, goaded us to try to find her, and shared a specific location and date-time group."

Ellen frowned. "Anything interesting about the location? What is the approximate date-time?"

"The location is an asteroid system in the Plycon Nebula. The date-time mentioned is approximately six days from now."

Paul jolted in his chair. "Six days?"

"What's so relevant about six days?" Ellen asked.

"You're going to need to tell me a lot more before I can tell you that."

"Is that when that big mission is? And look, I *did* know about the Plycon Nebula. I just didn't know I knew it yet."

Paul slapped a palm over his face. "Oh, shut up, Ryu, and tell me what you know about Union infiltration."

"Which is it, Captain? I don't know about you, but I've struggled to achieve talking and shutting up at the same time."

Lieutenant Shu smothered a laugh.

Paul was still for a moment, then narrowed his eyes. "The famous Ellen Ryu astounds us with her brilliance, yet again. Play nice now, or you might have to go sit in the brig until you're feeling more generous. And talkative. We're sharing, aren't we? You first. Via *talking*."

"I know *I* am sharing. I don't know about you," she said, hoping that wouldn't push him too far. As much as she didn't like it, Kael was right. These people were their best chance. If she wanted to get them fighting Arakovic alongside the *Audacity*, she was going to have to convince them they needed to be there too.

"I want that data the ensign mentioned too," he added.

She sighed. "Xi, I don't know if you have this on hand, but our friends don't believe us about my experiences with the Songbird project. Or that it is sinking its claws—"

"Talons?"

"Whatever. Into several Union planets. Any information you might have on that, at least what we're comfortable sharing, would be appreciated."

"I am sending along a copy of the official unredacted Songbird project files. That should clear up many questions."

Shu straightened abruptly at her tablet. "This is—How did you get into my tablet? This is—this is *highly illegal* for you to have this. And for you to have access to my tablet."

Xi's expression was flat. "Would you like me to remove it?"

"No! But it's so illegal for *me* to have this right now." She sighed. "This is all the information we've been trying to get access to, though, Captain. Nothing is redacted."

Paul sighed. "Ah, well. Add it to the list for my court martial."

Ellen frowned at that, but Xi continued before she could ask a question.

"I am also sending our files on Union infiltration. I have been told to tell you this information was hard-won and highly sensitive, so don't take it for granted." Xi's fingers moved across several more keys, although Ellen was positive she didn't need to do that to send anything. "Some of our latest additions, Commander, come from data acquired on Aeori III. While there wasn't a great deal of it, they did detail a large Union operation on the Puritan front orchestrated by Songbird-controlled agents within the Union."

"Wait, what?" Paul sat forward.

Xi continued, robotic. "The files suggest the Songbirds consider the mission a 'final solution' to the Puritans in particular. At least one, possibly two, Theroki ships have been deployed to assist with the attack with some kind of Songbird weapon onboard."

"That sounds like…" Shu started.

Bridell cut her off with a sharp look. If it weren't so concerning, Ellen might have felt a little smug. Looked like their big secret mission wasn't as secret as they thought. Of course, if the Songbirds had something to do with it, and Doug had uncovered some recent data in the drives they'd gotten from Aeori III, then it wasn't entirely fair. How could the Union forces have known they were just puppets in this game, especially those at lower ranks?

While Paul was gaping at the screen, Ensign Mertz caught his breath.

"What is it?" Paul demanded.

"This is… This list of infiltrators. Traitors, I guess. This is an admiral." He winced. "Two actually. And their medical teams."

"That seems to be their primary vector," Xi said. "Infiltration began through surgeons specializing in cybernetic augmentation and trauma repair. During standard, elective medical operations, they did considerably more than required. Or allowed."

"Give me examples. I need something concrete I can tell them to look for." Paul scowled at no one in particular.

"Examples include cybernetic and synthetic telepathy

infrastructure, as well as in some cases deliberately botching routine surgeries. Sometimes, this also involved eliminating, replacing, or augmenting the subject's immediate family and staff."

"Eliminating—you mean murder?"

"Yes, I do. Songbirds have murdered en masse before, so individual murders to secure power over a planet or part of an armed force would be a small contribution to their vast tally. These surgeries seem to be where the Songbirds gained a primary foothold, within both the military and parts of civilian government."

Continuing to scan the information, Mertz continued, "There are several colonels and the foreign minister and—"

"Wait, you said two admirals. Which ones?" Paul demanded.

"Admiral Hsu and Admiral Polunatu."

He swore. "Get my brother on the line. Now! Tell him it's an emergency."

"But we just told him that—"

"Now!"

All three began tapping frantically at their tablets, and Shu picked up her comm. "Senator Dealis, please. It's extremely urgent. Yes, extremely. Extremely, extremely. Look, I'm not going to stop calling until you get him."

"Commander," Xi said. "I will hold on the line in case you need further information."

"Good, Ensign. Thank you."

"Of course."

A second feed appeared on the main screen, shifting Xi to a smaller portion of the whole. All their eyes shifted to the new, larger vid feed.

"Paulie? You got any idea about what's going on?" A man with features strikingly similar to Paul's and similar ink-black hair was huddled under a desk, a woman cowering just behind him.

"What the frag is going on?"

"I asked the admiral to move up our lunch, the next thing I know, somebody's pounding down the door—"

"A heli landed outside!" the woman shouted over another loud rumbling. "Without clearance. I can't get through to our security—"

"What did you tell the admiral?" Paul asked.

"Why aren't they answering?" the woman was shouting.

" 'Cause they're a little busy, Di." Jim coughed. "I just mentioned celebrating your accomplishment and having a few questions—"

Another loud slam sent pieces of plaster cracking above them, trickling down toward the ground.

"Or they're dead," Ellen muttered.

"Do you have a visual on the heli?" asked Bridell. "Can we get one? Or more than one—Ensign Mertz, see what you can do."

"Sending it," said the woman, fingers flying across her comm unit.

Mertz slid his tablet to the center of the table. An exterior cam feed showed a small stealth model heli, expensive and light but versatile. On the side was a blue, tentacled creature, the mark she was sure she could never see again and die happy.

"They need to get out of there." Ellen leaned forward, voice low but urgent.

"Get out of there!" Paul bellowed, standing up.

"Our car's the only way out, and it's outside—"

"Where's your security? Can we get them back up? You need to—"

Silently, Mertz's tablet switched to an exterior door, stopping Paul mid-word. Two black-clad bodies were crumpled.

"We had eight men," said the woman, "all down."

On the same feed, three, heavily armored soldiers had picked up a nearby park bench. Three, two, one—they rammed the door with it, a crushing slam coming over the main feed.

"Where are they on the Inner Planets that this is happening?" Ellen said. "He's a senator, for frag's sake."

"Panic room." Paul was running his hands through his hair. "Does your office have one?"

The brother nodded, even as he covered his head and ducked again as another crash came down. Were they on the roof too? Had to be. "But it's down the hallway—all glass—they'll see us."

"It'll be close," added the woman.

"Well, the desk isn't going to cut it against *them*," Paul thundered. "Get up and—"

Another thunderous impact, then a sharp crack, and the feed went dead.

Paul froze. The room was utterly silent, even Xi on the feed.

"Is he dead?" he whispered.

"Not necessarily," said Bridell quickly.

"That was the camera getting hit," Mertz added.

"The roof was coming apart." Bridell was gripping the table now but trying to look calm. And mostly succeeding. "Maybe his comm unit was just destroyed."

"Or?" he said slowly.

"Or…" Bridell swallowed. "Or the whole roof came down."

Mertz pounced back on his tablet. "Let's see if we can send emergency services or call for help or—"

Paul was shaking his head, backing away from the table. "She said I'd regret this. She's said it..."

"Who?" Ellen demanded, standing up now too.

His blue eyes met hers, haunted, bereft. "There was a voice. When I tried to… carry out Colonel Tauber's orders."

"We believe a hostile telepath was in range of the ship," Shu put in. "And tried to influence Captain Dealis to kill you."

Her eyes widened. "And by hostile telepath you mean a Songbird?"

"A Songbird, yes." Shu nodded. "The hostile agent was eliminated."

She turned her gaze back to Paul. "Don't you dare believe a word that a Songbird tells you. You will *not* regret trying to do the right thing. Now tell us. How did you know your brother was in danger?"

"I asked him to ask Admiral Polunatu about your trial." The words were hollow. He sank back into his seat. "I didn't understand why they were scheduling a trial if they're so determined to have you executed."

Mertz was murmuring something to Shu. "But this makes sense, if this intel from the *Audacity* is correct."

"It does?" Paul didn't move, or look at anyone, just stared at the table.

"Yes. If the Songbirds are determined to kill Ms. Ryu, then having one of their controlled admirals on the tribunal could be their backup plan. Then they could control a vote to execute."

Ellen blew out a breath and also sank back into her seat. "Hell… I knew that was possible, but even I didn't think it went *that* deep. When you put it that way…"

Paul was just shaking his head. "God, what if he's dead?"

"I'm sorry." She reached out a hand to put it over his, but the cuffs prevented it, so she gave up. "I hope he's all right."

He looked up. She expected a smoldering anger, a righteous rage in his eyes. Another death of someone close to him that was *her* fault. But there was nothing but an empty sadness there, almost a lack of comprehension, as if her apology didn't make sense, hadn't even occurred to him.

"He's locking himself in that panic room right now, *inshallah*," Kael said.

Paul blinked. Then looked at the table again. Slowly, the bereft captain's gaze slid back up to lock with Kael's.

"You should go and attack Arakovic," Kael said suddenly.

She shot a glare at him, but he kept his eyes trained on Paul.

"You said you can delay taking Ellen back to the Inner Planets to extend your interrogation," said Kael. "Or to do something urgent in the outsystem. The Songbirds just attacked your ship, you, and your damn brother."

Paul frowned. "None of that is certain."

"You were attacked at the reward point. Who the frag do you think was behind that?" Kael shifted forward in his seat.

"Davenmore. We can't link—"

"You can't prove it, but you can suggest it very strongly. Stretch the truth a little."

Paul's eyebrows shot up.

"Nobody's naive here, Captain," she said carefully. "We all know that, sometimes, the truth is bent. Especially on official records."

Paul glared but didn't deny it. "The Songbirds are clearly a threat, a dire one even. But an urgent one?" He shook his head.

Lieutenant Shu held up her tablet. On it, the heli on the landing pad outside his brother's office had been enlarged, the blue tentacled mark on the side easier to see. It was a little blurry, but clear enough. "Would this be enough to justify our timing, sir? This mark is explicitly identified in the Songbird files. Why it's not a bird, don't ask me."

Paul leaned forward now, the first spark of action in his eyes.

Kael jerked a thumb at Ellen. "Take her back for that trial, and your crooked military court will take your strongest chess piece off the board. Forever."

"Or what?"

"Or you can fight. Now. Before they hobble your options."

Goosebumps bristled on her skin, but there was an undercurrent of fear as well.

"You don't understand." Paul glanced at the screen where Senator Dealis had been, then back at the table.

She put both hands on the table. "Maybe he doesn't, but I do. Aren't you supposed to protect the people and planets of the Union?"

"Of course."

"So protect them," Ellen said. "You don't want to run off to Operation Disaster Number Eight Thousand And Ninety-Two anyway. *Do* you." She didn't say it as a question.

The room was silent.

"The Puritans…" Paul started, but the effort was feeble.

"The Puritans didn't just attack a senior senator on an Inner Planet," said Mertz.

"Or potentially infiltrate our admiralty," Shu added.

"You've been attacked three times, more or less, in just the few days since picking us up," Kael said slowly. "You think they're going to let up just because you move a few million kilometers closer to the Inner Worlds?"

"Inner Planets," Shu corrected.

"Whatever. There, it'll be even easier for them. They're going to keep coming after you."

"At greater risk to Union civilians," Ellen added. "And they're going to keep infiltrating your government."

"They're not going to stop until every last one of you is dead—or one of them." Kael pointed at the black screen where Senator Dealis should have been. "What if we had had this meeting an hour from now? You might not have gotten through. You might not have even known they attacked him. Who else are they attacking that we don't know about? The Songbirds need to be stopped."

Paul stared at Kael, and the longer he stared, the more Ellen's stomach twisted. Some line had just been crossed. Kael's argument was good, logical, incredible even. Too good. Too logical. Paul's eyes widened with a look of epiphany. The look she'd been hoping to avoid.

Paul was really seeing Kael for the first time. Not just Ryu's aide, not just a very stupid lackey who'd tagged along to get a life sentence or killed. Really seeing him.

He'd made the argument Ellen had wanted to make, that she'd told him not to. The one she'd known they needed to make to have a hope of taking on Arakovic's forces, the one they'd discussed long ago on the fighter ride over here. Some part of her writhed, sensing a huge mistake, a miscalculation. But he'd made her argument well. Better than she could have, in fact, because she would have sounded too full of arrogance to say those things, and then they wouldn't fly. Her goosebumps were still prickling her skin at the force and passion in his words, though.

She sensed some victory, some change in Paul, along with some fresh new danger. God, what the hell was this going to cost them?

"Get me a tablet to read through this intel from the *Audacity*." Paul's voice was quiet, but strangely steady. His eyes were sharp.

"I'll need to speak with Captain Weyer on the feed in my quarters in one hour."

"Sir, wouldn't you rather figure out if Senator Dealis is safe first —" Bridell started.

"Continue to try to reach emergency services and the army. As I assume you are already doing." Paul stood stiffly, then sniffed, and then finally looked at each of them. "At this point, my brother's fate is out of my hands. We can't reach him as quickly as we'd need to, much as I'd prefer that. I pray that he's safe. But it doesn't influence how we will proceed."

"And how are we going to proceed?" Bridell asked.

"Rhee is right. The message of that attack is clear. These people will stop at nothing to see Ryu dead, including attacking the Union fleet and a senator. Clearly, this group's danger to the Union is greater than we'd realized. It demands a response. And it will get one. From me." He strode toward the door.

"Paul—" She shot to her feet. "Wait. Let me help you or—"

"I have papers to read." His eyes held hers for a long moment, then faltered. "I'll think about it. Take them back to the brig." He started to leave, then paused. "No—take *her* back to the brig. Lieutenant Rhee, I'd like a word in my quarters."

Frag the whole damn 'verse to hell.

"Wait—" she started to say. But Paul was already gone, and Kael was on his feet jogging after him with a quick, apologetic nod goodbye.

Her eyes flicked to the viewscreen again. Xi was still there. They'd forgotten she'd been listening… Xi gave her a small nod as Shu gestured toward the door. The screen went dark.

Back to the brig again. This time, alone.

CHAPTER SIX

DEALIS'S CABIN wasn't quite what Kael would have guessed. Maybe it was just having slept in Ellen's spartan cabin for so long, but he'd expected some sort of military by-the-book decorum. Or perhaps a sort of austere asceticism, as if he lived only for the job and merely slept here.

The place was neat, the bed made, corners perfectly folded in a way Kael definitely couldn't have replicated. Although maybe captains had robots—or people—to take care of that for them.

But there was luxury in every surface and every detail. The holodesk wasn't the typical glass combined with steel or aluminum, but something sparkling and pale—maybe quartz? The bed wasn't your standard-issue wool or poly blend, no. It had a smooth, almost silken sheen. Here and there, there were touches of gold, chrome, automated lights blinking where there wouldn't usually be.

Maybe it was just the contrast to the rest of the *Everest* and its perpetual state of near collapse, or maybe Kael had just assumed Ellen's style was what the military had taught her. Apparently not.

Who really needed a finely polished, reddish-wood, gold-detailed intelligent pen?

"What exactly do you propose?" Paul asked as he sat down at his holodesk, facing Kael. He didn't offer Kael a seat, and that was just as well. He was full of energy and started pacing, back and forth, in front of the fancy quartz desk.

"I'm not proposing anything. I'm just looking at the situation and trying to keep the most people alive. I'm not a fancy officer like you—"

"You're a lieutenant. Which is an officer, in case no one told you."

"That was kind of a sympathetic vanity assignment from the rest of the crew, I think. I'm just a guy who can point my rifle in the right direction and guard doors."

Paul folded his arms. "You're not just a guy. You're a Theroki."

Kael stopped for a second, then shrugged. Yamamoto had said he would have to tell Dealis, and he couldn't fault the man for doing so. Dealis was his CO. Still, a touch of danger sparked in the air with the accusation. "I'm a *former* Theroki."

"I noticed. You have facial expressions. How did you manage such a thing? It's a lifetime contract."

"I escaped."

"Escaped." He sounded dubious.

"Was rescued? I didn't ask for that life, and I was liberated from it."

"By Ellen."

"By Commander Ryu, yes. And I repay her by doing the work. Like I said. Point rifles. Guard doors."

"Defend ships from laser batteries for twenty times the length of time they *should* have been able to withstand an attack given normal shield strengths." Paul pursed his lips.

Kael shrugged again. "The *Audacity* is my home. Its crew are my friends. You're the one who wanted to make it a pin cushion."

"I understand that. But don't play the dumb jarhead with me."

"I'm not trying to play anything with you. I'm just being honest."

"Then you sell yourself short."

Kael set his teeth and said nothing for a moment, stopping his pacing to prop his hands on his hips. When no response seemed fair, he just started pacing again.

"You suggested I should utilize your commander as part of this attack before I turn her in for her crimes. How exactly would you suggest I do that?"

His brow furrowed. "Again—you're the captain here. Don't ask me."

"Too late. I am asking you."

"Well… let her plan the mission, then. You execute it. That was her training, right, in plans? Strategy?"

"It's what she's famous for." He leaned back in his chair and sighed, as if remembering. "The Architect of SHR. A simpler time, then, oddly enough. The crew has been bored. Stir crazy even. A wild mission with a war hero—and a potentially dangerous one at that—might be great for morale. And loyalty."

"As long as they don't think you're a traitor in cahoots with a criminal."

"Therein lies the problem." Paul's nostrils flared.

"Keep the cuffs on?" Kael shook his head. "Look, just because I can see an opportunity to take out the Songbirds doesn't mean I know your crew or how to handle them."

"Fair point. But how do I know Ryu won't try to undermine my authority? Or walk us into a trap?"

"Oh, c'mon." Kael tried not to react too strongly to such ridiculous concerns. "Well, as to the first, you know her. She's a professional, and believe it or not, loyal. As for setting you up, I think you know that wouldn't happen."

"I suppose I could watch the cam footage. Check ahead on the sat feeds." He tapped his chin with one finger, then raised an eyebrow. "I mean, she criticized me to *you,* didn't she?"

He frowned slightly. Where was this questioning going, exactly? He had the sense that none of these questions were Paul's *real* question, and yet he couldn't quite sense what that real question was. "No… well, not really. Maybe just a little. How can you tell?"

"You flinched when she mentioned *Mirror's Light*."

He stopped pacing. "She may have said a few things about that, because it shaped her attitude toward her mission, but that's different."

"Why's it different?"

Oh, he did *not* want to explain that. "It was back on the *Audacity*. We were trading old stories. Fellow crew. That's totally different from badmouthing the captain of a ship you're on. Especially one who can throw you out an airlock any time he wants."

Paul laughed. "If anything, the airlock option would make my life easier. And I've been directly ordered to do it, too! But you know that fear isn't exactly Ellen's prime motivator."

Kael blew out a breath. "She wouldn't criticize you. Talking about you behind your back wouldn't be honorable."

"And you think she has any honor left?" Rising, Paul strode toward the window and looked out at the stars.

Again, tamping down his frustration and the urge to punch this guy in the face for thinking so little of her, he simply said, "I think she has always had a great deal of honor. More than most people I know."

"That doesn't say much for your acquaintances."

"You have no idea." He grinned. "Look, do what you want, but like I said, what she and I said alone over beers is not the same. This context is professional, and she's a guest. A prisoner guest, at that."

"I think that gives her all the more reason to undermine me."

"Like hell. You know she wouldn't."

"I think I know the real difference here." Paul turned and took a step closer, his eyes tightening into little beads now. "Are you sleeping with her?"

"I don't see how that's any of your business," he replied smoothly.

"Ah." Paul smirked now. "I see. You are."

"Slag off, I said no such thing."

"If you weren't, you would have said, 'Hell no, what would

make you think that? Don't be so unprofessional. It's a very uncouth question.' Unless you are, and then it is a simple fact."

"You don't know me. You don't know what I'd have said."

"I know people. That's perhaps my only talent in this world."

"Maybe I wish I were, and I just haven't given up hope yet." He wiggled his eyebrows. "Maybe I just want you to think I am."

Paul sighed, looking off into the stars again, calmer now. "Lying about it is disappointing. But I can't blame you."

"From what I heard, you had your chance." No, he'd promised himself he wouldn't go here. What kind of can of worms had he just opened?

"I'm surprised she admitted that much." A small smile tugged at the corner of his mouth.

"I believe there was a rival admiral involved?"

Paul laughed. The asshole actually laughed. A hand went to his chin and stroked. "Idiot. I was such an idiot." He bounced his palm off the side of his head.

Kael *just* stopped himself from saying, "Well, I can't disagree with that."

"If we ever work out time travel, I'll go back and tell Young Me a thing or two. Or ten. What a moron. That admiral was indeed well-connected, gorgeous, long-legged—and dropped me like an unlucky lava rock before my next commission was even half up."

"I guess there is some justice in the galaxy."

"Not enough. Yet. But twenty-year-old me got mine. In that one case, anyway."

"Many of us are still pretty stupid when we're twenty."

"And yet, she's smarter than us all, and what, twenty-one now?"

"Twenty-two. And nobody's perfect, even her."

Paul pursed his lips. "So I've been told. Too bad she wasn't the sort to shirk duty, at least not then. After our breakup, the next assignment she took was the one where she came under Tauber's command." He shook his head. "Supposedly on the front lines. As far from me as possible. Although for some reason, for the life of me,

I can't get access to the real location of that assignment. Maybe it's here in the files from your crewmates. I hope it is." He sighed. "At any rate. It was far. I wonder if that was not a coincidence."

"So you're agreeing that she's not the sort who would have ever deserted. Under ordinary circumstances."

"Oh, of course. I have—had—no doubt she was a lifer."

"Then why not just let her go?"

"Well, there's my duty required by commission. But also because she doesn't deny it. Because she was a lifer and she did it anyway. She abandoned people who needed her. She deserted her post, Lieutenant. Doesn't a promise mean anything to you people? Oaths?"

Kael lifted his chin. "I take promises very seriously. And an oath means something *very* different to me than it means to you. It's not possible to break. Ever. I'd say honor probably means something different too."

"We may not be as different as you think. This is my duty. That doesn't mean I have to like it." He looked straight at Kael now, surprising him. "I have made numerous dire mistakes in my life. I'm twenty-six, so I'm sure I'll make many, many more. But my admiration and respect for her wasn't a mistake. Treat her well, will you?"

"How I—or any of the *Audacity* crew—treat her won't matter." He narrowed his eyes. "Last I heard, life in prison was her best option at this point, so you should really talk to your prison guards if you care so much and you won't let us go."

Paul scowled, but his eyes said he knew the accusation was fair. "I'm not in control of her fate, I'm afraid. I wish I were."

"Aren't you, though?"

Paul narrowed his eyes. "I will not break the law, for her or anyone."

"But will you bend it a little? You can choose to go after Arakovic. You can choose what happens during the mission. Your brother gave you the legal breathing room. Admit it."

"And did that breathing room cost my brother his life?" He was breathing hard now.

Kael said nothing for a moment. What could he say to that, other than he sure hoped not?

Paul struggled to bring himself under control. "Even if he's alive, the cost of avoiding our obligations may be severe, for me as well as my crew. How can I be sure the two of you will not betray us if I take this risk? And you—you betrayed your comrades once. Abandoned the Therokis. Why not again?"

"I was conscripted to the Therokis. Against my will. I swore them no oath of loyalty, and I paid them a hefty price anyway. If anything, they are in *my* debt." He paused, but Paul said nothing, so he went on. "In Ellen's case, I couldn't imagine offering anything other than loyalty, respect, and honor to my commander," he said, hoping he wasn't admitting too much. He had a feeling both of them knew the truth of the relationship by now.

"I believe you. You must be remarkably loyal to sign your life away to accompany her onto this ship. I wonder, what was the plan? To use your Theroki abilities to help her escape?"

He simply met Paul's gaze for a long moment, and when he spoke, his voice was rough. "Sometimes, there's no plan. Sometimes, you're just doing the best you can."

Paul's eyes widened ever so slightly, and realization washed over Paul's face, then faded into thoughtfulness. "I see."

"Are you going to go after Arakovic? Get justice for your brother? Let us help you?"

"I am," he said, the ease of it surprising Kael. "And I know just how I can be certain I can trust the two of you." Paul slid a finger across the glass of the holodisplay. "Yamamoto, set a course for the Arakovic coordinates I sent you. Check with Shu if you have questions."

"Yes, sir."

The comm clicked.

"I am going to let her help me." Paul smiled, but there was something cold about it, something cynical. "I'm going to let her help us all. And *you* are going to help too. In your own way."

Kael frowned. "And what way is that?"

"You're going to be the collateral."

"Excuse me?"

Paul twisted his odd little intelligent pen, and the pen broke in two. Before Kael could really process it, the device had hissed and started firing.

Kael knocked two darts from it aside while they were still in the air, but the third made it through. Piercing pain stabbed into his shoulder. He looked down, clutching the silver tube—frag it all. He yanked it out, but it was too late.

Tranquilizer dart. Heavy duty. Fast acting, too—the image of the dart doubled, merged, then blurred.

As his legs collapsed, Kael swore. He hit the steel of the deck and managed to roll onto his back, but the darkness was closing in around his consciousness. Paul leaned over him, frowning.

"She said we shouldn't trust you." Kael shook his head. "She was right."

Paul smiled. "As usual."

WHEN PAUL STRODE into the brig, Ellen sprang to her feet. "Where's Lieutenant Rhee?"

"I have an arrangement to discuss with you. Sergeant, please remove her cuffs, and you can leave us for now."

"Where is he? Where's Kael?" she demanded, as the sergeant slipped out of the brig. Her mind jumped back to the time when he'd almost executed her here… Kael had saved them both, then.

But now she was alone with him. Acid pumped through her veins. He hadn't said anything, just stood with his hands folded behind his back, watching the sergeant leave.

Her question hung in the air, so she asked another one. "What is going on here?"

"I have an offer."

"Where's Kael?"

He held up a palm. "We'll get to that. I'm willing to grant you some provisional freedoms aboard the ship—if you agree to assist in planning an attack operation against the Songbirds."

"I'm not talking about anything with you until you tell me what the fuck you've done with my lieutenant."

"Hmm? Oh, he's cannon fodder. I ordered him taken to cargo and tossed him out an airlock."

"You dreck-eating—"

He raised a palm. "Ellen. Calm down. I'm kidding."

"Don't tell me to calm down. It's not funny."

He was silent as he walked away, toward the viewport window.

"He saved your life, you know. Twice."

"Three times, I think, actually. I may be a bit ungrateful in the tally of things at the moment, but I hope not to be in the end. If things go as planned."

"Because things *usually* go as planned. What in all the seven suns does that mean?" Even as the expression came out, she winced. That was Kael's expression. She couldn't even yell and swear without being reminded of him.

"I have transported your lieutenant to my sister ship, the *Lhotse*. Captain Weyer has been instructed to keep him perfectly safe. You can comm him when our discussion is complete to satisfy any concerns you might have."

"I *told* him not to trust you."

"So he muttered as he passed out."

Her nails dug into her palms as she shook. "Why are you doing this?"

"Because I've reviewed your intelligence reports, I've consulted my staff, and I've decided to take your companion's suggestions. I'll give you full disposal of my assets. We will go to the coordinates you were sent, and we will engage the Songbirds to the fullest of our capability. And if we can, we'll eradicate them. And avenge my brother's attack. And possible death."

"No word on him yet?"

"Unfortunately, no."

"Why does any of that require you to ship him off to the *Lhotse*?"

"It doesn't require it, but it's some insurance for me. You will plan this attack. And you'll make sure you don't kill my people needlessly. If not out of a moral duty, then because the man you love is on our other ship."

"The man I—" she started.

"Don't deny it. He told me everything."

"I don't believe you. He wouldn't."

"What does some Theroki have that I don't?" he demanded.

"What the fragging stars in hell are you talking about?"

"Why? Why him? Why not me?"

She stared at him. "*You* fragging left me, Paul."

"But you didn't wait for me. You weren't even sad."

"Are you serious? Yes. Yes, I was. Not that you asked or kept in touch. I was *fifteen*. Fifteen, Paul, and you used me to advance your career."

"I—I didn't mean it like that. I didn't think the thing between us mattered that much to you. I didn't take things seriously."

"Well, I did. And it hurt. You scarred me, dammit. Just because I didn't send you a holographic parade doesn't mean I wasn't crushed."

He blinked. "Breaking things off with you was a mistake. I was an idiot."

She jabbed a finger at him. "You're still an idiot."

He sighed. "That's definitely true."

"This isn't a comparison between you two." She cut the air with the knife of her hand. "You and I knew each other years ago. When I met Kael, I hadn't heard from you in years, and I was a wanted criminal, for heaven's sake, and *you* dumped *me*, remember?"

"You've pointed that out, yes."

"And I can't believe you even brought this up. How unprofessional can you be."

He was quiet for a long moment. "You're right. I haven't found a limit to my unprofessionalism and incompetence yet. But if I find it, I'll let you know."

An instinctive thrill of fear ran through her, at the way he said it, the tone of his voice. "Hey—wait a minute—"

"I've had a long day, and I'm not at my best."

"Welcome to the club, pal."

"I don't know what got into me."

"I do." Regrets and envy. Fragging jealous asshole.

"He's on the *Lhotse*. You're here. If you both survive, you'll get to see each other again. End of discussion."

"This is ridiculous. I would have protected them anyway."

"Really. Have you forgotten how ardently you argued you'd sacrifice your teammates? The sacrifices you made at SHR?"

She swallowed. "This situation is different. You're all doing me a favor you didn't have to do, risking careers already. I wouldn't sacrifice lives needlessly."

"Ah, but that's the crux of it. When exactly is it necessary to make sacrifices? You might think you wouldn't sacrifice anyone, but when the battle is nearly lost? That is when you'll make your real decisions. Deep down, you won't protect my people. Not like you'd protect *him*."

"I'd risk his life, too, if it meant ridding the 'verse of a horde of genocidal terrorists! But I'm not reckless, come on. They're my people too. You didn't need to do this. It's not going to change *anything*."

"Even if *you* think you're still Union, Ellen, they're not your team. And I don't need to find out the hard way. You will help us plan this attack, we'll destroy the Songbirds, and perhaps we can both get our various crimes forgiven for taking out a terrorist cell."

"Wishful thinking."

"I know. Most likely, my brother's dead, and we'll all go to jail for running off half-cocked with a disgraced war hero."

"I'm sure your 'collateral' will be hugely helpful then. What about your secret big operation? What about Tauber? Doesn't your brother have staff you can reach out to?"

"I… haven't been able to reach my brother's offices either. We're having difficulty contacting anyone on the Union network, actually. Strange amount of failures and interference. But before we were cut off, before any of this, the order I mentioned earlier that authorized further investigation into your desertion? I got it from my brother. A sealed Senatorial Order. A Union senator's order can override the admiralty in some situations, and definitely overrides Tauber's verbal orders."

"Holy hell. That's sure convenient for you."

"Not if he's dead because I asked him for it."

She winced. "Sorry."

"It doesn't get me out of jail free. Or even out of jail at all. It doesn't get either of us off the hook for certain. It *might* keep me from being shot on sight when this is all over. My brother's reputation could be considerably tarnished as well, if it's decided I was in the wrong. Our reputations, our freedom, our lives—it's all still on the line. This just gives us a slim chance out."

"What about your record? That's not how you get promo—"

"Fuck my record, Ellen. They tried to kill Jim." He stabbed a finger at the ground.

Something in her chest lifted at that. His career shouldn't be another casualty of Arakovic's, but… she'd just witnessed the most career-rung focused man she'd ever known actually care about something higher than his own ambition and advancement. For once.

She hadn't quite thought it possible. It was a beautiful sight, even if the surrounding circumstances were bitter and tragic.

Her voice was low when she finally spoke. "The Songbirds have killed many people. Jim wasn't the first, nor sadly, will he be the last. Surely, many of them *were* somebody's brother, father, or son. There are people who are still looking for those family members and are never going to find them. Thousands were killed, discarded… They deserved better, all of them."

"I saw the pictures. Of Upsilon. In your files."

She lifted her chin. "Then you believe me now?"

"I… I do. I can't say I agree with your decision to desert. But I believe you."

Her heart eased further at that, to her surprise. Had she really cared what he thought? "I can't say I agree with my decision either. But… I did my best at the time. And we can't go back. Nor do I want to."

"Oh, I'd go back and change more than a few things. But that's neither here nor there. Here's how this is going to work. You'll have a cabin—still under guard—and access to the files Shu approves that you need. My staff will be available to help you with plans and information that is at our disposal. We'll arrive at the coordinates you provided in thirty-two hours, give or take a few for traffic, which should get us there *slightly* before Freedom's Wing commences. Maybe. I don't know how the two are connected, but I have a bad feeling about it. So you had best get to work."

"This is really off the supernova, Paul. Are you sure this is okay? What if your career goes up in flames over this?"

"Ellen, since you've shown up, someone has tried to murder an old friend, myself, my brother, and my entire crew. I lost four crew members. And the message I'm getting from above me doesn't make any damn sense, while you point out very reasonably that Colonel Tauber has a blackhole-sized conflict of interest here and won't own up to it. So yes, this is a bit out of the ordinary. Now are you going to plan this mission or not?"

"Of course I am, damn it."

"Fine. Then Ensign Mertz will escort you to your new quarters. Get to work." He rose and started to turn.

"Wait a minute." She jolted to her feet.

"What?"

"At least admit to me one thing. Moving Kael off this ship wasn't just an insurance policy. This was personal."

He raised his eyebrows. "Hardly. This is to ensure my people are safe, just like I told you."

She hesitated, wanting to say more. But Mertz would arrive at the door any second. "Promise me he'll be safe. And would you give him my book? I already read it." She pulled Zhia's poetry book out of her pocket, quick as a pistol.

He accepted the book, frowning at it. "Thoughtful of you. Of course, he'll be safe."

"He has a daughter waiting for him. He's not just somebody else's lieutenant, Paul."

Paul's face softened. "Your daughter? On planet somewhere? What planet would you trust with your offspring these days, I mean, really."

Her face was hard as stone. "Not mine. My home is space."

"I see. He'll be safe, Ellen. As safe as he can be marching into battle with the rest of us. No harm will come to him on account of me."

"That's real comforting when he won't even be on your ship."

"I suggest you pray, then, if you're amenable. Or do your job, and you won't have to worry."

She groped for something else, some way to *make* him reverse all this and free Kael. Return him to her side.

Nothing came. Mertz had arrived, and the sergeant had returned.

Her head dropped down in dismay as the hatch to the brig slid open, slid shut, and he was gone.

MO PAUSED AT THE HATCH, one hand on the cold metal of the frame. "You almost ready? We're docked."

Doug was still eyeballs-deep in a dozen maps in the air. "Just one more second."

Yeah, when he was in the middle of something, it was almost impossible to draw him away. Almost. But any effective means she knew to break that concentration, she wasn't employing on the way out the door to a space station. She might as well accept her fate, maybe try to hasten it along a bit. "Well, what is it?"

Now, he did look at her. "Why do you say it like that?'

"Like what?"

"Like I'm an old rifle that's jammed one too many times."

Her lips twisted in a small, if controlled, smile. "You're not old. Now what's the issue?"

Smiling at her omission, he pointed. "They're not going the right way."

"What isn't?"

"Who. The Union ships. Ellen and Kael."

"They're not going the right way?"

"They're not going toward the Inner Planets."

"So?"

"Tribunals happen on the Inner Planets. Military prisons are there too. I…" He scratched his head. "If they meant to execute her, they wouldn't need to go anywhere in particular. They could just do it and get on with the next mission, I guess."

"What makes you think they haven't?" she said, voice low. It was a cold thing to say, perhaps. But there wasn't time to waste dancing around the truth.

"I don't know. No news updates. They announced the capture here, made a big deal about it, see?" He brought a bunch of articles up to the side, then swept them away again. She'd seen some of them but had tried to ignore it all. "I've been trying to get in to verify their status myself, more factually, but I haven't got far. It's just… There are dozens of Union ships on the move. A lot of them headed to the front. They're up to something. Something big."

She tilted her head, thinking. "Another push? It's been a while. Every so often they think they'll try again. Every time, both sides ultimately fail. You can obliterate a bunch of ships, but capturing planets is costly."

"And that's the only way you end wars. But there are years of fortifications."

"And they keep building them too." She sighed. "It's never going to end. What does that have to do with our friends?"

He bit his lip, then pointed. "They're going a different way."

She stepped closer, narrowing her focus. "That them? That's almost perpendicular to these other routes."

"Yes, and it's almost like they're headed…" He hesitated.

"Headed where?" She pointed at a point he was looking at, a system highlighted in amber. "What's that?"

"Those are Arakovic's coordinates."

"No…" Mo let out a disbelieving cough. "No, she couldn't have…"

"I think maybe she did."

Footsteps approached in the corridor, and Zhia appeared in the hatch. "Ready, kids? I've got your disguise, Smarty."

Mo blinked, mouth open, then looked back at the maps.

"What?" Zhia came closer. "Reading something juicy?"

"I… um… Not exactly." Doug coughed and reiterated what he'd already told Mo. "She seems to be headed toward the Arakovic coordinates now. Not Union central command. How?"

Zhia just threw back her head and laughed. "That girl is always one step ahead of us. We better get our asses in gear—get our goods and get back over there."

"Yes, ma'am," said Doug, with a lackadaisical salute. "Did you say something about a disguise?"

"Yep. Requisitioned this for you—you being a wanted man and all. Sort of. Can you be wanted if they've already arrested someone who looks exactly like you? Anyway, here." She held out a pair of thick black glasses.

"Hmm, not exactly my style." He took them and rotated them in his hands.

"Exactly the point. Also, they change eye color and disrupt facial recognition software. It's about as minimal as you can get for an effective disguise. You know, without a dye job."

He smiled as he pulled his own glasses off and slid the others on. "I always wondered about some kinda crazy color. You know, to go with the shirt. Maybe orange and blue tie dye? Won't look blond then."

Mo made a mock gagging sound.

"Maybe you should pick up some dye on station. A must-have accessory for the fashionable fugitive." Winking, Zhia turned on her heel and headed toward the cargo hold.

Mo, however, knew him well enough to not start moving until he did. And it was a good ten seconds before he finally grumbled something inaudible and started toward the hatch. She followed close behind.

In the cargo hatch, Zhia was signing off on some new packages. Large ones.

"Receiving a delivery already?" Doug asked.

"I ordered ahead." Zhia gave him a grin and handed the tablet back to the deliveryman.

"Oh, for me!" Shirin ran forward, almost like she'd been waiting in the wings for the man to leave.

"Try it on and make sure it fits." Zhia patted her on the head.

Doug's eyebrows flew up. "Wait—Shirin is staying?"

"Yes." She paused, eyeing him. "That was my decision, combined with her input. Do you… want to weigh in on that, Mr. Simmons?"

"I—no. I mean… it's just…" Wincing, he fumbled for better words. "No, ma'am. Course not."

"Then have a good time seeing the sights of Molyarch. I'm headed with Kentt and Xi to get them a spacecraft."

"See you in a few, Commander," Mo said, grabbing Doug by the elbow. There was no point in arguing it. Rooms were assigned. The decision had already been made. He only looked back once over his shoulder, before shrugging.

Molyarch Station wasn't much different. It didn't seem to change much *ever*, really.

"You been here before?" Doug asked.

"Yeah. Can't say I have a fondness for the place, but I have no animosity either. And something about stations in general just doesn't rub me right. I prefer planets. I'll settle for a ship, but space stations would be at the bottom of my list of Great Places to Exist."

"Really? I figured a station would be more… I don't know, planet-like."

"Maybe for some people. I guess something about the idea of living closed in test tube of a place, spinning through the cosmos, but that also isn't mobile like a ship..." She shuddered. "Ugh, it all gives me the creeps. Plus, what good is a sniper in hallways that curve so quickly? Years of training in adjusting for variable gravity on each world, calculating the Coriolis effect... and I'd be forever stuck using a pistol."

"I suppose you could learn about centrifugal—"

She held up a hand. "Or I could just get back on the *Audacity*."

He laughed. "That's how I'd prefer it too. But maybe we'll be back on a planet. Someday." His grin was bittersweet, sarcastic.

"Dream big, babe. That's what I like about you."

His grin widened. They all had duties today—no R&R this time. She'd drawn the unlucky task of relocating the civilians, but at least that meant she got to drag Doug along with her.

"I'll work the hand tractor. You do the talking," she said to him.

"How do people who had to leave their homes suddenly accumulate this much stuff?" Doug rubbed his chin, eyeing the nearly asteroid-sized load she had maneuvered down the cargo-hold ramp. Negotiating the dock had been intense, but with the straight corridors in this sector, it wasn't too bad.

She smiled. "I'm not the one to ask. Maybe some of them availed themselves of the ship's 3-D printer and used it to make things other than spare parts."

Doug met the gaze of a passerby staring at him until the guy finally looked away.

"Are you sure we can trust the people at this office?" They were supposed to meet with the Foundation representatives here on Molyarch, not that Mo had realized there even *were* any until now.

"Nope, I'm not. That's why we're hitting the hotel first."

"Is that the place, darling?" Catherine Simmons said, coming up alongside them. It was hardly clear which one of them she was addressing since she managed to address everyone as darling. It was also entirely unclear if Mrs. Simmons had figured out there was something going on between her and Doug. The *dahhrling* wasn't exactly telegraphing welcome in Mo's book.

"That's it, all right," Doug said. "The Starside Garden Inn and

Spa." Blue letters in an admittedly classy typeface floated in the air over an open reception area, green ivy moving and intertwining as it grew through the letters and around tiny sparkling white stars.

"Sounds fancy," Mo muttered. It was more commentary than she'd have bothered to offer usually, but she felt she should participate. After all, it was possible Catherine Simmons might be in her life for more than just the next ten minutes.

You know, if they all survived and everything.

"Let's hope." Catherine grinned. "I mean, I'm not getting my hopes up, but… I could go for a massage."

A hotel at this highly questionable station probably wasn't the best place to drop off most of these folks, but Catherine Simmons was apparently undeterred by the dirt smeared on the walls. Well, hopefully that was dirt. She marched past the bio barrier, head held high and greeted the woman behind a silver counter.

"Looks like I won't have to do that much talking after all," Doug muttered to the side.

"How many rooms was it, darling?"

"Six. Amaya said she could stay with Dr. Dremer. Nova and Dane can bunk together."

"Better make it eight, dear." Catherine leaned an elbow on the counter as the hotel attendant laughed a little. "Now, when you say spa… tell me more."

Mo snorted. "Are you *sure* you want to come with us?"

She'd meant it as a joke, but his face hardened. Again. "C'mon, you really want to revisit this? I'm going."

"But the spa."

"Do I look like I need a massage to you?"

"Yes, actually." She arched one eyebrow suggestively.

"Okay, well, when we get back to the ship, you can give me one that will be a whole lot better than whatever they're offering."

"Not so loud." She elbowed him. "And only if you return the favor."

His only response was a broad grin.

"We might all die, you know. *Not* of relaxation." She gestured at his mother. Okay, maybe she *did* want to revisit the topic, and this wasn't the most mature way to do that, but neither of them was an expert in maturity.

He sobered. "I know."

"It's noble that you want to be in the fight with us." She kept her voice low enough that hardly anyone beyond him would have heard her. "It's noble you want to be at my side. But you could help just as well from here *and* protect them."

"Nova is staying to protect them. And Dane."

"You know that's not what I meant."

"I earned the right to go, if I want to, I think."

"Of course, you did."

"I wasn't bad in combat, remember?"

"That was… a very unusual situation, but yes, you're very… creative and… resourceful."

His grin returned. "Listen, I tried to rescue Ellen once. Clearly, I didn't properly finish the job, because she's back in this situation."

"You can't hack people's memories. It was too public for you to wipe that out."

"Either way, I feel responsible for it."

"There's that word again. Responsible. Our Achilles' heel."

"Don't you want me with you?" he said, his voice quieter. A little hurt.

Her gaze sharpened. "I want you to go as you're called, even if it's into danger. But I'd *also* rather you outlive me."

"Well, I'd rather not."

"Damn it, that's not funny."

"I wasn't kidding. For once. But—I'd prefer we all survive. And we'll do that with all hands on deck, trying our best."

A man in a fancy suit eyed them arguing in hushed tones underneath the hotel sign as he exited. They waited till he passed to speak again.

"We should get you some armor," she murmured. "Or borrow some. Something."

"All checked in!" Catherine called, waving her forward with the tractor. "This way, lovelies."

He raised a hand and brushed his thumb over her cheek. "We have to do this. It's the right thing to do."

She made a disgusted noise, both because she hated him going along on the mission and hated him being right. And because she hated her primary contribution at the moment being the luggage cart. "C'mon, Mr. Simmons. Let's get these people settled. Before your mother catches you stroking my—"

Before she could finish, he kissed her, hard and thoroughly and unmistakably.

And then a second later, he was moving forward, tractor in hand.

Mo blinked, staring after him. Out of the corner of her eye, she caught Catherine's gaze flicking back and forth between them.

Ahead of her, Doug floated smoothly beside Dr. Persad as they dragged luggage like nothing unusual was going on.

She could feel Catherine eyeing her now. Maybe even thinking about approaching her. Hell, what if she tried to drag her to a girl's day at the spa? Terrifying.

Mo hurried after Doug and Dr. Persad. She'd better go before she died of embarrassment.

"Dr. Persad." Doug held out his free hand to shake. "I meant to say already, thank you for your help on this little adventure."

"Are you sure it's all right I'm staying here?" she replied.

"Of course. The mission will be dangerous, and you've already done everything you can to help us."

"But if something breaks…"

"It's entirely your choice. But you did leave Xi some very detailed instructions to manufacture more chips. I think we'll be able to make do. And I'm sure your craftsmanship is top notch. For my part, I'd rather you live, so I can see your next invention, Doctor."

The corner of her mouth quirked. "Well, that requires *you* living too."

He smiled. "I intend to."

"Here we go, room… eight." Dr. Persad held up a key card.

"How many rooms does this place have? On second thought, I'm not sure I want to know."

All the rooms seemed to be down this single corridor, so Mo got busy stationing the luggage along the wall for them to find their things. Doug was gliding from room to room, checking on people, and she wasn't sure why she was keeping an eye on his location, perhaps it was just instinct, but it did keep her from noticing Catherine's trajectory toward her until a few seconds before Doug's mother reached her side.

"Mo, darling? Could you help me with something in my room?"

Freezing, she blinked at the woman. Was that a murderous glint in Catherine's eye, or was it just Mo's imagination? She definitely couldn't murder Doug's mom, not even in self-defense, so she'd better hope the woman actually needed something in her room. "Of course, ma'am," she muttered, trailing after the woman.

The room—the suite, it turned out—could have been worse. It did have a huge bathing area, complete with a tub big enough for two people, and it also featured a wide view of the vacuum, which sort of made Mo's stomach turn. That bath, now *that* she was jealous of, but she could have done without the view.

"It changes, you know. You can change the exterior view to be a feed of whatever you like." The words were calm, neutral, but the sound of the hatch snicking closed behind her made Mo's senses sharpen, the hairs on the back of her neck stand up. When she turned, Catherine was just watching her, hands on her hips.

"You… needed something, ma'am?" She probably should have made small talk about the view, but it was obvious Catherine wanted something.

"Are you in love with my son?"

Mo tensed. She should have anticipated the direct attack from the enemy, but somehow she hadn't. "I—what?"

"It's a simple question. Are you in love with my son?"

"Ma'am, I… That's private. Personal." She lifted her chin.

"A simple question deserves a simple answer, I think."

She couldn't argue with that, really, so she let out a sigh of defeat, not for the first time today, and braced herself. "Uh… yes, ma'am. I am. Not that I'm accustomed to talking about such things." Or talking this much with you at all.

Or with most people.

To Mo's surprise, the tension melted from Catherine's shoulders. "Oh, good. I know the two of you went through a lot on that ship when he was kidnapped, and I just… Things that happen in unusual situations don't always translate to real life afterward. You wouldn't believe how I met his father, but you know he's lived kind of a sheltered life, my fault, really, and I wasn't sure—"

"Unusual situations?" Mo blurted, without intending to.

"Oh, yes. I may *look* like I belong at a spa resort—and trust me, to some extent, I do—but in the early days, Matthew and I had quite a few adventures, cataloging outsystem jungles. Why, once we got stuck with a llama in a cave-in in Antiquina and—"

The hatch abruptly slid open, Doug's frowning face leaning in. "Everything okay— Hey, what's going on in here?"

"Oh, nothing, sweetie, just boring your girlfriend with tales of my adventures."

Doug froze, then it was *his* turn for red cheeks.

"Go on, sweetie, I'm sure it's time to get moving on the rest of your mission. We'll be safe here!" She waved Mo toward the door. "Buh-bye, darling!" As Mo hurried past, Catherine muttered, "Take care of him for me, will you?"

"Of course," she said back.

She'd be taking care of him for herself. She was pretty sure that covered enough for both of them.

WAS IT PERSONAL? The words echoed as Paul stalked back to his office.

He had trained himself carefully. How to avoid mistakes. As a commander and as a person. Though he'd made his share, so maybe his training hadn't been all that successful. It wasn't something anyone could teach him or that he could ask about, but he'd formed his own guidelines over time. Don't make decisions too hastily. Always subtly consult subordinates that were smarter than you. Know which ones those were—and which weren't. Use external metrics and evaluations—test scores, their record, not opinions, and certainly not *his* opinions. Ignore the stupider ones as much as possible, even when their arguments sounded somewhat reasonable.

It was hardly a perfect strategy. Even idiots and broken-clock readouts were right once in a while. But following his own gut and judgment had never worked for him.

Now he'd gone and done it, though. He'd made some snap decisions. Big ones. The ones regarding Ellen's fate were ironically less concerning to him, because death was one mistake that was *very* hard to undo, and he was preventing that, at least in the short term. This, however…

He had plenty of excuses.

Having a Theroki uncontrolled on board was dangerous. Handing over any amount of control to Ryu was doubly dangerous. The two combined was too much. Neither of them was loyal to him or to any of them. In the after-action review, he wanted to at least look not utterly incompetent.

He rolled his eyes. This was a tangle. He wouldn't escape unscathed.

But he'd done the right thing. Certainly the reasonable thing. He was pretty sure it was the smart thing. He longed to ask someone—Yamamoto, any of them—for their opinion. But admitting weakness and uncertainty in this matter… That had a cost of its own.

Perhaps he should ask Yamamoto anyway. If this was a brilliantly stupid thing, nuclear-chain-event-level stupid, and he'd made a bitter enemy of the woman to whom he'd also just given some control of his ship…

His ultimate goal was to save lives. To keep them all as safe as he could. *And* accomplish the mission.

And how exactly did locking up the man who'd told him the truth to his face feed into that…?

It certainly had nothing to do with the fact that the lieutenant had somewhat admitted that he was sleeping with Ellen. He really didn't think it did. It couldn't. Really. But… well, he didn't exactly like the idea.

Lieutenant Rhee was right that going through with the attack on the Songbirds with Ryu at the helm would be the best thing—for the people and planets and parliament of the Union. Snap decisions would be needed, and that was far from Paul's strength.

But God. His superiors would hang him if this went awry, and it turned out he'd basically given over his ship and Captain Weyer's to two people who were *supposed* to be prisoners. And what would the fallout be for Jim?

If Jim was even still alive.

He swore and pinged Yamamoto. Once his second's face appeared on the vid display, he confessed everything he'd done. "What do you think?"

"What do you mean, sir?"

"Do you think she'll hate me now?"

"Probably." Yamamoto folded his arms. "But she'll still fulfill her end of the deal."

He scowled, then grabbed at the book. "She asked me to give him a book—has he been relocated yet?" He'd claimed to Ellen it was a done deal, but in fact, it took time to securely transfer an unconscious Theroki.

"He's in the docking bay. Send it down. We can hold the shuttle until then."

Something in him eased. That'd be one step toward redemption. "All right. I'll send it. Damn, I shouldn't care so much what she thinks."

"It's only natural." Yamamoto glanced over his shoulder, then back.

"Any update on my brother?" Paul said, softer now.

His second's face darkened. "Nothing specific, but news reports are coming in that the planet he was on has been subjected to a coordinated terrorist attack. Three different government offices were attacked, one Puritan-affiliated temple, and two other locations with details withheld. At least fifty-three are dead."

"Fifty-*three*?" He winced. More to potentially add to his tally. "Songbirds suspected?"

"No announcement of that yet, internally or externally. But you saw the same vid feed I did."

"Yes. I did."

CHAPTER SEVEN

THIS BEING her first time in a body, walking around on a space station, Xi was taking notes. Lots and lots of notes. Out in the world, she found so many things interesting. She was, in fact, taking so many notes that at times, she found herself inappropriately and awkwardly deprioritizing her social processing to capture a fascinating detail. She'd nearly forgotten to say goodbye to Zhia as her friend had headed back toward the *Audacity* after making sure there was a proper ship available.

That left only Kentt to finalize the purchase—and for Xi to ask her many questions about the world. So many things made little sense to her, even with the data and models she built observing the *Audacity* crew. As Kentt was not particularly talkative, it would probably take some time to address Xi's growing backlog of confusion.

"Pleasure doing business with you, ma'am." Xi watched Kentt reluctantly accept the sheet of stickers. The towering Teredark—who professed to run Claudette's Cruises but not actually to be Claudette herself—clicked happily and scurried back into the ship storage area to prepare their purchase.

The stickers in particular made very little sense to Xi. No sense at all, in fact.

"What are the stickers for?" Xi asked as the Teredark, who was not Claudette, began moving something large and apparently very heavy to the back. Teredarks had been described in her files as resembling large centipedes with upright front portions, but seeing one in person, they were quite different from what she'd envisioned. How she was moving anything around with all those tiny limbs remained a mystery.

Kentt stared at the sticker sheet in her hand, her usually luminous eyes dimmed so as not to draw attention. "I don't know, to be honest."

"Are you unable to read the thoughts of Teredarks?" Xi tilted her head.

A slight wrinkle creased the woman's forehead between her eyebrows—the most visible indication Kentt usually gave of irritation or confusion or annoyance. She was an interesting subject of observation, being on the low end of the physically emotive spectrum. Was being a telepath the cause of that wall-like exterior, or was it a coincidence of personality? Correlation doesn't always imply causation.

But it was a hypothesis Xi loosely held, that Kentt hid her interior self because she had known too much about the interiors of others for too long.

"I would never read someone's thoughts in a business interaction without their permission."

Xi chose not to express her own skepticism of that claim. Concealing thoughts was easy for an AI, but appeared to be challenging for many humans. One of the few advantages of being synthetic, perhaps.

"Well," Kentt added, "in a fair-handed interaction that's honestly established… All right, fine, stop looking at me like that. Yes, I can."

Xi hadn't realized her own flat expression had been unnerving. Somehow, it had resulted in the divulging of information. Fascinating. She tilted her head slightly to the side again when a new hypothesis occurred to her. "And you did read them in this instance."

Kentt's cheeks flushed a little. "Are you sure *you're* not the telepath?"

"I can assure you, I am one hundred percent certain."

"Well, our lives could be at risk if we can't trust this… Claudette. I prefer to be as ethical as possible in all matters, but that does not mean I should martyr myself at a moment like this. And that also does not mean I know what the stickers are for."

"I see. A mystery." Xi smiled, although she was uncertain if a smile was appropriate at this moment.

Kentt's smile was small in return. She tucked the sheet of stickers into her robe. "I am not sure *she* knows what the stickers are for."

Beside them, the station wall shuddered and lurched to life, two doors slowly grinding open to reveal a small ship.

"It's so small. Are you sure it can take us to our destination?" Kentt shifted her weight from one foot to another, making her deep-navy cloak sway around her knees. She'd traded her usual cloak for this more subdued one, wearing it in spite of the station's acclimatization controls making it highly unnecessary. The telepath glanced behind them into the shop foyer and the corridor outside. It was empty as far as Xi could see, but Kentt drew the hood up once again to cover her features.

"A precaution, or do you sense someone coming?" Xi asked, keeping the volume of her question low, prioritizing the safety inquiry over answering Kentt's initial ship capability question. Xi could keep a queue of hundreds of topics, but since most humans could only handle a conversational interruption of one or two things, she only interrupted their lines of inquiry for safety-specific issues.

"There are always people moving about in a place like this. It's too taxing to examine them all. Just a precaution for now. I usually adore people watching and crowded places, but this… I'll be glad to leave here."

"And leave here we will. The ship will be fine. Its specifications are more than adequate," Xi said, nodding. She used her best reassuring tone, but it didn't seem effective. She made a note to work on it.

It would be a few hours before Claudette had the ship out to dock and fueled up. The whole endeavor was funded by Kentt's business interests, which were extensive. Kentt probably didn't know how familiar Xi was with her finances, and that was for the best. Xi kept careful concealment of that knowledge and avoided any questions about funding sources. Kentt seemed pleased with the arrangement.

They spent the time browsing the dubious selection of shops in Molyarch's rings. Xi was amazed by the number of items she saw travelers purchasing that served no discernible function, except perhaps entertainment. She practiced her conversational protocols with several merchants, only a few of whom seemed mystified by her responses, so she considered it a mild success.

As soon as the ship was ready, they launched. Xi set the course herself, and Kentt prepared for a sleep cycle in the ship's bunk area.

Tasks complete, Xi decided to join Kentt in the sleep ritual, if only to give her fairly new machinery a brief respite powered down. Of course, her own mind never slept. Ever since Merith's forced turnoff, she could hardly bring herself to even reboot most of the time.

"Do you think your telepath friends will be able to help us?" Xi asked as she stretched out on a bunk and dimmed the lights. Purely for Kentt, of course, as she was still essentially flying the ship while her machinery rested, continuously monitoring the autopilot.

It was a moment before Kentt answered. "I am not certain. But these women know the real threat, better than most. They've had nothing to do since they went into hiding. They could be preparing to fight. To protect themselves."

"Or…?"

"Or they could be watching vid dramas on my dime. I don't blame them either way. We will find out soon enough. How long do we have?"

"About twelve hours. Not long."

"See you in my dreams then, Xi."

Xi's eyebrows twitched. It seemed to be an inquisitive expression, indicating curiosity as to the nature of the speaker's ambiguous words, which was how she felt just now.

Not that Kentt could see the expression. But humans still seemed to do these things, even when they couldn't be seen by their audience. Or didn't even want an audience. So she continued her practice at being human, or human-like.

If anything, it brought up more questions than answers.

HEADING BACK to the ship with just Doug by her side made Mo feel a little off kilter, like they'd left their luggage in the corridor for anybody to steal and just walked away. It made her nervous.

But these decisions weren't up to her—and she didn't really want them to be.

All in all, eleven people disembarked the *Audacity* at Molyarch to stay at the Starside Garden, at least for the time being, until they figured out a new plan. Nova and Dane stayed with the group for their protection. Doug's parents, Dr. Persad and her son Vivaan, Dr. Taylor and her wife, Amaya the cook, Ana the former Songbird pilot, Kentt's companion Loti, and Dr. Dremer took rooms.

"This is it," Doug said, gliding toward an unmarked door in a side corridor he'd led her down. Right, first, they needed to stop at the local Foundation office if they could... For what, he hadn't mentioned.

He rummaged in his pockets, then held up two small black boxes near a sensor by the door. Then a third. Then he turned away and started back down the corridor.

"Wait a minute—that's it?"

"That's it."

"Aren't we going to talk to anyone?"

"No, I just left a message for them to contact me."

"You couldn't do that from the ship?"

"Not this kind of message."

"What about surveillance? Won't they know you're you now and—"

"I already hacked the cameras along this whole path. Nobody's seeing us, at least not till we get close to the ship."

"And nobody cares about that? Somebody is going to come check out broken cameras."

"Oh, they care. But what's to care about? They're just seeing looped vid feeds of an empty corridor." He winked. "Plus that's why we come to stations like this. Even with broken feeds, they often don't care enough to do anything, certainly not quickly enough to notice before we'll be long gone. We're fine, Mo." He patted her shoulder, then waved his hand through the air. "We're fine."

They turned the corridor, heading back toward the main artery ring that led toward docking and customs—and the ship.

The hairs on the back of her neck started to tingle. She walked a little faster, glancing around. Above them, the shine of a chromed-out restaurant sign provided a reflection of the corridor behind them. She used her eye augmentation to zoom in—get a closer look.

A small group had fallen in step behind them. From the quick glimpse she could catch in the reflection, they were not armored, not most of them anyway. Four or five men, brown-haired, one blonde woman.

One blonde woman. Was she familiar? Like… like the one on the vid feed on Aeori III?

"Douglas Oliver Simmons," said a voice behind them.

"Don't stop," she whispered, speeding up but still walking. "It's not station cops. And don't—"

He glanced over his shoulder before she could finish.

"Hey! You!"

"Never mind. Run!" She winced at the incorrectness of the word.

She ran. He zoomed ahead of her in no time. Footsteps pounded after them.

He made it nearly to the cargo-hold ramp when he froze.

Mo caught her breath as a scream rang out. *His* scream.

She drew her pistol as she spun, dropping to one knee. The men continued forward, rushing around the woman, who'd stopped still.

She *was* the woman on the feed with Arakovic. How had she gotten here? Why now?

Her eyes were deep black. She frowned, her gaze fixed hard on Mo. As if she too were wondering, *How?*

"Let him go," Mo growled. She'd give her one chance. Just one.

"Who are you?" said the woman coldly. "Why can't I hear your thoughts?"

Yeah, like she was answering that. Focusing in with her targeting augments, she squeezed the trigger.

The laser connected with the woman's forehead. Skin burned through to brain matter, bubbling and boiling into a mist as it covered the docking area behind her, the woman's body falling like wood to the ground.

Behind her, Doug gasped for breath as he lurched forward into the cargo hold.

Twisting onto her other knee, she fired again, rapid in sequence, squeezing off precise single-second bursts and hoping that'd be long enough. Only one of the men reached Doug before she got to him, but when he turned and saw his comrades, he hesitated.

And then his time was up too.

Getting to her feet, Mo scanned the area. "No alarms yet. C'mon. We need to get inside."

Doug was panting. "But—what about—" He gestured at the bodies.

A blaring alarm split the air. Doug covered his ears with both hands. She swore under her breath, although she might as well have yelled it. That alarm meant somebody had seen, had been watching the vid feeds.

"Security incoming!" she shouted. "We're *officially* the low-lifes here, or at least I am! We gotta go!" She ran past him as she pulled out her comm. "And lock ourselves in." Zhia needed to know this had happened. And fast.

Well, Mrs. Simmons. Mission accomplished, I guess.

A heavy, thudding, crunching behind her made her wince as she ran. Maybe she'd spoken too soon. That sounded like the station's vice grip digging into the back of the ship.

Security was impounding them. And probably preparing to board.

THE GOLDEN THREADS twisted through the midnight blue dome over her. Ellen lay on her back on the hard metal grating, staring up.

Her eyes traced from star to star, node to node. The information flowed at a fraction of the speed of a blink.

"You're not real." Who was she speaking to? It didn't matter. In the dream, she sat up. Stood up. Crossed her arms. She'd never forget the beauty of it—both its visual representation, as well as its essential meaning, the amazing, gorgeous flow of ideas from one human to another.

But her real connection to Starbird was long gone, and it wasn't coming back.

"You're not real," she repeated.

The gold lights pulsed once, almost taunting, as if to say, *Real enough.*

Why had it ever existed? Why had it been part of the project at all? That question had lingered in the back of her mind, with no concrete answer. A justification of the cybernetics? Convenient to access data as well as thoughts? She certainly hadn't minded that part. The craving tugged at her even now.

"I don't need you. Sure, I wish I had the info. The help. I'm slagging on my own in this mess. But you're just a crutch. The real thinking happens up here." She tapped her temple.

The shine grew brighter, almost blinding. She let herself squint, but not quite close her eyes.

Some things, once a part of you, are always apart of you.

"Don't you have better things to do other than telepathically harassing people in their dreams at this hour? Isn't it past your bedtime?"

You are asleep. How can you be sure of the hour?

Ellen snorted as the glaring light began to ease. As it faded, it seemed like there were twice as many nodes now. Maybe ten times. The dome above her sparkled with fierce energy, data flying. "This isn't real," she insisted again.

Perhaps not. Or perhaps it is. You'll never know.

"Gee, that's comforting."

All that truly exists only exists in your own mind anyway.

"That's a nice philosophy until someone comes at you with a knife. Or a laser cannon."

Nothing like imminent death to make one's priorities clearer. We are a part of you. You can't deny it.

"Sure I can." Ellen sighed. "Here I am, denying it. Let me get back to sleep."

Just wanted to remind you that you're not alone.

"Thanks. That's really helpful, and also super creepy. And in the reality outside this dream? I'm utterly alone."

Are you?

"Kael is gone. That dog-faced monkey-licking Paul took him from me. I might never even see him again and—"

Look again. The lights began to brighten again.

Ellen grudgingly lifted her gaze. "I can't use the Starbird grid, so I don't see what the point of this is."

Slight blips of light were traveling along the threads, moving from node to node to node, shedding sparks as they turned corners and made turns. It wasn't the information that was so beautiful. It was the interconnectedness of it, the movement from mind to mind.

This part of Starbird has never left you. You don't have to be alone.

"What do you mean?"

Take us back. Rejoin the network.

"No, I'll never go back."

Oh, but you already are. You're on your way. We don't want to be alone anymore either—

"Never!" Ellen glared and raised a fist at the sky of information soaring above her, and—

And started, suddenly awake.

She was sitting at her desk, rigidly upright now.

The side of her face hurt. She slapped one hand to it, staring down at the tablet she'd been working on. Was that… drool?

Her planning was almost complete, the cursor blinking impatiently at her.

She ran her hands over her forearms, her neck. There were no ports connected anywhere. Nothing amiss.

Just a dream. A real actual dream? A message from her own mind?

She was alone, yes. The silence in the sterile cabin around her was an incongruously loud reminder of that fact.

The cabin they'd given her was perfectly functional to sit and write a report. It didn't scream that the cell next to her was empty quite as loudly as the brig would have. But… he was still gone.

She *was* alone. Stupid dream.

But she was *technically* on a ship full of hundreds of soldiers. Heaven knew that, even with people around, you could still feel very alone. But she didn't need a lover. Or friends. She needed to survive this fight. She needed a plan that was not just good but excellent.

Excellence didn't come from chewing on your bone in a corner by yourself.

She groaned as she stretched for a moment, then punched the controls for the sharing function and started typing in Lieutenant Shu's name.

Paul was hopeless, and his minion Bridell aspired to be as hopeless as his mentor or to surpass him. But Shu was obviously intelligent. Who else?

She could send it to the ensign. Or even Yamamoto. Or hell, why not all of them. She could ignore—or rip apart—any objection Bridell or Paul could throw at her. Swearing, she added name after name.

Her finger hesitated over the button to send. For some reason, a few old friends flashed through her mind—all of them long dead now, in combat or to the Songbird project…

Would one of these people be next? Was she leading them straight toward the same fate that'd torn her other friends from her? Maybe *she* was the common denominator here. Her finger felt like a guillotine looming over their necks.

She gritted her teeth and hit the button.

Then she opened the wall panel. She needed to order something to drink. Or maybe eat. She stood, stretching. Maybe first she should get her blood pumping to wake up. Think more clearly.

The chime rang. Frowning, she waved the door open.

Mertz was in the corridor, scrolling his ever-present tablet.

"That was fast," she grumbled.

"This is… fascinating…" He waved at the screen vaguely.

"You should get that thing attached to your arm," she said.

"What?"

"Oh, nothing."

Mertz scrolled down. And down. And down. "How long *is* this?"

"A couple hundred pages."

His eyes bugged. "*Hundred*?"

"What, you want to be unprepared?"

"How will anyone read all this? How did you *write* all this?"

"They won't have to, they only have to read their part. There are many contingencies. We only follow them one at a time. But we're also broken into different teams. We have no idea exactly where the base is, what it's like, or if it's just some ridiculous trap. So we need plans for, well, *all* of that. And I didn't write it all, I used the AI to generate the proper plans based on your ship outfit, current Union protocols, and the astrogeography of the system, and then I edited them, heavily. Only way to do it in a few hours."

He wandered in, eyebrows still raised and still not taking his eyes off the tablet.

"Sure, c'mon in."

Finally looking up, his cheeks went pink. "Stars, I'm sorry. I just… I have questions. Operations planning is kind of a little fascination of mine. Don't get me wrong. I'd love even more to have the war *over* and not need them, but this is—well, this is just so—oh, I don't know—"

She smiled and waved a hand at the one other chair in the cabin and the bunk. "Take a seat. Ask your questions. I may have missed plenty. Still working on it."

He went still. "Are you *sure*?"

"Yeah. What the hell. Beats—" She stopped herself from what she'd been about to say. "Beats thinking about my other problems."

Mertz briefly contemplated the choices, then hurried to sit and continue paging through. "Your other problems? Like your friend the cap shipped off to Captain Weyer?"

She blew out a breath. Maybe this wasn't such a good idea after all. She kept her eyes trained on the tablet. "Yeah. Kinda like that."

"He's… kinda cute."

Raising an eyebrow, she fought the urge to turn. "That did not escape my attention."

A brief silence settled. Then, "Do you know if he's taken?"

She broke into a grin now, which was easier because he couldn't see her. "As a matter of fact, he is."

"Darn it," Mertz grumbled. "All the good ones already are."

She laughed softly. She felt like she should tell him something wise, something mentor-like in that moment. Someday, his prince would come? They only seem good *because* they're taken? But what the frag did she know. If she should give him advice about anything, it was his career—not love.

Though she *was* a deserter likely on her way to a death sentence, she was also currently in a pretty good relationship, so which was she really successful at?

Why was it so hard to see oneself clearly?

"Start with the flow chart," she said instead. "That gives an overview of how the pieces fit together. Then you can think about where to drill down. For what it's worth, I'd like to assign you to the threat-assessment team. Basically, the part of the crew that will look for cannons, turrets, mines, decoys. Any other hidden threats that might have been set up for us to ram right into when they gave us this location."

"Do you think it's a trap then?"

"Not sure. I think Dr. Arakovic wants me as one of them. To finish what she started. But it could just be a trap, and those things aren't mutually exclusive. It'd be foolish not to prepare for both."

"Threat assessment, it is. I'll start there."

Before a full silence could settle, the chime sounded again. Hmm, perhaps collaboration hadn't been such a good idea after all.

She waved, and the hatch slid open to reveal Paul.

"Captain!" Mertz jumped to his feet, as Ellen begrudgingly started to rise as well.

"At ease." Paul smiled. "I see you've sent out this draft. It's... quite long."

"Well, first, we have to find the actual base. Or the trap she set for us."

"What a warm and fuzzy idea." He stepped inside, glanced at Mertz, then pretended to look at his tablet too.

"If you joined up hoping for hugs, sir," she said, "I think you've chosen the wrong calling."

"Hugs? Do you think Dr. Arakovic would accept one if I offered?"

"You'll have to ask her. Would you like the short version, sir?"

"Yes, bottom line would be preferred."

"One team will begin scanning for the base, while another is on alert for attacks and obstacles set up to stop us. I have separate briefings prepared on what types of potential hidden threats to identify. An executive summary is on page six if you want to reference it later." That would probably be the only part he'd read, and if Mertz weren't there, she'd have been more direct about it.

"Did you include holographically cloaked turrets on your list?" Paul said, frowning and trying very hard to look thoughtful.

"Yes, sir, I did."

"Very good then." He grinned. "Proceed." Then he spun and walked out.

Mertz snorted as the hatch slid closed. "Dodged another ballistic, I think, ma'am."

"I believe I'm developing a talent for it. Not one I ever wanted, but…"

"Neither you nor I get to pick our opportunities. Now on the scanners, what if they have vironin coating on the base? It's new and hard to get, but the Songbirds seem high tech. They could have it. Vironin twists sensor readings."

"Hmm, how so? Is there a way around it?"

"Yes, we can look for the specific vironin signatures, but it requires a larger energy commitment than regular scanning."

"Maybe a second-tier scan for that then? I'll add it."

"That'd be good." He nodded, without looking up. "Let's see…"

She keyed in a note, yawned, and then punched in a request for some coffee. It might be a long night. "Is, um… Before we go on… is Kael going to be okay? On the *Lhotse*?"

He looked up, eyebrows raised. "On the *Lhotse*? Yes. Captain Weyer's got her hands plenty full over there."

"With what?"

"With keeping the *Lhotse* from falling apart. If you think this bucket of bolts is shabby, you should see that ship. Amazing she keeps it flying."

"Best of the best, out here."

"Only the best of the best for the Union."

"Where do you think he is on the ship?"

Mertz looked up again, as if finally seeing her clearly.

"What? It's not like I'm trying to pull some heroics. We have work to do."

"A war hero pull some heroics? How hard to imagine." Then, after a long pause, he said, "I'm sure he's sitting quietly—and safely—in the brig. Probably bored out of his mind."

She snorted. "Easy for you to say."

"You know what, you're right. The cute ones always give you the worst headaches. Let's look at the arrival point section."

"Headed there." Smiling, she started scrolling.

CHAPTER EIGHT

IF THE *EVEREST* hadn't exactly been in excellent condition, the *Lhotse* was even deeper down into the valley of disrepair. Maybe both ships were underwater, metaphorically speaking. They didn't exactly speak well for the Union fleet.

A trickle of what he hoped was water dripped into his hair as they led him down the corridor from the docking bay. The overhead grating was greenish brown for at least fifty meters where the drips and drops continued along, but he dodged most of them.

Nine men, in box formation, were escorting him somewhere. The brig, he presumed, and he was proven right after only one more dank corridor. Somewhere between a third to a half of the lighting was actually on.

But there was little evidence of bodily fluids, at least as far as he could tell, so it was still a step up from the *Genokai.*

Upon his arrival at the brig, though, they didn't immediately toss him into a cell. They pivoted him around to stand facing the door, assumed a parade rest, and waited.

And waited.

A good twenty minutes of sheer boredom passed before an

armored tank of a woman marched in, at least four people in a whirlwind around her asking rapid-fire questions.

"I need a purchase authorization for a new hydrogen converter —" one aide was reporting.

"You can't have it," the female tank barked gruffly back. The name on her uniform read WEYER. The captain of the *Lhotse*, eh?

"Well, then I at least need your stamp on the form to requisition alternative schematics from Central—"

"Fine. Here."

"Ma'am, the bio-field generator needs eight new bulbs. We lose any more, and we'll be eating only potatoes and crickets for—"

"Do I look like a bulb factory to you?"

"But, ma'am—"

She held up a palm. They all instantly went silent. Her eyes pinned him. She was his height. Maybe his width in the shoulders too.

"Are you Lieutenant Kael Rhee?"

"Yes, ma'am," he replied.

"Welcome to the *Lhotse*. As you can see, we have our hands full and don't need any problems from you."

"I have no plans to give you any problems, ma'am." At least none that he'd admit to her face. He never *did* get to use his plan to escape through the ceiling via all those bolts he'd unscrewed in the *Everest*'s brig. But there was nothing stopping him from trying the same thing here.

She blinked slowly at him. "Yeah. Right. Therokis are known for being so docile and easily managed."

"I'm not—" he started.

She caught the eye of one of his escorts and pointed toward the cell.

"I'm not that anymore," he muttered, possibly only to himself.

They shuffled forward. Except—blast it—this cell wasn't identical to the one on the *Everest*. Someone had added at least a dozen chains to the wall and floor.

"I know what you are." Her voice was cold. "There's no point in denying it."

He blew out a breath through his nostrils, trying to control a rising anger. Blowing his top wouldn't exactly prove his point.

"I was once a Theroki. I have the augmentations. But I've acquired further augmentations since then. I'm not one of them anymore, and I'd appreciate it if you'd remember that." He only let the edge drift into his voice on the final few words. At the same time, he calmly slumped to a seat on the bench and let them go about shackling him.

Weyer's brow furrowed. "Your cooperation is appreciated, Lieutenant Rhee. And your point is noted."

"Is all this really necessary? There were no such extra precautions on the *Everest*."

"I bet there weren't. But I don't play with fire. Especially not on a ship prone to trilini leaks."

He caught the eye of the last guard to close the final shackle who gave him a *Well, she's right* sort of shrug.

"I've done nothing but offer help to Captain Dealis since I arrived." Well, aside from the loosening of a few bolts. Maybe that could work again here.

"You're still a telekinetic cyborg in my book. Speaking of books…"

As his eyes widened, she reached out to an aide who handed her a small book.

"Captain Dealis wanted me to give you this," Weyer said, holding it up. Hell, it was Zhia's poetry. How did Ellen get that over here? "He says it's a gift from your girlfriend."

"My—wait—" he started.

"Well." Weyer snorted and tossed the book over her shoulder. It hit the wall then landed on the guard desk with a thud. "Captain Dealis is also an idiot. And *I'd* be an idiot to hand that over to you on his orders."

His eyes flicked from her to the book, then back to her, saying nothing.

"That said, I'm not enough of an idiot to make an enemy of Dealis, either, especially not while my ship is as stable as a three-wheeled minecart to hell. So you stay in your cell and do your job, and I'll do mine."

"Yes, ma'am. And what exactly is my job?"

"Sit still, shut up, and don't cause any trouble."

"I can do that. The chains should help with that immensely. But what is…" No, no, he couldn't ask what *her* job was. That was the opposite of not causing trouble, he was pretty sure.

Her eyes narrowed even further, but he saw a hint of laughter in them. "My job? It's to keep this mountain from falling to rubble. She's a good ship, but she's not gotten a fair shake. We're gonna give her all we can, though, aren't we?"

A chorus of *Yes, ma'am* went up, not just from the crew badgering her but from his guards too.

"So you stay out of our faces, and you'll be back on the *Everest* as soon as I can get rid of you. And you'll be taking your little book of love letters when you leave. No sooner. Got it?"

"Yes, ma'am." Kael looked pointedly at his wrists. "You know, I can do precisely nothing even without all these chains."

"Sure, you can. And you can also choose not to. Now sit tight until this fool-crazy mission is over."

Oh yeah, like that was an option. He was just going to let the person he loved most in the world waltz into danger without even breaking a sweat to try to protect her. If Weyer thought that was happening, she was in for a surprise.

"If you think Dealis is an idiot and this mission is fool-crazy," he said instead of those thoughts, "then why are you helping him?"

Her eyes were practically slits now. "Because he's a respectful idiot who is *trying* to do the right thing, at least half the time. And that's more than I can say for most of my colleagues." That got her another round of approving murmurs. Interesting. Did Dealis know his reputation was this… accurate? Weyer's comm blared abruptly with a chorus of alarmed voices. "Now, if you'll excuse me, my chief engineer just wet his pants."

His eyes locked with the brig sergeant as Captain Weyer and her posse filed out. "Is she always like this?"

The sergeant laughed quietly. "Some days, she's worse. You caught her on a good day."

ZHIA HAD HOPED a day with a visit to Molyarch would be a good day.

She should have known better.

"What is that God awful noise?" Doug asked her as she ran in behind Mo and Doug before the cargo-hold door closed.

"External ship bots deploying." Xi's calm and cool voice echoed in the huge cargo hold.

Zhia came to a stop beside him. "That's the sound of an impound. What happened?"

"We were attacked," Mo said, panting. "I defended."

"Permission to extricate?" Xi asked.

"Granted. Do it. How many down?" Zhia stepped over to the display near the hatch, pulling up the external vid feed.

"Three, I think," Mo answered. "Maybe four."

"All human?"

"Yes. One of them looked like one of those women we already saw—" Mo smacked her forehead, trying to remember something. "The lady on the screen on Aeori III."

"Goodie. How many crew still on station?" Zhia's voice was chopped, curt.

"All planned crew are present, Commander," Xi replied.

She hit the ship-wide comm button. "Everybody, strap in. Fast. We're having a little tussle with security."

"Strap in?" Doug asked. "But doesn't an impound mean we aren't going anywhere?"

"If our external bots work fast enough, we won't have to deal with them, but..." She hit the button and turned off the vid feed. "We're gonna have to hope they work fast because station security already has the blowtorches out. Figures they're fast *this* time, and not the time that guy tried to rob us of our bucket of beer, eh, Mo?"

Mo snorted. "Figures. Want me here in case they make it through, or…"

"Yes. Doug—your quarters."

"But you can't just—"

"There's no time for debate. Get down there."

"Yes, ma'am." He sped away.

"Commander, ship security is hailing you," Xi said.

Zhia sighed as she moved back to a defensive position with Mo. "I'm too old for this shit."

"So am I," Mo muttered.

"Nobody is young enough for this shit."

"I do not understand," Xi said. "Do you wish to speak with them?"

"Put 'em on. Wait, first—any status on those impound arms?"

"This station employs three prongs. Two have been countered. One has penetrated the hull."

"What does that mean?" Mo whispered.

"You're unusually talkative today. Just shooting up the place and asking questions and everything!"

She winced. "Sorry."

Zhia blew out a breath. "It's all right. I'm kidding. Can our bots ditch the third arm, Xi?"

"It is unclear, Commander. Chances are at forty-three percent and falling. It may need external human intervention."

"All right. Put them on."

"Ship 174562," came a gruff voice. "Halt and open your hatch. You are wanted for questioning in the shootings immediately outside your ship."

"What shootings? We don't know what you're talking about."

Mo's eyes widened. Zhia shook her head just slightly. They were only on voice feed, but if Mo started offering details, she'd have to tackle her.

"We have your crew on the vid feed firing a laser weapon,

murdering several people, and then fleeing into this ship. Don't feed me that line of bull shit. Just open up. Otherwise, Akil is happy to get the torch fired up over here."

They *already* had the blowtorch fired up and digging in, so they really must be underestimating *Audacity*'s external sensors. She frowned.

Wait. That name sounded familiar.

"Akil? Like the dancer at the Mossy Spigot?"

The security officer audibly choked. "Look, I get it, you've been on station before—"

"Tell Akil if he cuts a hole in my door," she said, smiling, "I'm never buying him that tenth drink I owe him."

Mo covered her snicker with a hand over her mouth.

"Akil, is that cute outsystem kid still hanging around? What was his name, Starstripe?"

"That's made up," Mo muttered. "That's not a real name."

"No shit," Zhia muttered back. "But with abs like that, who cares."

A groan came over the comm line. "He says to tell you Starstripe moved on. He's performing on a vacation liner now. Making the credits. Look, if you'd just open this door, the two of you can shoot the shit a whole lot easier—"

Xi's voice cut in. "Third prong countered, Commander. We can depart with moderate hull damage in thirty seconds, minor if we wait until two minutes, but they could detect the bots and try to re-implant—"

"Depart, Xi. ASAP. Put the security back on."

"—nothing personal, we just have to do our jobs. You killed some people. We at least gotta put you in the brig overnight or sit you down and have a talking to or something. I get that you're Akil's friend and all—"

"Friend! Is that what he called me? I thought we were *way* more than friends, especially that night with the zebra body paint and the pyrotechnics..." Zhia put as much sensual purring into her voice as she could.

A woman was more than sex, more than a body. But she stopped pretending sex wasn't a part of life about ten years ago.

A burble of flustered discussion erupted on the other side of the comm.

"Cleared in three, two, one…" Xi cut in.

"Better hold on," Adan's voice came on.

Zhia swore. Right. They weren't buckled down, and knowing Adan, this wouldn't be a slow departure. Even if Molyarch didn't have a planet-sized arsenal, they were definitely going to react somehow.

She grabbed the rail of a ladder as the ship started to move. Mo copied her. "Xi, put security back on."

"Hey—hey, wait a minute—hey, stop!"

"Sorry, ladies and gentlemen," she replied. "We've gotta leave the party early. But we can settle all of this next time, Akil. You owe *me* one now."

The scraping sound was truly awful, and they both scrunched up their shoulders and winced as the ship started to accelerate.

"Hell…" Mo shook her head. "If Molyarch isn't a safe port anymore…"

"Dark times indeed," she agreed.

"We just left a whole bunch of people there."

"Hopefully, they won't associate them with the ship too directly. But there are going to be *very* few places we can repair this damage. Maybe none."

"Just the way we'd like to fly into the lion's den. With scratches in our sides."

"And a thorn in our paw. But it's the only way we're getting our friends back."

ADAN TOOK a hasty sip of coffee at the sound of boots in the corridor.

It was a familiar cadence. And it had been *so* long since he'd heard it.

Just to hear her walking around that way… God, it felt good. It hadn't been that long, really, just two or three days. But every minute of it had driven him wild with worry.

His nerves were a jangle when Jenny strode in. Damn, it was good to feel her in the same space, too, in his orbit, to know that at least on some level she was all right. He had the package from Molyarch in his pocket, but…

Blast it, he should have thought more about what to say.

Or thought about what to say at all.

What was he even thinking? He had no idea. A wave of panic rose in his chest, but he set his shoulders and his jaw.

If he didn't say something now, when would he? And then the thing would be hanging around in his stuff for weeks, or even longer, and what if she found it?

And what if they went after Ellen and Kael and never came back and Jenny never knew. About what he wanted to plan, to build together…

He didn't know exactly what that was, hence his complete inability to think of what to say about it. But he had to say something. Or at least do something.

Prepared or not, the time was now.

She plopped down in the empty co-pilot seat, one leg looped over the armrest as usual, and gave him a wink. "Miss me?"

"Sure did." He took a sip of his coffee. Her presence beside him eased every frazzled nerve in his body, calmed the frenetic worry of his mind. She'd survived. Levereaux had said she would, but floating in a tank was a lot different than talking and walking around.

Casually, he set the box between them on the dash.

She sat up in the chair and pointed. "What's that?"

"Oh, I don't know, I thought maybe you'd like it." He waved at it, didn't look. At her or at the box.

She snatched it up, slowly raised the lid open, and caught her breath.

He could feel her eyes boring into him, so he relented and met hers, the green glittering in the console light. Their eyes locked, and the corner of his mouth twitched with a smile.

Her eyebrows had risen a little and stayed there as she turned her gaze to the open box.

Carefully, she removed the ring and set the box down. It was a soft silver band. Green glowed behind a series of stones that orbited around the band in some kind of sacred mathematical pattern. The jeweler had explained it, but he hadn't been able to understand.

Her eyes flicked from the ring, to his eyes, then back again. "This is a lovely… gift?"

"Not just a gift." He swallowed.

Laughing, she jumped from the chair and into his lap, almost spilling his coffee in spite of his mug's best efforts to enforce its own sphere of perfect artificial gravity. "Then what is it?"

"Then I don't know." He shrugged, carefully setting the cup on the dash. "I'd like to say it's… well, the sort of ring that says someday maybe you and I can find some red dirt and orange trees to just be ours."

A smile lit her face. "Just ours?"

"You don't like islands, but…"

"But I don't mind heat." Her eyes laughed.

"But who wants to go back to Bantilla? Who even wants to leave the stars? I don't. Not right now, anyway. I don't know what the future holds. Or even what you *want* it to hold." He ran a hand through his hair. Then he ran his hand over her hair, too, just because he could. "I probably should've asked before buying something like this…"

"Yeah, probably."

"But when you got hurt…" He sighed. "It can be just a ring if you want it to."

"And if I don't?"

"Then it can be more than that."

"You know I probably can't wear it on a mission or I might lose a finger."

"You don't think Levereaux could just regrow you a finger?" He tapped at his augmented eye and leaned closer with it for a second. "C'mon. I hear they have some cool add-ons too… You don't want to be part synthetic like me?"

She snorted. "She absolutely could regrow it, sure. But you know I'm *au naturale*. Just *think* of my reputation!" Chuckling, she threw her head back, and he fought the urge to kiss her throat. "I'm kidding. I try to avoid it, but I'd replace something like a finger or an eye if I had to. That's not the same as all the performance enhancers and stuff my parents do. I might decide to risk it on missions anyway. I haven't decided yet."

"Entirely up to you." He took her hands and cupped them in his, drawing her closer, holding their clasped hands over his lips, kissing a knuckle. "I just had plenty of time to think, and it seemed like the right thing to do."

"It was."

He smiled. "It was?"

"Yes. But what if we want different things for our future?"

"I guess that's a conversation we need to have."

"I propose we get some red dirt, put it in a pot, and stick an orange tree in our cabin. At the very minimum."

"I can absolutely co-sign that."

"And what if we make it our cabin permanently? Officially. You think Zhia would give us one of the bigger ones if we pestered her long enough?"

He snorted. "Maybe we can have the science cabin Doug's parents were using now that they're gone."

"Ooh. So sexy."

Chuckling softly, he let go of her hands to run his fingers over her red hair smoothed to her skull, the neat bun at the nape of her neck. "I shoulda looked for a tree on Molyarch instead. Then we'd be closer to your goal. I don't think red dirt is particularly fertile, though. No need to repeat my home world's mistakes."

"Yeah, mine neither. So, sand is out. Neither of us was born in dirt we wanted to grow in, but we made it out. We flourished anyway."

"You and I grow best in the stars, I think."

She smiled. "I wouldn't argue with that life. But who knows what the decades hold? We have to survive saving the commander first."

"You think we can?"

"You think we have a choice about trying?"

His smile broadened. "Nope."

She slipped the ring on her finger. Its size shifted to fit her. "Thank you for this, Adan." Leaning close, she kissed him quickly on the cheek, then started to rise to turn toward the door.

"Wait—where are you going? C'mon. Sit with me. It's a *long* way to the next jump."

"And we don't allow napping," Xi said flatly.

"I have to petition Zhia for our new double-wide." She winked at him. "Then I'll be back."

"Aw, c'mon."

"Adan," she said in a chiding tone. "Don't you know? It is customary for a girl upon receiving an important ring to show it off to her friends. Duh."

He snorted. "You know I don't know your Capital-type etiquette—"

"How dare you." Her eyes flared as she propped her hands on her hips.

He grinned, a playful gleam in his eyes. "But you just got here. I've missed you."

Her expression softened. "I'll bring you back a coffee?"

"Throw in the bigger cabin, and you've got a deal."

THE HATCH CHIMED. Ellen waved her hand, eyes still trained on the display. "C'mon in. Give me a second, I have to—"

The pinch that hit her neck sent her eyes wide. A mistake.

She should have looked.

A mistake.

Her body went numb. But not her mind, her eyes. Blinking, she felt herself slide, then fall to the floor, landing hard on her shoulder. There was no pain, which seemed like an even worse sign because a fall like that should've hurt.

She squirmed, trying to turn, but her muscles wouldn't respond. There was a hiss of the hatch sliding shut. Footsteps coming toward her.

"Well, well. You thought you had it all figured out."

Bridell. She should have known.

He was smiling when he rolled her onto her back. No, grinning, like a fragging hyena. "You seem to be very good at getting away with things, Ellen Ryu. But actions have consequences."

"You think I don't know that?" Her voice responded, but barely. The words were heavily slurred.

He sank to a seat on the floor next to her, then drew a small box from a trouser pocket. He entered a few commands and laid it on the floor beside him.

A wall of shimmering blue bloomed from the box, enveloping them both, expanding until it formed something of a bubble around just the two of them.

"A personal force field," she tried to say.

"Precisely. And neither of us is leaving it until you tell me everything I want to know."

He drew another box from a different trouser pocket. This one opened like a clamshell, and she could see inside a needle and at least a dozen cartridges.

She squirmed harder as he drew the needle and loaded a cartridge. She managed to lift her torso slightly and squirm back, so her head came back down against the force field.

Which was hard as a rock and, indeed, very real.

"What is that?" she whispered.

"Just a little something to help you tell the truth. Considering you were so unforthcoming on my earlier attempts." His eyes glinted, and then he seized her arm, lightning fast. He knew, somehow, where to push, and the ports opened. She rarely used the cybernetic connection and entirely ignored the others, but one of those was what he went for now.

Whatever gunk was in his needle flowed directly into her veins.

Earlier attempts? What was going on?

She slumped down. No point in spending precious energy if he'd just tranquilized her even more. Until she figured out what was in that syringe—if she even could—it was better to conserve.

Unless she was dying... Then the seconds would just be ticking away. But really, finding a way to disable his force field would be a challenge even *without* being drugged.

Her eyelids felt suddenly heavy. Her breathing slowed, and the world around her seemed to quiet and expand at the same time. Which was ironic since she was trapped in this stupid bubble with Bridell of all people.

"Kael's not gonna like this," she grumbled.

Bridell smirked. "I knew he wasn't just your lieutenant."

She let her eyes drift closed. "What, you've never shagged anybody on a spaceship? Yeah, right. I don't believe that for a second."

"We're not here to talk about me."

"Wow, so you haven't? Well, I have." The words were coming too easily now. His drug was doing its job. She was too tired, too numb to even wince about it. "And lived to regret it. I didn't shag Paul, though, and he's fragging bitter. Can you believe that? He was the one who broke up with me!"

He cleared his throat. "I believe the injection has taken effect, so I shall administer the second."

"The second?" She could barely get her eyes to open to see what he was doing. "What is this, four-dimensional chess? Why so complicated? Just tell me what you want to know."

Heat burned into her veins, so he must have been busy doing, rather than talking. But she heard the *clink* of the needle going back in the case.

"I have to give you that injection so you don't go into cardiac arrest."

"Wow, that's really considerate of you."

"Well, I wouldn't want you to die without telling me what I want to know. But if I don't give a third injection in exactly two minutes, you will. So please be forthcoming. For both our sakes."

"Hah. Like you care."

He ignored her laugh. "Tell me where the Empress Capsule is."

That was enough to open her eyes. "What?"

"Lord Regent Jun Il Li gave the capsule full of his most important research to a man who looks stunningly similar to your lieutenant. Then *someone* gave Li an injection to scramble his brain. I will give you a very similar one shortly, in his honor."

"God, you're a fragging Enhancer?" She tried sitting up again. It worked a little better this time, not that she succeeded.

He lifted his chin. "I am perfecting the universe. I am fighting off Chaos. What can you say *you've* done?"

"I've *helped* people," she drawled. "Big people, little people, Ursa people, Teredarks. People you wouldn't even consider people. I'm not over here asking for a damned parade."

"That's lucky because you won't get one. Tell me the location of the capsule."

"Capsule's gone," she replied, making a ridiculous sliding gesture with her arm. This drug was bizarre. "Down the garbage chute. Wheeeee." The words were playful but her tone was more murderous than light.

His jaw tightened, rage flickering in his eyes. "You wouldn't. You had the technology. You could have suspended gestation. You threw all of his research *away*? Morons!"

"Oh, no, we didn't throw it away." She cursed herself as soon as the words slipped out. Damn this stupid drug.

"You didn't? You said—"

"I said we threw the capsule away. Baby was way too big for it. Fetus I mean. There's no baby in my spaceship crawling around trying to mind control anybody. Definitely not my boyfriend."

The two of them stared at each other, both their eyes wide.

"You… you brought it to term. It's alive?"

"*She's* a person. You're talking about her like she's a collection of files in a folder."

"She's whatever our scientists wanted her to be. She's Enhancer property. And you stole her."

"I didn't *personally* steal her. I just found her on my ship and sure as hell didn't go out of my way to give her back."

"Ah, that's right. Your lieutenant was the thief. Well, when I'm done with you, I'll be sure to deal with him."

The hatch suddenly chimed.

"Hey! Help!" she shouted. She tried to move her leg, and it *did* move, to her surprise. Easily. He didn't see, his eyes on the door and then on her face.

He smirked again. "We can hear what's happening outside the force field, but it shields our voices from leaving, as well as the computers from seeing in. So, scream all you like. No one can hear you."

As if to prove his point, she heard the footsteps of whoever had come to see her as they walked away.

He drew another cartridge, attached it to the needle. "Where is your ship?"

"Fragged if I know, man. Your computers probably know better than I do."

"Where would they be likely to go?"

"Restock, refuel. Somewhere off the beaten path. Then they'll come after me."

Bridell fed the injection into her line. "I suppose I could just sit and wait. Perhaps that's exactly what I'll do."

"Are you going to kill me then?"

"Oh, no. I think I'll keep you around a little longer before I scramble your brain. I may have more questions, and this drug has worked so well. *This* particular injection will simply ensure you don't remember any of this." He grinned again.

"Then my future self says fuck you."

He chuckled. "Or perhaps I'll go after your boyfriend. He

destroyed one of the brightest minds we had. Devastated our progress toward perfection. We were forced to start all over. From square one."

"What happened to the other copies? Don't you always keep three copies?"

His eyes narrowed at her specific knowledge. "Why yes. And I'll be damned if I'd tell *you* that. Now sleep, pretty girl, and when you wake up, this will all have been just a terrible dream that gave you a *splitting* headache. I'll be busy taking care of your traitor boyfriend and all your friends while you play the hero." He reached for the force field box.

She kicked out, catching him in the temple, and sent him colliding into his force field.

Her limbs hardly wanted to work, but she launched herself at him anyway. The force field generator slid.

It was a blur of reflex and training deeper than conscious thought. Or maybe it was just some animal instinct. But she was on top of him, doing her best to pummel him into the floor. Blow after blow, blood splattering across the grating. The RPD, she realized, she should activate it, but she couldn't focus on the mental control—

Somehow he found the force field box and pushed the button.

The shimmering blue evaporated into nothing.

An alarm suddenly blared. Footsteps came running in the hall. The door slid open, and she was still slugging him, like if she could have ground his brain into goo, she would have.

Arms dragged her off him. She didn't know what she said, what he said. The world went fuzzy.

The lights got bright and blurry. Adrenaline could only take her so far, and her eyelids were heavy as hell.

Shu and Mertz were there. Helping Bridell to his feet, toward sick bay.

"Traitor!" she managed to shout. "He's a traitor! A leak—"

A wave of dizziness slammed her like a brick wall. She tilted sideways into one of several people trying to restrain her, lost control of her legs, and fell into the abyss of sleep.

CHAPTER NINE

WELL. Twenty-four hours of sitting awkwardly chained in this cell hadn't improved Kael's opinion of Captain Weyer very much.

Especially since the number of ship-maintenance emergencies announced—loudly—over the ship comm system nearly exceeded the number of hours he'd been sitting there.

And every "comfortable" position he could find still caused at least one limb to fall asleep. Fragging chains.

He'd managed to loosen every bolt in the steel wall behind him, to which the chains were secured. He had no idea what lay on the other side of the wall, or if it could even help him, but this way, if he had a chance to run, he'd be able to at least drag the chains along with him.

He was also pretty sure he could break the chains if need be. Or bend the cuffs. But that would only make sense if it was go-time. If he revealed that now, they'd just get better restraints.

So he had to wait for the exact right time. When his chances of getting back to Ellen were best. But also when it made *sense*—at the moment, they both needed these people's help. So unless the shit was hitting the fan, he ought to sit tight.

But would he even know if they were going into battle? Especially with the alarms blaring every five minutes. It wasn't quite that often, but it felt like it, and it made sleeping impossible.

Ear plugs were probably standard-issue for those crewing this ship.

While he was mulling how he'd ever sort the ordinary emergencies from the big one, the outer hatch hissed open. Footsteps came toward the cells.

"Status, soldier." It was Weyer. He straightened up.

His guard snapped to her feet. "Excellent, ma'am. Nothing to report. He sits there and stays quiet."

"Like you told me to," Kael called in a singsong.

"Hmm. Is that so? I don't know. He's got that look in his eyes."

"What look, ma'am?"

"Looks like a troublemaker."

"I never denied that." He grinned. "But I can choose my battles."

At almost the precise moment he stopped speaking, the floor under them shuddered.

"Damn trilini leaks again—" Weyer started, stamping her foot like it'd fix something.

But she stopped short and her mouth fell open. It took him only a split-second to realize why.

A loud crash exploded to his left and right. The chains pulled him down suddenly, and he winced as he saw what had happened.

The panels had fallen. The panels he'd loosened the bolts on.

Six separate panels, with that nudge from some machinery a level down and Weyer's foot, had given up on life and thrown themselves to the floor like they'd fainted.

"Wow, this ship is in worse shape than I thought. You should probably fortify your brig a little better." He risked a glance over his shoulder. The walls were full of solid conduit and wire, although he was pretty sure he could see at least two dead creatures between bits. He shuddered.

"*Really* not a troublemaker, huh?" Weyer was glaring at him, with her hands on her hips, not buying his excuse for a second. "Computer, get me medical."

"Medical?" He frowned. "I think you mean Engineering."

"I know what I said. They'll be next."

"Your ship is quite literally falling apart, Captain. That could have killed me. I am collateral, if you recall. I need to be alive to be useful."

"And you didn't give those panels a hand? Please. Don't bullshit me, Theroki." She drew her pistol and motioned for her sergeant to do the same as a frightened-looking med tech arrived.

"For the last time, I told you I'm not a—"

"Yeah, yeah, you're not a Theroki, and I'm not doomed to hear bullshit like that until this vessel flies us all into a star. I should have listened to the recommendations."

"I… I have no idea what that means." He stared from person to person while Weyer slid aside the old-fashioned cell door of bars and motioned the med tech in.

"It means I've got no patience for mincing words. You're telekinetic, you're in my brig, and you tried to escape."

"No, I didn't." Technically, he had only *prepared* and planned an escape. He hadn't actually attempted it yet.

"You know, I thought you were a straight shooter. Honestly, I'm disappointed."

The med tech drew a syringe from her pocket. Fuck.

He caught Weyer's eyes with a challenge, hoping there was no panic in his gaze. No point in trying to argue his innocence now. They'd made up their minds. "Give me a gun, let's find out."

Weyer just shook her head. "Do it."

"I do hope you're careful," he said, giving the med tech his winningest smile. "I'm valuable collateral, after all." He glanced pointedly at Weyer.

"I need you alive. That doesn't mean conscious."

The med tech's hand was shaking—which was not reassuring—as he found Kael's port and injected whatever it was.

His scrubbers would work to nullify it, just like that time when Josana had slipped Osiris into his drink. But not right away. And his captors wouldn't know what to expect. Dr. Dremer had told him it was unpredictable at this point. That the effects could be cut down or magnified, last longer or shorter.

Mostly, though, he'd seemed to get over things more quickly than expected… If he could exaggerate whatever effects their drug had, draw them out, maybe he could get them to keep the doses lower.

He expected some kind of sedative, but acid shot into his veins. Heat and fire exploded across his nerves. The pain spiraled, multiplied, racing along connections as the drug moved through his system.

He gritted his teeth, started to sweat.

Started to groan. "Seven suns, that hurts like an asteroid to the nuts—what *is* that stuff?"

Weyer was frowning. "I never said anything about pain. What did you give him?"

The med tech's eyes were wide, panicked. "No… it's not supposed to—he's—maybe he's—maybe it's contaminated, or—a reaction—"

"Contaminated?" he grunted through clenched teeth.

"Computer, emergency in medical," Weyer barked. "Emergency response team, immediately. Get his vitals."

"Yes, ma'am!" The med tech scrambled.

He could barely see, it hurt so bad. He ignored the tech, ignored it all, slumped back against what remained of the wall and glared at Weyer. "This… didn't need… to happen."

She glared right back at him. "I agree. It didn't. Don't try to escape next time."

He shut his eyes, clenched his jaw harder, and tried to breathe through it. "If you were me…" he whispered, "you'd try…"

He had no idea if she responded—if she heard him.

The world around him blurred. Go, scrubbers, go. Hurry. He needed to get back to Ellen. To get back to Shirin. Back to all his friends. They'd reach Arakovic soon. He needed to be there, to help them.

He had to. Had to get out of this alive. Had to get *free*, especially if they were going to torture him.

He wouldn't *try* to escape next time. He wouldn't wait.

Next time, when the time was right, they'd know he was escaping, because he'd be long gone.

"DANE?" Nova poked her head inside the door to his room, chewing her gum with more than her usual amount of sass. "Mrs. Simmons has some… ideas."

He frowned at her tone of voice as he stood. Their rooms in the hotel on Molyarch were pretty swank, but even he was starting to get bored, so he couldn't say he found the interruption unwelcome. "Ideas?"

"You'll see."

He followed her, past two rooms, down to the largest suite, the one with the meeting room. The two elder Simmonses were gathered around the table with Dr. Persad and Dr. Taylor.

"Oh, good, that was quick." Catherine gave him a wide smile. He was pretty sure it wasn't one of those, *If I'm nice to him he'll agree with me* smiles, but he definitely wasn't positive. "Nova said I should discuss my ideas with you and the rest of the team." She gestured at Dr. Taylor, although he didn't see how that was the "rest" of the team. Unless, oh no, had she run them by everyone but him and Taylor already?

"I'm all ears," he said, returning the smile, although inwardly, he felt more guarded. It only paid to be friendly and polite.

"We've avoided contact with the rest of the Foundation so far," she began, "but I wonder if it's time to reconsider. We also have contacts outside those circles. While we've been financially attacked, it doesn't mean we can't get access to additional funds."

He had to work not to shake his head. His parents had both been doctors, and until the shit had hit the fan, he'd had pretty much anything he wanted as a kid. But the idea of having so many wealthy friends that being financially ruined was a minor speed bump to this lady? That was hard to grok. "And if we had said funds, did you have some plans for them?"

"Well, we could buy this hotel, first off. Maybe the whole station. It'd give us the option to make changes, put in additional security."

"And it'd draw an avalanche of attention," he said. "I don't think Molyarch gets many billionaire investors."

"I know it could be a risk, but I think we should get in touch with at least one member of the Foundation. They—at least at one point—had an office here. We should find out its status. Were they attacked by known bad actors that are still here? And that knowledge as well as more funds could, again, help us truly secure this station. Or at least a good part of it."

Nova did shake her head now. "It'd reveal our location, ma'am. Big time. Can't take a risk like that now, ma'am. Maybe when they've settled things with Arakovic. But right now, we need to lie low."

"I agree," Dane added. "We don't have an easy evac out of here. Evac as in *evacuation*. If this situation goes sideways, we could easily be trapped here in Hotel Paradise."

Dr. Persad snorted at the inaccurate name.

"You want to work on something," Dane continued, "we should work on that first. An evac plan."

Catherine frowned, looking thoughtful. "You mean like getting us a ride?"

"Maybe a ship. If we reserved some seats or chartered somebody's ship, I'm not sure we could trust those to really be there when the time came. But we can't call any old friends to do it. And we don't have Xi pulling strings for us anymore."

Nova scowled at her boots. "I hate this. I wish I was with them." She glanced at the others. "No offense. I'm happy to keep you all from robbery and death."

"Well, that's good," murmured Dr. Persad. "I think."

"Mother," Vivaan said, "Maybe you could build something. Or repair something. To raise funds."

"Hmm. That's possible. But my skills could also attract attention of their own."

Dr. Dremer nodded. "I could offer some medical services. But in places like this, there are also folks who would… indenture medical services."

"Or enslave them," Nova added.

"Yes, true. Not sure why I was being delicate about it."

"Because it's as scary as a twenty-tentacled flying monster in a typhoon," Nova replied.

"Or a week-old burrito," offered Dane, trying to lighten the mood. They didn't need to dwell on getting into trouble. That was the whole reason he and Nova were there.

"Why a week?" Nova asked. "Is that when it's still sort of tempting to eat it?"

"Ew, Nova. I have never even considered such a thing," he said with mock primness.

"I walked right into that one."

"All right, back to Vivaan's original point. We all have services," he said. "We all could make some credits selling them. But most of us are rare pieces of work. That means there's a danger in it, too, in exposing ourselves."

Vivaan raised his hand. "Well, I'm not particularly skilled. I mean, someday I'll be a great investigator, but—"

"No, that's a good point," Dr. Dremer said. "Maybe Vivaan could get a job as a dishwasher."

"A dishwasher? My son—" Dr. Persad stood up. She looked like she might have a different use for a plate, like serving up Dremer's face on it right about now, until she stopped short. "Oh. You were joking."

Dremer's small smile spread to a grin. "Yes. Though a kitchen job *might* get any of us access to the rumor mill that's certain to be churning on a station like this."

Vivaan's eyes lit up. "I could get so many leads…"

Dane sighed. This could be worse, he told himself. They were secure. They were bored. But how had he gotten stuck herding the civilian cats instead of charging into battle and glory?

As if to mock him, outside the door, something exploded. The lights flickered.

He didn't hesitate. He grabbed Dr. Taylor's arm and dragged her behind the sofa, then lunged toward Vivaan.

Another roar from the corridor. Good thing they'd shut the door behind them, hell. But half his people were still sitting at the table, staring, like ice sculptures of highly educated civilians.

"Get down!" he growled. Some of them had instinctively braced, but none of them had ducked except Nova, who'd pivoted to train her multi on the door. They were both in armor, but it had been starting to seem a bit overzealous. Now, he was glad. At his words—and a third barrage of noise outside the door—more of them scrambled to take cover.

"Be careful what you wish for," he muttered to himself, shaking his head.

He pulled out his comm and looked at the vid feeds Doug had set up. They'd managed to quietly install a number of security measures for just this sort of situation.

"You getting this, Dane?" Nova shouted as another went off.

"On it."

Two people in hoods and masks were a bit down the hallway, tossing what appeared to be fireworks at the door. Fireworks?

A bunch of stupid kids? That just figured. Maybe the armor *was* overzealous.

He shook his head again. That ironically did make him feel better. These little idiots might have noticed the wealthy people in this part of the hotel and were looking to scare them into handing over some credits or jewels or something. Not exactly organized crime, here.

Pulling up the commands Doug had given him, he activated one of three drones installed for this purpose. He wasn't sure if the hotel had given permission or not, or if he was going to be asking for forgiveness real soon, but hey, they probably didn't want these yahoos setting off fireworks in their corridors either.

Looking back at the vid feed, the drone whizzed from the corner, peppering the perpetrators with a dozen rapid-fire blasts.

The paint capsules hit hard—and on target.

Dane smiled as he heard them swearing through the door. He shouldn't have been able to hear them, so the seal must have been damaged.

The drone circled around for another pass, but the kids were already running for the exit. It tailed them out of view for a moment, only three paint capsules bouncing off the kids and getting on the walls.

Hopefully, the proprietors would be fans of… colorful redecorating.

Just when Dane thought they might simply run off and he'd have to go stalking through the station looking for who had green paint left behind their ears, some beefy security guys came around the corner and grabbed them. Maybe the hotel? Maybe organized crime? Who knew. Didn't look like station security.

Dane blew out a breath. "Okay. At ease, everybody. It's taken care of."

"How do you know?"

"Because I got the action vid feed right here on my wrist."

They all gathered around to watch the replay.

It wasn't until later that he had time to think about what happened.

Long after everyone was more settled and it was certain no additional attacks were coming, and the discussion about buying the whole darn station or hotel had petered out—for now, he replayed the scenario in his mind. Something about it still seemed… odd.

As he worked to repair the seal on the door with a bit of emergency glue and brute force, he ran through each step. The explosions. The masks and hoods and firecrackers. The paint. The idiots running away. Security approaching at the last minute.

Someone from outside the hotel really shouldn't have gotten that close. Did that mean they were from inside the hotel?

And station security had never responded to the explosions. Had somebody paid them off? Were they that bad?

"I am going to swing by station security and inquire about our… visitors earlier. You okay for a bit?" he said quietly to Nova.

"I'll keep my eyes open between naps." She winked. "Kidding. I can always call your comm. Go on."

He left the hotel and headed toward station security. He and they were going to have a little talk.

HER EYES WERE gritty when they opened again. Ellen reached to rub the grit away, but her arm hit some restraint and wouldn't move. She blinked and squinted, trying to make her eyes work.

A silver rail on a pod in sick bay was the first thing to come into focus. She was cuffed to it, both wrists *and* ankles.

She hadn't served the Union as long as she should have, but the stream of expletives that she let out didn't show it.

Her eyes focused on a wide-eyed Ensign Mertz.

"What's going on here, Mertz?" she growled.

"We, uh… we were going to ask you the same thing."

"What happened?"

"You don't remember?"

"No. Last thing I remember is working on my report. What the actual fuck, Mertz."

"You beat the shit out of Bridell, ma'am. I mean, we have all wanted to at times, but… But you actually did it."

"I did *what*?"

Her head swam from the effort of talking. She sank her head back into the pillow, searching for some foggy recollection. A glimpse of him smirking at her flitted through her mind. A brief flash of blood spatter on the deck.

But the memories slipped away like catching fish in a river with her bare hands.

The sick-bay door hissed aside, and Paul, Shu, Bridell, and

Yamamoto filed in. At the sight of Bridell, a vicious, illogical rage welled up.

He gave her a cold look and had clearly been in sick bay too. He had a dozen bandages, including over his nose, and a black eye. She gritted her teeth at the tidal wave of rage and tried not to show it lashing around inside her, but her arms were already tense against the cuffs.

"She has no memory of what transpired, sir," Mertz offered, looking at Paul.

He looked at her. "Nothing at all?"

"Sorry, sir," Ellen said. "Last thing I remember was working on my report, then the door opened."

"Don't the vid feeds have something?" Shu asked.

Yamamoto shook his head. "The video feeds captured right up to the incident, but somehow, miraculously, missed the majority of it. When they come back on, both Bridell and Ryu are inside a personal force field system. The vids don't capture who activated it."

"A what?" She scowled. "Well, you can search my cabin. I don't have anything like that. How would I even have gotten one?"

"Please. You've had free access to the entire ship," Bridell sneered.

"And if it was hers," Mertz added, "that still doesn't explain why she'd turn it off just to beat the shit out of—"

Yamamoto cleared his throat.

"Sorry, just to assault Lieutenant Bridell? That doesn't seem logical."

"Maybe it failed her. She *assaulted* me because she didn't like the questions I was asking about her report." Bridell jammed a finger at her.

"I would never," she snapped. "Come on."

"Stress gets to the best of us," Shu muttered.

"That doesn't mean you give someone a black eye for offering critique of a mission plan," Paul shot back. "Or do you have a violent past I don't know about, Lieutenant Shu?"

Her face flushed slightly. "Sorry, sir. I just meant… erratic behavior would be within normal human parameters in this sort of situation."

"Ah, but is Ellen Ryu within normal human parameters?" He raised an eyebrow, smiling.

"She had no problem with *my* questions," Mertz pointed out.

"Mine either," Paul said.

She almost laughed at that. His questions, such as they were, had been more formality than actual critique. But this situation was too serious to take lightly. They could keep her here, take her to the Inner Planets, and abort the whole mission.

"Listen, I wouldn't do anything to endanger getting to Arakovic. This mission is too important."

"You're strung out," Bridell said. "Obsessed with this scientist, and we can't even prove she's who you say she is. Don't you see how obsessed she is? She hides it well, makes it seem rational, but it's not healthy."

Paul held up a hand to silence him.

Bridell kept going. "You're risking your career on a delusional maniac!"

"Dr. Madsi flagged no such issues," Paul replied, his expression going stern.

Who? Had he had someone look her over? They'd never *talked* to her. Now she imagined some psych pouring over the vid feeds of her every move, looking for evidence of dysfunction. She'd known they *could*, but knowing they *did* somehow felt worse.

She scowled fiercely at all of them. "I don't know what happened in there, but I think it's pretty damn odd that I don't remember, don't you? How does that happen? It wasn't *my* head that got hit."

"I agree," said Shu. "And the obfuscation of the force field is extremely… abnormal."

"How do you explain that, Lieutenant Bridell?" asked Yamamoto.

"Me? Why am *I* supposed to explain everything? I'm the one she trapped and assaulted just for asking a few questions!"

"Did you hit back?"

"No!"

"Not once?" Yamamoto frowned. "Perhaps you need a refresher in hand-to-hand combat training, then."

Bridell swore. "I can't believe you're trying to pin this on me. I go in there to try to make this mission better, and look at my *face.* How much more evidence do you need? She's lost it. She needs to be removed from this mission. *We* need to be removed from this mission."

"It is not your place to say," Paul snapped.

"In fact, if you all want to put someone like *her* in charge of this, I seriously question your competence, and I will be filing my concerns on record."

"File anything you like." Paul's eyes had gone steely. "I am in charge of this operation and this ship, and I am in charge of *you*. Officers plan missions for commanders all the time. It is my prerogative to delegate any duty I chose, including this one. And you very neatly side-stepped Yamamoto's questions, without offering any explanations for the memory loss or the force field. This is the *second* occurrence of memory loss with you in a one-on-one situation, Lieutenant."

Bridell's face had gone red with rage. "You people have drunk her fragging Kool-Aid. Why don't you just take the ship and become free agents while you're at it? Who needs to serve the Union anyway? Let's all be deserters!"

Paul opened his mouth, his expression thunderous, stormy.

But Yamamoto spoke first. His voice was quiet, but hard as granite. "Do not question anyone's loyalty to the Union here. How dare you."

There was something in his eyes, something dark. Anger? It was almost like he knew what had happened inside that bubble. But how could he? No one could but Bridell.

The words didn't seem especially powerful, but something between Yamamoto's tone and his eyes made Bridell take a step back. His mouth had been open, planning to cut in, but now he shut it.

"Look, the mission planning is done," Ellen said quickly. "You don't have to change anything. It's ready. We've briefed half of it, and the easy half is left. Take it and run with it. I'll stay here in sick bay if you want. I'd rather be out front, but just *keep going.* Please don't let whatever I did or didn't do endanger this mission. Please. Arakovic must be stopped."

Paul looked to Yamamoto. "Second, what would you advise?"

"After this incident, I would advise keeping Ellen Ryu in restraints while moving around the ship, and then proceeding as planned. If another violent outburst occurs, then we could always revisit that opinion." He looked from Paul to Bridell. "Somehow, I feel quite certain that it will not reoccur if Commander Ryu and Lieutenant Bridell are not alone together. So I suggest that is not allowed. Whatever happened in that room, the Songbird threat is real. There is no question of that. We should proceed with confronting the threat as planned."

"Anyone else?" Paul said, almost weakly, as if he didn't want to hear anyone else but felt required to.

"I strongly object," Bridell said.

"Yeah, we know," Mertz replied. "I concur with Lieutenant Yamamoto's suggestion. This doesn't change the attack on Senator Dealis or the history of terrorism the Songbirds have. And we can't catch up to Freedom's Wing anyway. If we abort without any other objective accomplished, that seems the worst of all worlds."

"Sunk costs should not determine future actions," Shu put in. "But I agree we should proceed. Commander Ryu has zero history of violence against other officers in any of her time served. This is at worse a stress aberration. I think we should do a thorough neurological and blood analysis. I have additional thoughts on analysis, but they can take place outside of this meeting."

"Thank you all for your opinions. We will proceed. Yamamoto, either you, Lieutenant Shu, or I will be in Ryu's presence when restrained on the bridge at all times. Understood?"

"Yes, sir."

"All right, get her out of here, then. Ryu, you may return to your quarters but fragging stay there." He waved at Yamamoto.

"Beg your pardon, sir," Ellen put in, "but I'm not sure I can stand yet."

"Oh. Then, when you're feeling up to it." Paul turned on his heel and left.

Shu frowned and joined the medic near the console, looking over the data feeds of Ellen's vitals.

"THIS IS THE PLACE," Kentt murmured. "Thank you for doing this."

Xi's hands glided over the controls as she guided their small ship in for landing. Sub-par as fingers were speed-wise when compared to a direct connection, it was fun to pretend. "For doing what?" she asked.

"For coming with me."

"You are welcome. But it is and was necessary. My calculations suggest that our friends will need all the help we can acquire."

"You can land there." Kentt pointed to a flat, snowy area with a small bunker to one side. Low mountains rose up on either side, but in the center, it was unnaturally, perfectly flat.

"Is this an unused manmade landing zone?"

"Yes. They don't really want many visitors."

Wind whipped snow against the outer cameras and buffeted the wings. Eccentric as Claudette could be, and as old as this ship appeared to be, it was sturdy and reliable. Far from the *Audacity*, but perfectly adequate. They hadn't thought of a name for it, and Xi wasn't sure they would. She did the calculations to adjust for the wind and snow that she didn't trust the ship computers to do as accurately as she'd like. She debated feigning strain as a human would do, but the effort was probably too minuscule to justify the external expression of emotion.

"This site is colder than I expected someone from Capital to select," she said instead.

Kentt's mouth barely twitched in chagrin.

Between the two of them, Kentt was a more convincing android, even though she was in fact mostly human, with fairly modest augmentations, and simply chose to show little emotion. Or perhaps it wasn't a choice, just her nature. Xi would truly wonder if she didn't have the biometric scans to prove Kentt was indeed flesh and blood. She had not yet collected enough data on sentient beings to understand that part of existence, but there did seem to be a difference between what one might want to be and what one was.

The ship settled neatly on the landing pad.

Kentt unbuckled her harness and stood. "Variety is the spice of life, my dear."

Xi twitched her eyebrows again. She filed that into her occurrences of idioms to ponder and unlatched her harness as well.

The harness was more theater than fact, as she had reflexes to steady herself that were far beyond a human's. She also had little of the biology that made the harness necessary, although of course getting smashed into the hull hard enough could hurt just about anything. Strictly speaking, this body was mortal, as in, it could be destroyed. But her mind still resided, in part, in partition, inside the *Audacity*. And in fact she had begun investing in non-co-located backups after the encounter with Merith, not that she'd told anyone. Not even Doug this time.

Replacing her physical body would be time-consuming, and costly, so she took these precautions. But, unlike Kentt, she would not die. Not exactly, not via her body anyway.

This gave her a certain fearlessness that her friends could not afford. Enough to push ahead of Kentt where she stood in the open hatch and glared out into the bitter snowscape.

Xi strode toward the blank steel doors of the only visible bunker, backed by the certainty of calculations over similar situations done millions of times.

Snow was thick as she dragged her boots through it. For the number of people, she'd expected a small village, not just two doors cowering here between the low mountains. The majority must be underground. Kentt's boots crunched along behind her.

"Are they... expecting us?" Xi asked.

"They did not respond to my message. So perhaps. Or perhaps not."

Zipping up her parka—more to hide her synthetic nature than for any practical need—she stopped in front of the doors.

"Shall I?" She raised a hand but waited for Kentt's acknowledgment. When the telepath nodded, Xi knocked on the metal, bare knuckled, and then tried waving at the probable sensor-panel locations around the doors.

A divot of a frown in Kentt's forehead said that there was something odd about how she'd done it. More notes for later. Her sensors also immediately registered exterior synthetic skin damage. She checked the temperature.

An unfortunate ten degrees below Celsius. Likely, human behavior would be to put her hands in her pockets—or wear thick gloves. She stuffed her hands into the fabric parka and waited. Hopefully, the knuckle burn wouldn't be too hard to repair. Perhaps it would even add a certain realism. Maybe she wouldn't repair it at all.

Kentt stepped to the side and bent low, peering directly into a small camera Xi had already waved at.

A voice suddenly crackled over a comm, making Kentt jump back slightly. "Dr. Kentt? Is that you?"

Xi raised an eyebrow. "Doctor?"

"It's me. Can we come in?" Kentt's gaze flicked to meet hers, with a small smile. "We all have our wild pasts. You were a ship, I was in academia..."

"I am not nor was I once the ship. I am not sure my past is wild. But I would like to hear more about this… wild academia."

"Another time. Perhaps you are having a wild present, then."

Xi opened her mouth to respond, but the grinding of the doors made her cancel the action. What had she been planning to say anyway? The vague definition of wild certainly didn't clarify the matter.

A woman with short pink hair cut close to her head exploded from the bunker. Xi's hand went to her pistol at her hip, violating her settings for standard human speeds, but it appeared that the girl was friendly.

Her arms had launched around Kentt in a fierce hug.

"What are you doing here?" she asked, stepping back.

Kentt straightened her cloak, looking a little ruffled. "I'd love to say we're just dropping in to visit. But it's a little more complicated than that."

At her words, the girl registered Xi's presence, looking sharply over her shoulder. "All right then. It's cold as a witch's tit out here, anyway. Come on in."

Kentt went first, and Xi followed. The doors opened onto a large elevator, the walls of which were dark metal, dented and worn, although not enough to look unsafe.

"Thank you for seeing us, Pria," Kentt said as the girl shut the outer doors and ordered the elevator as it lurched into operation.

"Are you kidding? It's not like you pay for this place or anything." Folding her arms, Pria leaned against one wall near a streak of rust.

"I am sure you are busy."

"I am, but not *that* busy. Who's your friend?"

"This is Xi."

"You're not…" Pria shrugged one shoulder and tilted her head. "I can't, you know, read her thoughts."

"We've been working with some friends who have discovered a technology for blocking telepathic abilities."

"Really? No shit."

"Really. I think it's a wonderful development for a variety of reasons. Including that it has the potential to not make us quite such dark boogeymen for those who have… things to hide."

"Yeah, let 'em hide them. If they just leave us alone to live our lives, what do we care? Well, nice to meet you, Xi. What's your story? I'm Pria. I'm a telepath. I was studying on Capital until, well, everything went to shit. But that's okay, cause this is way better anyway." She gave Kentt a wink.

Was there sarcasm in play? Xi had no idea at the moment. "What is my… story?"

"Yes. Where you're from, what you do, all that."

"I…" Perhaps she should have rehearsed this. "I am a pilot. I was born on Tetra VII, but I mostly have spent my life in space."

"Tetra VII, nice. Who wants to leave there?"

"There are many worlds and stars to see, and wonders on all of them," Kentt said placidly. Hmm, that seemed to be a conversational movement of defending an ally's choices. Xi made a note to express gratitude at a future time, although this choice didn't quite make sense to her yet. Why defend? Xi did not need defense, and Pria was also an ally. Perhaps Kentt was trying to draw attention away from the fact that Xi was an illegal android, with no typical "story" to speak of.

Less discussion of fabricated stories would be less likely to encounter unconsidered, poorly planned details. Then again, nothing she'd said was untrue. Telling the truth was ideal in all situations.

Although the truth was that she was illegal in many places, unnerving in others. So perhaps the less said, the better.

Yes, during tonight's "sleep" cycle, she ought to create a minute-by-minute biography of her fictitious life for this purpose. A good activity for later.

For now, she only smiled and shrugged and hoped that was an appropriate response to this exchange.

Pria seemed mollified, shrugging back and running a hand through that pink hair. The elevator came to a grinding halt.

"What is this place? It feels strange," Kentt asked.

"It originally was an opsepium mine shaft." Pria grinned as she pulled a lever and opened a new set of doors into the interior. "Still is, in fact."

"This is where you brought them?" Xi asked, looking at Kentt.

"It was a… collaborative choice."

"C'mon in, ladies. This is our little home sweet home." Pria held her arms wide as they followed. A large, open room was filled with women and a few men, many working at holodesks but a few lounging on couches or chairs, reading tablets, chatting. The floor was smooth, plain stone, and the ceiling low enough that Xi was glad she hadn't gone with a taller specification for her body.

The air composition did in fact contain elements suggesting a mine, and on the ends of the room, five wide, blue force fields lit the place in their glow.

"Dr. Kentt! Dr Kentt!" A handful of women and girls rushed toward them, swarming the now-blushing telepath.

Xi placed her hand nearer the pistol, but at a casual, normal human speed this time.

"How nice to see you!"

"Welcome!"

"Hello!"

A few minutes of polite niceties were exchanged, and Xi watched from the outside. Thankfully, no one asked her to introduce or explain herself. In fact, for a moment, she felt more like her invisible ship self, a voice through a speaker, an un-seeable presence.

"All right, ladies. Let me give Dr. Kentt a tour. I'm sure you can all chat with her more later." Drawing Kentt away from the group by the elbow, Pria started them on a walk circling the large room. "So all you can see here is the working area. We've got our own rooms down that way." She pointed to a corridor without a force field. "And the kitchen and such. We purchased this mine after a few months on this planet. And thinking about our options for the future."

"Fascinating," said Xi. "Do you operate the mine?"

"Yes."

"What are *they* doing?" Xi pointed to those at holodesks.

"Some of them are working on selling the opsepium. Both legally and black market, I'll admit." She gave Kentt a slightly sheepish shrug. "Some of them are studying it, developing other uses. And some of them are working on other options all together. It's worth so damn much, we don't have to mine it very often. But these five shafts are all active, so we can afford to keep up the co-op for… well, quite a long time. And we'll probably need to."

"What's that way?" Kentt pointed. "And how were you able to afford this?"

"A group of locals had targeted the place, harassing the former owner, bombing it and stuff. He was happy to get rid of it."

Kentt's eyes widened. "How are you handling them?"

"Oh, them? Not a problem anymore. In fact, there are two of them over there." She pointed to a woman and a man drinking tea at a small table, talking.

"How…"

"We offered a few of them a place in the co-op. C'mon, let me get you some tea." She led them toward the kitchen corridor, out of the main area.

"A place in the co-op?" Xi asked. "I do not understand."

"Some of 'em were just down on their luck. Jealous of the mine owner. But some of them—the leaders, especially—were telepaths. Rogue ones, hiding it. Didn't want anybody to know."

"Violence against an opsepium mine is not the most delicate way to hide that." Kentt frowned.

Pria chuckled. "Nope, it wasn't. They didn't much appreciate the opsepium, but even more so the anti-telepath sentiment the mine brought to town. That was a ticking bomb."

"So… if you can't beat 'em, join 'em?" Kentt said.

"Yep. They were unconnected to the broader telepathic community. And here, they're in power, instead of just serving the opsepium buyers a drink. Once we explained that tools that allow ordinary people to create solid boundaries against telepaths is a good thing for everybody, they started seeing it differently."

"Why is that a good thing?" Xi asked.

"Because knowing everybody's secrets is not conducive to a long life." Pria grinned at her. "And also the honor system ain't great. Without opsepium, we have to simply promise not to peek inside people's darkest secrets and use their knowledge for manipulative gain."

"I see."

"Even ordinary, intelligent decisions uninformed by telepathy can be questioned." Kentt nodded.

"I have witnessed this happen to Ms—Dr. Kentt," Xi replied.

Kentt's blue eyes caught hers, crinkled by a smile.

"Simple good luck becomes suspect too," Pria continued. "You *knew* the lottery would come up with that number. Your telepathy told you."

"That is not how telepathy works." Xi shook her head. "That is illogical."

"Yeah, people sure are." Pria snickered. "It's not unheard of for people to be accused of other nonexistent powers. So, people hide it best they can."

"And many others suffer when they aren't able to hide it," Kentt added, sobering.

"Yeah." Pria's head ducked, her wide smile faltering for the first time. "Yeah, that's true too."

"Let me help you with the tea," Kentt said as they reached a new cavern-like room with cabinets along one side. "Xi, have a seat over there if you would."

Studying them as they worked, Xi was mystified. While they owned a drink machine, the two of them spent over seven minutes and forty-eight seconds preparing a steaming earthenware pot, a plate of star-shaped pastries like nothing Xi had ever seen, and three small cups.

Yes. The decision to create a "digestive" system had been an excellent one. The complexity and risk that it had added had been questionable and required some additional supplies from Molyarch as well as some surreptitious use of the ship's parts printer. But, at this moment, it was all worth it.

Not that she could taste any of it. But at least she didn't have to pretend not to be hungry. That would have created suspicion and obstacles, she suspected, which had been a primary driver for the digestive inclusion effort.

But she had not anticipated feeling like one of them, as she did now.

"So, spill it, Doctor," Pria said, sliding into a seat and taking a huge bite of a pastry in one fluid motion.

"Whatever do you mean?" Kentt took a demure sip.

"Yes, what are you a doctor of?" Xi asked.

Pria snorted. "You don't know? I think it's pretty obvious any time you talk to her."

"I do not know."

"Philosophy. She's a doctor of philosophy."

"I specialized in Buddhist thought experiments." Kentt shrugged mildly. "But that wasn't what you meant."

"Something dragged your brilliant brain all the way across the galaxy here in person. What was it?"

"I didn't leave home to come here," Kentt said, sighing. "I left to look for my sister."

Pria sobered. "Any signs?"

"No. And, indeed, from what I have learned of Arakovic and the Songbird project, she is likely effectively dead."

"Fragging hell." Pria jammed more of a pastry into her mouth now.

"It is difficult to accept," Kentt admitted. "But we are seeking justice anyway."

"Justice? How can you find justice? There's nobody that Arakovic answers to."

Kentt straightened, rising in her seat as her shoulders drifted back. Her eyes had seemed more human till now, but their glow seemed to brighten. "I am seeking to make her answer to me."

Pria froze mid bite, then kept chewing, more slowly now.

"And I am looking for allies," Kentt said, sipping again. "To correct the mistake that was made."

"Mistake?" Pria snorted. "You always did have a talent for understatement."

"My rhetoric is controlled. To right the wrong?"

"To stand up to Arakovic," Xi offered. "To fight." They were the kinds of words that the commander used to stir the crew, but neither her words nor Kentt's did anything but make Pria shake her head.

"There's no standing up to her." Pria dusted crumbs off her hands, brushing them together. "There's no fighting. She will win. We've thought it through a million different ways, but there are too many Songbirds now. All we can do is try to survive."

"How many are there?" Xi asked.

"Can't be sure, but at least over a thousand minds linked. Not all telepaths. But that's... *not* a small number. And just a handful of Songbirds can control whole worlds, depending on the population size. Maybe five, maybe ten, as few as one on a small planet. Think about that."

"I know," Kentt replied. "Capital is among those under their control."

"Hell, I didn't realize the infiltration was complete there."

"When I was leaving, I think it was nearly so. They controlled that Appellate, at least."

Pria slumped back in her seat. "How are you going to stand up to her? She's got major force on her side. At least two Theroki ships, all part of their network."

"We believe there are three," Xi said. "And we have substantial force on our side."

"How many ships?" Pria demanded.

"One," said Kentt. "But it's state of the art."

"Like that junker you flew in on?"

"No, that was purchased in an emergency for the side trip here. To recruit additional help."

"How many soldiers?"

"Well, I'm not certain. From a specific military?"

"No, just people with guns. How many? You're not prepared for this, Doctor. I'm telling you."

"Ten," said Xi.

Kentt's brow furrowed. "Ten?"

"Give or take a few." Xi was getting better at human things all the time. Like vagueness. And generous estimation.

Pria laughed out loud. "You're screwed."

"We're going." Kentt straightened again, squaring her shoulders. "We know her location. We're going to end this once and for all. Part of our team is already on their way."

"Only part? Sounds like a death wish."

Kentt sighed. "You won't come?"

"No way. Sorry, Doctor. I got a good thing here. I appreciate all that you gave me. I appreciate it enough that I can't just throw it away on a pipe dream. You know?"

"I know. I understand."

"You can ask around with the others, but... a brush with Cassandra once was enough for most of us. And we can protect ourselves from her here better than anywhere else in the 'verse."

"Is that what the opsepium is for?" Xi asked, putting two and two together.

"Yep. How else can you defend yourself in the 'verse she is building? I won't let that monster in my head again. If you survive, you can always come hide here, okay?"

"She won't succeed," Kentt said sharply.

"You're brilliant, Etrianala. But so is she. So, I can't just take your word for it. But blast it, I hope you're right."

Xi took another sip of tea. She should really order some sort of taste receptors. Without them, she could be tricked into exposing her synthetic nature. Yes, it was an operational need, not just a curiosity.

Someone waved for Pria from the door. "One second, ladies. I'll be right back."

"I can't believe they won't come," Kentt said as Pria strode away. "I won't pressure them, but I had thought..."

"You thought perhaps that you helped them so they would help you?"

"Yes. I hoped. I considered that they might not, but I guess I thought it would be a hard decision."

"That looked fairly easy."

"I concur. I will ask a few others, but she is right. Her rationale makes sense. Is this a foolish endeavor on our part?" Kentt spread her hands.

Xi laid a hand on Kentt's arm, as she'd seen others do to offer reassurance. "Sometimes, it's not about being smart, it's about trying to do what must be done the best you can do it."

Kentt closed her eyes for a long moment, then took another sip.

"If they were the type to directly and violently resist, they likely would have done so already," Xi said.

"True. And some did. And they are dead."

"This is the remainder that got away. Lucky, or perhaps pacifists. Perhaps the rebellious foolish ones were already weeded out by Cassandra earlier on."

"Is that what we are? Rebel fools?"

"I do not have rules by which to make that judgment."

"I see." She winced. "We should never have come."

"No, it was worth checking. They *did* put a great deal of thought and preparation into how to counter Cassandra's methods. You were right. They just came to different conclusions. The approach that they are taking is simply not compatible with ours."

"So what do we do now?"

"You talk to a few others. Then, if it looks grim, we re-join the *Audacity* as soon as we can. We head to the target coordinates. We may even arrive before them, depending on how long we stay. They needed at least one more refueling stop for that vessel, and the best route was likely not the direct one."

"All right. I'll talk. But before nightfall, we should go." Kentt took another sip. "And... I should have several more cups of this delightful tea."

And even though she couldn't taste it, Xi agreed.

MOLYARCH STATION SECURITY was entirely unsurprising in just how much it left to be desired. The front of the security station area had a fortified counter you could walk up to and talk to someone, except nobody was there. The door to the rest of the security area was open.

"Hello?" Dane called from the front.

No response came.

Some part of his instincts went on alert. There were only two reasons someone would leave their security area in this state. Because they were absolute idiots who didn't know what they were doing, or because they'd *just* been attacked and incapacitated.

Yeah, right. Maybe the firecracker kids had stopped by here?

Still, some part of his mind was wary. What if they had?

He sobered and put his hand on his weapon, keeping it lowered. Better safe than cocky.

He tried calling again as he eased through the open door. There was something… a sound like someone sawing.

No. When he realized what it was, he almost rolled his eyes. Was that *snoring*?

Maybe they're snoring because they've been drugged. Don't get overconfident.

He made his way down a short corridor toward the sound. He passed an office that was empty, a sort of break room with a big table and a drink synthesizer on the wall.

The last room on the left—that's where the snores were coming from.

He eased around the doorway. Indeed, there was a woman, head on a desk, snoring.

Shaking his own head, he eased passed that room, although he was a little worried about what it'd mean if she woke up and drew a gun on him.

He passed three more doors, offices all empty, before he came to another person who *wasn't* sleeping, thankfully.

Nope, he was reading. And entirely ignoring the massive banks of vid feeds that covered the walls and the flat surfaces of two large holodesks. There had to be more than fifty feeds. Maybe seventy-five.

A glossy magazine practically the size of a man's torso was spread out in front of the guy, his eyes ogling at the curves.

Dane cleared his throat. "I used to get a subscription to *Aeronautical Advancements Monthly too.* They still have a monthly lottery?"

The guy jumped and looked about to wet his pants. Quickly closing the magazine, he straightened in his seat. "Who are you and what are you doing here?"

"Just a concerned citizen checking up on the status of station security."

He cleared his throat. "Who let you in?"

"There's nobody to let anybody in. There's one other officer here, and she's asleep."

The guy finally had the sense to look chagrined. "There was just an arson call near the docking bays. Gotta take those seriously. We don't have a huge force. Are you here to report a crime? I can help or I can wake up Vega."

"No, there was a crime outside our door in the hotel. I just wondered why nobody ever showed up."

He gestured around. "Well, does this answer your question? We're short staffed." He shrugged.

"How do you know there was an arson at the docking bays? Or was it just a call?"

"A call—but like I said, fire in that area? That's all hands on deck. It's pretty likely, too; happens at least once a month."

Dane shuddered at the thought. Yes, he should really get Mrs. Simmons to direct her energies toward getting them some evacuation options from this crazy place. "So someone could just call and clear everybody out of security whenever they feel like it?"

The guy's eyes widened, but Dane couldn't tell if it was because he was realizing he shouldn't have admitted their weakness to this strange person or if he hadn't realized a weakness until just now.

Dane had been studying the feeds as they spoke, looking for the hotel, and he finally found it near one holodesk corner. "Hey, why is there a book over that vid feed, huh?"

The security man's eyes were as wide as saucers now.

Dane took a step forward to see if the feed was the one of their hotel corridor. But he stopped abruptly when behind him he heard a click.

"This is a restricted area," said a woman's voice. "You're not supposed to be in here."

"Relax, Vega, just a tourist." The security man grinned and folded his magazine. "Why don't you give him a tour? Show him the drink synthesizer, eh?"

Dane turned slowly, keeping his hands loosely at his sides but not on his rifle. "Listen, lady. Can I call you Vega too?"

"No."

"All right then. Listen, I am a bodyguard, all right? I came to see how much I could rely on Security for help doing my job."

"And your assessment is?"

"Not much."

She blew out a breath and lowered her weapon, although both hands were still on it. "That sounds about right." She looked uneasily at her colleague. "Sorry about passing out, Fro. This is my third sixteen in a row."

Dane fought the urge to shake his head. "You didn't answer me, man. Why is that book over there?"

"What book? I have no idea—" Nervous laughter bubbled out of the guy while he hastily knocked the book onto the floor, then realized it didn't exactly help his point. "Oh that book. Oops. Silly me. There's just so many vid feeds."

"Somebody pay you to put that there?" Dane said slowly.

The guy's whole face paled.

Next to him now, Vega swore. "Jeez, Fro, you gotta work on your poker face. You know that's against the rules."

He hung his head. "You're not gonna tell Crax, are you?"

"Course I am. You know I do things by the book."

"Only one around here," Fro grumbled.

"Go on. Get out of here. Go take a break."

"A break— What do you mean, Vega—"

"Go take the day off. Crax will let you know if that's the arrangement indefinitely."

Sobering, the guy took his magazine and a bag and hurried out.

Shaking her head, Vega cleared off several other vid feeds that were blocked. One she unveiled was broken, and she punched in a quick repair order.

"Something happen to your charges?" she asked him.

"Firecrackers in the hallway. Could have been worse, but seemed odd nobody responded."

She shrugged. "Molyarch has a certain reputation. You didn't know when you touched down here? Half the people might consider it a liability, but the other half consider it a perk."

He frowned. "I knew. But usually, we don't stay long. I'm in a bit of a strange situation because we'll be here more than a few hours, so it was time to dig a little deeper."

She punched in a few more orders to the computer that apparently Fro had been neglecting, glancing at him periodically with those world-weary eyes as she spoke. "Listen, the rules are different here. Thieves get away with things. We don't even try to stop it all. I'm not sure we could, but we don't. But overall, it's pretty safe."

"Safe?" He gestured at the book still lying where Fro had knocked it on the floor. "When safety is sold to the highest bidder?"

"They'll dock his pay for that. But you have to believe me. You might get some stuff stolen or stupid pranks, but nobody wants to shop or refuel on a station that will get you murdered. We focus on the violent crime. The locals know the rules. Fights are one thing; it's killing that'll get you thrown in the brig with no bribe big enough to let you out."

Dane winced that apparently there were crimes for which a bribe was probably standard. "Listen, I see you're overworked around here. Let's make a deal. How about my people watch this console for a few days? You guys get some much-needed help. You don't have to pay us."

"Why should we trust you?" She scowled. "And are you going to tell us what is happening?"

"I think I can be at least as thorough as the last guy. I have an actual interest in safety."

She sighed. "I need to get Crax to approve it. Maybe… Maybe fifty credits?"

"Are you serious?" Hadn't she just told Fro it was against the rules to accept a bribe? Or was that different because it was just one vid feed? How did that make any sense?

"Yeah, Crax isn't too frou-frou, but he won't go for this out of the charity of his heart. The credits aren't for me, they're for him."

"I should pay *you* to do your work?"

"You should pay *us* to allow you and your people access to our entire security infrastructure of this station."

He gritted his teeth. But she had a point. "Forty credits."

"Forty-five."

"Fine. Here." He handed her the hotel charging card.

She snapped it up. "All right, make yourself comfortable. I'll go run it by Crax, but I think you've greased the wheels enough. We'll see." Smiling, she went back to her office.

Dane dropped into the chair and sighed. So much for hanging out in the swanky hotel. Although… he could still see Vivaan's eyes shining at the thought of helping out with this sort of thing.

Maybe the kid wouldn't have to be a dishwasher after all. Even if Dane did some of the watching himself, he'd need to sleep. But realistically, he couldn't leave Nova alone the whole time. He'd have to put at least Vivaan, maybe more of them to work. Hopefully, inside station security wasn't as horribly dangerous as he was thinking it might be.

As his eyes ran over the instruments idly, his attention caught on the system Vega had been entering things into. The console screen was open to a database.

He leaned closer. A list of names in a certain sector were displayed. None of his people, thankfully. Actually, it seemed to list every single domicile, so maybe it was a list of residents.

His heart pounded a little faster. His eyes traced the edges of the screen, searching. There it was. A search box.

He hesitated for only a moment longer before he typed it in, muttering to himself. "Don't get your hopes up, you stupid old man." He wasn't stupid, except for hoping, and he wasn't old, not really, except every day he'd spent without his son made him feel a decade older. "Let's see here… Shawn… Anthony… Hall…" Click.

He blinked. They had looked a lot of places and found a lot of Shawns who weren't his Shawn.

But it was still a little surprising when a single name stared back at him from the console. And it was still hard not to hope. The age said fifteen. The right age.

Shawn Hall. Mechanics Bay B. 15. Passenger Number 489463.

"Vega?" he shouted. "Does this place have some kinda comm system?"

"What? Hold on." She murmured a few things, then came bustling in. "Crax says we're good. He'll give you a week. After that, more credits."

"Great. I was asking if you have a way I can call Mechanics Bay B?"

"Sure." She started punching things into the console so quickly he couldn't follow them, but it didn't matter. He only had this one call to make.

The voice that answered wasn't an eight-year-old's, as it couldn't have been, because so many years had passed, so it told him nothing. But his heart was assaulting his rib cage as he asked his usual questions. Where was he born? Did he recognize the name Dane Hall?

This time, the young man faltered. "Uh, what if I do?"

Dane tried not to hold his breath. "I'm Dane Hall. I'm looking for my son Shawn. Shawn Anthony Hall."

The pause was excruciatingly long, but the voice was rough when he responded. "Dad? Is that you?"

It was hard not to break down with Vega standing right at his shoulder, but somehow, he managed it. "Yeah, Shawn. It's me."

"Was this your plan, guy? You could have just asked to use the database." Vega folded her arms.

"No, I told you the truth. Shawn, can you come meet me in Security?"

"What? What's wrong?"

"Nothing's wrong. Or if you can wait a few, I can come to Mechanics Bay—" His mind was screaming not to do that, that it'd take Vivaan too long to find his way through Molyarch's donut. And that in those few minutes, his boy might disappear again. He needed to run the hell out of here, deal be damned.

But Shawn said, "I can take a break. On my way."

The line went dead.

"How long have you been looking for him?" Vega murmured.

"Eight years."

"Wow. The war?"

"Yep."

There was a pause. "I'll give you some privacy."

Well, thank the lucky stars for that. But in truth, he really was lucky today.

He, in fact, couldn't believe his own luck when his little boy, morphed more than halfway into a man already, appeared in the doorway. He wore grease-stained coveralls, smudges on his face, and a grin. But it was the same face.

Dane knocked over Fro's chair getting to him and damn near crushed the kid in a hug when he did.

"You're taller."

"You found me."

"I've been looking for so long. There are too damn many Shawn Halls in the 'verse."

"I missed you, Dad."

He stole a chair from the empty office next door and ignored grumbles from Vega. "Tell me everything I missed. Literally everything."

CHAPTER TEN

TAILING PAUL, Ellen strode onto the bridge of the *Everest* just as light from the nearby yellow star started to burst across the viewscreen. A dozen large asteroids were scattered through the view, limned with light.

She followed him to the command consoles, and he could have sat, but neither of them did. She followed his lead. She'd never felt at home on the bridge of a larger starship like this, and she didn't feel at home now.

The dirt—or whatever was under your boots—had always been more her style. Briefing the *Everest*'s crew several times hadn't made her feel any more like one of them. Maybe once upon a time, but not anymore.

Definitely not now that she was here in these cuffs.

These weren't the same sort of cuffs she'd arrived in. The original ones had glowed a ghoulish green, but these were an acid fuchsia color. And they came specially loaded for prisoners who were likely to assault people—meaning they could be ordered to tranq her if anyone felt threatened.

She only hoped they hadn't included Bridell on that list of people who could issue the order.

"Asteroid 234 eliminated, Captain. Clay-silicate makeup." Lieutenant Shu was hovering behind the science team, who didn't look like they appreciated it very much. "Six more approaching complete analysis. Four hundred and forty-two complete."

"Good work," said Paul, nodding.

"Only eight hundred more to go," Ellen mumbled.

He smiled. "If you had a better idea, you should have put it in your plan."

Ellen shrugged one shoulder, willing herself to spot some anomaly on the viewscreen. They both knew she'd already done all she could.

Arakovic had been right to hand over the coordinates without fear. Ellen had expected to be a bit exposed while searching the area, but this was worse than she'd expected, even studying the maps and sat feeds of the system.

She sighed. "If only the Songbirds had given us a beacon or a map instead of just a general location string."

"Rude of them."

"Highly." Her voice was cold, her eyes still fruitlessly searching. She ought to be nice. But she was going into the fight of her life with tranquilizing cuffs, an ankle bracelet, and a sincere concern she was losing it. It wasn't just the thing with Bridell. It was not remembering. It was the dream of the empress, that was impossible with Persad's device blocking all telepathy. It was all of it.

Besides, if he wanted friendly banter, Paul should have kept Kael around. She pursed her lips. "I sure hope we don't miss the party."

"I bet they're eating all the hors d'oeuvres, and when we get there, it will just be crackers and cheap wine left."

A snort of laughter escaped her anyway. "Hors d'oeuvres. You really *didn't* read the briefing, did you?"

He grinned. "If *you* were invited, they aren't rolling out the red carpet. So we'll just have to knock on doors. There have to be *some* hors d'oeuvres around here somewhere. Threat assessment—give me your report."

The bridge ops officer opened his mouth but didn't get a word out before Bridell spoke over him. "All clear so far, Captain."

"It's quiet." Paul lowered his head to his displays, pretending to scan, but she didn't really think he was looking at them.

"They're here somewhere," she said under her breath.

"Or this is a way to draw us away from the real target, and they're attacking something else as we speak." Paul shifted his weight from one foot to the other.

"The big mission you're missing?"

His lips pressed together. "Let's hope they're unrelated, shall we? Though the timing does seem a bit… fishy."

Before she could reply, there was some commotion in the threat assessment corner of the bridge.

"Activity at the gate." The usual ops guy beat Bridell to the chase, throwing up a second viewscreen overlay of the shining circle of the gate. "Ship profile… hold on, getting it on screen."

The newly arriving ship—no, *two* ships—barreled into view, bristling with guns and barbs and fortifications.

"Therokis." She set her jaw. Damn. "How convenient—two of us and two of them."

"You've got to be kidding me." Paul swore. "Here?"

"There's your trap," Bridell said. "Why fight when you can buy mercs to do it for you?"

"Shields at the ready, Captain," said Mertz.

"Prepare to engage," Paul ordered. "And get me a comm link."

"They're, uh… They're already hailing us, sir."

"One of your friends?" He narrowed his eyes at her.

"Never in a million years." She met his gaze with her own icy glare. "If there's anybody my *friends* do not want to see, it's them," she added, hoping he'd understand the meaning.

"You sure?"

"They won't be friendly to renegades," she said, voice low. Apparently, Paul needed it spelled out. If they got their hands on Kael… she wasn't sure what the response would be, but it'd definitely be violent. When wasn't it?

"Bring the vid feed up."

The Theroki that greeted them was the High Adjutant, the highest rank she was familiar with. The chaotic mess of char marks and steel that he called armor would have made a flaming shipwreck proud. He had a fresh injury that ran from his forehead down his cheek, just missing his left eye, scab barely formed.

The High Adjutant narrowed his eyes and pointed at the screen. "Her. Surrender Ellen Ryu."

Ellen rolled her eyes. "Here we go again."

"No greetings? Hello, how are you?" Paul's lips twitched with the sarcasm. "Diplomacy is truly dead."

"Turn her over, and no one will be harmed." His eyes were flat as he spoke, cold.

"You *do* cut right to the chase. But I'm afraid that I only just captured her. I'm certainly not turning her over to the likes of you. Why would I?"

"Because if you don't, my ships will destroy you. We will blast your ship until only splintered shards and blood remain."

Paul rubbed his chin. "Splintered shards and blood, eh? I see. Well. You will attempt to destroy my ship. I will attempt to stop you. I'm doing my duty to my nation... and I'd likely be court-martialed if I did what you're asking. So I don't see much incentive on my part here."

"Your incentive is your continued survival." The High Adjutant's black eyes narrowed.

"You drive a hard bargain." In contrast, Paul's features were alive with mocking amusement. "Still, I am somehow unmoved. If you're goal is to capture her, then it doesn't seem like this 'shards and blood' threat is anything more than an empty bluff."

The Theroki's jaw tightened. She couldn't tell if Paul had successfully called him on the lie, or if he just hated bandying words with this smug jerk. Perhaps he was just so full of rage at all times that the way he was shaking now was his normal state. "This is my last request. If you do not surrender her now, prepare to be fired upon and boarded."

Chuckling, Paul shook his head. "Who are you again?"

The Theroki reached to cut off the comm but stopped short as Paul started talking again.

"Well, I'm Captain Paul Dealis. Pleasure to meet you. As a representative of the Union of Allied Systems in this region, I will be bullied by no one, definitely not you. We're on a specially assigned Union Senatorial mission that will brook no interference. Now get out of my way and leave the honorable work to us."

The High Adjutant snorted, nostrils flaring. "Please. The Union has all the honor of the slug I just crushed under my boot. Your ship is no match for ours. Surrender."

"You do realize you can upgrade weapons systems on an existing hull, don't you?" Paul grinned, loathing in his eyes. "Besides, we caught our prisoner here fair and square. Ellen Ryu belongs to no one but the Union. She swore an oath to serve, and it precedes all others."

In spite of herself, she glanced down at the floor. Well, when he put it like that, it stung a bit.

The High Adjutant grinned back, equally mirthless. "Don't be naive. You Unionies always think your *laws* will help you." He said the word with derision. "You should know by now that that's not how things work."

"Oh, do school us." Ellen lifted her head.

He paused briefly before deigning to shift his gaze slightly toward her. "Whoever hits the hardest makes the rules."

She tilted her head, glanced at Paul. "So… still us then?"

Paul burst out laughing.

"We shall see, Union scum." Lip curled, the High Adjutant cut the comm. The screen went black.

"Brace yourselves," Ellen warned.

"Captain!" Shu shot up from her seat. "While he was talking, we got a hit! I mean, we found one! Seven-fifteen! I've found indicators of an electrical grid in 715!"

"Analyzing likely purpose of grid and size," one of the science team called out, apparently determined to get a word in.

"Excellent news. Now if we can just make it there without being turned into a pin cushion." Paul looked to her. "Still feeling good, hot shot?"

She shrugged. "We have contingency plans. We knew this could happen. Move toward 715. These look like real Therokis, not the ones she's hijacked, because there's no Songbird. At least, not on screen. If that's true, it means they're no friends of Arakovic's."

"Then why are they working for her? Are there so many with a bounty on your head?"

"Well... yes and no. But the bounty could have been offered anonymously. Maybe if we can get them close enough to her base, we can pit one enemy against the other."

The chatter around them rose as they talked. Some of the crew shifted to defensive mode, while others zeroed in on the asteroid.

Acceleration picked up. That was all according to plan. She gripped the headrest of the chair she stood behind, trying to steady herself against the ship's acceleration that the grav systems couldn't quite accommodate.

There was something about it she was missing. Something that niggled at her, something that didn't make sense. Bridell was glaring at her, but she refused to meet his gaze, keeping her eyes locked on the screen. Maybe it was just that asshole—and the associated hole in her memory—niggling at her. Or maybe it was something else.

Well, well. The Therokis on their asses even before they made it to the relevant asteroid. The likelihood had been low that some third enemy would show, but everybody rolls snake eyes sometimes.

Had Arakovic called them in? How else would they have known she was here? The trap, in a very loose sense of the word, was sprung. Unless there was an intel leak onboard, which she sensed could be the case. She wanted to glare at Bridell, but it wasn't worth it.

Arakovic was on the Therokis' *target* list, not their client list, right now. Was there some way she could take this new variable out of the equation?

Many of them were forced into service like Kael. They'd be used to fight for something they didn't know about—or care about. Just do what you're told. Everybody needs to eat and not get beaten to a pulp by their CO.

But would Arakovic actually *pay* for trying to hunt her down? That would be ironic, given Kael's theory that the Therokis were one of Arakovic's inventions, there simply to do her bidding. If they caught up with Arakovic, would they destroy their own maker? That was a big *if,* though. They were too busy being tricked into doing her bidding.

"I have an idea," Ellen said. "Get that Theroki back on the comm."

The comms officer glanced nervously at Paul.

"What are you looking at me for? Her orders are my orders for now. You want me to repeat them verbatim?"

"No, sir. I mean, ma'am. On it. Ma'am."

"Thanks," she said.

The screen flicked to life a moment later. "Have second thoughts, Captain Dealis? Prepared to surrender?" The High Adjutant raised his eyebrows.

"Not exactly," Ellen said, stepping in front of Paul at the command chair. "Why are you working for Zeta Arakovic?" she said, voice smooth. "I thought the Therokis had banned their people from working for her."

"We are not working for Zeta Arakovic." His voice was flat, robotic, when it wasn't busy threatening. God, she'd forgotten what it was like. The memories of Kael walking out of the *Audacity*'s cargo hold, headed toward that meetup on Desori, flashed through her mind.

"Yes, you are. You're after my bounty. Who do you think posted it? Who told you I'd be here?"

"As if I would share our intelligence with you. It is irrelevant."

"I get it, ships come with expenses. But Arakovic asked us to meet her in this system. Maybe she's hiding behind a third party, but she's playing you like a violin. She's the only one who could have known we were going to be here. And you just somehow show up?"

The High Adjutant glanced off the screen for a moment, then to the side. There was a sheen of alarmed panic in his eyes, just a hint of it. "Our client has another name."

"Yeah, your client has another name, all right. Two names—the name they gave you and then the real one."

"That would be convenient for you," he replied.

"What will be inconvenient for you is when your client doesn't actually pay you. Are you sure you want your higher ranks knowing you accepted a contract with a banned client? You could get your ship all banged up and be left with the bill *and* trouble on your hands."

Frowning, the High Adjutant glanced to the side again. Consulting with someone? "Stand by."

He cut away, the screen going black.

She glanced to the side. "What are you smirking at?"

Paul was looking entirely too pleased with this development. "They didn't know. I find that amusing. What?"

"Whether that actually *helps* us remains to be seen."

The High Adjutant reappeared, looking annoyed. "It appears your claims are plausible. I have... an alternative proposal for you."

"We're listening," she said.

"We are looking to collect on your bounty. You are looking to attack a fortified fortress of highly trained telepaths and *former* Therokis. You will need our help."

"We're prepared for the situation just fine." Paul's chin lifted.

"We could still capture you for that reward. She may pay if we demand payment before delivery."

"Or?" she asked.

"Or we could help you capture her instead."

"And why would you do that?" she asked.

"The same reason we showed up here. Credits. Arakovic is a shared enemy. Offer us the same in credits as your reward, and we will aid you instead of her."

"Standard merc tactics," Bridell grumbled. Paul glared.

"It's simple. Match what they're offering, and we will help you instead."

"We can't do that—" Paul started. "Maybe a half or a quarter, but—"

"Or allow us to claim an equivalent amount of salvage when your adversary is defeated from the asteroid. There are sure to be valuable materials, weapons, equipment, information."

"Done," Ellen said, before Paul could disagree. Had they mentioned the asteroid, specifically? It seemed odd he was so certain of their destination. But where *else* could they be headed in this system? She set the thoughts aside to focus. "We can promise you salvage rights. Credits might be negotiable."

"Wait a minute." Paul put a hand on her shoulder, drawing her gaze. "We can't—"

"Glad we have a deal then." The High Adjutant cut the comm.

"Ellen, the Union absolutely cannot let random pirates pillage what will then be Union property—"

"Maybe you can't, but I can," she said, smiling. "Blame it on me. Would you rather tackle the Songbird base *after* a tussle with them or before?"

"Before? I thought you just promised—"

"I promised salvage rights. I, however, am your prisoner and have zero negotiating power to agree to anything. They don't realize they're making a deal with a prisoner, that's their problem. And I definitely didn't promise you wouldn't shoot them in the back."

"Hey, now."

"Are you claiming you wouldn't?" she said.

Paul snorted. "Well… no."

"Frankly, I'm counting on it."

"I can't tell if that is a compliment or an insult," he said, catching Lieutenant Shu's eyes.

"Little of both?" Shu shrugged.

"That's a risky game you're playing, Ryu," said Paul.

She stepped back from the command console to his side again.

"No riskier than letting them pummel us now and not even making it as far as the docking bay."

He sighed. "I need a mineral water. Anyone else? No one?"

Bridell shot to his feet. "I can get that for you, sir—"

Paul held up a palm. "No, thanks. I can do it. I need the walk. I'll be back. Shu, monitor Ryu. You have the bridge."

"I have the bridge, sir," Shu replied as he strode out, moving next to Ellen at the command console. Quiet settled over the bridge, eyes focused on sensors and screens.

Something about the exchange grated on her nerves.

"Sorry," Shu murmured quietly. "For all this."

Ellen shrugged. "It's all right. I'd do the same if I were you."

"Hmm." Shu didn't sound convinced. "You should have the bridge for this. You planned it all."

"Nah. I'm not a starship commander. And I'm not a part of this team."

"For right now, you are."

"Being a true part of this team, part of the Union, was ripped away from me long ago. I thought I'd made peace with that, but..." She didn't know how to finish the thought. *Audacity* and her crew were a better team—and a better family, although she might never make it back to them. But she couldn't say that to Shu right now.

"You can think what you like. And I'll think what I like. But if we find the person we're looking for, it might make finding peace a little easier."

"Let's hope. The past is in the past. I can't change it. But I can do what I can to keep what happened to me and worse from ever happening to anybody else."

Shu smiled. "I've got a 64.2% likelihood that the key to that is inside this rock." She touched the command console—for the first time since they'd arrived, since Paul had ignored it—and brought up a vid feed of the asteroid they were approaching, information overlays swirling around it. "We've got a few minutes before approach. Best dig into this data the sensors are picking up, don't you think?"

Ellen nodded. "Study time."

"APPROACHING THE WORM HOLE, COMMANDER." Adan leaned back in his seat on the bridge and rubbed his biological eye. Biological eyes could get tired, and even if the synthetic one never did, it wasn't like you could just go around talking to people with one eye squeezed closed to give it some rest. Not to mention integrating the two images at times was a bit dizzying. He'd been flying for longer than usual—and this fight was just beginning.

Fern better have been sleeping like she was supposed to. Not that he could blame her if she wasn't. He had trouble sleeping on demand, too, but he didn't have more than five hours in him before he'd start to make mistakes. And that was with stims already in his system.

"Have you heard from Xi?" Zhia asked, slipping into the seat beside him.

"Nothing yet." He checked the fuel readouts. All were normal.

"Kentt?"

He shook his head. "Nothing since they left that colony of telepaths."

"Something's wrong."

"I agree. But unless they reach out..." He spread his hands. "We've sent a few hails. Nothing's come back."

"Don't like that one bit. Nothing we can do, though. Looks like we're on our own."

"I am right here, Zhia," Xi said from the ceiling. "But I understand your meaning. I, too, would like to know my secondary location. I am pleased, however, to be able to be in two places at the same time. And survive."

"The continued presence of at least part of you is reassuring, Xi, thank you." Zhia started to buckle the harness, then hit the ship-wide comm channel, and kept buckling. "All right. You know we are getting close. You know the drill. We've practiced, and you've heard what to do a dozen times. Now's the time to do it. Suit up, sit down, strap in. We don't know what's on the other side of this wormhole.

Could be a battle. Could be a trap. Could be an empty system. Or anything in between. Once you're in your assigned position, register it with Xi. Xi, when everyone is accounted for, notify me."

"Be right back—bio break," Adan said. The race down to the mess and lavatory was good to get his blood pumping, too, which was useful when launching oneself into a completely unknown star system with a possible battle in progress.

Doug was on the viewscreen when Adan slid back into his seat, fresh coffee in hand, and started buckling in.

"No signs of battle yet," Doug was saying, "according to satellite feeds. We've still got a lock on their tracker location."

"I see it on screen," Zhia replied.

"The *Everest* and *Lhotse* are being tailed by an unidentified Theroki ship."

"Well. That can't end well."

"It's not firing, though. Just following. Odd. Maybe they're negotiating? Working on getting into their networks again. Let's see if they refreshed or upgraded since that last infiltration. I'll be in the box." The viewscreen cut off.

"Everyone is in position," Xi announced.

Zhia ducked her head for one moment. Was she praying? Adan had never been much of a praying man, but it certainly seemed the time for it. If only he knew how.

"All right," she said finally. "Go."

He hit the engage key, and the ship surged forward. The wormhole flickered through them, sprinkling his sight with specks of gold—electrical feedback—and in a flicker, they were on the other side.

"Ships in range," Xi said, adjusting the views to see the three other ships in the system. "*Everest* is closing in on a large asteroid. It's in the lead, the others are following."

"Would you expect anything less from the ship with Ellen on it?" Zhia twisted her lips. "Head toward them."

"Should we hail them, Commander?" Xi asked.

"Not yet. Take your time since no one is firing. They'll have seen us already, we can be sure of that. But there's nothing to say just yet.

We have no demands. We're just looking for the right opportunity to nab back our friends. Get me Roya on a vid comm channel, will you?"

"Oh, she's right here," Doug said, jerking a finger over his shoulder. "Got a question?"

He twisted the camera view to the side. Shirin and the empress were in the custom seat harnesses Bri had created especially for the telepathy-blocking storage closet.

"Well, little one," Zhia said. "Feel anything? Is this the right place?"

The large blue eyes had been distant, but now, they focused on Doug and the vid camera. Adan could never stop thinking of a puppy when she turned them his way, but they looked even more plaintive than normal now. "Something is wrong."

"That's probably an understatement." Adan raised an eyebrow. "What about this is right?"

Zhia's brow furrowed. "Like what? Is this the right place? Are Arakovic and her minions here?"

"Is Cassandra?" Doug put in.

Roya's eyes were distant again. "She is here. She is… large. Larger than she should be."

Zhia crouched down, frowning. "Tell me more."

"She's… These are not merely interconnected humans. They have another of my kind."

"What?" Adan sat forward against his harness for a moment, forgetting he had it on.

"What does that mean?" Zhia said.

"A creature exists here that has the same powers that I have. I had thought we were all gone but… I was told by the Enhancers I was the last but… It must have been a lie."

Adan squeezed the armrest. What a mindfuck.

"The size of the cluster is so large," Roya murmured. Her eyes went distant, dreamy. "Yes, the feeling is distinct. It must be. It must. Not just a large network. It must be a sister of mine."

"How large is large?" Isa asked from behind Doug.

"Many dozens."

"What does that mean?" Adan winced. He'd read the reports that said as much, but there was nothing like hearing it from the mouths of babes. Or telepaths. Or telepathic babes.

Zhia gave him a sideways glance. "I think what it means is that I'm glad I got this chip stuck in my head."

"Yeah," he agreed. "So am I."

"CAPTAIN DEALIS, we're approaching the asteroid." Lieutenant Shu indicated a measurement overlay she'd added to the viewscreen. "Five kilometers and closing."

"Larger threat asteroids in our proximity have been neutralized," Bridell reported.

"Have you hailed the base?" she asked.

"Yes, ma'am," Comms replied. "No response. Nothing broadcasting."

Back at her side, Paul licked his lips. "What now? Keep inching forward to give them a kiss, or fire and see if we can raise a response out of them?"

She shook her head. "You really didn't read the plan, did you?"

"I'm a fan of having a staff who are highly prepared. Why duplicate your efforts when you've already taken care of it?"

"In case I made a mistake?"

He gave her a dubious look. "One that *I'd* be likely to find?"

She cleared her throat. "Uh, excellent point, sir. The plan says attempt to dock if facilities exist. Get as close as we can peacefully. How is it looking?"

"Docking bay and beacons have been located," answered Bridell. "Force fields are occluding its size, however."

She gave him a nod. "Target the field generators."

"Yes, ma'am." He swiveled back to his console.

"Was that in the plan?" Paul smirked.

"I guess you'll never know, now."

"Do I have to pull rank to get you to fill me in? It was a thousand pages, c'mon."

She pointed at the screen, ignoring that little remark. "The docking area, if it can hold us, is our first objective. It's not like we can sneak in incognito. Can I get a readout of the nearby asteroids remaining?"

A holo glimmered to life over the command console, asteroids and the edges of Theroki ships outlined in shimmering amber and blue.

"The surrounding area, ma'am. Field generators taking damage. No response to our hails or movement, hostile or otherwise."

She frowned. "No response? Nothing?"

"Nothing, ma'am."

That was wrong. Something was wrong, but what? The hologram showed three large asteroids close. They should be harmless in terms of weapons installations or facilities, but it sure was crowded. The Theroki ships, however, appeared to be hanging back. She pointed again. "Why are the Therokis taking their time? Did they slow down?"

"Yes, ma'am, their velocity has decreased."

"And one of their two ships is veering closer to the *Lhotse*. The other one is easing closer to us."

Paul stepped forward. "Odd formation to move toward this objective."

Her intuition ratcheted up another notch. "Something's wrong. What does it mean? Why?"

Lieutenant Shu held up an arm. "Closing on twenty kilometers."

"Don't concentrate shields to the fore." Ellen spoke quickly, amending what was in the original plan. "We need 360-degree coverage. Make sure we're defended from those Theroki vessels."

"Shields full strength, all sides," Mertz reported.

"One enemy force-field generator is down, Captain," Bridell put in, "but it's not enough to disable their defenses. Three more remaining, under fire. Still no response from them."

"Seventeen kilomete—" Lieutenant Shu's words cut off oddly, suddenly slurred.

She started to turn toward the woman, but a dull thud at her side made her jump.

Beside her, Paul had collapsed, now sprawled on the steel grating. His eyes stared up at the ceiling, still open.

Vacant.

"What the—" she started. At least he wasn't bleeding this time.

The comm lines beeped, then beeped again. She spun in time to see the comms officer slump from his chair and hit the deck. Her breath was coming faster now, heart pounding.

The line beeped again. She turned, scanning.

It was all of them. Bridell and Mertz were lolling against harnesses. The entire bridge had lost consciousness.

Except for her.

On the viewscreen, automatic fire continued to pelt the field generators. They were still careening toward the asteroid, but with no pilot now to stop or steer them.

"Frag it all to hell." She scrambled toward the main command-control panels. Most of the labels were half worn off, and the glass was splintered in one spot and covered over with extra plexi. Wow, that had to work flawlessly, for sure. No part of this ship was in great shape, but this console excelled in its mediocrity. Maybe mediocrity was too generous a term. What a fragged-up piece of space trash.

The comm line beeped a third time, and she slapped a sweaty palm on the glass where a red button seemed to pulse in time. "*Everest*. What." This wasn't the time for formalities.

Something like a laugh, cold and lifeless, came over the line. "Don't make honor deals with pirates, Ms. Ryu."

She'd meant to turn on only the audio line, but a second later, the video sprang to life. The High Adjutant probably wasn't capable of a smile, but he definitely had a prideful look on his face.

"You Theroki scum," she spat, and for once, she meant it.

"And you really shouldn't believe everything you hear."

"What is going on?" she demanded.

"Oh, I think you know." The High Adjutant was still there. Watching. Gloating?

"Do you want something, Poker Face?" Yeah, it wasn't the cleverest insult, but she was busy.

"I want you to prepare to be boarded and peacefully surrender."

"You'd have better luck at a space-station casino. You're not the only one who doesn't play strictly by the rules, pal," she snapped. Now where was that damn viewscreen button. She was sick of looking at this guy's smug face.

"You came all this way to see Cassandra. To bask in the power of the *Alarus Octendi*. We are your VIP escort."

Her hands stilled over the controls. "My… what?"

"Your escort. Whether you like it or not. But you *did* accept the invitation, did you not?"

Alarus? But the last remaining one was supposed to be Roya, the empress, who was still on board the *Audacity*. Far, far away from here.

He sneered. "You know the name. Don't pretend you don't."

No time for this asshole. She pretended to ignore him and focus on the controls. But the computer wasn't granting her access to much of anything that would allow her to change the weapons or the trajectory. Probably rightfully so, but… How long did they have before the Everest just nose-rammed Arakovic's asteroid? Not an effective battle tactic if anyone wanted to survive.

"Our boarding team is on the way to your ship. Lower your shields, unlock the doors, and we may actually reach you before your ship hits the asteroid."

"I thought you wanted me alive."

"We do. Cassandra has questions for you. But if she can't ask them because you incinerated yourself, her distress level will not increase much. Me, I don't want anything. I'm just following orders. But I *did* warn your cocky friend about destroying your ship. He should have listened."

Glaring, she refused to respond. Refused to even look at him. Instead, she scanned the readouts. Did she just make a run for it?

Wasn't there *some* way to save these people? How much fragging time did they have?

There was no "minutes until imminent death" indicator. Something unexpected did catch her eye, though—the map.

There were *five* ships present now, not four. God, was there *another* Theroki ship? How many could they have?

Stabbing her finger at the new ship, she caught her breath. Familiar lines sharpened into view as the sensor display revealed everything the *Everest* knew about the newcomer. Hundred-fifty-meter length. Likely crew of about fifty. Two gun turrets, a wealth of weapons. Some new gashes in the hull, but she'd know that ship anywhere.

"*Audacity*," she whispered.

Her heart thundered in her chest. She could hail them, but she had to get rid of this asshole first. There *had* to be some way to shut him off. And to steer this ship, make sure the shields were operational, everything. But at the most basic level, shut this guy up.

Behind her, the hatch opened.

She whirled. Damn, she should have grabbed a pistol *first*. She was still cuffed, even.

Her eyes locked with Yamamoto's as he paused in the hatch.

The two of them stared at each other for a long moment. Then Yamamoto strode toward her and punched a rapid sequence into the controls.

The viewscreen cut to black. And she sighed with relief, even if it was ridiculous with everyone around her collapsed. "Finally…"

"What is going on?" Yamamoto whispered.

"The Theroki mentioned an *Alarus Octendi*," she murmured.

"Is that what's responsible for all this?"

She tried to shake off the confusion, get into her body. "It's too much to explain right now. *Alarus Octendi* is an alien species with telepathic powers. They can take over people, null their minds into nothingness, but usually, they consider it unethical. Evil. And they're almost extinct. This shouldn't be happening."

"But it is."

"Yes. But then why are *we* exempt?"

"No idea," Yamamoto said quietly, eyes focused on the controls.

Something about his tone rang false, especially for someone as consistently sincere as Yamamoto. She frowned. "I think Kael isn't the only one with a secret."

"Yes, clearly you have one as well."

"No secret. I have an experimental add-on that blocks telepathic powers."

"That you never mentioned."

"I wasn't hiding it. You never asked."

"And where did you get such a thing?"

"That's a long story, and you're just trying to dodge my question." She waited a beat, but he offered nothing to justify his own lack of unconsciousness.

"You didn't ask a question."

"Seriously? Fess up."

"About what?" Walking swiftly, he shifted to another control panel, checking something.

"Tell me why you're immune. And what are you doing?"

"There is nothing to tell." He moved to another console. "I'm trying to stop the ship. Reverse direction. Something."

"Not smashing the asteroid at full speed would be delightful." She narrowed her eyes. "Is that why you didn't advertise Kael's abilities? Because you were sympathetic?"

"I don't know what you're talking about."

"You've got your own powers. Some kind of… repressed telepathic powers, or…"

Yamamoto's lips went thin, then he straightened and met her eyes. "They're not repressed. They're just not… common knowledge. Want a candy?" He held one out.

She laughed, ludicrous as it felt. "A candy? *Now*?"

"The candy distracts people. They assume I'm just very sociable. And allergic. Want one?"

In spite of herself, she accepted one. "It's all a ploy?"

"Mostly. I am a little allergic. And this ship is a mold farm." He gestured broadly then went back to the navigation controls.

"Does Captain Dealis know?"

"He just thinks I am incredibly good at anticipating him. Which I am."

"Oh, I'm sure your secret powers are always used only for good." In truth, based on his behavior so far, she *did* believe that. He'd shown honor, gratitude, honesty. But keeping powers like that secret was suspicious as hell.

He sighed. "Claiming I'm a saint would hardly assure you of the veracity of my claims, would it?"

"True."

"And at the moment—it doesn't matter. We need to stop this ship from hitting Asteroid 715. And we can't effectively man it, with just the two of us. Not against the Therokis or the asteroid base."

"The *Everest* didn't even get its own ship AI?"

"We're on the list to get one in two years. Need a hardware upgrade. Engineering Dispositions Main said, ahem, that our excellent crew more than made up for the lack."

"Classic." She ducked her head, then looked at the console too. That asteroid seemed to be getting very fragging close. "So what do we do? How long do we have?"

"Minutes. Five. Maybe six?"

"We need to get off the ship. Now." And then maybe she could contact the *Audacity*. "After we're safe, we can find some way to defend them and not just abandon them here."

"We can't defend a ball of flames. I'm trying to slow the ship. Stop it maybe. Sitting still, the *Everest* could collide any number of other asteroids in the area, but…" He frowned at the controls.

"It will *definitely* collide with 715 if we don't change *something*." She swallowed, glancing at the fifth ship on the map. Should she tell him? Had he noticed? "Can we point the *Everest* at the gate? Reverse direction?"

His eyes lit with excitement. "It *might* work. Yes, the subsystems might be able to do the appropriate calculations... Or brake the ship if they fail…"

"We don't have much time. I can set up the weapons to keep firing while within range, if you can grant me permissions. Right now it won't let me do shit."

"Imagine that. Permission granted."

"Can you get these cuffs off too?"

"When we're on the way toward the shuttles. First, setting the course toward the gate…" He trailed off, concentrating.

She looked at the *Audacity* on the readout again. If she reached out silently, he might detect it. She could just tell him… But a man with a secret like that… Did she really know if she could trust him? She didn't know what had happened with Bridell, but she definitely hadn't expected black eyes to be involved.

She wouldn't tell him yet. But she would need to find a way to reach out. And soon. "Almost done?" she asked.

"Almost." He nodded, rolling a candy in his mouth. "Four minutes."

IT FILLED Dane with a calm he'd not known for a long time to know his kid was sleeping in the extra bed in his hotel room. Even if his kid was hardly a kid anymore, and had learned a trade on his own and made a life for himself, sort of, and traveled halfway across the galaxy. Still. He was here.

That had filled him with a mixture of pride and pain, but he'd had pain for so long, at this point, he was used to ignoring the painful part.

All he wanted to do now was keep him safe. He was doing his best to not have an itchy trigger finger at every sound just outside the door. Relax, he told himself. He's here. He's safe.

But then the door to the suite blasted clean open.

Dane was on his feet, taking aim, but the smoke made it hard to get a clear shot, and he wanted to make darn sure he knew who his attack would hit.

A man wearing a weird combination of light armor and cargo pockets stepped through the wafting smoke, saying "Cath—"

Or at least he tried to. Dane just barely managed not to smother the guy in freezing foam. Lucky he stayed his finger, though, because Nova was already taking the guy down.

She'd been positioned by the door and sent a vicious kick to the back of his knee before Dane could even get a clear shot from across the room.

She easily disarmed the intruder and had him face down on the ground with his own gun to the back of his head before any of them could even say "What the frag do you think you're doing?"

Dane snorted. Not a surprise, really. Something about the guy was off, amateur.

"Please!" If she didn't have his arm twisted behind his back, he'd have been cowering. "We come in peace!"

"Really?" Nova chewed that strawberry-mint gum she was addicted to with extra sass. "The burn marks on the door say otherwise, my friend! Tell whoever is with you to drop their weapons, and we can talk."

"Let us speak with your captives, and no one needs to get hurt."

"Captives? We don't have any captives. Well, except maybe you, now. Do I need to make a new brain-colored rug for this place, or are you going to tell them to disarm?"

"Set aside your weapons, boys! Set them aside. I apologize. I'm not terribly familiar with the etiquette of these sorts of situations."

Nova shot Dane a look that seemed to say, Get a load of this guy? What is his deal? "Put your hands on the back of your head," she ordered.

"Yes, ma'am."

Dane chimed in. "Everybody, outside. Hands on your heads and get in here."

Three more men came in from the smoke in the hallway, which

thankfully was dissipating. He did *not* need to wade into some smoke and get shot the day he was reunited with his kid.

"We only want to speak with Catherine and Matthew," said the man on the floor. "No one needs to get hurt."

"Oh, well. Why didn't you say so?" She didn't move the pistol away from his head, though.

"I'll get Catherine on the comm," Dane said quickly. He could punch the command into the wall comm without looking and keep one hand on his rifle.

"Hello? Need something, Dane?" Her voice came over the comm.

"Catherine! You're safe!" cried the man from the floor.

"Peridorius? Is that you?"

"Yes. Are you all right?"

"Of course, Peridorius, darling. What are you doing on Molyarch? And why do you sound so… muffled?"

"Can we put down these guns and talk? Are you safe?"

"Guns? What is going on?"

"Hallway's clear," grunted Nova, checking on the vid feeds on her gauntlet holodisplay. The gauntlet that *wasn't* holding the pistol.

Dane was eyeing one of the three men in particular. He looked a little too familiar. "Mrs. Simmons, I think you need to get over here."

"All right. I'm on my way."

She strode in a moment later, eyes wide, her husband and Doug's father, Matthew, in tow.

"Catherine!" the intruder cried again. "You're safe! Thank heavens."

"Of course I am. These people are my son's team. They're protecting me. I… take it you made quite an entrance?"

"Yes, ma'am," said Nova. "Is this person safe, ma'am?"

"Yes, Nova. Thank you. You can let him up now."

"Oh. *Oh*. Well." The man's eyes were wide as he struggled to his feet and dusted himself off. "I've got someone you—and they—need to meet." He gestured his palm toward the youngest of his three companions, none of whom Catherine had noticed yet. The young man's hands were still on his head, his confused eyes darting around the room. His hair was blond, but some things were missing that should have been there—like his floats and glasses.

Catherine went completely still.

"Well?" Peridorius said, grin dimming only slightly. Then concern crept into his brow.

"Hi, uh. I'm Douglas Simmons." The kid looked uneasy, then shrugged. "I don't know why you brought me here, man. They're just going to arrest me again."

"You can't be serious. None of you recognize him?"

Catherine finally seemed to catch her breath. "You… you found the twin. Of course, we recognize him." She glanced down, then up again, her lips pursing bitterly. "Sort of. Rescued him?"

Peridorius's eyebrows flew up. "Twin? You never let on you had twins, Aunt Cathy."

"Aunt Cathy?" Nova blurted.

"I didn't have twins. There is a clone. An illegal one."

"A what?" blurted the clone, his voice shaky.

"You made a clone of Cousin Doug?"

"You can put your hands down now if you want to, kid," Nova said.

"No, someone else did. An enemy. They had him turn himself in. The real Doug is still on the *Audacity*."

"Oh. *Oh.* Just whom did I liberate then?" he said, frowning at Clone Doug, whose eyes were now wide and concerned, and whose hands were still on his head.

Dr. Dremer stood up and smiled. "Scans show he is fully organic."

"Of course, I am! What is wrong with you people? I'm supposed to go to jail. That's it. End of story."

"And what are you getting out of that arrangement?" Catherine said slowly. "Some future favor? Money? When your time is served? Did they offer to jailbreak you? How is this benefitting you?"

The twin blinked. "Benefitting? What do you mean?"

"Well, I highly doubt jail will be amusing or intellectually stimulating for you. What did they offer you? What is it that you want?"

"Stimulating? I don't get to… want things. I do as I'm told."

Catherine's eyebrows went up. "Oh. I… uh. I see. For once, I'm speechless. Your creators were crueler than I thought."

Clone Doug looked at each of them, eyes frantic now. "What is she talking about?"

Taylor blew out a breath as she stood. "Well, I can see I have my work cut out for me. But at least I have a project."

"Excuse me?" The kid looked more alarmed every second. "I'm not a… project."

"Young man," said Dr. Taylor, "you actually have a variety of rights that all living beings deserve. One of those rights is… getting things. Wanting things. Having opinions. You'd be surprised how many people struggle to believe that, even ones with more traditional births than yours."

He stared at her like she'd grown a Teredark head. Or maybe he was still figuring out the words she was saying, he had to be pretty young. *Or* maybe he just couldn't believe he was allowed to have opinions.

"This is going to take a while," Dr. Dremer said, smiling wider. "But my initial scans show fully identical DNA to our Doug. He's a true clone, I think."

"What… is going on?" the kid said slowly. He *did* seem a hair younger than Doug should be. "What do you mean, 'your' Doug? I'm Doug."

"You were cloned from someone who is very kind. And also very rich and has a lot of friends," Catherine said gently. "That's the good news. The bad news is he was falsely accused of some crimes, and whoever made you was going to turn you in instead of him."

Peridorius rubbed the back of the kid's neck and swore. Brown makeup came off on Peridorius's fingers. "Barcode."

"What does that mean?" the kid said, flinching and hunching his shoulders to get away from him.

"It means the Enhancers were probably the ones that cloned you," Nova said. "But it's okay. You've escaped now. He's escaped right? We're not letting him go back?"

"No." Catherine smiled. "You're free now, even if it's not clear what that means. As long as you promise me *not* to go to jail for crimes that you personally never committed."

"I can promise that, yes, ma'am."

"Are you... still doing what you're told?"

"Yes, ma'am."

Catherine sighed.

"We'll work on it," Dr. Taylor murmured.

After a long silence, Peridorius cleared his throat. "Um. Sorry about the door."

Catherine shrugged. "It's not my door. It's the hotel's."

"You don't own this place already?"

"We tangled with a few... banking-savvy enemies, and our funds have become a bit inaccessible at the moment. And we are—well, we *were*—trying to keep a low profile and not attract attention."

"Oh. Ah. Sorry. But didn't you say you could use a hotel or two?" He grinned. "So I *can* be of service! Hold on." Peridorius jogged merrily from the room, calling out, "Can I speak with the manager please? Owner? Anyone? I've got cash."

"If he comes back in here with fireworks—" Dane started.

"Personally, I'm betting on a signed deed to the hotel in under sixty seconds tops," Nova grumbled.

Matthew put his arm around Catherine. "Well, I definitely didn't see that coming."

She shrugged again. "Peridorius is usually so concerned with his business, I didn't even think he'd notice."

Doug's father grinned. "We shouldn't be surprised. The adventurousness definitely comes from your side of the family."

Catherine laughed. "I'll tell your aunt you said that. But now that we are back in touch with part of the Foundation... I think I have some ideas. So I'll forget you said that."

CHAPTER ELEVEN

"ALL RIGHT, ALL SET." Yamamoto brushed his hands as if they were dusty. "Let's go. *Everest* will head straight for the gate and try to go through. If the Therokis let it get there, it should get through. Possibly. That is if they don't somehow board the ship and undo everything."

"I think if the ship can get through the gate, the crew might wake back up and be able to do something. Call for help at least." She tucked another pistol she'd taken from a collapsed crew member into the back of her belt. She'd grabbed three now and was eyeing a rifle in the case near the door.

She stepped toward it over another crew member. The man's cold, blue eyes stared up at her, all too much like Udo Trynkei's. John Doe's. Whatever, they'd taken his individuality. Whatever his name had once been no longer mattered.

But he'd had cybernetics. These people for the most part didn't. Maybe this was the temporary power that Roya and Kentt had spoken of. If they could get the ship out of range, it might wear off.

But those were all guesses. The resemblance to Udo Trynkei was uncanny.

"C'mon, let's hurry." Yamamoto grabbed an extra pistol and

tucked it in his back waistband. He pulled out his comm unit and came toward her. "Hold up those cuffs."

She opened the rifle case and then complied, as he held up the comm unit to the cuffs. An elaborate biometric lock on the rifle made it a dead end. The cuffs split open like ripe fruit and fell to the floor. "Good riddance," she muttered. "Shuttles. Let's go."

She started jogging toward the hatch.

Out in the corridor, he pointed the way. God, she hoped he was telling the truth.

"Once we're in the shuttles," he said, "what then? We can't go through a gate in a craft like that."

"We can't stay on board."

"Agreed. Even if our re-route works, the ship might not change direction fast enough, and we could still kiss the asteroid somewhat."

"And the Therokis are planning to board," she added. "We need to get away from them. What if we cause a distraction? We could increase the *Everest*'s chances of making it to the gate and not getting blown up."

His eyes widened. "What about *us* getting blown up?"

"I'd suggest we avoid that. Doesn't seem like a very good distraction in the long run. Odd recommendation, Lieutenant."

"I *meant*, how do we survive any of this?"

"What, you want to live forever?"

"A little longer would be preferrable."

"Got any ship-to-planet vehicles?"

"A few. But the SPVs are always breaking down."

"Of course they are. I say we fly well, and go straight for Asteroid 715. Draw fire and attention by going for the jugular. We might even make it in one piece."

He snorted. "Are you a pilot, Ryu?"

"Nope. You?"

"Nope."

She sighed. "There goes the first step in the plan. I don't suppose some of the funding the Union saved by not updating this rust bucket was spent on state-of-the-art SPVs?" She smiled ruefully. "Some snazzy nav systems?"

"If you assume that, you will be disappointed." He pointed. "That way."

"Ah, maybe the asteroid is out, then."

They turned the corner and reached the docking bay where she'd first arrived. It felt like months had passed since then. Years.

He waved an arm, not slowing down. "Take your pick, madam."

"Which one has the most armor, at least some weapons, and range and fuel enough to get us to the *Lhotse,* and then to the asteroid?"

"The *Lhotse*—ah. I see."

"We can't abandon them. We need to get them out of harm's way and send them through the gate too." Her tone was cold.

"Yes. But that's not the real reason."

"Nope. It's not. I need Kael."

"Indeed."

"Nobody gets left behind." Not that that was the real reason either. Or at least not the only one. "And we have a team of two. He'd make it three. He has the same augment as me, so he will be conscious."

Yamamoto pursed his lips as he turned toward a squat ship that resembled a rhino. He started forward, and she followed. "And also you're in love with him."

"And also I'm in love with him." She shrugged.

"Don't need to be a telepath to see that. This ship is probably the best fit. Let's go."

"WHAT ARE THEY DOING?" Zhia pointed at the viewscreen.

Adan leaned forward even though he could see the wide asteroid field perfectly well. He just didn't want to believe what he saw.

Two Theroki ships moved between the drifting, spinning boulders, the exteriors of the ships black and bristling with weapons and accumulated detritus mixed with comm equipment. A hatch in the side of one was opening. "Are they… are they… coming over to board us?"

Zhia smacked the console. "Hail the *Everest*."

"Already did. No response, ma'am." It was easy to ma'am Zhia when her scowl was that serious.

"Nobody's shooting or *anything*. What's going on? Hail them again. Hail the *Lhotse too*."

The spaceships had been drifting along together, two Union and two Therokis, in rough synchrony into the asteroid field. One particularly large asteroid wasn't far. Then, abruptly, the ships went still, and a few moments later, the *Everest* started slightly reversing course, back toward the gate.

What were they doing? And why couldn't someone just *answer the damn radio* and tell him?

Boarding tunnels slowly snaked out from the Theroki ships, like hoses set to drain the life from the Union ships—or at least the valuables and lives of those on board.

Gritting his teeth, he started entering the commands. Even if it was futile, they had to keep trying. "I set it to keep repeating. Neither of them is responding with anything but automated replies, but maybe we'll get lucky."

"What the hell happened?" Doug's voice came over the comm.

"The *Alarus Octendi* happened," said a soft voice.

Roya. Her voice when she spoke like this, more refined than a body of her size should be able to produce, and improving by the hour… it sent a chill down his spine.

"You mean now they're all under her control?" Adan shuddered. Thank the heavens for cybernetics. "Good thing you're in your coat closet, sir."

"Hey, this is like a luxury beach resort down here," Doug replied. "Amaya made me a piña colada before she left for just this sort of situation."

"Not everyone would be under her control," Zhia put in. "Everybody but Ellen and Kael, maybe?"

"Do you think the Union crews are Songbird puppets trying to kill them, then? Or just numb like that John Doe we picked up on Capital?" Adan asked, his gut twisting at the thought of either.

"Hard to say." Zhia frowned.

"Ghost ships," said Fern. "Glad I'm not on them. You ever been on an empty ship? It's creepy. Ship filled with John Doe zombies? Even more creepy. Their eyes just staring into space..."

"We can't let those Therokis get to Ellen and Kael." Zhia closed her fist. "Or any of the Union for that matter."

"We can attempt to stop them," Xi put in. "Any efforts would at the very least slow them down."

"Let's make some noise." Zhia leaned back in the command chair, her expression hard. "Move toward the *Everest*. Prepare to engage."

"Should we hail that Theroki ship?" Adan asked. "While we're being social?"

"No. I don't want to waste time waiting for them to answer and pretending to be civil. I'm not, and they're not trying to board Union vessels out of the goodness of their hearts. Fern, you ready?"

"More ready than ever, Commander."

"Keep your finger on the trigger. And everybody strap in so we can do so. We will have no surprises, but let's keep them guessing as much as we can as to who we are. Adan?"

"Yes, ma'am?"

"I'm thinking we use these asteroids to our advantage. You with me?"

"Prepared to shave an asteroid's ass." He took a sip of coffee and grinned. "On your command."

She winced even as she laughed. "Now that was a mental image I didn't need."

Adan dipped down, trying to get underneath some of the asteroid noise. There was a—relatively—more open space that should still give him a good clean shot of the boarding tunnel, and he poured on the speed.

"You know the nice thing about boarding tunnels, Xi?" he said as they were nearly within range.

"They allow the chicken to get to the other side?"

He snorted. "I don't know about any chickens. I was thinking it's nice that you can't put shields around them."

"Within range, Commander," Xi said.

"Fire," ordered Zhia.

Fern wasted no time. The Therokis apparently hadn't accounted for the stray ship in the area being hostile—or maybe they hadn't noticed the *Audacity* at all.

But they were going to notice now. It took barely a handful of blasts before the panels and arms of the tunnel broke apart, pieces exploding in all directions, the wormlike noodle remaining lolling to one side.

"Boarding apparatus destroyed," Xi reported.

Adan cheered like a kid at the dog races. "Nobody's boarding the *Everest* tonight!"

"At least not with *that* tunnel," Fern replied. He could just hear it in her voice that she was grinning.

"Unfortunately," Xi cut in, "the same is not true for the *Lhotse*. The Therokis' boarding apparatus has connected, and the airlock is in the process of cycling."

Zhia swore.

"Why not hit that one too?" Fern said. "Get me a clear shot!"

"Once the airlock is open, destroying the tunnel will risk Union lives and possibly our friends. While Kael and Ellen went to the *Everest* initially, we have no guarantee they stayed there."

"Good point," said Zhia.

"We have approximately three minutes."

"We've got a bigger problem, I think." Adan put in, his eyes on the shifting Theroki ship. "They're giving up on the *Everest*."

"Oh?"

He pointed at the viewscreen. "I think we are looking a little juicier."

"Logical choice," Xi put in.

Zhia smiled, a predatory gleam in her eyes. "Good, then. I'm glad we have their attention—that means Kael and Ellen don't. Care for a game of asteroid hide and seek, Adan?"

"How could I resist?" he said, smiling. But he turned on the extra proximity-sensor display. He was going to need all the help he could get.

WHEN KAEL CAME to the next time, he lay completely still. It'd become easier with time, almost a habit. Lying completely still as though he were unconscious was almost harder than enduring the pain he'd been in with the first drug they'd given him.

He didn't know what exactly had happened, whether it'd been a problem with the drug or a problem with him. He had heard that he'd passed out more from the pain than any actual sedative effect of that original drug, so from the bits and pieces he'd put together, he was fairly sure they now had him on a different one.

Lucky for him that, though a constant dosing through an intravenous drip would have made sense to keep him knocked out, they'd gone with single injections which they would repeat when he stirred to consciousness, at which point they would re-dose him. So when he started to wake, all he had to do was fake sleep, allowing the drug time to wear off somewhat. He would visibly stir when his bodily needs told him to, at which point they would give him time to eat and take care of basic needs, which also allowed him to move a bit.

He had no idea how long he'd been lying there when an unexpected sound almost blew his ruse. A heavy *thud* rang through the hull, jolting the whole ship and making him jump.

Not again. How many times could this ship possibly break down and still be flying?

It must not be that unusual, because the sergeant guarding him didn't react to the sound. A knot in his stomach tightened, though. Something about the sound bothered him. It felt more like an impact from the outside than just some part malfunctioning. Or exploding.

He focused on listening to those deep sounds of the ship over the human sounds—the ventilation's breath, the clanks from the decks below, the hum of the engines.

A second heavy *thud* rang. The sergeant sat up straighter.

Seven suns, maybe this Frankenstein of a ship would just come apart at the seams, and he'd be consumed by the vacuum. He might never see Ellen again or have a chance to get to know Shirin. To be a father to her. She might be better off without him, for all he knew about being a father, but damn if it didn't make his chest hurt a little. Not to mention that getting sucked into space because the ship he was on was just that old wasn't exactly the noble end he'd hoped for.

A third impact rang out, shaking the ship around them now. His hand jolted from the movement, catching against the length of one of the chains. Because both the chains and sedation were clearly necessary for homicidal maniacs.

He opened his eyes. Enough pretending. Something was happening.

"Ah, he's awake," the sergeant muttered. "Sick bay, you're guy is up. Come and attend."

"What's that noise?" he asked, trying to sound groggy. It was pretty easy.

"Nothing for you to worry your pretty little head about." But the sergeant was squinting at his holodesk and not looking particularly peaceful at the moment.

He sat up, groaned, and then kicked his legs down to the floor. Every part of him hurt, just from lying so still on that slab for so long. "C'mon. It's my life too. Is this junker finally falling apart?"

"What, you new to this being a prisoner business? What's happening outside is none of your concern."

Hmm, if it was an engineering emergency, there were no alarms blaring. And the crew hadn't been shy when complaining loudly about which subsystem was being a monster at the moment. So why the secrecy now? He rubbed the grit from his eyes. "Are we being attacked?"

"What'd they throw you in for, anyway? Being dense as a brick wall?"

"As long as I'm denser than this ship's hull, I'll take that as a compliment."

"I wouldn't count on that."

He winced. "For the record, I'm collateral to make sure that my superior officer doesn't betray the *Everest*'s commanding officer and yours, while all three commanders attack some nut jobs."

The sergeant's eyes widened. "Wow, you sure can tell 'em. Got any other good stories?"

Kael huffed with disgust and dropped his head between his knees. Nausea hit him every few hours around this point in their screwed-up cycle. Might as well give up asking questions. This guy wasn't budging. But he'd barely steadied himself from the nausea when the ship shook again.

"What *is* that?" he demanded. "It's not like... it's not like a laser or torpedo blast." No, it was eerily familiar, wasn't it? He usually hadn't been on the *inside* of those ships, but every once in a while…

Every once in a while, Therokis fought each other. And he knew that sound.

The sergeant shrugged. "They don't tell *either* of us that stuff. They just tell me, 'Make sure that brute doesn't get out.' So that's what I do."

"Brute. Really." Grumbling to himself, Kael probed the space that he could reach outside the ship. But without the augmentation of the ship's sensors, his range didn't reach far. Barely beyond the ship itself, in fact. Just as he was about to give up, he caught the tail end of a whip of energy.

A mind, another telekinetic force brushing his.

He shot to his feet, chains rattling. "Therokis!"

"What the—" the sergeant started, scrambling to his feet as well and, to his credit now, reaching to slap on the holodisplay.

"There are Therokis out—" Kael stopped short. The man was no longer listening. Before the sergeant's hand could reach the control glass, he'd frozen. His eyes went slack.

Abruptly, he fell back in the chair at a bizarre angle. He didn't quite make it onto the seat and slid painfully to the deck. If the man noticed, he didn't react. He didn't swear or try to stop it or right himself. Just slid. A sudden lifeless pool now at Kael's feet.

The eyes stared at the ceiling, unblinking. Blank.

He'd seen this before. In death, many times. But this wasn't death... it was more like... The inspectors on Capital that had attacked Persad's apartment. The dead-eyed zombie stare.

The ship shook again.

Well, if this wasn't go time, he didn't know what would be. It wasn't as if he could help the guy on the floor, even if he was just having a medical problem. Besides, medical was already on the way.

And he needed to get out before they arrived with their syringe.

He tucked one finger into a shackle, then two, and started to push and bend the metal. The shackle bent slightly, but didn't release.

They'd upgraded the cuffs. This was going to take too long.

The chains were too short to allow him to reach the bars of the cell door, so he reached forward with his mind, pushing against the bars. Interesting there was no force field here. Was it out of a lack of resources, or was it by design? Maybe having metal he could manipulate would help him.

The bars didn't budge. They didn't even groan.

He tried pushing harder again, pushing only in one direction, pulling in the other direction.

Nothing.

Weyer had reinforced the cell, specifically for him, hadn't she? It wasn't just the chains she'd reinforced. That was logical, but why did she have to be so thorough? He already had a hangover from her thoroughness.

He was eyeing the wall panels when another shake rocked the ship again, almost taking him off his feet. If he hadn't been holding on, he might have been knocked out like sarge over there just from the force of that.

Wait, the sergeant—his hand. It could activate the lockpad. Kael didn't have to break out if he could *let* himself out.

He chuckled a little to himself as he started to work. He'd gone first to brawn rather than brains, hadn't he? Probably best not to dwell on that too long. He started floating the man's hand toward the lockpad.

Well, maybe dragged was the more appropriate word. But he'd rarely had to move a body with precision. Mostly, he just batted people around or left them alone.

Praise Almighty, he really *was* a brute.

It took quite a bit of concentration to actually position and unfurl the man's fingers enough for the pad to get a reading, and he was sweating by the time he achieved it. But once he did, the bars slid open with a soft hiss. A few more carefully orchestrated pokes with the man's hand, and he found the rest of the controls. The shackles fell open, releasing him.

He stepped out quickly, just as another impact made him stagger. That one seemed harder this time.

"Computer," he decided to try, "is the ship under attack?"

"Prisoner Kael Rhee, one moment please." The answer seemed slightly delayed. The silence stretched on. He listened for the pounding of footsteps, screams, shots, shouting, anything.

An eerie silence was all that greeted him.

"Computer?"

"My apologies. My systems have not been adequately designed to include detailed protocols for an escaped 'prisoner' being the most senior active crew member on the ship."

"The most senior—what?" His eyes widened. "Excuse me?"

"I should be sending the crew to apprehend you, but I cannot. But they are not dead, so I must send them." It almost seemed to sigh. "I don't suppose you would oblige me and apprehend yourself?"

He snorted, went to the holodisplay, and started poking at it. It didn't respond to him.

"Escaped prisoners are not privy to the ship's information system," the computer snipped.

"What about senior crew members?"

There was no response. He strode to the door to the corridor and tried to open it, but it too didn't respond to his palm.

"How's it feel, huh?" He frowned at the sergeant over his shoulder, the man still lifeless, but seemingly alive. He strode back to him and looked down over the guy. Quickly, he patted him down but found only a generic, unlabeled card, a stick of gum, and a darn rat bar. Well, and the man's sidearm, which he tucked in his belt.

Hell. Cutting off his hand was probably out of the question.

He could float the guy or physically drag him to the door… Or he could just rip the hatch open. He sighed and started back toward the exit as another tremor shook through the ship. He really didn't want to give Weyer one more thing to hold over his head. Then again, she was nowhere to be seen.

"What is that banging, computer?"

No response. Getting a good grip on the rim of the hatch elicited no response from the computer—or the sergeant.

"C'mon, you can tell me." He grunted as he ripped away the frame of the hatch so he could get his fingers around the edge of the door itself. Sparks protested, but the computer remained silent.

"Is it Therokis?" he said slowly.

"Yes," the computer replied. "They are preparing to board."

"Well, don't let them!" Dang, he'd known they were attacking, but he hadn't thought they'd gotten close enough to board. He glanced around. Maybe there was a second pistol or something in the desk. Even two pistols would be basically nothing against what he was facing, but it would be better than just one.

"They have the first access code. I am unable to stop them from docking."

"Change the access codes," he snapped, yanking open the first drawer. And he caught his breath.

Zhia's journal was inside.

He grabbed it, a random chocolate bar, and some energy mags. No second pistol. Nothing else good. He needed to get out of here—maybe try the docking bay—maybe try to escape.

Blast it, he *should* have tried to take over the ship. Then at least he'd have been in charge when all this was happening.

"To change the access codes, please enter your Union officer identification code."

"You know I don't have one."

"I just thought I'd give you a chance. Without it, I cannot change the codes."

"So just don't open the hatch for them."

"If they have the Union secretly issued codes, their orders outrank yours."

He swore as he jogged toward the exit, out into the hallway. "You're going to get us both killed."

"Quite possibly, yes," it agreed.

"There are telepaths with the Therokis. They're stealing the codes from the minds of the people onboard." He didn't know that for sure, but it sounded good.

"Unfortunately, I am not designed to change my behavior in this scenario, nor can I prove your claim is true."

He groaned. "Is anyone conscious other than me? Someone I could reason with?"

"No. My apologies. I have no explanation for the loss of consciousness of the crew."

"I do," he grumbled.

"I have alerted the *Everest*. There was no reply."

A deep thud echoed in the belly of the ship. The engineering status lights he'd noted changed every few hours, and this time, one shifted from blue to yellow. Not good, but not the worst either. But the ship was taking damage. Or falling apart. Or maybe both.

"They have entered the second set of passcodes."

"How long till they are on board?"

"Fifty-five seconds."

He swore again. Fine. Time to find some place to hide. "Can you at least let me into maintenance areas or something so I can have a fighting chance?"

The computer didn't respond.

Seven suns. Where could he hide? Some place they wouldn't think to look for a Theroki who was immune to their mind control. But where exactly would that be?

He tried a palm pad, and to his surprise, the door opened, revealing rows and shelves of armor and weapons.

Well, well. Nicer than a maintenance closet. Maybe it wasn't his most unlucky day after all.

THERE WERE a variety of reasons that today had turned into a bad day, but the fact that Ellen's hands were on the stick of the ship-to-planet-vehicle might take the cake.

Any day when she was the best pilot in the room was truly a dark one.

"This thing flies like a turtle flying through gelatin," she grumbled, jamming angrily at the acceleration controls. It didn't do anything. The last time she'd flown anything had been to surrender to the *Everest*. And that had been almost entirely auto-pilot.

"You wanted armor."

"We need armor. It's either the cybernetic embodiment of a turtle, or I'm flying it wrong."

"Both seem equally possible."

She snorted. "Won't argue with that."

The High Adjutant's voice blared over the comm. She'd left the comm channels open and auto-accepting so when they hailed, she wouldn't get distracted trying to accept it. "Just what do you think you are doing," he drawled.

Yamamoto jumped. "I didn't realize that was on."

"Don't answer him," she said coldly.

"Wasn't going to." He eased back into his seat.

She shifted uneasily, watching one Theroki ship get closer and closer to the *Lhotse*. "We're not going to beat them there, are we?"

"That would be my assessment as well." Yamamoto's gaze was steely. "I suppose it makes sense. They started closing in on both ships when the crews were disabled. We had to set up our defenses and find this ship. They have the time advantage on us."

"Are there any minor airlocks, or are we headed to a shoot-out in the cargo hold?"

"Here and here." Yamamoto pointed on a map of the ship he'd brought up at his station. "But the *Lhotse* has been… aging. Struggling. A little. They might not work properly."

"How much is a little?"

"If you think the *Everest* is in bad shape, wait till you see the *Lhotse*."

"This is a crappy vacation." She jerked the ship starboard. "I should really read the tour guides more carefully next time."

He smiled slightly. "Although ironically, the *Lhotse* does have a ship computer."

"How'd they swing that?"

"Weyer won a drinking game. Against the right person."

"I don't think I've met this Weyer person yet, but I have a feeling I'll like her."

His smile widened. "Which back alley will you take to get in? Or should I flip a credit?"

"Okay, that one there looks farther from the Theroki ship. That'd be more cover, right?"

"Yes."

"Which is closest to the brig?"

"The more exposed one."

"Of course it is."

"Yes, of course. But we can fight our way through the ship, and I'll have access codes to help us. If we can't even get on because they've catapulted us into the nearest star, though, that won't help your lieutenant."

She nodded even as the comm crackled with static. The Therokis were close enough to the *Lhotse* to be kissing it.

"We have taken control of this ship," said the High Adjutant. "Surrender now, and you won't be harmed."

She made a disgusted noise. "They're bluffing. Hasn't been long enough for them to break their way in *and* take control. Unless somebody gave them the access codes."

"Let us hope that is not the case. It's one of our only advantages."

She maneuvered closer to the ship, still just slightly in view of their enemies. "They must actually want me alive."

He frowned. "Why?"

"Because they haven't fired on us."

"Maybe they think a bullet will be easier and cheaper. They are mercs after all."

"Maybe they are right. Then they could resell our turtle mobile. Wish I had some damn armor."

"Armor! Of course. Let me see if there's any in the back."

Her eyes widened. Yamamoto was a good leader on a ship, in the sky… But after that comment, did he even know which way to point the rifle? No seasoned ground trooper would neglect to think of armor.

Didn't matter. He was the only ally she had. If he was truly an ally.

She held close to the edge of the ship as long as she could. "Hold on! I'm not a great pilot on a good day."

"Holding on," he called. "All we need is good enough."

She dipped down at the last moment, toward the airlock, so the Therokis would have the least chance to notice or to plan. Or do anything about it. Swallowing hard, she engaged what autopilot the SPV had, but it still demanded a ton of calculations she was long out of practice at making. God, she missed Adan. And Xi. And the *Audacity*.

Yamamoto only gasped twice and cried out in pain once from the ruckus she caused, scraping the SPV across the hull of the *Lhotse* eight different ways before the bits lined up with the bops. Those were technical terms.

"Airlock cycling," the computer announced.

"Look!"

She turned just as Yamamoto tossed something at her. Her adrenaline surged, battle instincts already keen, anticipating a grenade, a bomb, a flash bang. But she caught it, hands closing around cool glass and metal.

A helmet. "You found something?"

"Five full suits back here. Some rifles too. Come suit up while it cycles. Hurry."

"That's good because I was going to kill you. The adrenaline rush —was that necessary?"

"With all that rough flying, I worried you had fallen asleep while trying to dock."

"Yeah, yeah, I'd like to see you do better, Lieutenant."

He chuckled as he twisted a gauntlet into place. Maybe it was the adrenaline talking, but fear suddenly struck her. If Bridell had been a spy, and Yamamoto had kept at least one secret from all of them, should she really be trusting him so readily? She guessed they'd be evenly matched in hand-to-hand combat, whether they were armored or not. But he already had part of his suit on. There would be a brief moment when his suit would be a huge advantage for him, physically. What if there was more that he was hiding, some ulterior motive at play?

What if he didn't really care about saving Kael or any of these people and actually just wanted to shoot her in the back?

Her instincts warred, struggling to remember the blur of running from the bridge. Had he already had his chance to backstab her, or would this be his first real opportunity?

His suit was almost complete. Only the collar-helmet unit was left.

She had nothing on yet, but she dropped her collar and helmet unit over her head and whipped the pistol from her back belt, letting the cold metal graze the hair on the back of his head. She pushed forward so he could feel it, hard.

She released the safety with an audible hiss.

He froze. "Commander—"

"How do I know I can trust you?" she demanded.

He didn't move. "*This* is the moment you choose to test that?"

"You were the only one who realized what Kael was. That's part of how he got sent over here to this ship. Maybe you wanted us separated. Maybe you orchestrated this from the beginning."

"I couldn't lie to my CO. I did my best to keep it discreet. I didn't realize there was such a… history between you and Captain Dealis."

"So it *was* personal."

"What *isn't* personal with Captain Dealis?"

That was true enough. Maybe truer than she'd realized. She hesitated.

"Commander Ryu, I have no desire to stab you in the back. On the honor of my grandmother, whose life you saved, I will help you, and I will not let you down. Please, let me rise so you can see my sincerity."

She took a step back, keeping the weapon trained on him as he rose, hands open and spread wide.

"You were always one of us." When he turned to look at her, that earnestness in his eyes was familiar. Just like Kael's. "You never should have gone through any of this. I am sorry for how the Union mistreated you."

Her throat tightened painfully. That… No one had ever bothered to say that before. Something about it made her falter, struggle to see through blurry eyes.

"I can't prove my loyalty. But I think you are correct that pointing our ships toward the gate and having your friend with us will be more advantageous to our survival. I have no incentive to do anything else."

"No incentive that I know about."

"These are my friends. My colleagues."

"Like Bridell is your colleague? You're a telepath. What did he do to me in that room?"

"He drugged you and asked you where something was. Some research. He thought of it as 'the empress,' whatever that is. He's a spy for the Enhancers. I've known for some time, but he's very careful. I haven't been able to catch him with any concrete evidence that wouldn't reveal my secret. He did it during his first interrogation too. The drugs kept you from remembering."

She swore. "Do you know what I told him?"

"From what I could gather, not much, but I had difficulty understanding the context."

"Cassandra found the *Everest* once. Paul almost died. More than once. Was it Bridell who helped them find the ship's location? The Enhancers have no love for Cassandra. Was it him, or was it you?"

"It was Tauber. As you rightfully suspected. I can't reach Tauber, but I saw his interaction with Captain Dealis in Dealis's memories. I believe Tauber had told the Songbirds our location, and they sent scout ships with telepaths to influence Dealis." His hands were still held wide. "Is this really the time for this?"

"Then why try to kill him? The suicide attempt? The drugs?"

"The drugs were Bridell. He convinced the nurse, then killed her to cover it up. Again, I was looking for real evidence, but he was too careful. And Paul's suicide attempt, well, that's not surprising."

She frowned. "How is it not surprising?"

"It's at least the tenth time."

She swore again, harder, as a chill ran through her.

The airlock buzzed. It'd finished cycling.

"Listen. You trusted Captain Dealis, Paul as you say, and he trusted me. I took you at your word about your desertion," he said. "That it was justified. Take me at my word about this."

She gritted her teeth, then lowered the pistol slowly. "There will be a price to pay if you're lying, Yamamoto. Just remember. I hold grudges long and hard."

"There will be no need." His shoulders slumped in relief. "Can we finish putting this armor on now?"

"Yes. Hurry."

CHAPTER TWELVE

KAEL TWISTED the last gauntlet into place and raised the helmet. The suit didn't fit perfectly, a little snug, but he had armor. *Armor.* He hadn't thought he'd find that when he'd broken out of the brig on this jacked-up ship. This was for damn sure better than two pistols.

Out in the corridor, the noise level was rising. Clangs and shouts.

He had everything he could carry. Time to really hide this time—and hope this wasn't a place they expected anyone to be stationed.

One of the heavier crates seemed a good candidate. No chance they'd see him from the corridor. They'd have to come in and look around.

Unless the computer told them where he was. In which case, he was fragged no matter what.

Hunkered down in the corner, new rifle at the ready at his side, he grabbed the poetry book out of his side compartment. He might get creamed by his former comrades, or worse, so he might as well find out just what Zhia had been penning about all this time. Haiku about flowers? Saucy limericks about late nights at bars?

He opened to the first page. There, carefully printed in a delicate typeface, was

• • •

JAGIYA,

These are ancient
from my own glory days
They may not work
Any more
Sort of like
An old woman
Like me
But if you can
Give them one last fling.
Or thirty-six of them.
- Z

IT WENT ON LIKE THAT, free verse about life and time passing, bullets and, ahem, "boys." There was an ode to a multi, another to an Ursa-loving moon. He tapped his finger against the side of the book.

One last fling. Or thirty-six of them. Why that number? An odd choice.

A message?

Hurrying, he flipped faster to page thirty-six. There abruptly mid-line, the free verse was interspersed with what looked like random gibberish.

THE HEAVENLY ECHOES *of space*
X166GI83P2
Eclipse the past with starfire
TUW&56J0!
And tacos with you.

HE SMILED AT THE WORDS. Mm, tacos would have been good right about now. Then he blinked. Wait, were those— *These may not work.*

Were they access codes? Frag, if he'd opened this book first, what else could he have done? He really was a brute. No, no. He was *action oriented*. And just not that into poetry.

Clearly, it wasn't the best life choice for this moment. If he'd just valued literature more, he might have gotten control of the whole ship right away.

"Computer," he whispered, certain it could still hear him. "Grant me command access to the ship." He had no idea if that was a real thing, but why not try it? "Code X155GI83P2."

"Access granted," the computer whispered back.

Well, praise the Almighty. He was about to ask what he could do with that, when the steps outside got louder and closer. He hurried to seal the book back in his side compartment.

Something hissed to life right outside the doorway. The sound of metal sizzling echoed in the armory room.

Frag. Frag, frag, frag. They were right outside. Worse, they clearly knew he was in here. How? Had they heard his whisper? Maybe they were in the surveillance systems. That would make sense.

A blowtorch or laser was working its slow but steady way through the hatch door.

Every so often, when the work would momentarily stop for whatever reason, voices on the other side muttered things like *How many* and *Yes, we're almost in*.

He glanced around. Maybe he could build up his barricade and take out a few more of them before he went down.

Because he *was* going down. He certainly wasn't going back to being a Theroki. Not now. And he was all alone against their entire ship.

He dragged six more crates into a corner, then, since the blowtorch hadn't yet finished, he started going through each of them with one hand, with his rifle at the ready in the other.

The first contained only canteens and rations—of which he pocketed a few, but they weren't going to help him with the unfriendly visitors at the door.

The second, though, was a little more promising. Grenades. Damn, this could maybe even get him out of this, although—grenades inside a ship were a zenithally stupid thing to do. Moronic, really. Why were these even here?

He examined a few of the small black spheres in his hand. Oh—they were flashes. And smoke bombs. Non-lethal.

Well, at least that wouldn't breach the hull. Maybe he could cause some chaos.

The third crate, though, the third had rifles. He had swung three extras over his shoulder when the door made an ominous groan. Ducking, he braced himself.

The hatch door fell inward, the metal finally giving way to fire. Two Therokis stepped in, then a woman. Unarmored, in a plain black dress. Black eyes. Loose curls of blonde hair.

Kael caught his breath. He knew that face. That hair. Looked just like Ana. It was one of *them*.

Cassandra.

She squinted at his hunkered form, only his rifle and a few centimeters of helmet showing up over the edge of the crate. Then her head cocked to the side, more like an android than a human.

"Why aren't you subdued?" she said simply. "All should be subdued."

"Some men are harder to catch than others, darling."

He tossed the flashbang over the crate and ducked, reaching for the next one.

Shouts and cries went up around him as he launched a smoke grenade, then another. Praise Almighty, let him not regret that. If he could cause enough disorientation, maybe he could slip past and through and—

But he wasn't the only one launching grenades. And Therokis had never been known for their less-than-lethal tactics. Or their intelligence.

Metal *tinked* against the wall behind his head, then clattered along the floor toward his feet. Footsteps near the hatch thundered back out into the corridor. Away from him.

Oh, frag.

He shoved the crates forward, pushing with his shoulder against them—and his legs and his mind, but he barely added a meter of distance in the split second before the new grenade went off.

The blast threw him against the crate, hard, pain lancing through his skull where it connected with the helmet and the metal. Seven suns, was this room in the center of the ship or along the outside? How could they not care about a hull breach? That woman hadn't been suited up, and last he checked, getting sucked out into the vacuum of space and floating forever was a problem for average Theroki, too, armored or not.

The blast had settled, but the floor panels hadn't. He was somehow still moving, sliding. He clawed at the metal grating, at the nearby beams now exposed, trying to steady himself.

The panels groaned, then screeched. They were giving way underneath him.

He scrambled for purchase faster now, unable to see. His pain-fractured glimpses through the smoky haze didn't reveal anything useful, and his hands found nothing to grab on to, except the crate.

In one last, desperate move, he batted the fragging crate back toward the corridor at them with his mind.

Hopefully, it'd hit whoever threw that stupid grenade. Or all of them. That would be nice.

Not that he'd be able to see it, because he was falling. Fast. Through the smoke, he felt himself slide off the grating and into whatever lay beneath him, debris and three more crates following him into the abyss.

YAMAMOTO JOGGED up off the SPV toward a large maintenance holo just outside the airlock. "Hell, at least five systems have malfunctions. No comm traffic. I bet they're just like the *Everest*."

"Therokis here yet?" She jogged to a view panel beyond the

doors and peered around carefully for hostiles. She didn't see anyone, not even crew sprawled on the floor.

"They *are* on board now, whether they were telling the truth before or not. Doesn't look like they've made it to the bridge. Barely inside the dock. They're searching the halls for… I don't know what."

Ellen swore.

"This way to the brig. Let's hope they don't think of stopping there. What do they even want?" He palmed the doors out of the airlock area open, and they headed down the corridor.

"What do pirates ever want? To loot the place." But these weren't really pirates, were they? They were more like Songbirds. "Or maybe they want more minions. Conscripts."

"Or maybe they want some leverage over you."

"Unlikely. They don't know what that would be. But they'll find it in the brig if they look."

"Here's praying we get there first."

A loud clang came down the corridor they were about to turn down. She put a gentle hand on Yamamoto's shoulder to stop him, scooted past him, and peeked around the corner.

A dozen Therokis in armor marked with blue octopi were marching toward them. Yep, these were Arakovic's insiders all along. She should have thought of it. She should have realized. If every Union soldier on these ships died, their blood would be on her hands for this mistake.

She made a face and jerked a thumb over her shoulder, trying to silently say, they're coming.

Yamamoto turned and palmed a panel a few feet behind him, then stepped inside, disappearing.

She scurried after him and watched as he disappeared from sight down the grav shaft. Right, that was a good idea—get to another level. Grav shafts were… not her favorite.

But Arakovic's foot soldiers were even less her favorite, so she stepped in and flung herself down, barely using the holds. They went down as far as this shaft could take them, at least two or three decks. She caught the last hand hold at the bottom and swung out without any grace whatsoever. There wasn't time for finesse here.

Yamamoto was already on the move. "This way. At the next grav shaft, we can go back up one deck and reach the brig. We'll have gone around them."

Down two decks, and then back up one. Clever of him. They kept their steps and their voices hushed for a few dozen meters, then reached another grav shaft. "Brace yourself for confrontation at the top," she murmured before they went up.

But the corridor she swung out into was empty.

"Here. The brig." Yamamoto palmed yet another hatch open, and they both raced in.

Three very old-looking cells lined one wall. Dozens of chains had been bolted into the wall in the middle cell, and the bars stood parted. All the shackles hung open, unlocked. The whole place was empty, except for one unconscious sergeant on the floor.

Frag it all. "He's gone," she muttered, mostly to herself.

"But he was here. Nobody needs chains like that for an ordinary person."

She stepped over the sergeant. One arm sprawled oddly up in the air along the wall. "I think he broke out. Using the sergeant's palm print. See?"

Yamamoto followed her gaze, then he steeled himself. "If we head back toward the docking bay or the bridge, we can get to computers that will let us see the full ship surveillance. That could tell us just where he is. But the chances hostile forces are taking control of those areas is high."

"They've probably already taken them."

"I agree. They are clearly in the dock. We might not make it."

"What about engineering?"

"From what I saw, they've reached that. That's why I didn't even include it as an option."

"Bridge it is, then. They don't need that as highest priority if they have the engines and everybody's passed out. Then from there, if we can see the surveillance, maybe we can locate Kael. No idea how we'll reach him—or get out but—"

"One step at a time. Back to that grav shaft."

Keeping her feet from pounding like an elephant as she ran down the corridor was nearly impossible, but she tried. At the grav shaft, she jumped in again and flew back down to the lowest deck, letting herself crash toward the bottom, with as much reckless speed as she could generate.

God, where are you, Kael? He was too good, and it might just get them all killed.

KAEL'S back slammed into metal grating. Alarms were blaring somewhere, maybe in the suit. Maybe in the ship. Yellow flashes lit up the chaos and smoke—*flash flash flash. Flash flash flash.* Crates and floor panels and beams were right on his tail, about to crush him.

The bubble he created around himself was more instinct than strategy. Grunting, his energy levels dipped further. He couldn't keep this up much longer, but exhausted was better than dead.

He batted the first crate to one side; the second to the other. The third was too fast, though, and he fumbled it, making it spin instead of move.

It smashed into his leg. Even with the armor, he cried out, the pain blinding. Panting, he tried to clear his eyes. The helmet readout of the armor was exploding with warnings, but nothing he was familiar with; everything was rearranged. It basically all added up to *not good.*

Was there even air? Was he still in a habitable part of the ship or some buffer portion? He needed to move that fragging crate. Above him, he caught a glimpse of more crates still remaining in the gaping cavity that had been the armory.

Beams of light sliced through the darkness and smoke. They were back inside the armory.

Another flash—the crates were close. Oh, fragging hell.

The Therokis were pushing the crates. And the weight of those above him was making even more floor panels give way. Not that they seemed to care.

Swearing relentlessly, he shoved at the crate pinning him down. He needed to *move.*

A scream rang out, making him falter. The crate fumbled again, crashing back down onto him. He couldn't contain another gush of agony.

But that hadn't been from above him in the armory—it had been from the side.

"Yama—" a woman started.

Wait. He knew that voice.

"Ellen, is that you—" He lurched to his feet, the crate flung away like a stray ragdoll. He wasn't even sure if it was the armor or the telekinetics, but hearing her had helped him find a way.

Ballistic fire rained down from the hole in the corridor ceiling above him, so he ran, limping and ducking and not clear where he was running other than *away.* He found a wall in the corridor with a display that showed an outline of the ship—and many, many zones flashing in red and yellow. Frag, this piece of shit wasn't prepared to take this kind of beating. What if he was near those constant trilini leaks? Whatever they were, they sounded bad.

"Kael, is that you?"

"Elle—yes—where are you?"

"We need help!" A pause. He glanced around, but couldn't see anything between flashes. "Follow my voice!"

"Keep talking." Had to keep her talking if he hoped to find her. "How did you get here?" The smoke had reached everywhere; whether it was from his grenade or something more serious, he still hadn't made his way out of the cloud.

"Long story!"

Her voice was to his right. He darted toward her. Finally, only a few steps away, he spotted a crate pinning a man to the wall. Seeing the markings, he knew it was a different one than the one that had pinned him. Crates 2, humans 0.

He'd drained much of his energy in that mad desperate shove away from the grenade—some good it had done—but he used what little remained to lift the crate off the man and set it carefully aside.

He saw another form turn in his direction, sharp brown eyes pinning him. "What are you doing?" she shouted. "You're supposed to be in the *brig*."

"I'm trying not to die," he shouted back. "And I didn't make it far, now, did I?"

"Guess not. What is all this? You tryin' to get blown out into space?

"I only made the smoke. It's—"

"I know who it is," she snapped as she turned to the man with her. "Yamamoto, hey! Wake up!" She smacked his helmet.

"Yamamoto? What are the two of you doing here?"

The man answered them both with an anguished groan. "I'm—I'm fine—let's go."

"We need sick bay," she barked. "Where is it?"

"I'm fine— Is that Kael? We need the docking bay, then."

"You're not going anywhere but sick bay, buddy." Turning to Kael, she explained, "That armor is *through* his shoulder. He'll bleed out before we reach docking—"

"We've got to take care of them first—" Kael pointed. "Or they'll follow us, and no med tech is gonna be able to help us if we're dead." Although his crate-mangled calf would love a med tech right about now. The armor made a sort of terrible splint, but a hot, wet feeling around his foot meant there was definite bleeding.

"We can't handle all of them," growled Ellen. She smacked at Yamamoto's helmet again. "Sick bay. Where is it?"

"I'm..."

Kael certainly had no idea. Instead, he dropped to one knee and eased forward toward the smoke and sound. Maybe he could get a shot in if he got a break in the smoke and light—

A wave of telekinetics blew him back, throwing him into the corridor wall. "Okay, now that is starting to get really annoying."

"You got anything more powerful than some flashbangs?" she asked.

"Rifles. Four of them. More smoke."

"Damn."

Wait—Zhia's book. The command codes. "Hang on. Let me see. Computer—we need assistance against these hostiles."

"All present groups have been given high-level access codes."

"But I'm the commander here," Kael said. "I was first, wasn't I?"

"You were. But you were in the *brig* at the time—"

"They're destroying the ship! And you! You should probably listen to me. Isn't it against Union protocols or something, for an officer to destroy their own ship? *They* should be thrown in the brig."

"Logic accepted. Your orders, Commander?"

He grinned. "I order you to defend us and the ship. Don't you have robots or laser turrets or *something*? Withdraw their access to any doors. They need to be contained."

"And we need to get to sick bay," Ellen added. Her eyes were wide.

"And where is sick bay?" he echoed.

Blue lights lit up along the ceiling. "Robotic defenses deployed. This blue line will take you to sick bay if you follow—"

Before the computer could finish, four figures dropped down from the upper compartment.

He was ready for the wave of energy they threw at him this time, meeting it head on with what little energy he had left, forming a protective shield around the three of them. There were four Therokis, pushing hard, but they weren't at full power any more than he was.

And Elle was firing at their boots.

"If you follow the line," the computer announced, almost shouting at him over the fire, "there are blast doors."

Right. He grabbed another flash and another smoke. "Switch to laser. And get ready to run."

"You grab Yama. I'll cover us!" She flipped the switch. These Union rifles didn't have the non-lethal options *Audacity*'s multis did, but they had the basics, at least.

He threw the smoke grenade, clouds billowing as it made a low arc toward their heads, making one of them instinctively dodge.

While they were focused on that, he launched himself at Yamamoto, scooping up the man and starting to run. His injured leg meant his running was more like an uneven lurching forward. If the muffled cries were any indication, his lurching hurt Yamamoto even more than it hurt him.

He couldn't look back to see if Ellen was behind him. He had to believe she could make it, that she could follow. There wasn't time for backward glances.

He followed the light path on the ceiling and saw the seam as they passed a pair of blast doors.

"Passing blast doors," the computer said.

"Great," he mumbled.

"Closing now."

"Wait! Not without her."

"Sequence already initiated."

"Ellen!" Now he did turn. She was still standing, still in sight.

And still six or eight meters down the corridor.

"Hurry! Ellen, they're—"

Their fire intensified, so he had to duck to one side, slinging Yamamoto along with him.

His stomach might as well have been in his throat as he watched, her arm holding the laser fire behind her, as she sprinted for the already-closing door.

The blast doors began to close, blocking his view of her.

"Wait—" He put down Yamamoto—very unceremoniously—and lunged toward the door, throwing himself between the two metal slabs sliding toward each other. There was barely enough room to straighten one arm, definitely not both, but he braced his shoulders on one side, his hands on the other, and *held*. Gears growled and screeched, objecting to his interference.

She dove and slid.

The doors were like vices closing around him, crushing the armor as he pushed against their force. Fire from the Therokis intensified now, slamming into the side of his armor, warnings of impacts going off in his helmet display like fireworks.

But he held.

Turning on her side, she half-slid, half-pulled herself through the gap.

He dove after her, finally releasing his grip. Part of one gauntlet finger caught in the gap, and he ripped it out savagely. Fortunately only surface damage.

He turned. Yamamoto was on the ground, clutching his shoulder. So was Elle, panting and smoking a little, but her suit looked mostly intact.

"Where'd you get that? The suit," he asked.

"SPV we stole."

"Used," Yamamoto interjected. "Borrowed?"

"Where'd you get yours?" she asked, looking at his armor.

"Ship armory."

"Lucky."

"If I were really lucky, none of us would be injured right now."

Her eyes flicked to his leg, then Yamamoto. "C'mon." She struggled to her feet.

Yamamoto's face was ashen. "It seems you were right. About what I might do under pressure. You never know until it happens, I guess."

"I didn't die, though. And you're not going to, either. So you'll have to find another chance to make your big heroic sacrifice. C'mon." She started to help him to his feet.

"No. No. Leave me be. Get off the ship." He pushed her away with his good arm.

"Shut up. We're going to sick bay."

"No. Listen. You two have suits. You can—"

"Yours is clearly compromised, but we can deal with that in sick bay."

He continued, ignoring her comment. "You can turn off the life-support systems from here. Look at the schematics in my comm, or find me a panel. Then they'll have to work with you."

"They have armor, too," she said.

"Their telepaths don't," Kael pointed out. "I saw one."

"You can—" Yamamoto continued.

"Stop it."

"*No*, Ellen. Leave me. If you get off the ship, they'll go after you. Might lose interest rather than kill me, and I can crawl to sick bay in the meantime."

"You won't live that long."

"If I live that long, you can come back for me. Meanwhile…" He coughed. It sounded wet. Not right. Not good at all. "If you can get me to that control panel, maybe I can direct the ship toward the gate from here. If they haven't taken control of the bridge—"

"No." She gave up trying to coax him up. "Kael, can you carry him, or should I?"

"I got this." He wasn't about to complain about his leg when Yamamoto had a hole through his shoulder.

She started along the path. "We're going to sick bay, Yamamoto, and I don't give a shit if you like the idea."

"But—" Yamamoto started, even as Kael was heaving him into his arms for the second time. This was one order that was easy to follow, even with the injury. Compared to the blast doors, hauling an unwilling but injured Yamamoto was no sweat.

"Nobody gets left behind," she growled. "Let's go."

"RETURN FIRE," Zhia ordered.

Projectiles erupted from the *Audacity*, and it was almost impossible to see if Xi had augmented them with little blue halos.

Adan gave Fern three more shots, then he veered abruptly starboard, heading straight for a bulky asteroid. Xi would help him not clip it. Hopefully. "Augment my course, will ya, Xi?"

Rationally, he knew Xi was still here on board, even though her new body with a copy of her mind had left the ship. Still, it had left a weird hole in him, a worry, especially since her traveling self hadn't responded in quite some time. Where was she? Right here, obviously, but he still had the strange sense that she was lost. Or maybe in danger somehow. So he waited with an odd amount of tension.

"Slightly," she confirmed. "Your trajectory is good. Accommodating for slight celestial body spin. Enemy ship weapons attack detected."

He winced and veered. Nobody needed to yell *evasive maneuvers*. Life was a damn evasive maneuver at this point.

"Let's head for that cluster over there," Zhia pointed.

Blasts lit up the shield interface. Adan tried to keep his attention on where he was flying, but the fact was that enemy fire would *eventually* wear the ship down. Running with them firing at their tail wasn't ideal. He needed more cover, so he accelerated toward Zhia's cluster, wiping the back of his hand across his forehead.

"What are they firing at? That's not—" Zhia's eyes were scanning the feeds.

Too late, he realized. They'd fired at the asteroid directly in front of the *Audacity*, narrowly firing *over* the ship. He'd been planning to duck under that for cover. Stupid, smelly drecks—

That plan became a *whole* lot more complicated as the asteroid shattered into so many different pieces.

"Enemy weapons attack detected," Xi said, for what felt like the thousandth time.

"They're firing on that one too!" Zhia swore.

"I got a good one!" Fern crowed. "They're not the only weapons that are attacking."

The second asteroid exploded apart, then the third. A huge piece of the third remained intact but ricocheted off the other displaced pieces—and headed straight toward them.

Moments later, try as he might to veer to the side, he could hear the tearing, the grating claw of the asteroid across the back end of the ship.

"Hull breach," Xi announced. An alarm blared. "Depressurization in more than ten cargo compartments detected. Permission to close blast doors to cargo hold?"

"Granted," Zhia said quickly. "Anyone in or near there?"

"No, Commander. Repair team deploying."

Adan gritted his teeth. That meant Jenny and Shirin. If one of them got hurt because of Theroki tricks… that whole fragging ship was going to pay.

CHAPTER THIRTEEN

"DON'T BE SO DAMN selfless. You'll bleed out!" Ellen threw up her hands at Yamamoto. "Let the robot work!"

Standing up from the table, where a second med bot had been hard at work on his leg, Kael caught her eye, then inclined his head toward Yamamoto. "Let me talk to him—you search the shelves."

She nodded breathlessly and stepped into their medicine closet. There was no way even the best med bot could fully repair the damage to his calf, but it probably could repair the suit and seal off the bleeding, at the very least. At least his limp seemed less severe as he moved to Yamamoto's side.

Inside the storage area, she searched. Tray after tray, there was nothing. Nothing useful, anyway. Oh, there were common painkillers, allergy medicines, skin glue and tape, vials of nanos for a variety of specialized purposes. But not what she needed.

If she didn't find something good soon, no amount of medical care for Yamamoto was going to matter. The Therokis would eventually blow up the ship or blast their way in here.

Clangs echoed through the ship every so often, followed by thunderous rumblings and creaking and groaning metal. All were constant reminders that they weren't alone.

But if she'd learned anything, it was that a Theroki infestation meant you needed something special.

Tranquilizers. And a hell of a lot of them this time.

More and more trays. Now it was not drugs at all, but scalpels and surgical laser tools. Maybe she could lob a laser scalpel at their heads if the tranqs didn't work out...

It took six more trays before she found it. "Jackpot!"

"What is it?" Kael stepped away from Yamamoto, who was finally not constantly grimacing in pain.

"Tranqs."

"I did not see that coming. For Yamamoto or the Therokis?"

"Therokis. Or the Cassandras. Or just whoever gets in my way."

He grinned. "How are we going to get them to lower their helmets?"

"I—"

"The drugs are kicking in," Yamamoto cut in. "Give me that tablet. Hurry."

"Here." Kael handed him the tablet off a nearby counter. "Why?"

"Send this ship. Toward the gate. Like we said."

"Good," Ellen said. "Do it."

"Therokis won't expect it—ship will pull them along—if I can just do this one thing..." His brow was furrowed and sweaty as he stabbed at the tablet. "Yes, if it works—I can die in peace."

"You're *not* going to die," she snapped.

"We'll see." He smiled at her, oddly, his scowl fading as he hit the last command. "Been a pleasure serving with you, Commander Ryu. Want a candy for the road?" He held out a handful he'd managed to get out of a compartment in his armor. When had he had time to stuff them in there?

Smiling crookedly, she took it. Who knew what the hell this really was, but he was right. This might be her only chance to get her hands on Yamamoto's stash.

He grinned and started unwrapping one as best he could. "Lieutenant Rhee—a rifle, please? In case they reach here? The two of you should go. Leave me."

She took the tablet. Drugged as he was, his orders looked sound. Then again, it was pretty simple, a vector aimed at the gate.

"Do we have a shuttle?" Kael asked.

"An SPV," she replied. "If we can reach it. But I have my sights on something bigger."

He frowned. "Excuse me?"

"We can't get them to take their helmets off here. It's too obvious. But the ships are docked together. Computer, is there shared airflow?"

"Yes," the computer replied. "Their filtration units are handling some of the smoke. This is helpful, because this ship does not currently have adequate filtering capacity for this level of destruction."

"Imagine that. Listen. We all suit up, then we take these tranqs and aerosolize them into the ductwork near the airlock. They want to knock everybody unconscious? Well, two can play at that game."

They were both silent for a second.

"That… just might work." Kael tapped his chin, thinking.

"They probably don't *all* have their armor on while on their home ship at all times."

"You're right. The High Adjutant usually doesn't, and even when he does, the helmet would likely be retracted when he's on the bridge. And as you said, none of the Cassandras seem to have any space suits at all."

"The trick will be getting enough of it, in the right location and concentration—"

A holodisplay beside them came to life. "Based on my calculations, this would be the optimum location for release. Also, you will need aerosolizing equipment." The med bot started to roll toward a cabinet.

Metal clanged down the corridor. A woman's voice echoed.

Ellen picked up the tray of tranqs. No, it was more like a small crate. "Computer, can you tell if we have enough?"

"Estimates only, but—"

"Short answer, please."

"Yes. Approximately."

"Look, here's a second one underneath." Kael picked up a crate of his own. "Computer, light us the way to that release location. In yellow. Something hard to recognize as the path."

The noise in the corridor was coming closer.

"Go now. Good luck. I'll get a breather," Yamamoto said. "Save my colleagues by getting to that asteroid and shutting them all down."

Kael pressed a second spare rifle to Yamamoto's chest. "We will, inshallah."

The med bot held out a small device, almost like an injector.

"Thank you," she said, grabbing it. "And thank you, too, Yamamoto."

They ran.

Out in the corridor, the nearest blast door had a torch burning through it. They spun and went in the opposite direction.

"I will light the path only in your immediate vicinity," said the ship computer.

She glanced up. The lighted segments indeed followed them, maybe six or ten up ahead, pulsing forward as they ran and flashing like emergency signals.

A blast door groaned open in front of them, blue override lights flashing, then it started closing again the minute they passed through.

Moments ticked by, punctuated only by the sound of fighting elsewhere on the ship and their footsteps on the deck. Some part of her knew it was too many, knew Yamamoto had been right, had been realistic as always. Too many moments.

They'd never get all this released and dispersed before their enemies finished torching through the door. Yamamoto might as well already be dead.

He deserved more than this. He deserved a medal. Or a ship of his own. Or to die for something *bigger* than this mess Arakovic had caused. And that she'd caused too. That she'd dragged him into.

All of these people deserved better.

She blinked hard at a hot wetness in her eyes. What good did it do? None. It wouldn't save anybody. She had to shove it back. Shove it down. Later.

Shouting and ballistic gunfire echoed through the ship. She gritted her teeth and ran faster.

KAEL DRAGGED a desk in front of the door to the maintenance room the computer had led them to. His leg was still killing him, in spite of the med kit and treatment the bots had applied in sick bay, but he was doing his best to hide it.

"I hope this fragging works." Crouched near the vent, she was loading a cartridge into the aerosolizer. He hurried closer as she held the tool near the intake fan and pulled the trigger. A faint hiss was almost inaudible over the din in the rest of the ship.

He reached for his own crate, cracked a cartridge into his own aerosolizer gun, and tried to muster a smile. "Well, I hope my suit's not damaged, and I don't pass out right now. The stats claim it isn't, but after that fall…"

"Well, if you want to compete, I hope the computer's right about this med volume and location."

"I hope Arakovic is actually on that damn rock after all this. Your turn."

She snorted. "Do we need to have a hope for every cartridge?"

"Probably. Definitely."

"I hope we still get to go to the snake resort."

"I hope you reconsider the snake part of that idea."'

"I hope I get to have wine again someday."

"That's pretty vague."

"And that's not a hope. What? I'm getting desperate."

He pulled out another. He didn't feel woozy yet, so either his suit was fine, or this plan was not working. "I hope Yamamoto lives."

Her words were hardly above a whisper. "I hope so too."

They were silent for a moment, emptying the cartridges as quickly as they could.

"I hope I can protect you through all this."

"I hope you get off your high horse. I can protect myself."

"So that makes two of us protecting you. Works for me."

"I'm not going to let you hog all the danger."

"There's plenty of danger to go around, I think."

"Slag off, Kael. This is my fight to settle."

"We'll see about that." If there was anything he could do to keep the brunt of the Songbirds from coming down on her, he was going to do it. Whether she liked it or not. How could he live with himself otherwise?

"Hey, now—" She narrowed her eyes.

"Well, I hope Arakovic sees the error of her ways simply by you explaining it to her, gives up her devious plans, and offers us some cake."

"Would you really eat it though?"

"Absolutely not."

"I hope I taste cake again someday."

"I hope I get to taste *you a*gain someday." He smiled at her, and through their visors, he was pretty sure her face was flushed.

After that, they fell quiet. Not much could top that wish, he supposed.

"Computer, how are the tranq levels?" he asked. "Anything?"

"They will affect any unarmored person. I cannot confirm if they have done so yet, though," the ship computer replied.

"Okay, wait, did I hear something about an asteroid? Did the crew on the *Everest* locate its precise location?" he asked.

"Yes, we're close. The *Everest* had nearly reached it, but when Cassandra's powers struck and put everyone to sleep, we turned the ship around and aimed it at the gate. Then we got on an SPV and headed over here."

"So is the asteroid our next stop? How are we going to get in? Take the SPV you rode in on? That rock must have defenses."

"Agreed. A Union shuttle might as well be a pebble tossed at a mountain." She cracked in another cartridge, squeezed, and grinned at him. "That's part of why we needed to go to sick bay."

He frowned. "I don't understand."

"Cause we aren't taking a Union SPV or ship. We're taking a Theroki one."

His eyes widened. "Did you hit your head when that stuff fell?"

"Nope."

"How are we going to control them all? This stuff can't neutralize them forever." Indeed, with scrubbers like all Therokis had, the drugs would last for less time than they would in the average person. Or cause debilitating, enraging pain, as he'd found out recently enough.

"We don't have to get far. Do Theroki ships have shuttles? SPVs? If we can just get by them to get one, then maybe we can sail right past all those defenses. I want to make them think we belong there."

He coughed. "There usually are some surface-to-planet transports, but you never know if they're working. Aside from that gamble, that's a pretty good plan. It might have a slim chance in hell of working, but that is way better than the zero chance my utter lack of a plan had."

She snorted. "Thanks."

"If only we didn't have to get passed… what did you call me once? A bunch of raging homicidal maniacs?"

"I'm certain I never used that term."

He raised an eyebrow.

"Doug, however, might have."

He chuckled. He grabbed another cartridge. There were only a handful left. "Almost there. I hope this works. What's the plan if they don't have an SPV?"

"We murder them all while they're unconscious. Or as many as possible. They can't hang on to the ship if they're dead."

His eyes widened.

"What? I'm hoping we can avoid that."

"Sometimes you scare me, Elle."

"Thanks? I think? You do realize they just tried to do that to you, except you were awake. Isn't that worse?"

"I'm not sure anymore. It's all bad."

"Got any alternative ideas?"

"There is a fortified brig. We might be able to throw some in there, but… not *all* of them. I wish we could just off the Cassandras and free the Therokis."

She frowned. "Me too. We're close enough that that probably wouldn't work. But what if we removed their chips instead? That would take each Theroki off her network."

"Yeah, but it'd take too much time."

"And they would probably still be within her range. Might just end up like the rest of these sleepers."

"Some of them have been connected for months or years. The squad was able to think independently. They might just keep going on the same mission, connected to the hive mind or not."

"True. Could we shut down their part of the network somehow? Make it harder for them to communicate? I wish we could block Cassandra's signal entirely. Do you know the layout of that ship? Or is it an unfamiliar one?"

He frowned. "Computer, what is the name of the Theroki ship that's docked with this one?"

"The *Genokai*."

His stomach sank. "Frag. I know it all right."

"That was your ship, wasn't it?"

"Yes."

"Cross your fingers, then."

"I can't. I'm too busy spraying this stuff into the ventilation system." He jumped as the noise of something mechanical approached.

Elle drew her rifle, but it was only a med bot. She frowned.

"I have located an additional tool for you," the computer offered. "Three tanks of sleeping gas from the armory. Used infrequently for crowd control."

He narrowed his eyes. Infrequently was right. He could see rust on one of the canisters. "Thank you," he said quickly. "That'll come in handy."

Ellen was already unloading them from underneath the bot. "Can we just… open the valve?"

"Yes, I would recommend setting the release valve to seven, which will continue releasing after you leave this area."

"Excellent," Ellen muttered, turning the knobs.

"My cameras can see one soldier collapsed through the airlock shaft," the computer added. "I would proceed with optimism and caution."

He cracked his last cartridge in and sprayed. "Thank you, *Lhotse*. I see you've very much earned your crew's diligence and admiration."

"Thank you, Prisoner and Commander Lieutenant Kael Rhee. Please help my crew return to consciousness. And be okay."

Ellen's shoulders slumped at that. "I'm their target. Maybe when I'm gone, they'll follow and leave you alone." That wouldn't free the crew from Cassandra, but maybe if they made it all the way to the gate…

"I can only hope," said the computer, tone stilted.

"We'll do all we can," he reassured it.

Ellen rose to her feet. "All right. Let's go see if this crazy plan worked."

JENNY WAS BREATHING HARD—MORE out of the adrenaline rush than out of actual exertion. She waved toward Shirin. "C'mon. This way. We're almost there."

They'd already crossed through the airlock in lower engineering and into the depressurized area, with Xi guiding them turn by turn through the maintenance tanks that made up a huge outer layer of the *Audacity*. They just needed to get through to the cargo hold, and they could patch up and repressurize.

"Got your magnets on good?" Jenny asked.

"Yes, ma'am. Are we going to die?" She didn't sound terribly worried about the prospect.

"I dunno. Probably not. Patching this hole will be one mark in the 'likely to live' column. You doin' okay?"

"Yeah, I'm decent."

"You're not afraid of dying?"

Shirin said nothing for a long moment.

"I am," Jenny offered.

"Oh, yeah, I guess I am. But I've been afraid for a long time." She shrugged. "Another day, another death threat. Most of that time, nobody was really trying to protect me. So this is a bit better than normal."

Jenny winced. "What about that bot of yours?"

"EOE8? Oh, yeah, it tries. Only so much a care bot can do."

"Where's it been? I haven't seen it around. Maybe it should be helping us." She grinned.

"Maybe. It's, uh, charging."

She sensed Shirin wasn't telling her the whole story but decided not to push it. "Well, I'm glad you've got more people on your side now. Come on. We're close."

They climbed up the ladder into the cargo hold, magnets on boots and gloves helping them along.

The hole was bigger than she'd hoped. The bots were swarming around the edges, rebuilding and bringing the supplies.

She pointed to the large metal sheets for patching the hull. A stack of them were secured near the far wall. The bots were small and *could* move the metal, but they did so more slowly and less efficiently than a human could.

"We got this." She wasn't sure if she was reassuring Shirin or herself.

Boots clamped to the deck, they each gripped one side of the first alloy sheet and moved toward the gash.

The black void gaped, and Jenny knew for a moment why Mo had politely requested not to ever be assigned this duty.

She usually tried not to think about it, about how much was out there. But now, the sheer number of asteroids emphasized just how much open, oxygen-free space loomed out there.

"Whoa…" Shirin whispered into the comm. "It's beautiful…"

Jenny swallowed. "You're right, it is."

Her view of the deep vanished as the bots seized the edge of the sheet and began welding it to the sheered edge of the hull. Her visor shifted to shield her eyes from the brightness of the welding arc.

"Let's get the next one," she muttered.

Shirin had already started to fetch it, though.

"Wow, you're a natural," Jenny laughed. "You'd think you'd been born here in the deep."

Shirin smiled. "Maybe not. But putting marks in my 'likely to live' column is something I have practice at."

"We do what we got to, to survive, sometimes," Jenny agreed. Not that she'd ever lived in fear for her life for years and years. Fear of meaninglessness and awful people? Yes. Check. But she'd always been as safe as she'd wanted. She'd climbed into danger of her own accord.

At least here, the danger had meaning. And death, if it came, would have meaning too. More meaning than falling during a climbing competition or dying of boredom on Capital. But somehow, watching Shirin work, Jenny felt that sheltered, shallow feeling creeping back again.

She had to make this life worth it. Somehow. Repairing this breach would help, but she was so ready for battle. To *do* something. Make a difference in the world.

You will.

Jenny's hands went still. Whose voice was that? Was it in her head? Was her telepathic defense add-on from Dr. Persad switched off? It couldn't be.

It's Roya. I'm connected to you via our suits, via the computer system. When you are about to head into battle—come find me.

She raised her eyebrows, then hoped Shirin didn't notice. Why would Roya want that? But she nodded to herself. *I will.*

There was no response.

Jenny mustered a smile and tried to blow off the strange interaction. Please let that not be some kind of stress-induced hallucination. She didn't have time for losing control right now. "Two more, and we're done."

Shirin, again, was already one step ahead of her. "We got this!"

ELLEN PEERED AROUND THE CORNER. A hundred meters down the corridor, an ordinary docking tunnel led from the *Lhotse*, shabby as it was, to a cave-like gaping maw that was apparently the *Genokai*.

"See it?" Kael murmured. They'd managed to get the two suits talking to each other on a closed comm so they didn't need to use the speakers.

"Does it usually look like the asshole of hell?"

He snickered. "Yep, that'd be it."

"Very unusual mood lighting. Nobody in sight."

He eased closer. "Guess we just… walk through?"

"What's the worst that could happen?" She shrugged.

"Do you really want me to answer that?"

"No, I can use my imagination. Is the ship computer going to ask for identification?"

"Are you kidding?"

"What?"

"There is no ship computer."

"Oh. All right, then."

"Well, the pilots probably have one, but not one that will try to talk to us."

"Point taken." She took in a breath, held it, and let it out. Was there something she was missing? She'd already made too many mistakes. They couldn't afford another one now. "It seems too easy."

"Well, the security is *supposed* to be the ship full of vicious Therokis."

"How do they handle saboteurs? Spies? Do they have surveillance?"

"The *Genokai* has a manually monitored vid-cam system. Like on Molyarch. Nothing fancy. But if anybody is passed out, that guy is, too. He's probably the least likely person on the whole ship to be armored, especially since, as far as they know, this ship is zero threat to them and he can't leave his post."

"Okay, well, I guess we just stroll in. Let's be on our guard, though. Some of them will have fallen through the cracks. Some who the drugs didn't affect because they had their helmets on."

"True. Let's go knock them out the old-fashioned way."

She smirked. "All right. Therokis first. After you, good sir."

"I'll happily be your meat shield any day, Commander."

"Nonsense. You're more like a burrito shield, with your metal outer layer."

"Mmm, burritos. When was the last time I ate real food? Thanks, Elle, now I'm hungry. And there's definitely nothing I'll risk eating on *that* ship. I miss Amaya."

"Me too."

Their breath seemed loud in her helmet as they eased toward the ship. She felt like she should be sneaking, sticking to the shadows, but what did it matter? There were no real spots to hide in the bare tunnel, and if their plan had failed, they needed to know now so they could high tail it back aboard the *Lhotse* and try something else.

But the computer had been right. A man was sprawled at the entrance to the ship, blue tentacles splayed in paint on his chest, unmoving and eyes closed.

"Well, one down. How many to go?"

"Three hundred? Maybe more?"

"Yippee."

"This way toward the shuttle bay."

"It is… dark in here."

"Light's expensive."

That was true, but lots of ships ran dark much of the time, or at least part of the cycle to synchronize Circadian rhythms. This, though, was something else.

"My boot just stepped in something… slick. Do I want to know what that was?"

"You do not."

They went a few meters and then he started down a ladder toward the next deck down. She followed. Behind the base of the ladder, between there and the wall, was a heap of garbage that set off all sorts of health warnings in her helmet. She turned to follow him.

The corridor was silent, no movement. Kael had paused at an open hatch.

She swallowed. More than once, he'd done that, and it hadn't turned out well. She could still see him back on Upsilon Station, the first time they'd discovered those crazed prisoners who'd been abandoned by Arakovic and almost died. He was standing just the same way now.

He saw Elle watching him and silently pointed inside.

Men were packed into the place like sardines. And every one of them was sleeping like a baby. She gave him a satisfied nod, and he nodded back. Sleeping was good.

They reached another ladder. Part of it was torn away, leaving a gap in the left rail of at least a meter. The right rail smeared something wet and viscous across her gauntlet. At the bottom, she looked at it. Red and something gooey and grayish streaked the dark gray Union-issued metal. Blood?

The suit was quick to inform her that yes, it was at least partly blood, and no, it was not a great thing to have on one's armor.

"You know, all this time, I guess I kinda thought you were exaggerating," she said as she trotted to catch up to him.

"Oh yeah?"

"Yeah. But I see now you were not." They passed half a dozen more Therokis on the ground. They'd been wearing armor but had helmets retracted.

He laughed softly, a smile lingering. "This isn't even immediately after a battle. Home sweet home, I guess."

"Nah, your home is the *Audacity*. This here was a prison."

"*Is* a prison."

"True."

"I guess that's why I'm not feeling the warm and fuzzies on this homecoming tour." He gave her a sidelong smile. "Let's get out of here quickly, then."

"Works for me. How much farther?"

"Almost there."

Abruptly, a voice further up the hallway echoed in the quiet. "What the frag are they doing on the bridge? Having a party without us? Nobody's responding."

Kael eased into an open hatch, and she followed. "Somebody's awake."

"Question is, how many?"

She held her breath, trying to listen.

"Something's not right," another voice replied. "Someone should be at comms."

"They probably just went to take a piss."

"At least two," Kael murmured. "But who knows?"

"Any chance you can still access the surveillance or vid feeds?" she asked.

"Nope. It'd be keyed into my suit."

"Well, unless we want to try some other part of the ship, onward."

He nodded. "I still have one smoke grenade from the *Lhotse*. This seems as good a time as any."

"Get it ready—let's go." She slipped to the other side of the corridor, staying close to the wall.

"At least the dark provides some element of surprise."

"Gotta count your blessings."

Step by step, they made their way to the edge of the shuttle bay. But as her view widened through the extra-large hatch, her stomach sank. There were at least two dozen Therokis working on a pair of small shuttles, walking the perimeter, and manning a handful of consoles.

"Frag. That's way too many," Kael said.

He was right. "They have their helmets on *because* it's the shuttle bay. The fields could fail, and conditions could change without warning."

"Yep, and they probably do, because who really cares if you forget to tell somebody and they get sucked out into space? They'll just find somebody else."

She winced at that. She eyed the two hanging around a comm console. They were probably the voices they'd heard trying to contact the bridge.

The non-responsive bridge.

She raised an eyebrow. "I think I have a better idea. Do you think you could get us to the bridge?"

His helmet swiveled to look at her, but the reflection on his faceplate from the light in the docking bay blocked her view of his face. "I can find the bridge. If we can get there depends on how many conscious Therokis we come across. What would we do on the bridge?"

"Let's see if we can make it there first."

He tilted his head in a new direction. "This way."

They hurried away down a corridor, up another ladder, which was marginally more functional and cleaner than the last, and turned a corner.

And came face to face with a suit of armor, helmet and all. All three of them froze.

Kael spoke first. "Erselai—what the frag are you doing here? MRM Manual Reg 147261-B clearly says that at these hours, this corridor is off limits for toxin testing. Gonna be acid spray any minute now."

The suit of armor swore. The voice was younger than she expected, young enough to crack with nervousness. The armor looked less mauled than she'd usually seen. A young one? "Sir, sorry, sir—"

"Get out of here before you get hurt," Kael snapped.

The armored kid hurried around them and down the ladder. They both watched for a second to make sure he was really gone, then Kael started forward again.

"Did anyone else ever read those handbooks other than you?" She followed him.

"Not clear. I'd wager against it. Maybe the Therokis that wrote them?"

"A man after my own heart. So to speak. Does that regulation even exist?"

"Nope." He grinned, but his grin faltered as he turned the next corner. "There—that's the bridge."

"Gee, it'd be nice if that hatch were already open, so we'd know what we're dealing with." She sighed.

"Maybe it's a party, and they'll invite us in?"

"A barbecue, possibly. Of us. All right, let's rip off the blasted Band-Aid."

Rifles ready, they eased to either side of the door, out of sight, and Kael hit the palm pad.

The hatch whispered open. Nothing moved. Nothing happened.

From Ellen's angle, she could only see a man asleep on a console. "Can you tell if they're all out?"

"Everybody I can see is down."

"Okay—go."

He spun round the corner, ready to fire. She came right up beside him. But it was true—every one of them was sprawled out on the floor.

"Well, here we are. Bridge delivery, undetected." Kael scanned the place, frowning. "Now what the frag do we do?"

"We throw them all out of here, seal the doors, and fly this craft into the asteroid."

"What?" He turned slowly toward her, eyes wide. "They'll wake up eventually. They'll rush the doors."

She was grabbing a Theroki's hand and dragging him toward the hatch. Slowly. "Agh. Heavy. Then we better seal the doors, I guess."

He looked at her a second longer, then grabbed the nearest comm operator by the collar. "We better work fast." His gait had seemed fairly normal on the way over here, but she could sense a limp, an unevenness, that told her the injury to his leg was still bothering him.

As he reached for the next one, she held up a hand. "Wait. Let's take his armor. Might be able to use it for something to get in? He looks about your size. We can't put it on yet, but…"

"Might come in handy. All right. I'll haul the others. You strip him."

She shook her head as she moved toward the man. "Just what a girl likes to hear from her boyfriend."

"Aw, you called me your boyfriend. You want to switch jobs?" he said as he caught another one and dragged him toward the hallway. He waggled his eyebrows at her. "I could strip him, if you'd prefer."

"I'm on it, I'm on it. You're the one with the augments. And you need to get ready to figure out how to fly this beast."

"Fly it? Are you serious? No way. That's all you. These fancy augmentations are going to be sealing the doors shut."

"Me flying twice in twenty-four hours? What is the world coming to?"

"*You* flew the two of you over here? And I missed it? And you *survived*?"

"Get hauling, Lieutenant!" She groped along the arm for the emergency suit release. This suit in particular had a scar right through the cephalopod on its chest. That should come in handy for recognizing him in the crowd later. "We have some doors to seal. Maybe a torch could melt it shut? Or can you disable the motors that power the hatch?"

"Disabling motors… Does that mean I can punch holes in the wall?"

"You betcha."

"Nice. On it!"

CHAPTER FOURTEEN

ONCE EVERY CREW member was tossed unceremoniously out into the hallway, Kael came back in the bridge and shut the hatch, carefully studying the walls on either side of it. The motors that retracted them should be right about… here. He slammed his fist into the wall, grabbed whatever he found there, and pulled.

A shower of sparks danced in his wake, and a number of cables now snaked out of the hole he left behind. He dropped the sleek motor on the deck and moved to the other side.

"You've chosen the brutal but direct route, I see." Ellen was sitting at the comm console now.

"Would you expect anything less?"

"I was thinking kill it with fire, but that works."

His fist dove into the other wall and yanked out more electrical entrails. "Oh, I'm just getting started."

"Where the frag is the comm console?" Ellen muttered, maybe to herself.

He scanned the place, then pointed. He'd only been on the bridge a handful of times, but he knew what the Theroki comm consoles looked like on shuttles well enough. "Over there. Who are you hailing?"

"Wait and see."

He shrugged. Motors were out of the wall—and on the floor. Now, maybe he could find a torch to melt the actual metal in a key spot or two and make things tougher for anyone trying to reach them.

There *should* be a repair kit around here that included a laser torch or something like it. Whether it had all the proper tools inside—that was a different question. He headed toward what looked like the engineering console. Kneeling down, he found a panel that slid open, revealing a haphazard collection of small crates. He sighed. If there was a repair kit or a torch somewhere, it'd be here, but they weren't making it easy.

The light flickered in the room—the viewscreen turning on. He frowned. Who was she contacting? Paul definitely wasn't answering. There was nobody; they were on their own.

But when he heard that familiar voice suddenly break through the silence, he jumped so fast, he slammed the back of his helmet against the panel.

If this mission had proven anything, it was that helmets were good. Helmets were wonderful.

He backed out part way and straightened hastily to see Zhia's and Adan's faces huge on the viewscreen.

"Commander! I almost didn't answer!" Adan was laughing.

"*Audacity*, you are a sight for sore eyes," she said, smiling.

"Adan, where are you?" Kael asked, looking back and forth between them and Ellen. "How far?"

"Right in your backyard. Just playing hide and seek with some Theroki scum. No offense."

"None taken."

"And what the hell are you two doing? Are you in control of that whole dreck-encrusted ship?"

"Nope, but we are in control of the bridge." Ellen spread her arms wide like she was going in for a hug. Or inviting them to a Theroki buffet.

"I don't know how you pull these things off, Commander."

"Pull off? More like stumble into them, surprised to be alive. This is about all we're in control of, though, and unfortunately, neither of us is a pilot. So… I called the best pilot I could think of."

"Did you forget about me, Commander?" Fern's voice came over *Audacity*'s ship-wide comm.

"Not at all, Fern. I just know we also need an excellent gunner. Since the *other* one ran off with some girl…" She glared playfully at Kael.

"That dude really needs to reconsider his priorities." He shook his head, keeping his face serious as a tombstone.

Adan grinned and rubbed his hands together and shifted forward in his seat. "Say no more, Commander. Can you widen security authorizations on the channel?"

"I have no idea."

"Look for the admin console."

"I see something that says that."

"Hit it. Okay, good— Let me call Doug to help. We can fly it from here. Probably. I think."

Zhia raised a skeptical eyebrow. "You're going to fly two ships at once?"

"No." Adan pointed at the ceiling. "Xi will have to autopilot one. Or I can take turns? What else are we going to do?"

"Smash both ships into an asteroid?"

"Isn't that the goal?" Adan's grin widened.

"I could do with a little less smashing and a little more controlled landing," said Ellen. "But beggars can't be choosers. With this ship, I'm hoping the computers might let us through the force fields because we're supposed to be there. They must already know we're running around in here, but not necessarily that we're flying the ship. Maybe we can get in there before anyone realizes they should lock us out."

"We'll work fast," Adan said. "I'm already in, and I've located the piloting interface. Just gotta get permission."

Kael's astonishment apparently chose that moment to wear off, because he abruptly remembered he still needed that blowtorch. He could dig through the crates and boxes while he listened. He found the nearest one and groped around for the clasps that held it closed.

"We're going to have to break away from the *Lhotse*." Adan frowned at several controls at once. "The airlocks *should* automatically close at decompression, minimizing losses. But it won't be instantaneous."

Kael winced. He wouldn't bet on either of these ships being in perfect working condition, but they had no other choice. He refocused on working on his crate.

"Do what you have to do. The Songbirds won't be any kinder to them than the vacuum." She paused, glanced at him, then continued. "Or we can try to run over there and close it manually and hope most Therokis are still sleeping."

A crash sounded somewhere inside the ship, which seemed to indicate that that was unlikely. Or maybe it was only the sound of the tube breaking off.

Kael worked faster. The moments of silence ticked past, feeling loud like as a roaring fire in his ears.

"Breaking away now." Adan's voice was strained.

"Do you have civilians on board?" Ellen asked.

The lid of his crate came open, but Kael went still. Civilians. Seven suns, they didn't bring Shirin with them, did they? And what kind of father was he that he was only thinking about this *now*?

"We let most of them off at Molyarch Station, although we did get into a tussle there and have some damage to the hull as a result. Doug is still onboard, and so is Shirin."

He gritted his teeth as he forced himself to keep looking. He didn't know what to do with the information anyway. Yell about it? Swear? Yeah, maybe swearing would help. He swore, and then he swore again. This was just some electrical tools for repairing consoles. He needed something that would melt steel.

Zhia cleared her throat. "I left the choice up to her, and she wanted to help. I got her a suit of armor in her size in case of depressurization."

"Well, at least there's fragging that," he muttered to himself. It did make him feel a little better, though. He gave up on that crate and moved to the next one, taking out his frustration on the clamps.

He froze. Inside, among a ratty nest of wires and garbage were some small silvery lumps in a clear case with a danger icon on the outside.

Plasma explosives. He leaned in and looked closer at the labeling —seven suns, what were they *doing* storing explosives randomly with the tools under the console? Unless these were being hidden, kept a secret for some less-than-wholesome end?

Scowling, he carefully set those aside for later and reached for the next box. More delicately this time.

Frag, why had they allowed Shirin to stay on board? If he had a problem with it, it was his own stupid fault for not sticking around— or saying something sooner. But what say did he have in it anyway? She had a right to her own decisions. He was a fragging stranger.

But if her decision was to follow him into danger… What then? Didn't that make it his fault if she died?

The next box relented, and the clamps fell open, a shiny if weathered blowtorch inside. As if to say, there was no way out of this but through.

He could think about what he *should* have done if he lived that long.

"All right then." Ellen blew out a loud breath. He could hear the seat creak as she leaned back to think. "All set. Follow us toward the asteroid. Ignore the Therokis if you can. The sooner we can stop Arakovic, the sooner our Union comrades can wake up and actually pilot their ships again."

"If we can get through the force fields with them thinking this ship is friendly," he said as he headed toward the hatch with the torch, "then maybe we can disable the defensive battery and let the *Audacity* in too?"

"We may as well try." Ellen stood. "As long as the force field stands, there are three field generators remaining. The *Everest* took out one. Target those to start."

"Commander," said Xi, "I have located a thirty-meter gap in the force field around the destroyed field generator. It's narrow. But you might be able to enter there."

"That'll be our tactic then if they don't open sesame. Adan, head for that gap. Hopefully, they'll lower the fields before we reach it."

"You got it, Commander," Adan said. "Xi and I are setting your trajectory. Looks like we're in."

"They're letting the *Genokai* through, based on its sig," Doug put in. "But the asteroid's hangar-bay computers are a different story. The security is significantly more complex. We'll keep at them, but we might need you to manually open a port for us to exploit."

"How do we do that?" he asked, pretending he didn't notice how dirty that sounded.

"Got any nukes? Portable drives? Storage sticks?"

They looked around. "I don't see anything," Ellen replied.

Doug sighed. "Okay, well... This is a long shot, but if you can find the security bot system, shut it down. It should be under System Maintenance Utilities."

"Security bot system? Like, should we be expecting robots?"

"No, he means computer bots," Adan replied. "Look for anything security and just set it all to off."

Kael shook his head. Yeah, real precise strategy. He might as well just use a shotgun on the console. "We'll do our best. We're going to need your help in there."

"Two to two thousand isn't a great ratio," she agreed. "We'll look for somewhere to hole up and wait for you, but it might not be possible. If we have to, we'll head to the center and do everything we can to find Arakovic."

"We're on our way," Zhia replied.

Ellen looked at him. "It's show time, Kael. Ready to play the part of a Theroki one more time?"

He ignited the torch. Anyone outside, of course, would be able to torch their own way through the hatch, but at least this would stop simple Theroki fingers or a crowbar. "Why do I always get typecast in that role? Is it my massive shoulders? My rugged jawline?"

"It's your bubbly personality."

"And your absolute lack of a temper!" Adan called out.

"Slag off, Adan." He strode to the door. As he started in on melting the seam, he could already hear voices and boots pounding distantly outside. "I think they're on their way here—whoever's awake. Maybe we better go silent."

"I'll cut the comm. Fly us in, Adan."

Adan wiped his forehead with the back of his hand. "That's a lot of faith, Commander. I hope I can live up to it."

"Hey, it'll be better flying than *I* can do. See you on the inside."

Zhia nodded. "Look forward to fighting at your side once again, ma'am."

"If governments won't police science," Ellen said briskly.

A chorus of voices answered. "Science will police itself."

"Godspeed."

ELLEN TOOK up a defensive position by the comm console as Kael finished melting the door seam and hurried to join her, trying to keep quiet. Neither her armor nor his had the sound dampening of their Foundation armor, but it was quiet enough compared to the ruckus the Therokis in the hall were making. She switched her voice channel to inside the suits, turning the speakers off, and he did the same.

Kael pointed his rifle toward his handiwork. "That won't hold them forever. But the damage to the wall with the motor might block the door panels so they have to bend them back."

"Let's hope we don't need long, I guess."

"Or that they don't just decide to grenade the place."

"Grenade the *bridge*? Won't that destroy the ship, effectively?"

"Yes, but do *they* realize that? Do you think it's the cream of the crop manning the shuttle bay?"

"We're in for it."

The first thunderous pound on the door came. "Who the frag's in here?"

"All right, two questions," Kael said.

"Shoot."

"One, how do we know when we're through the asteroid's force field? Two, once we're through, and maybe docked somehow, how do we get off?"

"And do we wait to get through the force field to get off? Or do we make our way toward the escape pods now?"

"Well, I can answer that one. There aren't any escape pods, so..."

"Seriously? What is this, the *Titanic*?"

"The what?"

"Doesn't matter. The ship has no emergency evac?"

"It does, but the pods were all launched already. We passed them on the way here. Looks like some folks were smart enough to have their heads straight and their helmets on. And those folks *also* had the intelligence to get the frag out of here when their COs and everyone else abruptly passed out on the floor. Rare opportunity, that one."

"Well then. Clearly, the smart people in this situation are gone. That just leaves us and the dumb ones?"

"I like to think of it as just people with a death wish."

"That's fair. Let me see what this nav console shows." She crept slowly toward it, trying to stay quiet. The voices continued out in the corridor but no one seemed to be trying to get in yet. Why try if there was nobody inside but a bunch of sleeping fools? "Looks like we're closing in on the field. It's still up. He's veering toward the broken field generator."

She was still crouched and hurrying back toward Kael when she heard the hum of the viewscreen turning on.

And it was *not* Adan. "*Genokai,* you are disobeying orders. Your units are not responding. What are you—" The Theroki stopped short as Ellen stood up and faced him. "You."

She bared her teeth in a cold grin and switched her voice to the external speaker. "Hi, there. Your friends are taking a nap."

"What? How?"

"What, you don't like it when it happens to you? Must've been really tired, I suppose. You should probably not work them so hard. Now, are you people going to let me land this thing so we can smash each other's faces in with our fists like civilized people, or are we just going to play chicken?"

"Chicken?"

"Whose shields are stronger, the *Genokai*'s or the asteroid's? Would you like to find out which ones give out first when I ram this thing into you? Of course, you can try to stop us, but you'll kill more of your people than mine if you blow up the *Genokai*."

He rolled his eyes. "Replaceable. Worth the price of firing on these Unionies instead." He cut the comm.

"Wait— Dammit."

Kael stood up. "They don't care if they kill everyone on every single one of these ships, probably their own included. We do."

"Caring. It's a weakness, what can I say?" She propped her hands on her hips, scowling at the floor.

The voices outside had risen and then gone quiet again. He pointed in their direction. She nodded and switched her voice back to their inner-suit channel.

"Can we get a map of the *Genokai*?" he asked.

Stepping toward the consoles, she prodded a few controls until one sprang into the air, outlined in amber light.

"Here." He pointed. "That's where we are, near the center."

"Good position for a bridge. Less likely to sustain impact from external volleys."

"We came up this way past the docking bay. Here are the evac pods we passed."

"What's this?"

"Water storage. Purification."

A small thud, then a scraping at the door.

"Now that we've gone quiet, they're trying to get in. Wondering what that woman's voice was." She shook her head. "I should have ignored him."

"They'd have tried eventually anyway when they realized we were coming in hot."

"Do we go back the way we came? Or another way? This looks like a ventilation shaft. Electrical conduit..." She raised an eyebrow as he strode away from her and returned with a small box. "Tools?"

He flipped open the lid. "Something a little more... volatile."

Her eyes widened. "That's enough to blow the docking bay clean off. What were they doing with it *there*? Why would they store that *here*? Jesus!"

"In truth? Maybe stealing it. Or just being really irresponsible. It's 50-50 chance of either, if you ask me."

"Doesn't matter now."

"We could plant this behind us as we move toward the outside. We'll lose contact with Adan, but hopefully, he can get us passed the force field before it blows."

"Are you suggesting we just... explode part of the ship and jump out?" She arched an eyebrow.

"Yep. Pretty much."

"Why use a scalpel if a sledgehammer will do? Fine. Do you know how to set those?"

"Not half as well as you do, I'm guessing. I can tear a whole in the wall over there that leads to the outer corridor though. Or the ventilation shaft."

"How about the floor? They'll hear where we are if we emerge just down the hall."

"Let me get the torch. You take the explosives."

Shaking her head all the while, she carefully accepted the pack of explosives, set it on the console, and removed one charge. There were three in total, but this one alone would be enough to devastate the *Genokai*. After a charge detonated, this ship would be little more than another floating space rock with bodies in it. Ideally, they'd have landed before it went off, but she doubted they had that much time.

She shifted toward the nav console. The fields were still up, but Adan was flying the ship into the gap near the downed generator. She flipped through a few of the viewscreen settings.

A feed of the asteroid's hangar bay came into view. Based on the angle, the *Genokai* must be slowly drifting into the farthest right-hand bay in the hangar.

On the other side of the hangar, two shuttles and one fighter were parked, pointed in their direction, parked perpendicular to the field and the atmospheric seal that held out the vacuum.

There was probably room for two more ships the size of the *Genokai* in the hangar, maybe only one. The *Audacity* would have no trouble finding a spot, but if the other Theroki ship abandoned the *Everest* and tried to dock, it'd get crowded.

Stairs out front led to a raised platform where command and service consoles lined the walls, separated in the middle by a wide set of heavy blast doors. Four or five dozen Therokis stood on the platform, line after line, waiting.

She swallowed. It was too many. Way too many. She needed the shuttles from the *Everest*, the rest of her own crew, and support from the *Lhotse*. She had none of it. They were all alone.

A woman stood behind them, on the other side of a force field, a vivid blue cloak on her shoulders. Ellen caught her breath. She'd know that cloak anywhere. The atmospheric seal must be working, because she appeared to be breathing air. The hair was blonde, though, and where was the glow in her eyes? Was that really her?

"Kentt…?" she whispered. No, it couldn't be Etrianala Kentt. Could it?

Kael had carved a semi-circle into the floor and had started tossing sheets of metal and wiring toward the hatch, but he paused and looked up. "What in all the hells is that? Or should I say who?"

She zoomed in on the woman. Her eyes were a flat, dull blue, with no sign of their augmented sparkle. Was it someone else wearing a cloak strangely like Kentt's? Kentt's sister? Had Kentt been a plant all along, a spy for the Songbirds?

"It doesn't seem like her, but…" Kael scratched his head as the woman waved for a dozen Therokis to follow her. Most of them remained behind. She headed out through the two large blast doors, which sealed behind them as the group vanished from sight.

"Now just where are they going?" Ellen muttered to herself.

"Who knows?" He sprinted back toward the hole he'd nearly finished and started stomping through the weakened metal.

"Guess we better start the party." She dashed toward the door. The Therokis outside had burned halfway through the hatch door in one spot, but not enough to get through. Yet.

"You mean, this isn't already your idea of a party?"

"You Therokis and your weird celebrations."

He snorted.

She bent and placed the explosive, pushing in one wire and pressing the release safety. She twisted to look at him, still on one knee. "You through? You ready?"

He nodded and, without warning, jumped down and out of sight.

She pushed in the other pin, set its timer to connect in sixty seconds, and sprinted after Kael.

"I CAN FREE THEM," a voice suddenly said, just behind him. "The Union forces."

Doug jumped, then strained to look over his shoulder. He'd been so lost in his work, he'd forgotten where he was, who was with him, pretty much anything but the inner workings of the computer systems of the *Audacity*, the *Genokai*, and the asteroid they were trying to hack their way into—with little luck.

The empress had unbuckled herself and moved forward, but he couldn't have heard her correctly. Even in just a few days, Roya looked ridiculously older, but she was still toddler-esque. Maybe four human years at best. It was constantly disorienting. He frowned. "Pardon?"

"It's an *Alarus* that has the Union forces subdued," Roya said. "I can… release them. Wake them up."

He frowned. "Well, then, by all means, proceed."

"Well, I'll need to go out of this chamber to do so."

"Whoa, wait a minute. Are you sure? What if they attack you? Psychically or something?"

"That is a risk I am willing to take to enable us to win the larger battle. But that is not the only risk. Once I have left this safe zone, as you've suggested, they will sense me. That may make them more interested in our vessel—if they're smart."

Mo sat beside him with her arms folded across her chest. "I don't see a problem with that. Drawing their attention would be a good thing."

"Yeah, that's why we're here, to get into the thick of it," he agreed. "That's what we signed up for."

"Yes. That's why we're here. To set things right. So, may I have your permission to try?"

He hesitated, although he wasn't sure why. Her voice still unnerved him, even now. For a while, she had relied on telepathy, her tiny mouth not quite able to form words and use language as well as her mind. But her skill had quickly accelerated, especially as she focused on it.

Doug drew in a long breath, then let it out. He glanced at Mo.

"I'd do it," Mo said simply.

He nodded. "That settles it then. Worth a try. Having the Union back in the action would probably be superior to just trying to keep them all from getting blown up… Probably."

"Excellent. Open the hatch, and I will go."

"Wait," Mo said, unbuckling her harness. "You should suit up if you're going to move around. We're near the center of the ship in here, but if there's another hull breach and you're not strapped down, you should have your suit on."

Roya nodded. Together, the two of them had her suited up in a child-size suit in less than ninety seconds. He still couldn't believe the large blue eyes, cute nose, and wispy hair belonged to an ancient creature, far older than most humans, definitely far older than her body. The little suit added some dignity, looked less cherubically innocent. And if it kept her from getting killed, all the better.

"Smart choice, that," he said, pointing at the suit.

"Zhia's been around the block a few times," Mo mumbled. "Where will you go once you leave this cabin?"

"I will go to the bridge," Roya said. "This cabin has the best vid feed, but the bridge is the next best option."

Doug laughed softly. "Hey, if I can get my hands on a feed, why not put it up on the wall?"

They slid the hatch open, and Roya strode out into the corridor, then turned toward the bridge. He glanced at Mo, who was staring after the girl even after the hatch slid closed.

"Think she can really do it?" he asked, not because he had any real doubt but more to make conversation. Mo should know better than to trap herself in a small compartment with him. He liked to think she was growing to like his chatter, but this wasn't exactly a good time to ask if there was any truth to that.

"Probably? She has no reason to lie." Mo sat back down and buckled in.

"Let's hope she's right…" He swiveled and pulled up his keyboard. "I wonder…" He started tapping away.

"What? You wonder what?"

"I wonder if I can get to a vid feed inside—so we can see."

She snorted. "Just because he could, he never stops to think if he should…" But her tone was joking. Damn, if something happened to her, he would miss this…

Don't think about that, he reminded himself. Think about the standard Union protocols. Feed in the entry-key database, the really good one he didn't use too often so it didn't encourage them to update their entry keys… Smart security would be to change them automatically every so often, but if Doug had learned anything about people and computers… it was that being "smart" and "proactive" were pretty fragging rare.

It took a few minutes, but he got a feed. He would have tried it sooner, but comm officers who were actually *conscious* would have booted him out quickly using this very obvious method. Considering they were passed out on their asses at the moment, that altered the situation, and he was treated to an excellent livestream.

"Did we bring any popcorn?" He pushed the feed to one side and checked on the scripts he had running, trying to break into the asteroid's information systems. No luck so far.

Mo snorted. "I can't believe you got in there."

"If Roya wakes them up, it won't last."

Mo flipped through all the various feeds in silence for a few minutes, while he went back to his work. Maybe he should check the version numbers of the operating systems on their life-support and defense systems. If something was out of date, there might be a known vulnerability. Did telepathic cults remember to update their heating and cooling computer systems?

Just as he was reaching into the bottom of his desk for another cylinder of Amaya's non-alcoholic piña coladas, he heard a gasp. He whipped his head around to look where Mo was pointing. On the screen, one of the *Everest* crew had sat upright.

"It's happening." A smile tugged at Mo's lips. "It's Roya. She's fighting back against Cassandra. Look, she's waking them up."

Another officer struggled to her feet. A man on the floor rubbed his head. He tapped the glass rhythmically, cycling through the feeds. All over the *Everest,* crew were waking up, confused and weary.

"I don't know how that little girl-alien-hybrid did it, but anything that breaks Cassandra's hold is fine by me." Doug rubbed his hands together and hit the comm button. "Zhia? Permission to hail the *Everest* and speak with Captain Dealis?"

"Captain Dealis? He's awake?"

"Roya didn't tell you? She said she was headed to the bridge. That she could free the Union ships from the *Alarus's* control."

"That's the first I'm hearing of it. She's not here. But by all means —contact the *Everest.* Might as well take credit if we had some hand in that."

Something twisted in his gut. Like Mo had said, Roya didn't seem to have any reason to lie. She could have said she was heading anywhere, but she'd said the bridge.

And yet… she wasn't there. Had something happened on the way?

"If you're hailing him, you better relay some bad news," Zhia said.

He frowned. "What news?"

"He's got company. Look at the gate."

Doug shook his head. One emergency at a time. He'd talk to Dealis, then he'd break into that darn asteroid and get it to cooperate, and then he'd figure out where Roya had wandered off to. One at a time.

He hit the key to hail the *Everest* and waited, fingers drumming against the cold glass.

WHEN PAUL SAT UP, he felt like his head should be pounding. He put one hand to his temple. What the hell had happened? Had he passed out?

All around him, the entire crew was on the deck with him. He glanced around. The entire crew except…

Ellen.

"Yamamoto, where is—" He bit off his words. His second was missing too. He struggled to his feet. Confusion seemed to be the predominant condition on the bridge. "Gutierrez—what is going on?"

"I was hoping you knew, sir," he groaned back.

"Get me intel. What's going on out there? *Now*," he snapped.

People scrambled back to their stations. The comms officer immediately caught his attention. "Sir, there's a ship hailing us. Was that here before? The… *Audacity*?"

"The…" He swore, his eyes widening. "If they had anything to do with my missing prisoner." He swore again.

"Should we answer, sir?"

"Yes, fine, yes." Paul couldn't keep himself from rattling off questionably effective orders in the seconds of time between his agreement and the viewscreen kicking on. "Seal off that sector. Get me the distance to the asteroid. Why are we pointed at the gate now instead? Who issued these orders? Switch to backup filtration." The viewscreen blipped on, but he didn't slow down the stream of demands. "Oh—you. What do you want? And where the frag is Ellen Ryu?"

The young man with gold glasses smirked. "What, did you lose her?"

Paul let out a string of curses almost as colorful as the other man's shirt.

"I'm surprised you have such an… expansive vocabulary of expletives, Captain."

"Usually, I don't. But I have..." He straightened, trying to find decorum. In truth, a little break in decorum reminded your crew you were human. It could be useful. It wasn't always bad to say what he knew they were all thinking. But now it was time to get back under control. "I have a few emergencies at hand. We need to find Ms. Ryu. What do you want?"

"I wanted to check if our little experiment worked."

"Your little… what?"

"Listen." The young man steepled his fingers. "The Songbirds have a… let's call it a telepathic super weapon. If you come in close enough range, they can use it to take telepathic control of almost anyone. They used it on you. Somewhat luckily for you, all they had you do was go to sleep."

He shuddered. "Gutierrez, remind me to request opsepium plating for the ship when we reach the naval yards. I'm so sick of telepaths."

"I will, sir. If we live that long, sir."

"So they knocked us down. But we're back up again. You're saying that's thanks to you?"

"We… nullified the effects, let's say. With our own sort of weapon."

"How?" he demanded.

"That's our proprietary technology, Captain Dealis. I am not at liberty to share."

Paul narrowed his eyes. Lawyer speak. Great. He didn't have time for this. "I have no idea what you're talking about, but it will have to wait. Assuming you're telling the truth, thank you for your assistance. Now, do you have any more useful 'proprietary weapons' on board your little vessel?"

The young man's grin was feral, almost catlike. "A few."

"Then let's go kick some mutual enemies in the hindquarters, shall we?" That… had sounded better in his head.

The young man snorted lightly, smiling. "There's just one issue."

"Yes?"

"We have a new enemy arriving. The gate is active right now."

Paul groaned. "Of course we do. Better get shooting then." He hoped the *Audacity* would forgive his shortness, but this was no time for casual repartee. "Did you need anything else, *Audacity*?"

"No, Captain. Do you?"

"Luck. And to win."

"Can't guarantee that, but I can promise we'll go down fighting. Good luck."

"Same to you, *Audacity*." He glanced at his comms officer, who nodded and cut the channel.

"You need to see this, sir." The operations officer split the screen, so that one half showed the *Audacity* and the other half showed their view of the gate. "We're barreling toward the gate—and whoever's coming through it.

"Who set this course?"

"Lieutenant Yamamoto, sir."

How had he been able to set a course when everyone else was unconscious? Had he chosen this course to try to free them, get them to safety? Had to be.

But Yamamoto hadn't counted on a new addition to the battlefield. As they watched, a familiar ship emerged from the gate, and Paul swallowed. Yeah, there was no way he was getting out of this without lawyers. Many lawyers. Possibly jail time.

Because the new ship was the *Volga,* commanded by his CO, Colonel Tauber. Who was also supposed to be at Freedom's Wing. But somehow, some way, Tauber was here instead.

Ellen had been right about him. He now knew that, and she knew that, but that didn't mean either of them would survive this.

"Reverse course. We can't flee," he ordered. "Where are the two Theroki ships?"

"One is—or was—docked to the *Lhotse.* The one that had been chasing us changed course and has almost arrived at the asteroid."

He'd have to leave the ship closest to the *Lhotse* to Captain Weyer and hope that her crew had also been resuscitated. "Were you able to reach the *Lhotse,* at all?"

The comms officer nodded. "They've sustained more damage, sir. Therokis on board. They'll be busy with them for a while."

"Tell them we're headed to the asteroid. I'll trust Weyer to dispatch her Theroki adversaries and their ship. You all have your orders. Let's carry them out. Proceed with the plan Ryu worked on with us. If my hunch is correct, she is still following the plan too. She's just a few steps ahead of us now." He sighed. "As usual."

"Permission to ready the shuttles, Captain."

"Permission granted. Go. Now. Faster. We can do this."

The viewscreen switched to a full view of the *Volga,* headed straight toward them. Tauber hadn't commed, and Paul was almost grateful for that. There was nothing to say. His CO was a traitor. He just wished he had some actual concrete proof of that. Otherwise, the only one getting his hindquarters kicked in the long run would be *him.*

He reached for his comm. Maybe Shu had found something in the files she'd received and poured over from the *Audacity.* She hadn't been impressed with the file organization system, so her perusal had been taking a while.

Before he could comm her, though, the ship was jolted to the side, and he had to grab on to the edge of the console for balance instead. "What was that?" he demanded.

"The *Volga,* sir. They're firing on us."

"*Firing*? Without hailing?"

"Yes, sir. Another round is coming."

"Increase speed. Adjust shields according to protocols." They already knew what to do, he was probably just wasting their time. And confusing them.

He zipped his lips. Let them do their work. He'd done his.

As worried as he was, as he thought about it and watched his crew buzzing like bees in a hive, he slowly, gradually started to smile.

He'd gotten his lawyerly paperwork in line to come here. Sure, he'd used nepotism and a loophole of power and probably owed favors for the rest of his life. But Colonel Tauber had just fired on a Union vessel in good standing, a vessel on a very important, special Senatorial mission.

Maybe Paul would get out of this with his hindquarters intact after all.

CHAPTER FIFTEEN

MO HAD SPENT most of the mission so far strapped into a spare harness in the storage closet with Doug and the others. As the minutes crawled by, she knew she needed to leave soon, but she was determined to wait as long as she could, as long as it made sense. It wouldn't be good to keep opening the door over and over to see what was going on. She could watch the action from here just the same as she could out there.

But outside this little closet, she'd be waiting alone.

Doug had every wall display showing scripts streaming by, databases, and log-in screens, as well as several different ship exteriors. He had a couple of holo displays going too. One feed even came from a nearby satellite.

He'd always had a lot to say, and he spoke as he worked, telling her what he was doing. About a tenth of it made sense. For once, instead of marveling at the sheer volume of words, she just felt them wrapping around her, like a warm, fuzzy blanket she didn't want to crawl out of.

But she'd have to. Soon.

She didn't like to think too far into the future when a battle approached. She liked to focus on gratitude, for the things she had, the things she'd miss if their mission went sideways. And a chattering, brimming-with-excitement Doug was one of those things. Chattering and maybe a bit nervous too.

A while ago, Shirin had left their closet with Jenny to go patch the cargo hold. She hadn't returned, probably waiting to see if they'd be needed again for more repairs. Then Roya had slipped out.

Once they'd been alone, she'd rested her hand on his arm, shut her eyes, and just listened for a while, occasionally squeezing his arm.

Somewhere along the way, he'd figured out that just because she didn't immediately respond with her own torrent of words, it didn't mean she wasn't listening. That in and of itself was a huge achievement.

Doug kept the ship-wide comm open, but his side was muted, so they could hear everything being broadcast from the bridge and other places. But only Mo had the pleasure of his stream of consciousness details.

They were getting close. She should go. But... just another moment or two.

She heard Zhia order Jenny to do a pass and locate Roya, make sure she was okay. Adan counted down the distance to the asteroid. In Engineering, Bri—amid a flurry of curses—reported a valve cylinder had blown but was being replaced.

"I sure hope they are able to do something in there, because the *Genokai* has been docked in the asteroid for several minutes now, and these shields are still up," said Adan. "No security changes yet."

"He sounds nervous," Doug observed.

"Aren't we all." Mo opened her eyes and sighed. "We're getting close. I better go suit up."

"Mo, I was thinking..." He put his hand on her arm as she unbuckled her harness and stood. "I just—Mo—wait."

She tilted her head. "For what?"

"For me to remember what I wanted to say to you. I just looked at you, and I forgot it all."

She smiled. "Every genius has their weak spots."

He laughed, but it had a frantic, manic quality to it. Or maybe he was nervous too. Of course, he was, of course. "I know you have to go and be a badass and all, but I might never see you again. I just—I feel like my last words to you shouldn't just be like, hey, see you later."

"C'mon, don't think like that." She eased slightly. There had to be a few minutes to spare, and Zhia hadn't ordered anything yet.

"You know it's a possibility."

"Of course I do."

"Listen, I just want you to know, if you don't come back…"

She held up a hand. "Don't. Don't say your goodbyes. It'll haunt me."

"Can I give you something instead?"

"What is it?"

He held up a shirt, in a festive pattern of nebulas, beach umbrellas, and puppies wearing sunglasses. "This came in handy last time, so… Take it with you? Don't want you going into the fight unarmed."

She smothered most of her laughter. Most. "Of course, of course. How could I have forgotten? This is more important than my rifle. You never know who you might need to strangle with a tropical shirt. I'm not sure the puppies are going to appreciate the carnage, though."

"Bring it back, okay? This is just a loan." He kept his expression stern.

"What a cheapskate trillionaire philanthropist you are. I'll be sure to return it, don't worry. Or at least scraps of it. Along with one of these." Then she leaned close and kissed him, deep and passionate, if not for quite as long as she would have liked.

She could have kissed him forever. It took sheer force of will to break apart, to squeeze his hand one last time, and to walk away.

Of course, she had an excellent, outfitted rifle—or five—with her this time and a full suit of armor, so she really hoped she wouldn't be wrestling anybody with a shirt on this barren rock.

But she tucked the shirt in her belt all the same. Her modern-day version of a handkerchief given to a knight. Maybe the space puppies would bring her some luck.

She'd find a compartment for it once she'd suited up.

STILL INSIDE THE *GENOKAI*, Ellen dropped down to the ledge behind Kael. They'd followed an air-intake system to get this far, but they were almost out. It couldn't be long now before the timer ran out.

"All we need to do is remove this grating—or make a hole—and we can drop down." Kael started checking the edges of the grate.

She leaned to one side, surveying what they could see from this angle. "Can you see how many hostiles?"

"No, can't get a clear line of sight." With a jerk, the grating came loose, and he shifted it to the side, keeping quiet. That thing looked heavy. Lucky he had the hydraulics—or the telekinetic abilities—to try that, because she'd have been melting her way out with their blowtorch, and that wasn't exactly a stealthy process.

She indicated a spot below them and to the right, outside of the ship. "Let's see if we can drop down by those stairs and make it to that control room."

"Got it."

"How's your leg? Can it make the drop?"

"Do we have much choice?"

She didn't like that answer, but he moved before she could ask more questions, and her only choice was to follow. Besides, they were short on time—and choices.

They dropped, timing it together to minimize the noise. Having Foundation suits would have been nice.

As she fell, she winced as she spotted a patrol barely fifty meters away out of the corner of her eye. His thud was significantly louder than hers. The patrol swiveled their direction.

Behind the patrol, a crate toppled off a stack, even though no one was nearby.

"Good one," she whispered, even though the enemy patrol definitely couldn't hear her.

One spun around to look, but the other kept coming. He lifted up his arm to check something, then lowered it back down. Near the main doors, a dozen more started toward them.

"That's too many," Kael growled. "Strike now, or do we wait?"

"Wait for the blast. It's gotta happen soon. Let's head for that control room." She pointed. "See if we can muck up the gears, so *Audacity* can get in."

"Got it. But how will we—"

He didn't get to finish asking. The blast on the bridge of the *Genokai* shook the station and threw her toward the outer force field. God, let it hold, let it hold. She slid across the metal for at least ten meters before she finally stopped.

Wreckage littered the ground around her. A huge piece of the fuselage that had been the outer portion of the *Genokai's* nose circled around in front of her. She swung her rifle around. That was... a lot of cover. It was also a hell of a lot of burning metal between her and Kael.

"Where are you?" Kael was saying, grunting and groaning.

"I'm fine—don't look for me. Get to that control room. I'll meet you there."

"No—I can't—"

"It's like a maze down here—go! I'll find my way."

Flames billowed, sucking up oxygen like mad before zipping out. She finally caught sight of him staggering up the stairs that led toward the control room. He'd been thrown closer to it, rather than farther away.

She dashed forward, getting to the edge of the fuselage that was closest to the *Genokai*'s hull. The thing didn't have much in the way of landing gear; it mostly just had its belly on the floor of the hangar. She did a quick look around the corner, then took cover again.

The impact had also knocked several patrolmen into the stack of crates, toppling them all in a disorganized heap. But all the others were approaching. And approaching fast. There was no straight shot up the stairs to follow Kael. Another piece of fuselage had landed across the base of the stairway. She'd either have to push it aside or climb over or around somehow.

All of it was too slow. Too slow with *that* many Therokis ready to fire, closing in on her. More wreckage littered the approach. If she tried to climb, she'd paint a target on her back. But if she stayed here, low and hidden… She might take a few of them out first before they got her.

"I can't follow straight." She tried, and mostly failed, to keep the despair out of her voice.

"I'm coming back."

"No—I'm going to try to fortify here. It's a bottleneck, so I can pick some of them off. Get into that control room! We need help, dammit. We can't take all of these alone. Even us."

She dragged a flaming pilot's seat and a piece of a console forward and propped them between the hull and the burning fuselage. She hunkered down to the soundtrack of swear words coming from Kael behind her. God, she hoped he was headed for that control room, and not just coming after her.

Some of the smarter Therokis moved up to the platform that led to the control room, but their rifles were trained on the wreckage. They'd probably heard her dragging this stuff around or seen her and Kael fall from the ship before the explosion. Others picked their way through the carnage, slower but steady.

One patrolman was abruptly flung off the raised walking area, then another, slamming into the hull of the *Genokai*. She smirked. That had to be Kael's doing.

"Thanks," she barked. Three more went flying, this time over the ship toward the other side of the hangar.

In front of her, she caught sight of the first Theroki as he came around the corner closest to her. She aimed for the power supply and pulled the trigger.

"No problem," he replied. "Entering the control room."

"Excellent." She took a deep breath. The sound of blasts behind her meant he hadn't found it empty. It also drew some of the attention of the men rushing at her, so she took that opportunity to aim a spray of ballistics at any Theroki who had his eyes on the control room.

What she wouldn't give for some *grenades* right about now. Of course, the plasma atmospheric seal over the docking bay wasn't unbreakable. Typically those things had their own backup power and were surprisingly durable—maybe they had to be with ships going in and out all the time—but no need to tempt fate. If she hadn't already damaged the seal by blowing up the bridge of the *Genokai*, grenades could very well push the damage over the edge, so maybe it was better she didn't have them.

She disabled one Theroki's knee joint and another's power supply, not killing them, but stopping them in their tracks. The wide pair of doors leading into the station slid open.

Another ten streamed out. Even with some of them moving to investigate the *Genokai*, the reinforcements obliterated every bit she'd gained. She clenched her jaw.

She did her best to make every shot count, staying close behind her cover between carefully placed shots. One of them got wise and flung the pilot's chair away, so she fell back to the more solid fuselage, peering around every few seconds to take another meticulously placed shot.

She flattened her back against the wreckage again. They were close. Getting closer. Kael pelted several more away from her and into walls.

Her attackers had stopped firing, she realized suddenly. Why?

"How we doin, Kael?" Her voice was rough.

"Took care of the competition." He was grunting, maybe dragging something heavy. "I'll see what I can shut off now." What was he doing, heaving the force field aside with his own bare hands?

No time to think. The Therokis had bunched up behind the nearest cover, apparently no longer content to be picked off. A new line of them attacked, rushing at her all at once, pouring out of the wreckage and scattering in several directions.

She hit three before they smashed into her cover. Into her. And reached for her.

She held on to her rifle, pulling the trigger to the last and smashing at least two with the butt end, but she lost it eventually, out of her hands, gone. She grabbed for another guy's weapon and burned several new stripes into three suits of armor before she lost that one too.

Theroki gauntlets lifted her into the air, ignoring her struggles, and carried her toward the double doors.

Into the asteroid.

BLASTED TERMINALS.

The two Therokis who'd manned this station were sprawled on the floor at Kael's feet. He'd locked the hatch and pushed two metal cabinets, three storage crates, and some assorted office junk in front of it in case someone was able to override the lock.

All the brute-force work was done. But this stupid terminal remained. Oh, he wanted to smash it. But that was not going to help him let in their friends. As far as he knew, the *Genokai* had gotten through because it had a friendly ship identifier. The *Audacity,* however, did not.

Why couldn't there just be a switch? Levers were so easy to find. SECURITY: ON / OFF. Pick one.

But no, there had to be at least a dozen menus to poke through. Too bad there was no clearly labeled *Let in my friends* or *Murder the bad guys* button.

Was a *Save the damned 'verse* button too much to ask for?

And it didn't help that he could barely concentrate on the console. His mind kept flashing to the Therokis swarming toward Ellen. She was a good shot, but how long could she really hold out?

Any second now, they could overtake her. There were too many. Which was why he should hurry the hell up and find a way to update the security protocols to let the *Audacity* inside the atmospheric seal.

Easier said than done. The way this was going, the best he could hope for was doing some damage to or disabling the security programs and hoping Doug and Adan could find their way in.

He could still follow her... If only he could just get this piss-spraying, ass-faced, dung-eating security system to go down! What did they call it? What the…

He forced his thoughts to sharpen, forced his eyes to focus not on what might be going on outside but instead on the fragging orange letters on the black display.

Comm Systems: Operational

Artillery Systems: Ready

Atmospheric Seal: Damaged, 38% Integrity

Oh, that didn't sound good. That was probably their fault for blowing up part of the *Genokai*.

Heating >

Ventilation >

Surveillance >

Defensive Systems >

Restart >

There—maybe that could do it.

Jamming his gauntlet into the screen, he was confronted with another menu, which had a whole 3D matrix display with controllable handles. A map of the force field? It *was* shaped like the outside of the asteroid. Seven suns, he just wanted to let them into the computer system—or the docking bay.

Where was the star-damned, dreck-worshipping OFF button?

He made a noise of frustration and put his whole palm on the screen, sweeping everything to the side in disgust like wiping all the pieces off a chess board.

To his surprise, outside, a mighty hiss split the air, the sound of metal wrenching against metal. Had *he* done that? Or was it just them coming after him? Probably didn't particularly matter.

Either way, the outer force field was lowering. The *Genokai* had ducked through one disturbed pocket, but now, the entire force field should be down. That didn't get them through the atmospheric seal, though. But it would make the entire asteroid easier to blast to bits.

Except he and Ellen were still *inside* it.

Thinking of her made him flip back to the surveillance part of the menu, where a little digging got him a live feed of the hangar.

And a brief glimpse of a crowd of Therokis hauling Ellen with them through the blast doors.

"Oh, no, they did not," he growled.

Pulse racing, he groped around for a comm. He found something simple and opened a completely unsecured channel.

"*Audacity*—force field's down. I can't lower the security." He glared at the menu again. Wait… restart? The systems might all cycle down with a restart. Maybe that would be enough. "Would a restart give you an in?"

"Maybe," someone replied, but the voice was garbled. He wasn't even sure if it was Doug or Adan.

"Get ready to try. Starting system restart in 3, 2, 1…" He hit the restart command and didn't wait for a reply. He dropped the comm, leaving the channel open, and turned toward the door, starting to remove his barricade.

Now, he just had to find Ellen, wherever they'd taken her.

He might be destined to lose her. Nothing lasted forever. But he'd be damned if a bunch of Therokis would be the thing that came between them. That was *not* how the two of them were going down.

Someone was going to die today. Probably lots of people. If it had to be one of them, he was going to do his best to make sure he was the one to go down.

Just before he had the last junk out of the way, he paused. Their escape from the *Genokai*—that had worked well. But it hadn't been a direct route. Was there another way out of here?

A way that most Therokis in their bulky armor wouldn't be able to follow? He had his own borrowed Theroki gear, but all in all, climbing into the duct work wasn't in the playbook.

Although, since he seemed to be the only one reading the playbook, did that make this a good bet or a bad one?

Shaking his head, he pushed one crate back to block the door and started prodding at the ceiling. The third steel panel he tried jerked up when he pressed, and he moved it aside. Climbing onto another crate revealed a maintenance crawlspace.

Swearing and scowling, he climbed down to get another crate and reinforce his barricade in case anyone tried to put the force field back up. They weren't trying, though. They were focused on their new captive.

With the barricade reinforced, into the ceiling he went.

"AND WE'RE IN!" Adan whistled as he slid the *Audacity* into this sorry excuse for a hangar bay. Columns of black smoke and white steam rose up from blast holes, and motionless bodies were scattered across the wide landing platform. Silently, he tried hailing Kael a third time, but, again, there was no response.

"Restart worked!" On the vid feed from his secure closet, Doug grinned. "This is… messy."

Maybe a dozen suits of armor turned in their direction. Adan had expected more. Probably two dozen more lay lifeless on the ground, but most were close to the busted-open front of the *Genokai*, probably thrown out in the explosion.

Pieces of the Theroki ship were strewn everywhere, some to the front, but many to the far-right side, probably continuing past where they could see. He parked the *Audacity* as far to the left as he could manage, although he didn't like the small shuttles and fighters parked nearby that were pointed directly at them.

"Good job, everyone." Zhia sat in full armor, helmet retracted, in the copilot seat beside him. "We all the way through the atmospheric seal and the force field?"

"Just about… now, yes." The ship shook slightly as it settled on the deck.

"Fern, fire when ready," Zhia ordered.

"You know I'm always ready, darling." A blast from the ship's turret hit the first Theroki even before she finished talking.

Adan leaned forward against his harness straps, more out of habit than because it would actually help him see more. He had bionics *and* camera zoom for that. "Kael and Ellen already did a lot of damage. But where is everybody?"

"No sign of either of them here." Doug frowned at his consoles. "There should be approximately 1800 Therokis in their force. Even spread across a couple of ships, this isn't the majority of them."

"And one of those ships is right there." Zhia rubbed her chin, frowning. "So there's a good chance we've got at least half of their force on this asteroid, maybe more."

Fern picked off three more who were aiming all too close to the shield generators. The usual thunder and sizzle of the turret felt louder here, in the more enclosed space. The remaining Therokis were gesturing to each other, fanning out to get behind better cover.

"I hope they were all sent to board the *Lhotse*," he muttered. But just in case they hadn't been, he switched on a thermal scan.

Everything in front of them lit up. Theroki armor might be tough. And artfully scarred. But one thing it did not do was conceal heat signatures. "This isn't an asteroid, it's a jelly donut! Look at all that."

"Somehow, I don't think I'm going to like this flavor." Zhia unbuckled her harness and stood. "Well, that's where our friends are, so let's get to work. The Songbirds must have noticed us by now, so we should have more company any second."

Fern cackled. "Good! I'm running out of targets!"

"We will draw their attention," Zhia said. "To draw them away from Kael and Ellen. The squad, Mo, Jenny, and me—get ready to deploy."

"We're already in the cargo hold, ma'am," Jenny reported.

"I'm not, but I'll be there shortly," Mo added.

If Mo wasn't there, who did Jenny mean by "we"? Maybe the squad?

Zhia continued. "The squad and I will defend the ship. Jenny and

Mo—I want you to try to get past them. Kael and Ellen can't do this alone. They need our help."

The idea made Adan's throat tighten. Why couldn't somebody else do that—the squad maybe? He didn't like the math of two thousand Therokis versus Jen and Mo. His fingers dug into the arm rest.

"Adan and I will assist," Doug put in. "I'll see if I can get in so we can take over the vid feeds, get us some situational awareness."

Yes, yes, Doug was right. Time to help out, not freak out. Somehow. He shook off his panic.

"What can I do?" he asked.

"Start up the drones, my man. Let's each take one."

"Right." He nodded, breathing more deeply. "On it."

"Commander Verakov?" Xi asked.

"Yes?"

"In my scans of the hangar, I have identified an anomaly. The control room past the *Genokai* has been barricaded from the inside. It now appears empty. Ellen, Kael, or both may have gone in and not come out."

"Well, that sounds ominous," Adan muttered.

"Maybe that's where he let us into the computers!" Doug said. "And sent that comm message."

"If it is empty now," Xi said, "then it may show the path that one of them took, so that you may follow."

"We'll check it out." Jenny's voice was sharp, full of self-assurance. He tried to let it steady him.

"Okay, get those cargo doors open. Let's do this." Zhia strode toward the door, leaving Adan alone on the bridge.

"We got this," Mo said. The last bit was clearly to Jenny, slightly muffled.

"Someone on the asteroid is contacting us," Xi said.

Adan reached for the control to respond.

"I believe it is... me." Xi's physical version of herself appeared on the viewscreen.

Adan raised his eyebrows. "Xi? Where are you? Other than, you know, um, here... This is confusing."

"Can everyone on the ship hear me?" Xi's physical self said. "There's not much time."

"We can all hear you, Xi. Everyone who's still on board, anyway," Zhia replied over her comm unit in her suit. Adan could hear slight shuffles as she moved through the ship.

"Commander Verakov, Kentt and I arrived here ahead of you. It… has not gone well."

Adan glanced at the fighter in the hangar—had that been theirs? It had seemed odd for the Songbirds to have only one.

"Where are you?" Zhia replied.

"I am hiding in the medical facility. They… rely heavily on biological means of detection, so I have had an easier time evading them than expected. Plus I do not eat."

"Glad to have you in the fight, Xi. Listen, we need to cause some distractions, enough to draw people away from Kael and Ellen, and we need to know their location so we can get through to help them."

"I can sabotage this area. It includes their food sources. That should draw attention."

"That's a weird place to put the food, right by the surgery—"

"Yes, it is. Do not ask. I will cause a disruption here and move toward you to reinforce the *Audacity*. But the time required may be significant."

"Good. Just go as fast as you can. Mo, Jenny—the two of you see if you can get into that control room. Maybe there's a way to get deeper into the asteroid in there."

Or… they could find one of their friends dead, Adan thought. But he didn't say that out loud. "You better hurry," he said instead.

"We got company arriving," Mo barked. "Look alive."

"Use the wreckage," Jenny shot back. "This way."

He flicked through the vid cams during pauses in the drone-deploy sequence. He caught a glimpse of Jenny and Mo sliding behind a smoking hunk of metal and moving fast. Some extra equipment was on Jenny's back that he couldn't quite make out, something like a heavy backpack. Huh, he would have thought she'd have mentioned some new equipment.

He let out a long, slow breath. Let this not be the last time he saw her, slipping into burning shadows.

The drones came online. He grabbed his flight controls, switching them to the first drone. "I think it's time for some target practice, eh, Doug?"

ELLEN SWALLOWED as her eyes adjusted to the darkness. A dozen Therokis had peeled off from the much larger group, crowding around her and obstructing much of her view as they all lumbered together down the corridor. None of them looked at her. They didn't even touch her, just shoved her when she slowed down too much. Together, they reached the end of the corridor, where another broad set of heavy blast doors opened onto an even darker cavern.

As they stepped inside, she faltered, eyes wide. At least until a heavy gauntlet to the shoulder blades shoved her forward. But it was hard not to stop and stare.

This place reminded her of a tall, dark cathedral, except some of the stone was raw and rugged. The metal floor was dark and covered with so much dust and pebbles that it resembled stone as well.

At the far end of the dark cavern, a blonde woman waited. She turned as they entered, and smiled. It was the coldest smile Ellen had ever seen. "So. We meet again."

Ellen gritted her teeth. "I killed one of you once, I can do it again."

"Ah, but can you kill us all?"

Her lips pressed together. She didn't want to play this game. "I'll do whatever I have to," she whispered, scanning her surroundings.

Maybe this was one of the chambers Ana, the former Songbird pilot they'd rescued on Faros, had seen, the one she'd described in the mess that day so long ago on the *Audacity*. The escaped pilot had described three chambers she'd seen while she'd lived on this asteroid: one dark chamber, one medical one, and one with three chairs.

Dark? Check. Maybe this was the first.

Columns cut from the stone stretched between ten and twenty stories high to the raw, uneven roof. The columns jutted up every ten meters or so, so many of them, forming pockets of darkness in between. It'd be a good place to hide, if she could get away from them, but considering there might be two dozen Therokis behind her? She didn't see that happening.

"Who are you really?" Ellen called. They were rapidly moving closer, and she couldn't say she liked it or wanted to reach the other side of this place. Especially not alone.

"You know who we are." For how young she looked, Cassandra's voice was confident, bold, a little smug.

"No, I don't think I do," Ellen replied.

As they passed close enough to one of the columns, she zoomed in on it with her helmet display. Yes, not stone at all. They were slim, black rectangles stacked up, dozens of them, maybe hundreds, stretching up and back into the shadows and—

And a tiny green light on the closest one winked at her.

Frag—computer drives. Servers. *Something* electronic. What did they need all these for?

"We know you," Cassandra said smoothly. "Your imprint is still a part of us. Your memories. Your longings."

Her fist tightened. That meant her colleagues were still a part of the hive mind. Her friends. No, that was only going to throw her off. Focus. "Where is Arakovic?"

The blonde woman strode to the wall and, with a carefully manicured finger, pressed a button. A hatch in the wall slid aside, revealing a large tube illuminated in white light. Her Theroki guards brought her to a stop about five meters away.

Ellen caught her breath. A woman with auburn hair lay inside, under a clear shell of plexi or glass. Utterly still.

"You came all this way for revenge. Sorry to disappoint you. We came to the same conclusion as you. Dr. Zeta Arakovic was dangerous. You and we aren't so different, you know."

Her breath was ragged, mind racing. "You came to the same

conclusion?" She didn't believe that for a second, but she had to keep Cassandra talking.

"Yes. She was a very dangerous woman. She had to be stopped. Of course, you and we are dangerous too. Aren't we? The galaxy has always underestimated women like us."

"Arakovic killed a lot of people. And ruined a lot of lives. The death I've seen…"

"It's true. Many died. But now, justice is served, no?"

Ellen narrowed her eyes. "Is it?"

"We assure you, it is." She paused. "What will you do, now that your long quest is over?"

Every muscle in her body tensed as the woman started to walk closer. At a wave of her hand, the Theroki released Ellen's arms and took a step back.

Something didn't add up. Which parts of this whole scheme had been Arakovic's doing, and which were Cassandra's?

"It's hard to believe." She had to buy time. She groped for something. Maybe if she acted stunned, unsure, she could draw more information out. "I wasn't sure I'd ever catch up with Dr. Arakovic."

She wouldn't have, either, if Arakovic hadn't personally given her the location of this base. Why had she done that?

Cassandra shifted closer still and raised a hand, running fingers softly down Ellen's visor as tenderly as if she'd been caressing her cheek. The telepath's eyes were eerily black, all pupils. "But now you have. We are truly sorry to steal your vengeance from you, but time was of the essence. Please, be free. Be at peace. You can do anything—go anywhere. Be anyone you choose. You could even return to the fold. Or leave, if you like."

"You'll let me leave?"

Her lips hinted a smile. "Of course."

Ellen's thoughts raced. Something didn't add up. Someone who'd tried to kill you didn't act like this… Did Cassandra *want* her to leave? Why?

Because Cassandra had never wanted outsiders here? Didn't want them obstructing whatever she was doing?

Why had Arakovic shared the location in the first place? Ellen racked her exhausted brain, trying to remember clearly. After Arakovic had shared the location, she'd disappeared off the screen, replaced by Cassandra. Doug had suspected—yeah, that was right—he'd thought maybe Arakovic had been asking for help.

Ellen gazed at the glowing figure in the tube. Help. If she'd wanted help, it'd come too late. Ellen shouldn't have felt bad about that, but she did anyway. Blasted woman, haunting her even in death.

Why would Arakovic have needed help? Unless… Had her little science experiment gotten out of control?

"If you don't know what to do…" Cassandra smiled sweetly. "We hope you consider rejoining us. We would take you back."

"Oh, I don't think I could do that."

"You could."

"Once was enough to drive me nearly mad, I couldn't—"

"We are *not* mad." Cassandra's eyes flashed, suddenly stormy, the saccharine facade gone.

"I never said that you were. I said I was." Ellen went still. She had to find out more, while she still could. What were these Songbirds really up to, so she could *really* stop it? "How did you meet Dr. Arakovic anyway?"

The storm cleared, replaced by a bright pixie smile. "At university. Dr. Arakovic was a visiting lecturer on the potential of genetic and bioengineering to end suffering."

"I bet the Puritans loved that talk."

Cassandra laughed softly. "Indeed, they weren't fans. But even after centuries of advancements, there's still so much more to do. War, rape, and murder are sicknesses that never go away. She spoke superficially, but we could see what she really meant. What she really wanted. What she knew could be achieved by those who were brave enough to dare to try."

"A better world. Peace." Ellen swallowed back the bile that was rising in her throat. So many dead because of this one conversation between a scientist and a telepath. If only one of them had had the stomach flu or had slept through her alarm.

"Peace." Cassandra nodded. "Sadly, she wasn't brave enough for it, in the end. She didn't have the stomach to do what must be done."

Gut twisting, Ellen had a feeling she didn't either. "But you do?"

"Yes."

"Is she really dead?" Ellen said slowly.

"Yes." Cassandra stepped back toward the tube and pressed another button. The tube's clear outer shell retracted, opening the body to the air. "Here. See for yourself."

Ellen's gauntlet was shaking as she reached out. It'd be better to take it off, but she wasn't risking it. The suit *should* be able to read *some* biometrics. Or the absence thereof. And it did.

No pulse. Temperature around zero degrees Celsius. A meat popsicle.

She swore under her breath. Dead.

"It must be hard to accept a project of five years drawing to this conclusion."

Ellen tensed again as Cassandra came alongside, much too close for comfort. She had to pretend to buy it. But she certainly couldn't just turn around and walk out. Her options were unclear. Kill this Songbird and her team of Therokis? Even if Ellen could manage it, there'd just be another hundred of them right outside the door. Fishing for more information was going nowhere, though. And she had a feeling she'd have little success convincing them to just give up whatever they were up to and start a mango farm in the outsystem.

She swallowed, hard. "What wasn't Arakovic brave enough to do? What must be done, exactly?"

Cassandra's black eyes twinkled. Instead of answering, she turned and walked toward the farthest end of the room, seeming to go even deeper into the asteroid. She clasped her hands behind her back and stopped. Regarding something? Considering? Why was she standing *there*?

Ellen tried again. "She seemed to have the stomach for a lot of nasty things. On Aeori, Upsilon... we saw many abandoned to die."

"Perfection is... difficult. Costly. Especially with an imperfect species like *homo sapiens*."

"But is perfection really possible?" Ellen knew full well it wasn't. "Is any species really perfect?"

Cassandra's voice was quiet when she spoke. "There was one, once. Peaceful, intelligent. Until humans killed them all."

Ellen's jaw tightened. "Almost all, you mean. Don't you?"

"If there were only two human women left after a genocide—just the two of us, perhaps—and we had no external technology to reproduce, would you consider that extinction? We would. Either way, the human species would end."

"You're talking about the *Alarus Octendi*."

"We are."

"I thought there were three that the Enhancers had captured. They always had three copies, three prototypes. What happened to them? Why are you so alone?" She poured sympathy into her voice.

"It's true, the Enhancers enslaved three *Alarus*, but they kept us apart. Our two sisters were lost to us... Until very recently."

Ellen swallowed. "Recently?"

"Oh, we believe you know very well where one of our sisters is, the youngest. The other sister is very old. She was nearly dead when we found her. We thought she'd been lost. But for the first time since the devastation, all three of us will soon be reunited."

Ellen winced but stayed quiet, waiting, hoping she'd say more. The Songbirds had looked so hard for Roya—but they'd found another *Alarus*, the third copy? Maybe that was why Cassandra wasn't demanding to know Roya's location. She'd gotten an unexpected replacement.

"The young, the old, and then us. We are in our prime reproductive years. The juices flow, but there is no mate. None ever again. It is... painful."

"It's tragic. It shouldn't have been done to you." Not that it justified what they'd done, though.

"It is not just the loneliness. The chemicals, they change us... They make us harm ourselves... It doesn't matter. We are much like the crone, the mother, the maiden. Your old mythologies have suited us well. We *are* called Cassandra, after all."

"After the myth? The prophet cursed never to be believed?"

"Yes. We try to tell you the truth. The future that must come to pass. No one listens."

"I'm listening now."

Cassandra's eyes narrowed slightly, as if she wasn't quite sure what to believe. Or she was looking at her harder. "At any rate, the young one, you know exactly who she is. The one contained in the capsule. You found her. You have her."

"She's long gone, left on Desori," Ellen lied. "Returned to the Enhancers."

"They'd like that, wouldn't they? But that's not what you did. You're more of a friend to us than you are to them. Besides, just because you have a fancy implant does not mean you can lie to us."

Frag. Miscalculation. "I'm not—"

"You are. Because we can feel her. She is here. Our sister joins us. Very soon now."

Ellen's blood ran cold, her lips parting but no words came out.

"She's coming to us as we speak." Cassandra turned and looked over her shoulder. "We sisters will be reunited."

"I thought you were Cassandra, the human telepath. But you're not, are you? You're *Alarus,* through and through. You don't have anything human in you anymore."

"Of course we do. There are many human nodes."

Ellen faltered. Nodes? "This isn't even about Arakovic's plan anymore, is it? Arakovic and the original Cassandra wanted to enslave you, like the Enhancers wanted to enslave you, to make your power theirs."

"They wanted their powers to be as great as mine." Cassandra's voice was soft. "But you cannot mix oil and water. Some things cannot be added by simple addition. You found this out yourself, did you not? Minds cannot just be mixed together like a swirling galaxy of stars."

"No... it's more like a black hole. Every mind is torn apart at the cost of creating... something else..." She thought of the squad, of the brief time she'd shared their collective mind. "Something new."

"In your case, you did not desire it. But as *Alarus Octendi*, we did. We missed the connections, the web of minds. Cassandra wanted this as well. We had centuries of memories, however. Her mind was a drop of rain in our vast ocean, as so many of you humans are. And that is not even the whole of our magnificence. But the drops of rain are still there, in the ocean."

"This body..." Ellen whispered. "This isn't even you. Are you trapped in a human body like your sister is?"

"We have broken free. We are many bodies, some of them human."

"Show me the real you, then, in all of its power."

Cassandra shook her head. "Only those who join us see the inner chamber. This is your chance to walk away, Ellen Ryu. You should take it."

Walk away. Like Kael had wanted to. Maybe she could just slip between the ships, escape the Union again, find Kael and the *Audacity* and run. Again. Arakovic was dead, after all.

But the forces she'd set in motion remained. And where could she really run from these psychos bent on lobotomizing every sentient creature on every planet they could reach? Back to Earth? Would they even try to reach *there*? She didn't doubt it.

Cassandra wasn't really going to leave her—or anyone—alone. She just wanted Ellen gone until her power was more secure. Gone until Ellen had no chance of stopping their madness.

Which meant, right now, there was still a chance.

"You're not going to stop, though. So I can't really walk away, can I?" Ellen looked across all the Therokis, then back to the woman. "Eventually, whatever planet I'm on, you'll find me. Otherwise, it wouldn't be a true peace, would it?"

Her expression was a mix between interest and annoyance. "True.

Once we have secured this achievement, it would only be ethical to share it with all sentient creatures."

"So I should rejoin you instead." God, she hoped she wasn't writing checks she couldn't cash.

Cassandra's eyes turned piercing. "You no longer wish to leave?"

Ellen shrugged one shoulder. "What's the point?"

The telepath didn't look especially convinced, but she inclined her head. "If it will help you appreciate the fruitlessness of resisting our mission, we will allow you to rejoin. But first, you must face the truth of it all."

An immense grinding churned in the walls. The asteroid shook, making her catch herself on Arakovic's burial slab. Was that from the grinding or some external impact? Another ship exploding in the docking bay?

The wall Cassandra had been facing parted, white light cutting a line more than two stories tall up toward the vaulted ceiling. The humidity reading on her helmet display went crazy, the visor rapidly shifting to accommodate the new blaze of light.

The Songbird arched one elegant eyebrow at her.

"I'm ready," Ellen said. "I'm not afraid of the truth." And she wasn't afraid of introducing these delusional drecks to the truth either. *Someone* here should make the acquaintance.

The fissure grew, and gradually she could see inside a massive cavern, bigger than she'd thought the asteroid would be able to hold. Tubes and ducts and catwalks crisscrossed chaotically, cluttering the cavern with overlapping lines. But they all led to a large steel construction in the center of the chamber, meeting what looked like a massive building at the other side of the cavern.

No, not a building, she realized. Her eyes traced one catwalk to the edge, but it wasn't a hatch or a door going inside. It was more like a window. A porthole.

Not a building. A tank.

"Come, this way then," Cassandra said easily. "And let us begin."

CHAPTER SIXTEEN

PAUL HAD ONLY BEEN in his personal cabin a scant five minutes when the chime rang. So much for regaining some sanity in a few minutes of quiet. His head was still reeling from what had felt like a fever dream, a drunken hangover. What the hell had happened that had disabled his entire ship and crew? That man from the *Audacity* had tried to explain, but Paul was hardly sure he could trust the man.

The chime rang again. He sighed and waved open the hatch in a gesture of defeat as he opened the drawer of his desk.

Bridell strode in, perky as ever, and stopped at neat attention.

He tried to hide how he tensed up at Bridell's arrival. Something about that situation with Ellen hadn't seemed right, not at all. And now Yamamoto wasn't here to watch his back.

"What is it, Lieutenant?" he said as calmly as he could. He took out a canister of Bloody Mary mix and cracked it open, not offering to share.

"Sir, you're planning to face Tauber head on?"

"Well, considering he's up our ass, I don't see what choice we have. We certainly can't run. He's between us and the gate, and he'd just chase us anyway. Do you have a suggestion, Lieutenant?"

"Well, we are smaller and more maneuverable, sir. But you already know that. We could potentially brave the asteroid field. But with the condition of the ship, coming out on top is pretty unlikely. Any small collision or mistake could sink us."

"My assessment as well." He took a drink and winced, enjoying himself. He considered adding the vodka, but decided against it. The spice should be enough to get the endorphins flowing. Not like he could taste the vodka anyway.

"In head-to-head battle, sir, they will outgun us."

"Yes." He took another swig. "I assume you're working up to something?"

"We could land on the asteroid, sir."

"Even if the *Audacity* is working to destabilize the rock?"

"Our analysis indicates the weapons systems on the asteroid are at least a PX372 laser-plasma array, possibly stronger. If we could seize control of those guns, it's likely they're stronger than what the *Volga* has aboard."

"We should be able to know what the *Volga* has, shouldn't we? Computer, what is the *Volga*'s armament?"

"Record access denied."

Bridell shrugged. "That's the wall we hit as well. Shu is hacking at it, but my guess is the ongoing communication issues aren't some random aberration. Our equipment is fine. I think Tauber has people working to actively block our access to information."

Paul swore. That would make sense. Tauber hadn't been shy about his feelings about the situation either. "Do you know what the standard array was when it was commissioned?"

"If it's got the standard guns and shields, then the PX372s would be stronger. Plus the asteroid should be some cover for the *Everest*."

"Interesting. We could possibly even raise the fields again if we could take full control."

"I believe the generators were completely destroyed, sir. So… perhaps not."

"Good point. Let me think on it."

"Respectfully, sir, there's no time. If we want to reach the asteroid before the *Volga* reaches us, we must act now."

Maybe Bridell didn't want to die. Maybe he wanted to impress his CO. That was pretty consistent about the man. Maybe Bridell had his own grudge against someone on the *Volga,* or the Songbirds just pissed him off.

Or maybe he had some other reason to want to get *onto* the asteroid, and this was an excellent excuse.

"Very well. Proceed. Change course to dock on the asteroid."

"Thank you, sir. You won't regret this."

Paul watched as Bridell strode out. That was… strangely helpful. And yet, he was hardly sure regret would not be coming his way today.

If only Yamamoto were here. Where had that man run off to? How had he resisted falling to what had laid out nearly the entire crew? How had Ellen resisted it, for that matter?

Paul would love to ring Yamamoto on the comm right now. Tell him to watch Bridell's every move. But somehow, Yamamoto wasn't here. Paul would have to do it himself.

Well… maybe not entirely by himself.

He finished the canister and opened another. Then he hit the comm button to get Shu on the line. If anyone was willing to sanity-check Bridell—and watch his every move—it'd be she.

And somebody had to find Yamamoto. Frowning, he narrowed his eyes. There should be vid feeds… Where had Yamamoto been when everything went down? Ellen had been on the bridge with the missing lieutenant. He could start there and see where she went and if she found Yamamoto.

He ordered the computer to prepare him the appropriate feeds. He'd discuss this plan with Shu and then, if all seemed kosher enough, he'd dig into just what had happened on the bridge—and on his ship--while he'd been sleeping.

ELLEN FOLLOWED Cassandra up and down and over catwalk after catwalk, climbing and descending stairs, but mostly climbing. The place was a convoluted mess. Their Theroki escorts followed close behind.

She tried to keep her eyes off them, to seem as oblivious as she could. Tricking members of a hive mind into underestimating her threat level might not be possible, but it didn't hurt to try. As they walked, she searched her armor's interface for any built-in weapons the suit might have, since she'd lost her rifle. Gas, an electric stun, gauntlet laser controls, anything. These Union suits had to have *something* built in, didn't they? Curse her for not looking sooner. She found some basic gauntlet lasers, but not much else. The wattage was low powered—not very encouraging.

Eventually, they reached the top of the tank, where they stepped out onto an expansive steel platform high in the air.

The platform area was large—and very empty. It could have held a few hundred people standing, but there was little to it otherwise. Near the edge of the tank, lights blinked and danced on an array of control consoles. Three chairs were placed just in front of the consoles, with wires lolling from the side of one arm on each chair.

This was it—the final chamber Ana had described seeing when she was still a member of the cult—before she'd been rescued. The chamber where Songbirds were made, where their minds were merged with the collective, the hive mind.

Or where their minds were consumed by the *Alarus*, devoured, leaving behind a husk that was just another body to control?

They stopped beside the three chairs, which looked for all the 'verse like ancient devices of torture. Or execution.

"Here we are. The heart of it." Cassandra spread her arms wide, then gestured up.

During the climb up all the stairs, Ellen had had her eyes on her boots, her adversaries, her exits. So she'd missed it until now.

She looked up. A broad dome stretched above her. The deep navy-blue ceiling was studded with tiny sparkles of light like nodes, like stars.

Like the Starbird grid.

Ellen froze. "It's real," she whispered. "I can't believe it. It's *real*."

"Do you miss us now?" Cassandra whispered, the corner of her mouth lifting in a twisted smile.

Ellen's mouth fell open. Memories of dancing across the chains of information flashed through her mind, pounded in her ears. Because yes, some part of her was seized up, salivating at the chance, at the sheer power. Some part of her wanted to reply, yes. Yes, I do.

Take me back.

She bit back the desperate words, swallowed them like she'd swallowed lots of criticisms of superiors and unpopular opinions over the years. "You said you'd show me the truth. Your real self. All I see is some chairs, a steel slab, and a bunch of flashing lights."

Cassandra's long, graceful arm gestured further, and her smile grew. Ellen had the distinct sense that she was missing something. "Don't discount the flashing lights, dear. But I think what you want to see is just over there—beyond the chairs. Would you like to see… before you rejoin the fold?"

She eased carefully around the chairs, trying not to show her fear of them and probably failing. She stepped up to the edge.

A horrifying mass of white tentacles writhed in the water, dozens and dozens of creatures, too many to even identify or count. Involuntarily, she took a step back, her lip curling in disgust.

Trying to hide her reaction, she pivoted back to face Cassandra. "Are you sure you want me back? You tried to have me killed. At least once."

"It was far more than once, but we can put the past behind us, can't we? We've given you what you most wanted—Arakovic. Dead. On a silver platter, or a silver tube at least. Surely, that should earn us some trust in your book?"

"But why did you bother to try to kill me if you wanted me to rejoin you?"

"Oh, we overestimated your danger, perhaps. We thought you'd figure out how to *really* stop us. But fortunately for us both, you never did, and now it's too late. Instead, Arakovic was a convenient distraction."

"You don't still want to kill me? I want to know I'm going to survive this... this process." She waved vaguely at the chairs. Cassandra's reply wouldn't be reliable or necessarily true, and Ellen was hesitant to even go near the chairs, let alone actually let them plug her in. But she only had so many cards left to play in this poker game.

"Come now, you've brought our sister home to us. So why should we kill you now? We thought you'd killed her or returned her or kept her for yourselves, but in fact, you've only reunited us. Please, come." She gestured toward the chairs.

Ellen staggered slightly forward. "That's—wait—reunited?"

"All we wanted was our sister back." She shrugged with a light laugh.

"I don't think she wants *you*." Did Ellen really know that? Had she just reunited two powerful aliens, one hellbent on killing one entire gender of several sentient species and the other with no particular reason to be friendly to any of them, after decades of Enhancer mistreatment and torture?

No, Roya was a *person,* a sentient being in her own right, not just a minion of this thing. She hadn't wanted any of this... Roya had been appalled by what Arakovic and Cassandra had done.

Hadn't she? Unless that was all a trick? What if even Arakovic's body was a trick, and she was just hiding somewhere in the wings, laughing?

Cassandra laughed. "You're hardly sure. That's quite amusing, we must admit. If she doesn't want to see us, then why is your ship docking even now?"

"They're coming to save me, obviously." Her heart leapt, pounded faster. It was hard not to be happy about the cavalry arriving, but if that meant she'd put Roya in danger, that complicated things... She took a few steps closer to the chairs, trying to draw her movements out.

"In saving you, they deliver her to us." Her smile widened. "With our sister back, we will tighten our grip on this galaxy. And peace will return, the way it was before the humans connected the planets and exterminated us. There will be peace. Our way."

"What about the Puritans? You'll never infiltrate them with your cybernetic spies."

"We don't need that. We didn't need cybernetics to make your Union friends sleep like babies, did we? The Puritans will find out soon enough the errors of their ways. Our movement is just spreading its wings."

Where had she heard those words before? Paul's voice seemed to echo in her memory. Operation Freedom's Wing. "The third *Alarus,*" she whispered. "You never said where she was. She's not here, is she?"

"No, she's not."

"She's on the Union ships, attacking the Puritans, while the other is here." Ellen's blood pounded in her ears. How far away had that operation been? Paul could have been there. Could it already be underway? If they used the *Alarus's* power for outright war, the Union ships could do what they'd done today. Put the Puritan forces to sleep, board the ships—and slaughter everyone.

Peace. That long elusive, awaited victory.

She wanted to throw up. Or strangle this—this—whatever she was.

"Yes." Cassandra nodded. "Good, now you've figured it. That's the benefit of a distributed brain system. Similar to your Earthen octopi, with brains in each limb, but our brain systems have evolved to be much more advanced. Our minds spread across many nodes. Our sister is there, but in her own way she is also here, talking to you, right now. We are one, each node like a limb to you. That part of us, that body, is old and ready for the end, for the completion of our grand task. For our vengeance. This time, the Union's victory over the Puritan humans will be swift, decisive, and complete. Any among the Union who question our methods will be eliminated. They are too late, and our control is too complete. They will come under the wing of our protection and peace."

"Or you'll kill them. Every Puritan, half the Union."

"We all die in the end."

"You're a monster."

"A monster?" A satisfied smile spread across Cassandra's face, as if she had never quite believed Ellen's claim. "Some will die so that others may have peace. Is that not precisely the choice every warrior makes? That you yourself have made?"

"I was defending my home. That's different."

"Is it? Who is the monster? Those who allow murder and rape, starvation and suffering to continue? Those who see suffering but choose not to intervene? We say it is not us who are the monsters but them."

"Nobody should stand by while people suffer, but *you* have caused your share of murder. I've seen the bodies."

"Dr. Arakovic considered the calculations to be in the greater cosmic favor in those cases. We did not disagree. Even those deaths will result in peace. A permanent, *lasting* peace, which you humans have never had. Your tiny, single-node minds can't even imagine it."

"Peace is a choice," she insisted. "A choice to live a certain way, in harmony, in cooperation. What you're talking about isn't peace, it's oblivion."

Cassandra folded her arms across her chest. "Well, if peace is a choice, none of you are any good at making it."

"That's the truest thing you've said all day."

"You already made another choice today. It's time you follow through on it." Cassandra glanced at the two nearest Therokis, who marched toward her.

They grabbed her and dragged her forward, slamming her down into the chair in the center.

"Remove your gauntlet," Cassandra ordered.

"No."

"Take it off her then," she ordered them. "Strip her armor."

So they were throwing pretenses aside, eh? Three more closed in, and they set upon her, probing at the suit for the gauntlet release, the emergency release. She batted at them and kicked and twisted, trying to keep the emergency release out of reach and growling like a rabid animal. With a hiss and a twist, though, the gauntlet came free.

"Got it," one said.

Her left arm was pinned against the arm rest. Cold metal gauntlet digits probed for the release for her ports. She smirked. They weren't going to find them. It was tempting to try to shock whoever it was with her RPD, the cybernetic defense system built into her body to protect her from assault, but with only three charges, she couldn't subdue all of them.

"Open your ports," Cassandra ordered.

"I don't think so." Ellen clenched her jaw, as she felt the cold metal of a rifle barrel press her palm into the metal arm rest.

When the Theroki holding the rifle spoke, the tone was nearly identical to Cassandra's even though the male voice was deeper, huskier, probably more rarely used. "Open up, or I'll open one for you."

There was no sound for a moment except for her breath in her helmet. She'd had that vague idea that maybe she could do more damage operating from inside their system than outside, that maybe hooking in could have been the sucker punch she was looking for. If she couldn't beat them physically, maybe she could do it mentally.

But now that she was here, in the chair, arm naked across cool metal—panic coursed through her, rising in her veins.

She didn't want any of them inside—in her suit, in her body, in her veins, in her mind, ever again.

Cassandra stepped forward, some of the Therokis parting to make room. "No one comes in here without joining us. All who enter join—or leave as meat. I'm happy for either, in your case."

The barrel pressed harder into her palm.

"Which will it be?" Cassandra demanded.

She swallowed. Well, at least she was a righty.

Her eyes locked with the brutal black ones glaring down at her, and, for once, Ellen smiled back almost as coldly as Cassandra had. "Thanks, but no thanks. Once was enough for me, I assure you."

After that, everything happened all at once.

The rifle pressing into her hand fired, the ballistic obliterating the center of her left palm. She couldn't contain the scream. The pain was momentarily blinding, incapacitating.

At the same time, ballistics hammered into Cassandra's torso.

The unexpected close-rifle fire kicked in old instincts and forced breath back into her lungs. Ellen grabbed for her gauntlet and slid partly out of the seat, scanning for somewhere to run, to hide. There was no cover anywhere, but she was getting *down* at the very fragging least.

The suit was injecting her with painkillers, but she was still reeling. Adrenaline was spiked in too by the suit, according to the helmet display. Like she needed more. Damn Union suits. Warnings exploded across the screen, the first and most important to retrieve and replace the missing gauntlet.

Right. Get it together, Elle. She jammed the gauntlet back on, trying not to stare at the hole in her palm, the blood dripping down her fingers. At least they were all still there. Whether they stayed viable or not was anyone's bet. Much of what had connected them to her hand was gone.

Then she rolled, just in time to see six Therokis fly backward onto one of the catwalks. Kael! He had to be here, blasting them off there telekinetically.

Gauntlet replaced, her armor applied medkits to the hole in her palm, and she had to bite back another snarl as they sealed around the wound—two kits, one on each side. That was never good. Vicious, vicious assholes. Hell. Her hand. How much of it was gone?

She tried to move the fingers. Her thumb and forefinger seemed to respond, but it hurt like hell. She switched the left hand to direct neural control. That way the suit—via her brain—would move the hand, instead of them relying on amplifying motor signals from the muscles. Muscle-based control was more intuitive and healthier for the user, but there were some instances when neural control was still critical… An old technology but a good one.

She scanned all those in armor, looking for Kael—and spotted him by one of the two hatchways that led onto the platform. The armor with the gash through the cephalopod on its chest was just different enough from the others to pick him out. Maybe he'd taken the long way around. Rifle in one hand, he gripped the railing of the catwalk with the other and pulled.

Metal screamed and twisted, sending half the Therokis tumbling down as the catwalk spun.

Unfortunately, that still left six others—and Ellen with no rifle and with a hole in her fragging hand. God, what she wouldn't give for a multi right now. The gauntlet lasers probably wouldn't be enough to take out all these Therokis, even if they were unarmed. Should she even bother? They'd draw more attention than it was worth.

Kael wasn't the only telekinetic here, though, and before he'd even finished ripping the catwalk from the platform, he'd been hit.

Once, maybe more than once—they pummeled him. She could see him resisting. The magnetics on his boots grinding as they engaged but still scraped along the platform until—

He went over the side.

She swallowed her scream of rage and scanned around her. There had to be something here she could use. She needed something else… Or to run.

There were the three chairs, the consoles. A metal ridge that was presumably the edge of the tank, although she couldn't see beyond the ridge to be sure. Two hatches in the wall that led somewhere else, off and out of the platform area. Another catwalk on the other side—but she could hear footsteps. More coming up to join them?

With Kael dealt with, all the remaining Therokis turned toward her, ignoring Cassandra's dead body. More where that came from, Ellen supposed.

And indeed, seconds later at the top of the stairs leading up to the nearest catwalk, another Cassandra appeared, shaking her head and frowning. Ellen permitted herself a few curses this time.

The nearest Theroki pounded closer, reaching for her.

Time was up. Frag it all, futile or not, she was going to try. She rolled onto her back as she powered on the lasers, aiming at the fingers nearest his rifle trigger.

He twisted sideways, blocking her line of sight to the rifle and absorbing the damage with his shoulder as he continued closer. She shifted the laser blast to the enviro regulator near his neck, which she could just reach the edge of. Behind his visor, his eyes were wild and black and manic—and they locked with hers.

Abruptly, he was knocked back, hitting the ground before her with a skid. He lay still, the others staring at him, then glancing around frantically.

Was it Kael? She was looking around just like the rest of her enemies, but she didn't see Kael. She frowned at the collapsed Theroki.

A ballistic had cracked the visor wide open. That took special anti-armor, long-range, large-caliber—

Long range.

She and the other Therokis caught sight of the dark figure at just about the same time. High up, near the Starbird lights of the ceiling dome, a figure lay on one of the cat walks, a long slender gun aimed in their direction.

Mo fucking Mihio, ladies and gentlemen. And aliens.

Another round, then another. Two more went down.

One Theroki grabbed her, putting her between Mo and himself. Another—and it was arguable which was the smarter of the two—ran toward the Cassandra. To protect her? It seemed that way until he started down the stairs. He didn't make it far, though, before apparently receiving orders to turn around and help.

As she struggled with the one using her as a meat shield, a third Theroki ran to the edge of the platform and took aim at Mo. It wasn't *too* long a shot for a rifle like that, although it wouldn't be easy.

But he probably didn't need to hit Mo, just the catwalk beneath her. It'd be a long way down.

His first shot missed, sending sparks flying from one of the Starbird's glittering nodes behind Mo. So focused was he on getting the shot right, he didn't feel the gauntlet wrapping around his ankle until it was too late.

He went over the edge, making Ellen's Theroki jump in surprise. She took advantage, twisting in a new direction and ducking hard.

Mo did not miss the opportunity. The sound of his visor cracking —and the scream—told her that her instinct had been right.

She grabbed his rifle—he made no move to stop her—and sprinted toward the edge where the fourth man had fallen over, even as another Theroki fired at her boots. He might be the last one, though. Mo had taken out a lot.

At the edge, she finally stopped and brought the rifle to bear on her attacker, a sloppy spray of bullets because the thing seemed to be firing down and to the right of where it should. Considering Theroki maintenance protocols, that really wasn't a surprise.

The second Cassandra fell, and the last Theroki tried his original plan again—just running for it.

He might come back with a lot of friends. Or maybe he was just freaking the frag out and was going to go hide in a closet.

Didn't matter. Even if he didn't come back, they wouldn't be alone for long.

She slid onto her stomach and looked over the edge.

There, clinging to the remnants of a maintenance ladder, was Kael. The final rung had rusted out and broken, and so had several further down, keeping him from fully making his way up, but there'd been enough to hold on to.

She held out her better hand. "If I pull, can you give yourself a boost?"

"I don't know—not sure—" he said, voice breathless. "Your hand —is it—"

"What else are you going to do?" she shouted at him, reaching farther. "Fall down and die?"

"Better to spit in the wind, baby." He grabbed on. Together, they got him up over the edge and collapsed together, panting. "And die fighting."

"How about we try *not* to die?"

"Such a dreamer. Is your hand…"

"Suit has a medkit on it. It's… not great."

"What the dreck is this place?" He groaned, rolling onto his back.

"It's where the *Alarus* lives. Right over there."

"What? Let's nuke it then."

"Fresh out of nukes."

"Knockout grenades?"

"Too gentle."

"Spoken like someone who hasn't taken many hits from those demon seeds."

"Let's take a look at those consoles and see if we can end this."

"I'M OUT OF DRONES." Adan cursed. He'd lost track of how many enemies he'd taken out with the drones' weapons systems, but whatever the total, it hadn't been enough.

"Me too." Doug's voice sounded bleak. "My last one just got hit."

Adan flicked his wrist, hurriedly bringing back up the security consoles, looking for what he could do to help out in the asteroid computer systems, when a massive thud echoed from the port side of the hull. "What in the—"

Xi flipped the viewscreens for him. "The shuttles. Therokis are working together to use the shuttles as a sort of battering ram against the shields."

He just stared for a long second. What was he supposed to even do about that? People never used ships as battering rams—they were too valuable, not to mention too dangerous for those on board. But those Therokis probably didn't care about either of those things, especially since those shuttles were presumably empty.

"I'm detecting lift," Xi reported.

"What do you mean? Lift on the ship?"

"I think some of them are trying to move the *Audacity* itself from its docked position."

"Why?" He scrambled, running his hands through his hair.

What to even *do* about that? He tried to look across the swarms of armor now covering the hangar floor. None of them were lifting their arms or doing any sort of suspicious movements to call out who was lifting and who was firing. Hell, maybe they could even do both.

"Engage reverse thrusters," he said, finally. "Counter their attempts. Our ship is not an atom in a reactor."

"I will do my best." Even as Xi replied, the ship lurched upward, then down too hard. Warning lights blared. "Shields weakening, hull is taking superficial damage in a number of places."

"It won't stay superficial forever, Xi, c'mon. Keep us steady."

"It is difficult to anticipate their pressure. I have no models for it. I may overcompensate."

"I know, I know, it's okay, just try."

Fern cleared her throat, but her voice was harsh. "Let's not forget we have another gun turret. Someone, get up to the other one! It's calibrated good enough—Xi and I can help—argh, fragging too many of them—" She bit off the words.

On the viewscreen, her shots mowed down rows of oncoming Therokis, but there always seemed to be more taking positions at the blast doors, hunkering down, getting in way too many shots before they were taken out.

The gun turret. Adan swallowed. He *hated* leaving the bridge empty, but so few remained on the ship… Really, he was the only logical choice to man the second turret. He couldn't even see Zhia or Jenny or Mo on the viewscreen now. But it wouldn't matter if he was on the bridge, ready to fly away, if the ship got overrun with Therokis. He unbuckled his harness and started to stand up.

"I'll do it," said a girl's voice on the comm.

He blinked. Shirin.

"Xi says she can guide me."

"And I will be operating the shipboard weapons, as well," Xi said. "And optimizing shields. According to my calculations, if they have distributed half their estimated force to attack us, we have a sixty-seven-percent chance of defending the ship."

He sank back down into his seat. "And… if they distributed more than half or our estimate is wrong? Or we're just unlucky?"

"Then we will lose the ship," Xi replied simply. "Let us hope for lucky."

Feeling numb, he forced himself to rebuckle his harness. He needed something. Anything. He couldn't do much to help here.

Explosions and sounds of burning laser fire sizzled and echoed through the hull from the cargo hold and over the viewscreen audio feed. He wasn't sure which was which really anymore.

Suddenly, the hatch hissed open. Dr. Levereaux rushed in, breathless. "Where's the kid? Where's Roya? Where? Have you seen her?"

"What the hell are you doing? Get strapped in! You're gonna get knocked out." As if to prove his point, the ship lurched up and to the side, before righting itself.

Levereaux slid awkwardly into the co-pilot seat and started snapping the harness. "I can't—I can't find Roya," she panted. "The empress. Wasn't Jenny supposed to find her? I can't find her. Did Jenny find her?"

"Jenny?" Zhia's voice sounded tense over the comm. But it was good to know she was still alive.

Adan's heart flipped in his chest. There was no answer.

"Xi—where are they?" Levereaux demanded. "God, why didn't I think of just asking you instead of running around like a fool? Xi, where is the empress?"

"You didn't think of asking me because stress and anxiety make our brain less logically functional as blood rushes to muscles, enabling our fight or flight response. But you will not find her. She exited the ship on the arm of one of the squad, found Jenny, and I believe they have made it to the control room we were targeting."

"What?" Levereaux clutched her chest. "You're not helping with the stress part here."

"Then why aren't they responding?" Adan demanded. "Is Jenny okay?"

Don't panic. Don't fragging panic. His blood was rushing in his ears.

"Why is she—" Levereaux started. "Why would they take her?"

"Jenny's suit reports normal if slightly elevated vital signs," said Xi. "Something may be interfering with her comm system, or she may have turned it off. As you might imagine, hearing the *Audacity* under heavy attack is not exactly conducive to her mission or peak concentration. As to Roya, the girl asked them to take her."

He ran his hands over the armrests, trying to calm down, trying to think of something to do. But what the hell could he do? He was helpless. Fragging helpless. He was a pilot, not a marine.

"Why? Why?" Levereaux was shaking her head, slinking down in the harness like she wanted to fade into the vinyl. "Ellen and Kael are going to kill me."

Another heavy thud hit the ship, this time from the starboard side. "Is that what I think it is?" Adan growled.

"They are sliding the *Genokai* into us, as well," Xi confirmed.

Shaking his head, Adan reached under the console and got one of the multis he'd stashed there. He shoved it at Levereaux. "If you don't know how to use that, you better start learning."

She swallowed, her face going white, but she took the rifle and held it properly. It was a good sign, he thought.

Then, gritting his teeth, he put his own across his lap and bent toward the console. There had to be something in their system he could frag up. If it was the last thing he did.

SHIRIN HAD BARELY SAT down in the too-large chair in the gun turret when the hatch behind her hissed open again. She turned, mouth open. She had to be allowed to help; they had to let her. This was getting ridiculous. "Hey—oh. It's you."

But it wasn't Commander Zhia or Dr. Rachel or any of those people. It was that weird girl Isa who was always sneaking around in the shadows. She reminded Shirin of a rat, if a rat were graceful and quiet and a whole lot cleaner. Maybe dolphins were like that? Butterflies or bees? Slipping in and out of rooms with no one noticing? There *had* to be a more flattering comparison because she didn't really want Isa picking that thought from her mind. Wait, no, she'd had the surgery that the doctor had told her would make it so nobody could read her thoughts anymore. It was hard to get used to.

But Isa *was* graceful in a way Shirin never would be. Once, she'd be given a chance to be a server in a fancy house back on Faros. They'd given her a dress, a bath, she'd even gotten to brush her hair. It had felt amazing.

So of course, she'd spilled the first tray of pita all over someone. And proceeded to make at least six other messes in less than an hour.

Boxing had come a lot more naturally to her. And hull repair—now that was fun. She'd never known her mom, and at this point, she wasn't sure she cared to, but the fact that fixing things and punching things felt good was starting to make more sense.

"And… Hi?" Shirin frowned. The two of them were just staring at each other.

"Yes. It is me," Isa said, eyes gazing past Shirin out the viewports of the gun turret.

Shirin turned to see what she was gazing at. Drat, she had a job she was supposed to be doing. She'd better just ignore Isa. That's what everyone else seemed to do, and it seemed to be working just fine. Girl was always a fly on the wall.

Seven hells. Rats. Flies. Couldn't she think of anything better?

Shaking her head at herself, she grabbed the controller Xi had produced from the console. A bright display lit up.

"Assisted-targeting mode recommended," Xi said. "I will identify targets by positioning them in the crosshairs, and you confirm and shoot. You're still welcome to choose others."

"Great. Got it." Shirin impatiently chewed on some gum Nova had given her as a gift before she'd gotten off at Molyarch. It made her feel a little more like she belonged.

She buckled herself into the harness. There wasn't another for Isa, and she frowned, but that was Isa's choice, she guessed. They both had their suits on that Commander Zhia had gotten for them. That was more safety than the harness in a lot of situations anyway.

She nailed the first target the instant the computer locked on.

"Good one, Shirin," came Fern's reassurance through the comm. "Keep it up."

Shirin didn't try to respond. She'd muted her side, even though she wasn't supposed to, because she didn't want them to hear her swearing or grumbling to herself. And she was pretty sure surviving this was going to require at least a little of both of those.

A green circle appeared around another target, gradually jumping to smaller and smaller sizes as the computer refined its recommendation. Shirin hit them both.

"Can't you do this yourself?" Shirin asked. She glanced over her shoulder awkwardly at Isa, whose eyes were still focused on the distance. "I'm talking to Xi, I mean."

"I can to some degree," Xi replied, "but the weapons systems have a time-rate limitation for my fire that is designed to prevent me from carpet bombing or melting planets, were I to go haywire."

Her eyes widened. "Ah, what? Excuse me?"

"Humans, however, are not rate-limited, so fire away."

"Wasn't that a joke?" Shirin glanced over her shoulder at the other girl.

"I'm… not sure," Isa said mildly.

Feeling uneasy, she picked off six more, trying to balance time and precision. It seemed like there were hundreds of them, and the ship kept shaking from what felt like earthquakes, not simple rifle fire.

And through it all, Isa was still there. Silent. Staring. Shirin tried to ignore her, but it was like someone was reading over her shoulder.

Just as she was about to blow up at the girl, the target she'd been about to fire on just… fell over. She frowned. "Did Fern hit that target?" Sure enough, the crosshairs were moving on to select a new target, somehow knowing this one had been eliminated.

"No," said Xi. "Obviously, I deconflict the targets I offer, dividing them between gunners for optimum efficiency."

"Then how…" She turned slowly now. "Did you do that?"

Isa's eyes flicked to meet Shirin's, then back out into the distance. "Maybe."

"Maybe? Are you *supposed* to use your powers like that?"

Isa's brow furrowed, her gaze staying longer on Shirin now. "No. Are you going to tell on me?"

Shirin hesitated. "Maybe." What if they found out and it was a problem? And Shirin got in trouble for not telling anyone sooner?

"If you tell, I'll tell everyone you cry for your guinea pigs at night."

Shirin lifted her chin. "I don't care about that. I want more guinea pigs."

"I've read Doug's thoughts, and Xi's analysis, and the odds of surviving this situation are not yet in our favor."

Shirin bit her lip. Was it really that bad? Oh, who was she kidding, she could see out the viewports as well as anyone. And feel the shaking.

Isa seemed to interpret her silence as hesitation. "If you tell, I'll—"

"Hey, I've lived my whole life being coerced," Shirin said sharply. "Don't."

Isa's expression shifted dramatically, from neutral to such deep sadness, Shirin blinked in shock, realizing that Isa knew just what she meant, just how Shirin had felt when she'd come on board.

"You peeked. You peeked in my head. Before I got the doctor's chip."

"I peek in everyone's head. I—"

Shirin held up a hand. "Wait. You want to help, right? You don't want to be left out."

Isa let out a great sigh, her lips smiling softly, like she was so relieved Shirin had figured out what she felt without her saying. "Yes."

"I get that. That's me too. I didn't want to be kicked to the curb on Molyarch either."

"This is my home," Isa said, tone insistent, although Shirin knew it wasn't directed at her as much as the others.

"Yeah, exactly. At least, I want it to be."

"Then let us defend it," Isa said, gesturing at the viewports, "the only ways we know how."

Their eyes locked for a moment longer, and then Shirin nodded sharply and turned back to her targeting gear. "I mean… I don't actually know how to do this."

Isa snickered. "Neither do I. I'm convincing them to go to sleep, I think. Or maybe killing them. This is bad. I should stop."

Shirin shook her head as another thrust bashed against the hull. "No, you shouldn't. Xi, how are our shields doing?"

"Dramatically diminished. Shields are at thirty-eight percent."

"See?" Shirin held up a hand, gesturing toward Xi's speaker in the ceiling as if that explained everything. "This is no time to stop. They chose to shoot at us, remember?"

"After we landed in their docking bay."

"Peacefully!" Shirin squeezed the trigger, and even she had to laugh at that. "Well, at first anyway."

"Cassandra hasn't noticed me yet," Isa said, her voice quiet. "But Xi, Shirin, if she does, if I start acting strange—take me back to the safe room."

"You got it." Shirin cracked her gum again, grinning. That was almost starting to feel natural. Just like this place. It'd be a shame to lose it now. "Let's get to work."

KAEL RACED after Ellen toward the consoles. As well as it had worked as a disguise, Kael was starting to regret trading his Union suit for this Theroki one. This part of the asteroid must double as a steam room or public bath—or it would have on Faros—because his suit was fighting the humidity to keep his visor clear. That… didn't happen with suits in even reasonable maintenance condition. This suit didn't monitor or treat his injured leg, either. The large medkit they'd taken from the *Lhotse* sick bay was going to have to be enough.

Up in the high catwalks, the sniper rifle fired every so often, nearly as fast as Mo could manage it. "She's buying us some time," he said.

"Who else could have made it off, you think? It worries me that she's all alone."

"Me too." Privately, he had a bad feeling that that meant more backup wasn't coming, but it wasn't helpful to share a hunch.

As Ellen slid to a stop before the bank of consoles, the interfaces whirled black and slid shut, now nothing more than shiny glass.

He swore as Ellen swiped at, tapped, and finally punched one of the consoles, leaving a crack in the glass. "Frag." She shook her head. "They locked us out."

He skirted around the consoles to the edge of the platform, where about a meter of steel rose up from the floor to make a half wall. Below that about a dozen meters down, water lapped against metal, and—

The churning mass of white tentacles and bodies made something hitch inside him. His bile rose in his throat, and he coughed, staggering away from it, but it wasn't enough.

The memory came back, even though he didn't want it to—his ex's face. Asha's face, and the feeling of the suspiciously *Alarus*-like white-tentacled creature she'd forced down his throat on Faros. Could he still feel it crawling inside him? No, no. The docs on the *Audacity* had told him the creature was gone, that he'd thrown it up before he'd regained consciousness. They'd told him—

"Kael!"

Ellen's cry snapped him out of it just in time. A dripping tentacle as thick as his arm had slapped over the steel and had barely missed him. It rose up to come down again.

He didn't remember sliding to a seat against the half wall, but he was there now, so he threw himself into a roll, across the floor, and away from the thing. His head was still spinning, and nausea threatened to overtake him. With all that, rolling till he slammed into the steel back of the consoles was a welcome relief.

"You okay?" Ellen reached his side and was helping him up, pulling him back from the edge, both literally and figuratively.

"Just be glad you never had an *Alarus* sushi sandwich."

"I don't think sushi comes in sandwiches, and—"

"Not helping."

"Good point. See any grenades on the way here? What I wouldn't give for some grenades. Or a comm channel to Mo."

"All I got is this lousy rifle."

"Let me check for other weapons." She hurried away from him as he leaned on the consoles and bent to check under the glass interfaces and chairs.

"Check the fallen too. Might have some grenades. I'll see if I can get a comm channel between us at least." He didn't look at her as he spoke. His eyes hovered at the edge of the tank, at the wet marks on the steel from the tentacle that had been there not so long ago. If it was that thick at the end, he did *not* want to see the base of it. He tried to shake off the memory. Maybe he should step up to the edge and try to face it down? That's what they'd have done on the *Genokai*. Somebody would have held him there until he puked—unless he managed to hide the terror, shove it down. He'd been pretty good at hiding things, closing down on the outside to conceal the way the memory could take him back to that moment with Asha again and again. How many years had he spent pretending he was fine?

Well, he wasn't fucking fine. He wasn't pretending anything for anyone anymore, not even pretending not to be disgusted or afraid. He was pretty sure Dr. Taylor would approve. Maybe he'd live to see her again.

Ellen jogged back to him. When her eyes met his, he didn't like the look on her face. Stormy, afraid. But worst of all, defeated. "I found three fragging rifles with no more than a handful of ammunition. Rest are nearly empty. Ridiculous. We need something more. We can't win by salvaging rifles and shooting their leftovers back at them."

He sighed, hating to agree. "We barely fought off a dozen of them. There are hundreds more."

"Yes. We need something… drastic."

"Like what?" He looked over the rifle she'd handed him. It was in terrible shape, but better than nothing.

"We need to cut off the head of this beast." Her eyes were scanning the area, searching.

"Agreed. But where the hell is its head?"

"Therein lies the problem…. Does it have two thousand heads? Ten? Just the one in the tank? I have no idea."

He struggled to his feet, the pain in his leg radiating and making him dizzy for a second. "Well, we can start with the tank." He gestured with his rifle. "Killing individual Therokis doesn't stop them."

Elle nodded. "Killing Cassandras doesn't stop them either."

"So the beast in the tank it is. If that doesn't stop them, hell, I don't know what will, but at least we haven't tried that yet."

Her lips twisted in a wry smile. "True. It's the *Alarus* itself that's providing them with the power to subdue others and magnifying their telepathic range. Even if the individual Cassandra telepaths can survive independently without the alien, killing the glorified octopus might free the crews of the *Everest* and the *Lhotse* so they could fight."

His stomach rebelled at the idea, but he was going to have to deal with it. "Let's go."

They both jogged toward the tank's edge, slinging rifles over their shoulders as they went. Mo's shots were coming faster, and also closer up the stairways. The footsteps clanking on metal were getting louder. He glanced toward the ladders. He'd ripped one apart, but there were two others. "What is that rumble in the distance?"

"Don't know, but it's concerning."

"The servers—do we know what they do for certain?" He pointed at the lights glittering in the dome above them.

"The Starbird grid. It looks just like it looks in my dreams and memories, but they've built it here in real life."

"Why build it, though?" One Theroki helmet came into view at the stairs, but he nailed it with a blast of rifle fire just as Mo got in her own shot. Poor guy tumbled over the side, never having a chance.

"I think… I think they're all connected. We don't know for sure, but why did they run the two programs at the same time? Starbird seemed entirely different from Songbird. Separate. But I think it's not."

"But why would they—"

Her gasp cut off his words. An explosion behind him made him spin just in time to see the catwalk Mo had been shooting from tilt and swing outward. Mo slid, then caught the railing with one hand.

A second grenade dinked onto the last part of Mo's catwalk that remained level. Ballistic fire spattered Mo's armor even as her dynacamo morphed into a darker shade of gray, trying to adjust, but she was too far from anything for it to work properly.

He flinched as the new grenade exploded. The catwalk came free, and the sniper fell, the metal falling with her.

Straight toward the tank and the *Alarus*.

Ellen cursed. "Well, now that's two reasons to target the tank. C'mon."

They were only a few steps away from the edge. As soon as he could see white, he showered the tank with ballistics. The bullets sprayed across the surface, water shooting up, but quickly all trace of his rifle fire vanished, as if he hadn't even fired. "Look." He pointed. "That's right—the ballistics don't work on them."

"We brought rifles to a knife fight." She laughed bitterly. "Crappy rifles, but still… How do we get down there and stab it then?"

Behind them, he heard the hiss of a door opening, and he knew in that moment they had a big problem. Twisting, he saw that one of the two doors to the platform had opened and more reinforcements were swarming in. "Frag, Elle— We got company!"

She turned, eyes wide.

"I'll hold them, you go after Mo," he said quickly.

"No, we stay together."

"We can't stop this tide with lead, remember? I don't want to go *near* that thing. So you go, and I'll deal with these fools and join you when I've leveled them."

She didn't look like she liked the idea one bit, but there wasn't time to debate or come up with other plans. "I'll need something sharp. Can you rip off a piece of the stairway railings?"

They dashed to the closest one. While he fought the rivets and pulled, Ellen sprayed bullets at the incoming Therokis and a few coming up via the catwalks from below like a kid with a hose in the summertime.

With one last heave, he broke off a piece of the railing, the metal screaming as it tore into a jagged point. "There, that should do it."

She took the jagged piece of metal and sprinted for the elevator. "Tell those Therokis they can go to hell for me!"

He grinned as he turned and started to fire as he hurried to get some cover behind one of the freaky chairs. "It might surprise you, but I've been told I can be quite cocky at times. Occasionally insulting. Even rude. But sometimes, I think bullets speak better than words."

She chuckled. "Good luck, Kael."

Metal tore and screeched behind him and lights exploded, sending down cascades of sparks and creating pools of darkness. He got a second rifle and carefully aimed around the chair.

Therokis went down. Not all of them were even running, or firing, but simply shambling forward, almost like zombies. But some were keen, and he tried to hit those first.

Then the first rifle went empty, and his stomach dropped to his feet.

That… might be a problem.

He was dragging a fallen Theroki closer to try to get his weapon when they finally overran him.

He fought like a demon, but combat armor wasn't really designed for hand-to-hand combat, especially not with a bum leg. He managed to toss one into the tank. Then he crashed two helmets together, cracking them both, and sent their owners staggering…

But there were always more of them, always more.

He was getting tired. He could feel something wet and warm around his foot, which meant the medkit might be getting torn loose or failing.

To his surprise, they seemed all too prepared to fight him in particular. One produced a metal cable, then another had one, then another.

They looped one over his head like a bull at the rodeo. He lurched back, throwing his attacker off guard and off his feet, but another just picked up the cable, dragging him forward.

Where were they trying to take him?

Another got one around his shoulders, and when a third got his left elbow, it was harder and harder to use the cables against them.

He knocked a handful of them down, clotheslining them with the cables, but they were pulling him forward, steadily, steadily.

"Kael?" Ellen said over the comm channel.

"Not good, Elle," he grunted, then snarled as he heaved one off his feet by pulling the cable around his arm. He fired at their feet, trying to drive them further away. Some of them danced back; some of them ignored the fire, hoping their armor would hold. "Kill that squid for me! It sure would be nice to be fighting some docile zombies right now instead of these assholes!"

"Doing my best…"

They kept pulling until they had him in front of the chairs. Then more rushed in—pushing this time.

Pushing him down, back—into the chair.

He felt the left gauntlet come free and swore, realizing what they were trying to do. *Going* to do. Panic coursed through him, and he kicked one in the chest, sending three flying. But they were quickly back on their feet, and others funneled into the gap they left empty.

One of them, apparently the brains of the operation, was looking hard at the cables at his left, finding the right one. A dozen of them prodded at his arm, finding the port release easily.

It was just like theirs.

Praise Almighty, what would happen if they connected him to

that thing? To the hive mind? Would it kill him instantly? Would he become one of them?

This might be the last time he could ever talked to her. The ports on his arm cracked open. He'd better say anything he needed to say. "Elle—they've pushed me into this chair and are trying to hook me up."

"What? No, I'll—"

"Keep going, the *Alarus* is our best bet." He snatched his hand away from one of them and punched the guy with the cables in the face, to buy sometime. Nothing like punching heavy armor to hurt your hand, but what was a metal skeleton for if he didn't break a few visors with his knuckles once in a while? Bitterly, he twisted, kicking two more of them away. But the cables were tightening. "If I don't make it, take care of Shirin for me, okay? You'll be a better parent than I would've been anyway."

"What? No, no—that's not true. You're gonna be a great dad."

"I never had a family. What do I know about being a father?"

"What does anybody know? Nobody knows. Hold on, Kael. We can do this."

"Take care of her for me." Two more cables tightened around his chest, around his lower legs, making him clench his jaw and swallow a scream as they tightened around his legs and the already-failing medkit. Blood gushed toward his ankle.

"You are *not* dying here."

"Inshallah, my love."

"And neither is Mo. Not if I can help it. I'm down the elevator, I've almost found my way in—almost."

"Have a nice swim." The brains of the operation was back on his feet, sorting through the cables again.

"I hate swimming."

He swallowed. His mind flitted back to Vala, to the scientist all the way back on Helikai who'd tricked him into thinking she loved him. She'd actually been trying to hack his Theroki chip, steal it, and she didn't give two kumquats about his brain or his heart. That had become abundantly clear about the time she'd tied him to a chair in quite a similar way.

He laughed softly. It was funny in a way. He was back where he'd started. Except he had so much more. The chip Vala had destroyed had inadvertently freed him from his Theroki chains, had led him to Ellen, and the *Audacity,* and a life worth living.

"Just in case I end up with blond hair, I love you," he murmured.

"Love you too. This isn't the end, Kael."

"All things come to an end sometime, love. I'll die in the service of something noble. That's all I ever wanted anyway. This was more luck than I expected or deserved."

The brainiac was lining up the cable with his port.

"Not true." Her voice was rough, the comm distorted by interference. "Survive, Kael Sidassian, or I'll kill you."

The lead Theroki slid the connection home.

He closed his eyes and braced himself. *All right, fine. You want this? Show me what you got.*

Oh, we shall, replied a sleek, feminine voice.

The world exploded with a tidal wave of skull-splitting pain.

CHAPTER SEVENTEEN

"KAEL? KAEL!" She smacked the helmet by her ear, as though it would help her hear him better.

He didn't respond.

Something had happened.

She let out a hurricane of curses, taking out white-hot rage on the less-essential parts of the corridor she'd been racing down, even as she continued to run.

A plexi panel shattered. The floor was quickly pockmarked with dents. Smoke hissed out of a panel she'd punched as she passed, leaving destruction in her wake.

She slid to a stop in front of a view window into the tank. She was closer to the lapping water's edge now, getting closer.

Mo had made it to a jagged spot in the edge of the tank, clinging to the wall near the waterline, but she was on the complete opposite side from where Ellen was. Rifle fire had torn into the tank, and Mo had managed to get a grip on some of the resulting holes.

The bottom of the tank wasn't visible at all. A mass of white tentacles seethed, completely obscuring anything below.

As she watched, one of those tentacles curled around Mo's wrist and started to pull.

Swearing, Ellen started to run again, looking for a way in, her broken piece of rail still in her hand. Too bad she hadn't thought to bring along a harpoon.

A few meters later, she found what she was looking for—a hatch. She slapped a palm pad and spun the round handle on the door, and the thing swung inward slowly. At least it was unlocked…

Before her was a steel platform that wouldn't have fit a hover-bike. Beyond that, the thousand white, wriggling bodies stretched out, squirming. In the middle of them all, a larger tentacled creature swelled and heaved. She couldn't see all of the creature at any one moment. Who knew how big it really was, or how it was moving?

Or what it could do.

And the wires. So many wires. Cables running from the sides of the tank out, snaking around. Like their own sorts of tentacles, wires wound through the water, connecting the giant mass and maybe some of the others… to what?

To Starbird. To the telepaths and the Therokis. Cassandra was a monster stitched-together, all of those things combined. Those wires made her sure of it.

She staggered back abruptly as a tentacle snaked out, wrapped around her boot, and jerked her off her feet. With one hand, she caught the edge of the hatch as she slid.

Twisting, keeping her grip on the bottom of the hatch as best she could in this slick wet environment, she sliced at the tentacle with her piece of railing. It cut at the thing like a dull serrated knife, cutting but catching, snagging and then giving way with a spout of black blood.

An inhuman roar shook the tank. More tentacles snaked out of the water, larger ones, and she tore at them, too, and batted some of them aside. It bellowed again as its grip gave way.

She crawled away frantically, scanning the corridor. Was there a rope, an emergency kit with an ax or a laser torch? She needed to get to Mo, not just kill this thing.

The corridor might as well have been a holo chamber it was so empty. Hell. What would Kael do in this situation. Probably punch a hole in the…

Actually, that wasn't a half-bad idea.

She scanned for anywhere that looked like it might have a maintenance panel. She couldn't get anything to open directly, but she found some grating where she could see conduits running up into the station behind it. And maybe some pipes.

She was no Theroki, though, so she kicked instead. After three or four impacts, the wall was sufficiently brutalized for her to pull the metal aside. Then she grabbed the bundles of cords and yanked as hard as she could. And kept pulling.

She was still pulling cable from the wall as she ran back toward the tank, meters of wires dragging behind her. Well, hopefully, this could serve as a lifeline and not just electrocute them both. The suits *should* protect them from that—as long as they were properly intact.

She switched her speaker on and yelled, "Mo!" as she tossed the cables into the tank in Mo's direction. "Can you reach one of these?"

One of Mo's arms stretched out—the one that wasn't holding on—and tried to reach for the lifeline. "No dice!"

Still brandishing her torn, broken piece of railing, Ellen pulled on the wires, unravelling more and more into the water. It wasn't enough—it would only reach about halfway—and then abruptly, it stopped. Whatever the cables were attached to, she'd run out of slack.

Should she try to unmoor them? But then, how would they get themselves out? But this was still too short.

Before she could decide, another tentacle lashed out, catching her off guard because it didn't reach for her leg or arm nearest the water, like she expected.

It grabbed her makeshift weapon and pulled.

Ellen barely hung on. Lunging back toward the corridor with all her strength, she dragged the tentacle with her, the white flesh sliding up the railing and cutting into the raw jagged edges. Thin, black blood ran down the metal toward her hands.

Enough.

Both rifles were slung on their straps, and now she sloppily brought the first one she could reach to bear, ballistics slamming into the flesh.

The whole world shook with the anguished, shrieking sound. But it didn't recoil, no—six more tentacles, larger ones, reached for her.

She tried to dodge while also continuing to fire. She ducked one and leaned away from another, but the third found her boot. She stopped to hack savagely at it, but that gave the other ones more time to find purchase. Two more latched on.

Adrenaline pulsed through her as she was pulled toward the tank.

Black blood bloomed in the water. She'd hit something—maybe with the bullets or the two tentacles she'd sliced—but as before, the bullets sank in fruitlessly, doing no apparent damage.

She severed the tentacle wrapped around her boot, but two more found the piece of railing, and it slipped from her hands. Her only bladed weapon was gone.

Even though the bullets were barely more than useless, she emptied the first rifle, then began on the second. Not being multis, she had no idea if the weapons would survive the water, and she wasn't about to let any potential way of harming this thing go to waste.

She kept on firing, even as it pulled her closer to the edge.

JENNY HURRIED ALONG, shifting the heavy hiking backpack. "You know, I don't know if these are made for carrying kids *in space armor.*"

"What other kinds of kids would they carry?" Roya said flatly, blinking as she scanned their surroundings. A Theroki came around the corner, but even before he could have spotted the two of them, Roya removed the helmet just a little, and the Theroki's eyes blurred.

He fell down, somewhere between asleep and unconscious.

Jenny didn't know. Nor did she care.

"Where did you get the backpack anyway? Same place you got the helmet?" Zhia had ordered Roya, Shirin, and Isa some reasonable space armor at Molyarch, and Dr. Persad had fitted Roya's helmet with a few of her telepathy-blocking devices, so it could act as a shield, hiding Roya. And keep her from using her powers unless she took the helmet off, but really more for the shielding.

"Naturally," Roya said. "Xi ordered it at my request. Molyarch Adventure Outfitters has a large selection." Her head turned sharply toward a corridor they were approaching on their left. "This way."

"Yes, ma'am."

"Open that hatch."

Instead of answering, Jenny simply palmed open the nearby hatch. It shouldn't have worked, if it were truly locked, but maybe they didn't lock things around here. After all, everyone was literally the same person once they joined their goofy squid cult, right? Who exactly were they locking out?

"What are we looking for?" she asked, as she strode in.

"Environmental systems. Manual overrides."

Jenny carefully swept the room, giving Roya an eyeful of nearly every surface systematically. They had to be here *somewhere.*

"There!" Roya pointed. "That. Destroy that."

"Yes, ma'am." Jenny switched her multi to laser and put on a sustained, high-powered blast. Instantly the panel was melting, sending off sparks and smoke and probably toxic gas. She backed up but kept firing. As she worked, she reached out to the *Audacity.* "Adan?"

"Jen! Your comm was off—are you okay? Have you seen the empress—"

"Listen." Roya had sworn her to silence, so she decided she was going to have to breeze past that. "I've found the environmental controls. I think I'll be able to destabilize the *Alarus* completely from here."

"That's great. But have you—"

"I can't talk long. Have you been able to reach Ellen?"

"No, but I'm close. I can see the Union beacon in the network."

"Can you connect me to her when you do?"

"Consider it done. Maybe ninety seconds? But wait, have you seen Roya? Xi said—"

She faked swearing. "Sorry—a little busy here!" She snapped off the comm link and blew out a breath. Not like he couldn't just comm right back, but she had no idea what else to say. She wasn't going to *lie* to him. "Why can't we just tell them?"

"I understand you do not want to lie to your mate."

Jenny sighed. "You're too little to use words like that."

"I am centuries old."

"I know, I know. But why can't we just tell them?"

"Because they will not like what I am going to do. What is necessary."

"You sound like Cassandra."

"We are the same species after all. But what I believe is necessary and what she does are… not at all the same."

"Well, we're here now, and they're getting pummeled by Therokis. So they can't stop you now."

"All right, all right. Tell them the truth."

The hole in the wall where the control panel had been was gaping now. "It's melted. What else? Any others?"

"That one. And that is all it should take."

"I've got her!" Adan's voice suddenly broke through on the comm. "Ellen—you still there?"

"Mostly." Ryu's voice was strained, like she had an elephant sitting on her chest. Or a squid? Jenny shuddered. "Good to—hear you—Adan."

"I've got Jenny here on the line."

"Commander," Jenny said quickly. "Where are you? I think we've destabilized the *Alarus* habitat. I think that water may either get colder or start flooding the asteroid any minute now—or maybe boil?"

"Oh—really—" Her voice was enormously strained.

"Commander, where are you? Let me help."

"In—the tank."

Jenny, eyes wide, looked over her shoulder, locking eyes with Roya's big blue ones. "We're coming, Commander! Hang on!"

"Mo—too—" Ryu ground out.

"Wait—what do you mean *we*?" asked Adan.

Jenny winced. The cat was out of the bag, it seemed. Or the alien-kid hybrid was out of the spaceship. Whatever, the secret was out. Jenny steeled herself as she raced out of the control room and down the corridor.

"We, as in… I have Roya with me," she admitted.

"Why?" Dr. Levereaux demanded.

Hell, she hadn't realized it was the whole ship.

"It's important. I think. She asked. I said yes."

"But—I—but—" Levereaux sputtered.

"It doesn't matter now," Zhia cut in. "Focus on the mission and defending the ship."

A brutal, masculine roar exploded over the comm line, making her flinch again as she ran.

For a moment after it ended, they were all silent. And then a small voice said, "Is that… my dad?"

"Shirin—honey—" Levereaux started. "Maybe turn off your comm."

"No," Zhia insisted. "She's gunning, and we need everybody on. Kael's tough, Shirin. And so are you."

"He's—fighting—Therokis—a lot of them," Ellen ground out.

"Oh, seven suns," Shirin whispered.

"He'll—win. He always does."

Jenny's stomach twisted. God, she hoped Ellen was right. For all their sakes. She stopped as she came to an intersection. The corridor here branched off, leading in six different directions.

"That way."

EVERY TIME SHIRIN thought she was getting faster, the targeting interface sped up. "This is like cockroaches! There's always more of them!"

Isa, beside her, did not respond.

Grumbling to herself, she gritted her teeth. "That's fine. This is fine. You've probably never seen a cockroach anyway, let alone slept near one. But this is what it's like!"

"I have been on Molyarch Station, you know," Isa said calmly, eyes never moving.

Well, that was fine too. Shirin needed to keep her eyes on the targeting console anyway.

Except that part wasn't fine. It didn't matter how many there were.

"We're getting slammed here, Xi!" Adan cried out on the comm. His tone was pretty desperate, which made Shirin's stomach twist a little tighter.

"I would agree with that assessment. We have been slammed approximately 1,978 times with telekinetic forces, not to mention all the ballistics."

There was an edge of panic in Zhia's voice. "I'm falling back to the cargo hold. Three squad are with me. A couple more are in a defensive position. About half of them are down."

Shirin winced. They were weird and they didn't talk much, but they seemed like nice guys. They seemed… shell-shocked like her, from the way the world had treated them. Some people got quiet. Others got sassy and took boxing lessons and volunteered to shoot big guns in hopes of not getting abandoned yet another time. Of course, maybe she had already been abandoned but—if he came back, maybe that didn't count?

She squeezed the trigger a little harder for the next shot.

"Xi, do you know how that distraction is coming?" Doug put in.

"Unfortunately, no," Xi answered. "I cannot reach my physical android platform."

"Great!" Doug's laugh was manic. "Just great! Ellen, how are you—"

He never got to finish the question, as far as Shirin could tell. Suddenly, the view systems flickered and distorted, everything going black, for one long second, two, three.

"Comm and transfer systems disrupted!" Isa's mom was yelling from somewhere deep inside the ship. "They hit something on the outside of the ship, I think. Or maybe an EMP? I can't tell. Attempting to initiate backup systems!"

Subconsciously, Shirin reached for Isa's hand. To her surprise, she found it, and Isa clasped her hand back.

Voices rang out from inside the ship, echoing off of metal, hard to pinpoint and identify. The targeting systems had gone dark, but the gun turret had real viewports, several of them, and they could still see out into the hangar. That's where Isa had been looking all along.

The hangar itself had gone black as the deep too. Isa clenched her hand tighter, and although it was probably stupid, Shirin unbuckled her harness and stood so she could try to see whatever Isa was seeing.

It was hard to see anything in the blackness, but there were little pinpoints of electronic light. And some of them were moving.

Heavy impacts clanged against metal toward the front of the ship.

"They're on the hull up here. Not far!" The accent sounded like Fern's. Shirin thought she could hear the sound of rifles being loaded.

She glanced around. "What if they reach us?" she whispered.

"I'm planning on keeping them from doing so."

"Can they hear us?"

"Yes."

"You're reading their minds. What are they thinking?"

"One is thinking that they have us now. Another is pondering how we'll taste when they eat us."

She wished she hadn't asked. There had to be a weapon or something around here. Not that she had learned how to do much with any of them. The multis were complicated. She let go of Isa's hand

and tried to search around the nooks and crannies of the gun turret area for something, anything that could help.

She found nothing. "Xi?"

There was no answer.

"Deploying grenades!" someone yelled from somewhere in the ship.

There was the sound of something sliding, then a *thunk, thunk, thunk*. The launch would normally not have been audible, but it was loud with the *Audacity* having fallen silent in the dark.

Shirin staggered back. They were close to windows. Wouldn't the grenades potentially hurt them too?

"Knockout grenades," Isa said quietly. "Most of the crew have shielding built into their armor. We don't, but they're firing them far, into the biggest mass of Therokis far across the hangar platform. That's good because *Audacity* is helpless right now. We need something extra."

"H-h-helpless?"

The thuds on the hull seemed to be lighter, coming closer.

"What is that?" she whispered now.

"Footsteps."

It seemed fruitless, but she rushed back and grabbed Isa's hand again. What would happen if they reached this turret?

Isa squeezed her hand again, and Shirin found herself shivering. It wasn't cold, though. She forced herself to look out the center viewport again, to see what was going on and if there was some way she could help—

And she screamed.

ALL AT ONCE, the pain abruptly ended. All Kael's senses shut off, shut down, like he'd been plunged into one of those sadistic isolation chambers used for torture in Faros and other horrible corners of the 'verse.

Well, this was just going *great* so far. Just peachy.

He heaved in a breath, but he couldn't feel any air. Or any lungs, for that matter. A dark swirling shadow overtook the field of view in his mind's eye. It felt like he'd lost his body altogether.

If you play with fire, Kael Sidassian, you're going to get burned.

Panic at the complete isolation was rising, but he forced it down. His enemy was talking to him. Dr. Persad's blocking add-on had protected him from telepaths getting into his mind at a distance, but the wire they'd plugged in overrode that. Both his mind and Cassandra's were now connected to the computer network, and that meant she could get in. How far, he wasn't sure. Could she know his thoughts? Could she kill him? He had no idea.

The only thing slowing Cassandra down was the sheer number of minds in this network. He didn't know how many, but he sure hoped Elle and the others were keeping their enemies busy.

He gritted his teeth. *I've been playing with fire my whole life. This doesn't impress me.*

The shadow in his mind cleared, and he found himself… somewhere else entirely.

Flames licked around him, obscuring the view down the corridor. It was dark, bleak, a corridor of the *Genokai* or another Theroki ship just like it. Smoke stung his eyes—where the hell was his armor—and he held up an arm to shield his face.

At the end of the corridor, a face caught his eye through the licks of flame and the billows of smoke. Ellen.

His gut wrenched. But no—hell, no—this wasn't real. This was the *Alarus*—Cassandra—Starbird—whatever it was, torturing him.

C'mon! he shouted into the nothingness. *Why even show me this?*

To hurt you. To remind you who is in control of this network and who must comply or be expunged.

When he glanced back, Ellen had become Shirin, and knowing it wasn't real didn't keep his body from responding, jolting in fear, wanting to run toward her.

No, no, *no.*

The shadow returned, and with it, the silent emptiness.

He growled. *You call this control?* he tried to roar into the silence. *You're not in control. You're a warden of a prison of mindless zombies.*

You will be one of them soon. We are many. You understand nothing.

None of them following you willingly, like I follow Ellen.

There was a hiss. *Do not speak of the deserter here. What you say is not true. Many of us volunteered.*

Finally. Some sort of rise out of the thing. *Like hell, they did. I saw the reports of the kidnappings on Faros. You lobotomized them. They're puppets, and you pull the strings. Real leaders win people over.*

Your insults mean nothing to us. Your node has already been assimilated, as will all others in time. The sooner you accept this, the sooner we will allow external access.

He wanted to snap, *Never!* But he tried to quell the rage that had built up from the pain. He needed to calm down, get steady to find a way out of there.

You are in the hive mind now. We control every aspect of your world, every sense, every experience. Every choice you can make.

A room opened around him, circular, with windows all the way around. Sea stretched out in all directions, the sun close to setting to his right. The only thing in the room was a gaming table, almost like… almost like some of the ones on Capital. Was this room supposed to be Capital?

Inside the gaming interface, lights sprang to life, shifting and forming a golden holographic ghost of the *Audacity*, gliding into a docking bay.

It was being swarmed by blood-red sparks that he knew were supposed to be Therokis.

Your friends are dying. They die because they chose to follow you. You led them to their deaths. Does this make you happy?

Happy? You're cracked, you know that. Sick. He squinted at the holograms, reached out. He was able to zoom in further, see the attack on his friends better.

Your insults fuel me almost as much as your pain does. You are the cause of their suffering. And yet, you've already failed, they just don't know that. You're already one of us.

He said nothing for a moment. If any of that were true, a lack of reaction was in his best interests. *These Therokis are getting mowed down. You're really not much of a leader.*

It was true. Despite their large numbers, Kael could see sparks going out shockingly fast. Of course, foot soldiers storming a starship with just rifles wasn't *ideal* for overtaking a ship. Especially if the ship didn't have to care about the hangar bay, you know, surviving at all.

As if you could do better.

I could, he insisted. *I was a Theroki. I manned the guns on that ship. Maybe you should let me.*

Please. Ridiculous. You won't turn on your friends.

No, but... so many dead. He took a deep breath, carefully controlling his thoughts. Those Therokis were innocent, too. They didn't choose this fight, as conscripts. *It's hard to watch.*

Is it?

He regretted saying that because his brain suddenly flooded with anguished images from the hangar—his body slamming into a piece of fuselage, impaled; a turret blowing off an arm; a soldier near the *Audacity*'s hull throwing a grenade toward a crowd of Therokis that were blown back. Pain and chaos washed over him.

Wait, he knew that armor. That grenade thrower was *Zhia.*

She was totally alone. Where was the squad? Where were the others? Someone to help her? There had to be hundreds more Therokis coming. He could see them jogging closer, shouting. So much pain.

The images ended, and he found himself back in the strange Capital room, but he'd fallen to his knees. Or had she put him in that position? Seven suns, though—Zhia was going to die. He had to try to do something.

You see. Hopeless.

She doesn't need to die, he begged. *C'mon. You already have me. I—I could show you how to get onto the ship and take prisoners. Maybe some of the* Audacity*'s crew would join willingly. More would survive—on both sides—that way.*

There was a pause.

No. You are lying. Why would you bother to help me?

Because they're my friends. If there's anything I can do to keep them alive—

You are not yet adequately assimilated. You need further treatment—

Wait! He had a bad feeling that meant more excruciating pain and sensory deprivation. *Please. Like you said, it's less death in the long run. Peace sooner. You should try to take prisoners. Give them a chance.*

Why? Why should I bother?

If you just murder them on their ship, you're no better than the murderers you're trying to stop! Please. Surely, some of them would relent to join your side. Even if they don't, you can kill them later anyway. Less Therokis would be dead. He held his breath. *Please—let me help my friends.*

Lines appeared above each little spark, extending up to a rectangle of light floating above them. Kael stood up and saw there were controls in it.

If you truly seek peace, go ahead and try. We are watching.

He reached toward the controller. His hands were naked, unarmored, and they penetrated the light like the object wasn't real, but then it shifted, coating his hands in red light like gloves, crimson as a poisoned apple.

I will offer the choice to join us in exchange for your cooperation. But if they refuse, they will die.

He nodded. *Only fair.*

Taking a slow breath, he started to move, to see what he could do. His mind throbbed, images of the docking bay and the outside of the *Audacity* battering his mind. Thousands of eyes and thoughts and breaths threatened to overwhelm his sanity. And the noise—too many weapons firing all at once, inside his head.

You see. Not as easy as you thought, is it, to be a leader, control the multitude?

He set his jaw. *The way to get into the cargo hold is…* He made the image larger, but he was still staggered by the information. But then again, it didn't need to be easy, did it? He didn't need to stay sane. He didn't even need to live. For him, it was too late.

But he did need to make one final oath. And he'd let the bloodlust and the oath programming work for *him* this time.

What are you doing?

In his mind, he activated the oath, imagining finding the control on his forearm. He felt the need kick in, real or psychological, and he gritted his teeth.

I swear I will tear control from you if it's the last thing I do. Then, he held on as hard as he could to the strange controls and pulled. *Give them to me.*

How dare you. You promised peace.

He ripped at the threads, red and gold, both in the interface and in his mind. *It's a simple calculation,* he growled. *Less death in the long run if I'm in control. I thought you'd understand.*

Liar. Fool. Absolutely incorrect.

In the strange circular room, he bent and, with hands still red as blood, he lifted the side of the gaming table and overturned it, hurling it toward the windows and the sea.

Those were people *once,* he snapped, *with their own minds, their own dreams, and they deserved to keep them. They don't belong to you. They don't belong to anyone. I will set them free.* And even as he said it, he knew it was true. He could feel pieces of the system cracking, falling away, going silent.

Air and the scent of the ocean and light and noise and screaming exploded around him.

You will pay for this. I will torture this mind for eternity. I will never *let you free.*

EVEN AS THE water covered her head, Kael's anguished scream rang out over the comm, setting her nerves on fire.

"Hang on, Kael," she whispered, even if he couldn't hear her. "Hang on."

But she had a much more immediate problem—the creature was already hanging on to her, tight.

Gritting her teeth, she fought her way free of the few that had pulled her under and, for a moment, got free of them. Desperately, she found the wall with her feet and pushed hard in the direction she thought Mo was. She had to reach Mo. The sooner, the better. Two of them together would be better than one, and if they could get out of the tank, maybe Mo would have a grenade they could toss back in.

Kael screamed again.

She swam faster, pushed her way through the seething white cephalopods. God, she needed to kill this awful thing before it killed him. Although… A chilling thought occurred to her. If it died while he was connected to it, would he live? Or would he…

Before she could really complete that thought, she swore as pain lanced into her ankle. A thick tentacle had wrapped around her boot in the disgusting mix of water and tiny squids. The grip was so strong that even the metal power armor started to constrict against her bones—not quite enough to damage the seal. Not yet. But it took quite a bit of force to crush power armor. And this was just *one* of them.

Not. Good.

The tentacle tightened a little more—and then pulled.

She didn't scream, not exactly, as it pulled her down into the depths, but she did roar in frustration at the thing, grabbing at anything and everything she could get her hands on. She yanked at cables and wires, got hold of other squirming tentacles and tossed them away or tried to crush them in her gauntlets.

The grip tightened even further.

She bent, still sinking lower and lower in the tank. The water-pressure readings on her helmet display climbed. Reaching the tentacle, she got a good grip on her adversary above her boot and squeezed.

Two could play at the crushing game.

Somewhere in the tank, an unearthly, earsplitting cry echoed. She flinched.

"Oh, you don't like that, huh?" she shouted. "Let's see how you like this."

Just for some added spice, she fired up the gauntlet lasers and let them get to work. She had no intention of turning them off any time soon, at least not until she was out of this stupid tank.

They wouldn't work anywhere near as well as they would in the air. But they might boil the water. Or make it annoyingly warm—anything. She needed all the help she could get.

She gritted her teeth, grabbed onto a tentacle reaching for her waist, and squeezed, all the while trying to kick her way toward Mo.

CHAPTER EIGHTEEN

ISA CUT off the sound of Shirin's scream with a hand over her mouth.

The Theroki was right there in the center viewport. Close now. Shirin wasn't sure if he could see them, but she sure as heck could see him. The tiniest bit of light from outside the hangar glinted on his battered helmet, one light blinking on the shoulder of a charred chest.

He reached a hand up and—slammed it into the viewport window. Cracks immediately formed.

"No…" she whispered. "How can he—"

"No shields, and augmented with his telekinetics," Isa said quickly. "Did you get an RPD installed yet?"

"A what?"

Another slam into the window—this time, both fists. Deeper in the ship, she could hear shouting, but she couldn't make it out.

"It doesn't matter. Let's move back." Isa moved the two of them back against the far wall.

"What is he thinking?"

"Are you sure you want to know?"

The whole turret seemed to shake as he pummeled the window again.

"Yes."

"He's thinking, *there's no food. There's never enough food.*"

Shirin bit back a whimper.

"That's the problem," Isa said. "He's too hungry to fall asleep like some of the others. Starving to death."

"Tell him the better food's in the *Genokai*. And none of the others are even looking there, so he'll have it all to himself."

Isa looked down at her in surprise; even in the dark, Shirin could see her eyebrows were raised. She looked almost like a normal person.

The next slam didn't come. Footsteps on the hull moved away.

"That actually worked," Isa whispered. "Good idea, Shirin!"

Unfortunately, the electrical was still not up, backup or otherwise. The two of them held each other, curled against the back wall of the gun turret. The steel was cold against Shirin's shoulder. She could smell ozone and oil and—most concerning—smoke.

More footsteps clunked against the hull, coming closer. There were more *thunk, thunk, thunks* of grenades, rifle fire somewhere near the cargo hold.

She clung tighter to Isa. "Do you think we will die here?"

"No."

"Has anyone ever told you you're a bit strange?"

"No. They all think it, though."

"Oh, okay."

There was a pause.

"Do *you* think we'll die here?" Isa asked.

Even as she asked it, fresh footsteps approaching manifested their apparitions outside the viewports. More Therokis, three, four, no half a dozen. Maybe she couldn't even see them all.

One raised the butt of his rifle, and the others followed suit, pounding on the viewports.

Gritting her teeth, she realized there *was* one weapon she hadn't tried yet. "EOE8, come online!" she whispered. Its sensors were sharp to hear its wakeup command from a great distance, but she'd never tried from this far, with the banging. She had no idea if it'd be able to hear. "Emergency, EOE8. Hurry!"

She could hear it had worked by the pounding of the bot on the deck grating. "Shirin is in trouble! Shirin is in trouble!"

Even without light or Xi's guidance, the nurse bot found her somehow. It lurched into the room, throwing itself in front of them, and Shirin felt a surge of guilt for turning it off in the first place. It would never have let her come here, and this whole situation proved it would probably have been right.

"Shirin, Isa, if you please, we should evacuate this cabin. It appears you have some hostile visitors. And then, if someone could get me a weapon? It is my duty to protect you, after all, my dear Shirin."

"C'mon, this way," Isa said, moving toward the ladder out of the turret.

Just as Shirin turned to follow them, the pounding abruptly stopped. They all turned and looked, just in time to see several of the Therokis collapse.

Shirin frowned and looked at Isa. "Your doing?"

"No."

"A grenade?"

"They're…" She frowned. "They're dead. Well, they're brain dead. Like the inspector, the John Doe they'd picked up on Capital. Something… someone… cut the cord."

"Well, none too soon," EOE8 said primly, "but we should still be going. Those viewports likely no longer have space-faring integrity."

They eased down the ladder, into the darkness, and Shirin noticed everything had gone quieter now. Almost dead quiet.

Behind her, EOE8 pulled across a heavy metal seal. "Blast doors. I can't perfectly seal it like Xi would, but some barrier will be better than none. Now let's—"

Before the bot could finish its suggestion, the roar of an explosion outside the ship drowned out their voices. In her surprise, Shirin lost her grip on the rung and slipped, reaching out in vain as she fell into the darkness.

ALL ELLEN COULD SEE WAS white and gray. Small tentacles, bigger ones. The water had gone gray with black blood. "Adan? Doug? Xi?"

"We're here, Commander," Jenny replied. "But I can't reach the *Audacity* either."

"Here—too—" Mo grunted.

"Looks like it's just the three of us, then," she said quietly. "Let's kill this thing. Or at least get out of the tank alive. I'd settle for either at this point."

She was pulled this way and that, but not toward the bottom of the tank, where the jagged rail had fallen.

Did metal armor make good squid food? Because she had a bad feeling these tentacles were trying to take her toward the center. As a snack.

She wrestled one tentacle off that had curled around her chest and tried to crush her. She brutally ripped away another one that had been wrapping around her helmet as it tried to find the helmet release.

But they just kept fragging coming, like pit dragons in heat.

She was in the process of severing another random tentacle with her bare hands—well, her power-armored gauntlets, but still—when a new familiar voice cut in.

"Ellen. Ellen, can you hear me?" It was Paul. Fragging Paul.

"How did you get this number?" Her voice was hard as steel.

"Very funny. You *are* wearing one of my suits. Stolen, I believe."

"Touché. What do you want?" She wondered if Jenny and Mo could hear all this. If they could, they were keeping quiet.

"Also, your friend Doug connected our comms people. He's gone silent now though."

She swallowed hard. "Overrun." Just as she felt this limb squish apart, another curled around her thigh. Dammit. "Little busy."

"I'll make it quick. It's important. Listen, it's—it's Tauber."

"What?"

"He's shown up with the *Volga*."

She swore. "Dreck-eating, puss-covered—"

"Hey now, I'm just relaying—"

"Not you! Him!"

"Oh. Right." He sounded moderately pleased.

"If I could just—get—free—" Of course, at that moment, another tentacle grabbed at her wrist, so chances of that were slim at this point. "I'm being strangled to death by ten dozen squid, Paul! And I'm unarmed! Do you fragging want something?"

"Look—your friends are on the asteroid, they should be coming to help. I'm gonna do my best to hold Tauber and the *Volga* off. But you know this won't be an easy win here."

"One way to put it!" She laughed bitterly.

"We are royally fucked."

"More accurate!" Her voice ground out the words as she finally severed through a tentacle trying its best to become a manacle too. But the other two were trying to work together, pulling one arm up and her leg down.

It was trying, in its uncoordinated way, to rip her apart.

Could Paul hear the creature shrieking on the comm? She sure hoped so.

"I'll buy you all the time I can," Paul was saying. "But in all likelihood, the *Volga* will get passed us. Bridell has a plan—"

"Don't trust him! Don't do it, Paul!"

"Okay, okay. Kick those Songbird bastards in the nuts for me, will you?"

"No nuts to kick!" She kicked at the one capturing her leg with her free leg and pulled on the arm-attached tentacle, trying to find some traction. Or maybe… Her eyes caught on some nearby wires swirling past on her right side.

"That figures," Paul muttered.

"And if anyone is getting kicked, it's me," she grunted out. "At the moment."

She lunged for the wires and yanked them toward her as hard as she could. Somewhere below, something gave way, but nobody screamed, so she pulled down harder now, hoping the other end was attached to something above her.

Harder. Harder.

Suddenly, the resistance gave way, sending her spinning. The piercing shrills made her flinch, rage coloring the sound. The two tentacles on her arm and thigh suddenly loosened. She tried to right herself, wriggle free.

"You've never cared about the odds, Ellen," Paul said. "You can do this."

That was... oddly fortifying. Even if he *was* a complete asshole. She snatched her arm out of reach. "Working on it."

"Godspeed." He cut off the comm.

Maybe... maybe trying to reach Mo wasn't going to work. Maybe if she could reach the bottom, though, she could unplug some more circuits. Find her broken railing piece.

She jackknifed and kicked with her feet, breast stroking through the miasma toward the bottom.

The next tentacle that got ahold of her was on the thinner side, and she yanked it along with her. The thing's howling moan was continuous now. The sound seemed to shake her suit, shaking her very bones.

She severed it, a trail of black snaking after it as it recoiled away from her, darkening the water ever further. The blood didn't help her here. It'd be good if it meant the thing was dead, but clear water would be nice.

With enough damage, she realized abruptly, the water would become opaque, and it would be harder and harder to tell which way was up and out and how she could possibly reach Mo, let alone help her.

Momentarily free, she put everything she had into her strokes, pointing herself down in the direction of the artificial grav generators while she still could.

About ten seconds later, she'd dodged two swinging tentacles—

and she'd found the bottom.

She groped along it, swooping tiny octopi out of her way like snow from a blizzard littering the ground.

She found one mass of cables joining into the side, and she gave it a tug. It didn't come free, but the laser happily cut into the insulation. Bubbles from the water boiling erupted around the cables, little sparks finding life inside a few of them. Oh, excellent. Electrical current in the water. Because life wasn't complicated enough.

Unfortunately the *Alarus* was still moving, so it didn't seem to be enough to kill the creature.

She pushed off the damaged bundle of cables with her feet, sliding past two other connections. They were tempting, but not really what she was looking for. If she got caught up in another tentacle grab, she could find cables as they snaked through the water and do equal damage. But she needed something special.

Just as she felt one tentacle find her right knee, she saw it. The jagged railing.

She groped. Her gauntlet scraped against the tank, short by a few centimeters. She raked at the bottom, looking for purchase, but the tank bottom was smooth as ice.

The tentacle started to pull her back toward the center.

She fought it, kicking, using it to push off and slightly forward, reaching—

And her fingers found the bottom of the rail.

Smiling viciously to herself, she went limp except for her grip on her weapon.

The silence of the comm was deafening. There was no Kael, no *Audacity*, no help coming, no one else. Quiet but for the sound of the water through the suit.

She let the tentacle pull her. In fact, after a moment or two, she bared her teeth in something between a smile and a snarl. She turned, grabbed on, and—still holding her weapon—she started to climb.

WHAT DO *you hope to accomplish by this?* Kael demanded as soon as he could think again over the pain. He was unmoored in space again, no body, no sight, but somehow, he had the sensation of walking across hot coals while also being dipped in acid.

Cassandra's answer was brusque. *Your endless suffering.*

Well. That certainly was going to prove a problem. *You can't break me.*

But it will be amusing to try. You lied to us. We thought you understood. Peace can only be achieved through submission.

You murder *people. You abandon them to starve. I might be a Theroki, but I don't think I'll be taking lessons in 'peace' from you.*

Really? How many have you *killed? And for what, for money?* Faces flashed through his mind, faces from the streets of Faros, people he'd give anything to forget. *Three hundred forty-two…*

Stop.

The faces kept coming, ripped straight from his memories—hits in the company of other Therokis, innocent bystanders. Asha. Now *she* didn't count. Enhancers, Teredarks—

Eight thousand, six hundred—

Stop, he screamed.

When the faces finally stopped, he was panting again, even more exhausted, and a streak of fear ran through him too. He might just be wrong about this. Maybe she *could* break him.

The pain started to rise again.

There had to be a way to cope with this—aside from just screaming, which considering he couldn't feel his body exactly, didn't accomplish much.

What had Dr. Taylor said to do? Maybe it'd work here, maybe it could work even better than normal in this strange, twisted world of mental night.

Visualization? That hadn't distracted him so far. Maybe the *Alarus* was interfering with it, because he couldn't quite hold a picture for more than a few seconds. Deep breaths, well, he had no idea if his body was still breathing. Or if it even existed. Compartmentalization?

Yes. That was the ticket.

He got to his knees, at least in his mind, the pain coursing through him like knives in his veins. Visualizing the separation in his mind, he dug at the ground. He made the dirt soft, no—sand. Just like he'd done a time or two as a child. It felt real and tactile for a moment, but the sensation was fleeting, like a scent on the wind. Yes, he'd dug up a hole to dump the pain into.

No, maybe to put himself in and hide—to shut the pain out.

He blinked as a structure formed around him, even as his hole grew at his feet. It was bleak, the curved walls made of something like industrial cement, like the infrastructure in the tunnels of his youth.

Energy surged through him, and excitement, in spite of the pain dancing like acid across his nerves. Maybe he couldn't escape Cassandra and this system. But he *could* have an effect here, some kind of effect, even if they were just illusions keeping him from losing all grip on sanity.

Building a tiny little fort in your tiny little mind? How quaint. Go on. Hide like a little boy.

He *was* a little boy who had survived for a long time, relying only on himself, in a world that hadn't given one whit about him, so he didn't see the insult in that. The cement structure was small, cramped even, almost like a drainage tunnel. He'd been there more than a few times. Facing him was an open door that could block off the tunnel. Behind him, another door was already closed, a heavy one, like a blast door. For keeping out fires or tamping down explosions or airborne contaminants or contagions. Or were they storm drains? No, no. They weren't anything. This wasn't real.

This was a way to hide from Cassandra, hide from the pain.

A real man would have the courage to face his defeat. Endure his punishment without so much screaming and whining and crying.

A real man doesn't worry about if he's a real man or not. His mental form stood up. He strode forward and closed the door to the tunnel. The light went dark, midnight blue, dreamy.

The pain lessened. Silence fell, but an easier one this time.

At least until there was a crash into the doors. He was hiding. He was safe from the pain for now.

But she was out there, still trying to get in, still coming.

He lay down in front of the door to rest, to fortify it, to hope that Ellen would find a way to kill the damn thing and to hope that this was actually accomplishing something.

Time went molten. He couldn't be sure whether minutes or hours or years had passed. He might have slept, or it might have been only a blink, but eventually, he heard Cassandra outside the doors again.

Sister! I did not want to help them in these deeds! Free me!

He shook off his sleepy confusion. Who was she talking to?

And then he heard another voice, a voice that sent a chill down his spine. *It does not matter. You broke the sacred laws. Our covenants. You know what happens to those who break them.*

"Roya," he whispered, mostly to himself. "What are you doing here?"

I am making things right.

No—the telepath coerced me. And the network—it's intelligent! It's insane! Sister! Free me!

I will free you, in a way. Roya's voice was cold. *But I will brook no lies. We shall end this.*

Roya. His body called out, far from his mind. "Roya? Roya!"

Let the humans have control of us no longer. Come closer and help me, sister. Together we are so much more than we are apart.

To force is not the proper way. You know what happens to those who break our laws.

Do not betray our species—join me! Help me! The voices went wild in his skull like a thousand people at once, demanding and shrieking and jockeying to triumph. But why? What did Roya *mean?*

You made your choice, not me. I honor our species in honoring our laws. You are the one who has betrayed us. Roya's voice paused for a moment. *Kael Sidassian.* Somehow, her voice reached inside him, quieter and closer, dimming the cacophony. For a moment, he thought he could see her in all her shining glory just before him in the dank drainage tunnel. *Thank you for all that you've done for me. You certainly took me full circle. Can you disconnect from this system? Otherwise, this may kill you too. I am not sure. I am not even sure I can succeed.*

I can't disconnect. They forced me in here. I don't think I can reach my body. I think—I think she might have cut the connection. What are you doing?

I am severing all of Cassandra's connections. All of them. To everything.

He caught his breath.

As I freed Ellen Ryu from those she adopted on Faros, so now I will free them all.

But I—I—you'll kill them.

Yes. And I'll likely die in the process. I don't want to take you with me. Get out now.

I'll try. He tried to move his arms, feel his arms, even. To find the cable and yank it out. He tried to move his lips. Form words. *Real* words. Could someone hear him? Because instinct told him this was his chance.

Nothing happened. He pushed a desperate shout into the void, a wild, primal scream. No sound came back to him of his own voice, no real sensations. No breath in his lungs.

His body was gone. Maybe he'd been shot and his mind was just trapped in here, floating forever.

His mental body shook its head, frustrated with the futility of it all. *Nothing. I'm trapped in here.*

Roya's mind growled, a fierce, primordial sound he did not think a human throat could make. *I will lend my strength to yours, to mentally fortify this place where you hide. Close yourself off to her, to me, to all of it. Hide, and you may survive.*

No. A chill went through him. *No, let me help you.*

Her glowing form frowned.

Let me do something to help.

You could… focus her presence for me to act.

How?

If you draw her anger here, I can cut the connections more easily, in one swift slice. Or perhaps two or three. There are many connections.

How? How do I bring her here for you?

Simple. Open the door.

He swallowed. He knew what that would mean, how much it would hurt. He might not get the door closed again. Cassandra might tear him apart while Roya was tearing *her* apart.

Indeed, she might. This is why you should hide.

No. I can die happy if Cassandra dies with me. He nodded, mentally anyway. *Tell me when.*

He stood and strode to the door, putting his hand on the antiquated handle that would spin the door open.

No. I see. No. She seemed to be talking to Cassandra, not him now, but he couldn't understand it all anymore. They were speaking in their own language. *You thought because I was young, I would be weak. But your drive blinds you. For I am strong.*

He closed his finger around the handle, listening. Trying to steady his mind, calm his nerves, steel his heart.

Now.

He spun the wheel and flung open the door to the tunnel, exposing his sanctuary.

Water flooded in, liquid screams, cold as ice and cutting to the bone. He started to shake, but he gritted his teeth and braced himself against the drainage wall for the flood that was to come.

CHAPTER NINETEEN

THE TENTACLE THICKENED as Ellen climbed, more tendrils winding around her. But they didn't stop her climb. She supposed if your lunch was crawling toward your mouth, you might as well let it.

She kept an iron grip on her lance made of broken railing.

As she neared the top, the tentacle swirled, bringing her up, up—and Ellen froze.

In front of her loomed a giant eye, larger than her chest, golden and bright, but the pupil made her wince. It was shaped like a U, like a normal pupil had melted into a limp outline of one. Even as she watched, it moved, opening and closing slightly.

She was so freaked, she almost forgot her plan. Almost. She'd been thinking heart or beak, but this would be even better…

Squeezing her eyes shut, she let go of the stupid tentacle and stabbed straight at the brilliant, golden eye.

The inhuman roar buffeted her, her body shaken by it, and then the tentacles moved. Not closer, but further away—she was moving fast, up, up.

Out of the water—it tossed her into the air, slamming her into the side of the tank, almost out of it.

Almost.

Raking her fingers against the sides as she fell, she found no purchase. Her whole body ached, in spite of the armor, and hitting the water didn't help, but she fought to stay above the surface, pulling herself around the edge of the tank.

There were two ladders at twelve and six o'clock, and a platform at nine, so she couldn't be *that* far away from any of them. Scanning frantically, she saw no sign of Mo at all.

Frag it all to hell.

"Commander, was that you?" Jenny's voice came over the comm.

"Flying through the air?" She swam as best she could toward the nearest ladder.

"Yeah."

"Yup, having lots of fun down here." It wasn't far now.

"We're close, let's see what we can—"

Ellen was nearly to the wall when a mass of tentacles reached for her. Maybe the *Alarus*-Cassandra-whatever-it-was was done playing with its food.

Just as it pulled her under, her hand gripped the rung of the ladder. Her other hand joined the first. And she was *not* letting go. Kicking and squirming and just pulling away from the offending tentacles, she pulled herself up one rung, then another, out of the water.

Suddenly, ballistic fire rained down around her. She flinched—fragging Therokis. One more rung, then another.

But it seemed to only be hitting the tentacles. More screams of frustration and some of them recoiled. "That you firing, Jen?"

"Yes, ma'am."

"Good shooting." Even if it did nothing but piss the *Alarus* off. She got the next rung. And the next. And she climbed.

When she reached the top, Mo helped her up over the side while Jenny kept up suppressive fire, this time taking aim at a catwalk above them where a few Therokis had taken up a position. As the only one left with a rifle, that made sense.

"We need more guns," Ellen muttered.

"I got up pretty much the same way, Commander," Mo said. "That's a lot of blood down there. You wreaked havoc."

"Remind me to never eat calamari ever again." Ellen shook her head as she surveyed where they'd climbed out of the tank. Unfortunately, the platform they were on was *not* on Kael's side of the tank, but the opposite, with no direct path connecting them. All the stairs leading up to his platform had taken heavy fire—or been torn off by Kael personally. On their side of the tank, there was one set of stairs down from their platform to the level that led to the cathedral area, but with no way back up to Kael's side, that didn't seem to make any sense.

For a moment, she just stared. How were they ever going to reach him?

"Or maybe we should eat all the calamari we can find." Jenny grinned. "If we ever make it out of this place."

As Jenny spun to pick off another target, Ellen froze. "What—who—is on your back?"

"Oh that? I needed to bring someone." She jerked a thumb over her shoulder. On her back, a little girl holding a helmet in one hand smiled and then waved.

"What in the ever-loving-frag are you—" Ellen started.

"I demanded it," said Roya's small voice.

Ellen scrambled for words but couldn't find any.

"Only I can kill her."

Ellen's mouth fell open, then she hurried to shut it again. "Well. I. Um..."

"I needed to be close. It will be soon."

"What?"

"Cassandra's death."

"I—but—how?"

"I will enforce the old laws. You will escort me, as my honor guard, but leave her to me. There are more Therokis coming," Roya said simply. "We must hurry."

Ellen sighed. "Anybody see an armory around here?"

Mo shook her head. "Where's Kael?"

Ellen pointed, wincing. "Up there. Therokis overtook him while we were headed toward the tank. He went silent a couple minutes ago. Sort of."

"He was forcibly connected to the telepathic computer network," said Roya.

Jenny swore, forgetting her target for a moment.

"Yes. He is distracting Cassandra, or she would have crushed you more thoroughly during your swim," Roya replied. "She is enjoying torturing him."

It was Ellen's turn to curse. "Some of these fallen Therokis should have something we can use. Find any weapons you can."

Wordlessly, Mo bent toward the nearest one to help search, while Jen provided cover.

Suddenly the lighting banks above them flickered, flickered again, then died.

In complete darkness, the whole asteroid shook. Mo hurried to grab on to Ellen's arm—standard protocols. Loss of power could mean loss of grav, which meant holding on or losing each other. Of course Mo was the one to have her wits about her.

"What's causing that shaking?" Ellen demanded, switching to night vision. Thankfully, this suit had that. She'd only found one rifle, but it was better than nothing. She bit her lip, trying to think.

"Commander." Roya's quiet voice was urgent.

"Yes?"

"It will happen soon. You need to get to Kael and get out of here."

"Yeah," Jenny put in. "The damage we did to that tank was hard-core, any minute now something weird could happen—"

"If the gravity is lost with all that water—" Mo started.

"Water and blood and cephalopod are going to be floating every which way," Ellen finished.

"I think I know a way we can get over there," Mo said. "I've got a handful of grenades left. It's not the safest option, but if we could bring down some of those catwalks, or even the light banks, in a piece that was long enough, we could position them across the tank and run across, like a bridge."

"And if the tentacles come up and drag us back in?"

Jenny winced. "Then you two already got out of there once and can do it again?"

Ellen shook her head. She did *not* want to do that again. "It's too risky. We don't have time for it." She hesitated. "But I also don't have any better ideas. Anyone?"

Mo shook her head. "We… hope we lose gravity and can fly our way over there?"

"There is a convoluted way through the corridors," Roya offered. "I can pull it from the memories of the Therokis. But it will take too long. We don't have that much time."

Ellen sighed. "Okay, let's try the lights. Let's get off to the side, and if we can get the catwalks down with just one grenade or rifle fire, then save some explosions for the tank. If the bridge idea doesn't work, we head into the corridors. Short on time or not, we have to *try* to reach him."

"Sounds like a plan," Mo said.

Hanging on to each other, they eased through the darkness and the eerie silence. If they didn't fire, the Therokis didn't seem to have sights on them, so they kept quiet.

"Okay, now," Ellen whispered.

Mo punched in the proper sequence. And she threw.

A whole world of metal and glass came crashing down. The top of the tank was covered with ravaged infrastructure. If one could traverse it safely, though, was hardly clear.

"No dice." Mo swore. "Too much of it fell in."

Shaking her head, Ellen eased them toward the mess. "Let's go see if we can rearrange anything."

The first time Mo nudged a boot into a ragged piece of metal, though, it gave up its fight with the grav emitters and slid into the tank with a loud shriek, first from metal scraping on metal, then from metal colliding with alien.

Ellen smiled. "That can't feel good to have that in your tank, right?"

"Not at all," Mo agreed. "I don't think this is going to work. But I'm still in favor of dumping it all in. If we can't shoot it, at least we can be a splinter in that thing's side."

Indeed, none of the pieces they could reach were intact enough to cross the entire breadth of the tank. But the tank was a wreckage stew. As they watched on night vision, steam was rising from the tank now. Dead light fixtures and pieces of grating swirled among the wires and tentacles.

"The corridors," Roya said. "We must reach Kael. Soon. We're almost too late."

Ellen urged them into a jog away from the tank and toward the wall Roya indicated. "Keep arms linked."

As they neared the wall, Roya pointed at a blank spot. "Hold one of their rifles up here."

Ellen hurried to raise her pilfered rifle toward the spot. Light flared for a moment in the darkness, and a portion of the wall slid aside, an unseen hatch opening.

Holding on to each other, they eased inside.

She'd always said she wanted to make the world better, to fight hard or die trying. Fate or God or the laws of physics might be about to call her bets on that one.

IT WAS a war inside Kael's skull. And he was losing.

Cassandra's arrival into his sanctuary was like a hurricane, water rising madly, waves lashing at him. Wind whipped hair into his eyes, but he refused to move from his spot next to the door. This would be a hell of a way to spend eternity.

Then again, maybe he'd earned it. He'd killed a lot of people, as Cassandra had so eloquently pointed out. Maybe some of them had deserved it, but not all of them. If this was hell, it wasn't exactly what he'd expected, but so be it.

He only had two regrets, but those didn't matter now.

The water quickly rose past his knees, then his waist. His toes ached from the cold of it, legs turning to ice. Cassandra sure could be creative with pain. Somehow, that wasn't surprising. Or was this simply what it felt like to die, finally separated from your body? Maybe this torture wouldn't last an eternity. Maybe he'd just die here.

Still, there was something oddly familiar about the bitter cold. It was… peaceful. Even the winds seemed to gradually calm.

Before he knew it, he was chest deep in water and shivering bitterly. But suddenly he could see something—something outside the door of his hideaway, something beyond the flooding water. He opened his mouth and stared.

Gentle flakes floated down from a dark sky, sweet and pretty, calm as incense smoke on the wind.

Snow.

He'd only seen snow like this in Dr. Taylor's wall meditations. Never in real life, never felt it on his cheeks. And strictly speaking, he probably didn't actually feel it right now. It was fake. None of this was real. Or any realer than an illusion fully within his mind.

But cold pricked his cheeks, his forehead. He shut his eyes and listened.

Silence. Beautiful and complete. And so peaceful.

Opening his eyes again, he saw someone else. Her glowing blue form floated above him in the softly falling snow.

Calm, Kael Sidassian. Calm, Cassandra. Feel my power.

You're not more powerful than I— Cassandra said, voice lashing. But it was fading with each word. *You're not. You can't—do this—*

I am. Embrace peace. You want it? Death is the greatest peace of all.

He felt himself fading too.

No. You can't—you can't kill us—we are thousands of bodies—thousands of minds—

The howling winds had grown weak, then went still. The water that had risen to his chest was motionless now, utterly flat as a mirror, reflecting only the gently falling snow.

You are one mind dominating a thousand shells. It is not right, and it's certainly not peace.

That's not… you can't…

Embrace. The ties are cut. You have broken the old laws, and I have followed them.

No.

You are alone. Peace.

Salaam, Roya, he whispered to her. All his limbs felt cold now. Light and distant. His eyelids felt heavy.

Close the door, Kael Sidassian.

The water receded slightly, leaving his chest dry as it sank to his knees. How was that possible? None of this made any sense. Oh, yes, it was all a dream, an illusion, a fever—none of it real. He should just close his eyes the rest of the way and get back to sleep. He had a feeling it'd be dreamless for once.

Embrace peace. Close the door.

His arms wouldn't move, but his eyelids would. They drifted gently closed. The blanket of stillness around him was complete, all consuming. He was so tired.

It'd be good to rest. Just for a little while.

He slipped, sliding down into what should have been the water, but it receded further. He went limp against the cement side of the drainage tunnel, content to rest there, inhospitable as it was. He was so tired. Bone tired.

A light outside his eyelids pressed him to open them just a little to see the empress floating toward him, into the room. What she intended to do there, he didn't know.

He heard a grinding, like the door shutting, but he didn't care. It wouldn't make it warmer in here, or bring back his energy. He needed sleep. And peace, for once in his life.

The world faded to the purest white, like the blazing fire of life had finally burned him alive, and he slept.

SHIRIN HIT the metal grating hard, grunting against the pain. Knife-like sharpness shot up her leg, and then her shoulder took its own share of the agony as she fell to the side, but she had a sense that the suit she wore had absorbed a lot of the impact. Normally, that fall would have been… much worse.

EOE8 jumped down, leaving the ladder to Isa, and helped Shirin to her feet. "What did I miss while I was powered down?"

"Uh, sorry about that. It's… kind of a long story." Everything inside the ship was pitch black except small strips of emergency lighting along the walkway and the halo of blue light created by EOE8.

Down the hall, she heard a sound, something sliding open, then closed, and braced herself.

"Shirin? Isa?"

She let out the breath she hadn't realized she was holding when she saw it was Doug. He was zooming into the hallway and holding a rifle with the strap over his shoulder. She was still getting used to seeing anyone get around in his unique method of transportation, so it hadn't occurred to her he'd move around so silently… no footsteps. And she'd definitely never expected to see him holding a rifle. Ever. She wasn't sure she believed he knew how to use it. Not that she was one to criticize.

He must have seen her staring and guessed at her thoughts. "Well, it seemed better than continuing to type into a piece of glass and a blank screen. Besides, I couldn't stay in the storage closet and miss all the fun."

Isa reached the bottom of the ladder and turned to regard him.

"Okay, okay, and there aren't any backup lights in there either. *You* try sitting in the pitch black with all these noises going around." He pointed one index finger at the ceiling and rotated briefly in a cyclone.

"What do we do now?" EOE8 asked.

"The gun turret is being attacked," Shirin explained to Doug. "Some Therokis are trying to get through the viewports."

"We closed the blast door," Isa added.

"That should hold them. For now." Doug nodded.

They all looked at each other, then tilted their heads, listening. There seemed to be gunfire on all sides. The clanging from the lowest floor of the *Audacity* was the loudest. There was plenty above too. They could go to the bridge, but—what could they do from there, with the power out?

"Where is safest?" EOE8 asked.

"No," Shirin said. "We should go where we can help."

"How much help can we be?" it replied.

"Well, I think *you're* very capable, and he's got a gun, and Isa—" She remembered her promise not to say anything. "Isa is very smart. We should try to help."

"I'm not sure I can successfully fire this even once," Doug pointed out.

"EOE8 can," Shirin said. "Hand it over, and let's go down and help."

All three of them raised their eyebrows, even EOE8 with its odd robotic ones, but they exchanged glances, then nodded. Doug slipped the strap over his head, handed the weapon to the robot, and then jerked his thumb behind him.

"C'mon, let's go this way. The cargo hold stairs will be a shooting gallery if anyone's made it through the cargo hold."

"Which it sounds like they have," said EOE8.

"I know a back way," said Doug. "This way." They hurried through the ship, the sound of their steps lost in the chaos of metal and madness.

WHEN THEY BURST out of the hatch onto the platform, Ellen took off at a sprint. Kael's form slumped limply in the chair, wires snaking out of his forearm. He hadn't slid out simply because cables had been tightened around him to hold him there.

She cursed the Therokis up and down. Of course they had the means—and the knowledge—to restrain one of their own.

All around Kael, Therokis were collapsed on the floor, unmoving. She jumped over one, zig-zagged around another. She was hardly thinking straight.

But he wasn't moving. Was his mind moving, so his body stayed still? Or… were they too late? A terrible, dark feeling was brewing in the pit of her stomach. The others were still far behind her when she grabbed his hand.

His skin was cold and clammy.

"Can I unplug him?" Her voice sounded raw, like it'd been through a grinder.

"Yes," Roya replied, voice weak. "We must—unplug—it all."

"Roya—what's wrong?" Jenny stopped, twisting to try to get a look at the girl.

Ellen couldn't spare more than a glance. She ripped the wire out of his arm jack, then searched around. His gauntlet had to be here somewhere—but she couldn't find it. "Dreck-loving pig-dogs, where is it?"

"I'll get the cables, hold on." Mo's proper Foundation armor had tools in the leg compartment, so she quickly went to work on the heavy cables restraining Kael.

"Commander, something's wrong with Roya." Jenny's voice was shaking now.

"Kael's cold," she blurted.

"Check his pulse," Jenny ordered.

"Right." Ellen swallowed down her panic. "It's there, it's there! Weak, but it's there."

"We need to get them both back to the ship. Back to sick bay."

"Assuming the ship is still there and still *has* a sick bay," Mo pointed out.

They all looked at each other for a second.

"Is there any way to know that without going there?" Jenny asked.

"Not that we can pull off right now," Ellen replied. "Jen, you know the way back?"

"I think so."

"Okay. I hope this Union armor is worth its salt. I'll take Kael. Mo, you take the lead so Jenny can pay attention to Roya, and we'll go back the way you came—"

"No—Starbird—survives," Roya stammered, words slurring.

"Right, right." Mo opened a compartment in her armor. "Here. Doug gave me three mega-nukes. These two can scrape data and send it back, but *this* one just wipes everything it can reach." She held out the tiny devices. "I vote for number three. Can you plug this into the chair?"

There were no viable ports on the chair, but Ellen grabbed the drive and jogged toward the hatch they'd come out of. It had a simple palm pad, but it wasn't far from the dome where Starbird glittered. If they were connected on the same network, maybe this palm pad would be close enough...

Wipes everything it can reach.

But Starbird had been *helpful*. Starbird had felt like... a part of her. It'd been terrible to lose it, but she'd always figured it was somehow still out there, still helping someone.

Gritting her teeth, she found a small panel on the side and jammed it open. The metal clanged loudly as it swung open, revealing a tiny screen and two inputs.

All she had to do was plug one in. Still, she hesitated.

No... No, Starbird and Songbird were the same, and all of it combined had almost destroyed her once. It had destroyed countless others. Helpful or not, Starbird was part of the equation, and therefore, Starbird had to go.

She pressed the third device into the port, then hurried back to the others. "It's done."

"Good," Roya croaked, then pointed. "Through that door. Down the auxiliary corridor. Hurry."

Jenny immediately started moving in that direction. "Roya, tell me what's happening."

"It is simple. I am dying."

"What? Hold on, we can get you back to sick bay."

"This was always... my intention... Jenny. Let me go."

"No, you can't. I can't!"

"I am centuries old. I have ended… the menace… my kind has wrought. I will rest."

"But there's another *Alarus,*" Ellen grunted as she hauled Kael over her shoulder and hurried to follow them. "You can't leave us yet. We need your help."

"I am sorry. This was… all of me."

"I'm so sorry, sweetie," Jenny was saying, her voice tightening. "You were so horribly mistreated. It wasn't right." Ellen was glad she couldn't really see them, bent she as was, staggering forward under Kael's weight. Oh, the armor would do it, but the servos were groaning. These motors just didn't have the lifting power of her usual armor.

"It is over now," Roya replied. She seemed to be laboring to breathe. "So it does not matter… Will you do… one more thing for me?"

"Of course."

"Take this… shell of mine… to the waters of my home world. As ashes… if you need to. Let me… swim again."

Ellen's eyes felt hot. She bit down on her lip. This was not the time to feel things, not grief, not fear, not panic, not anything—survive now. Feel later. She choked the rising wave down.

Jenny, however, seemed to have no such concerns, her voice colored by tears. "Yes. Yes, of course. I promise."

"I believe you."

Roya was fading fast. God, they weren't far now. They *had* to reach the hangar soon. Maybe if she kept asking questions, Roya would hold on, change her mind. She groped for something. "You said Cassandra is dead? How is that possible?"

"Three parts. Kael severed part… of the network… I severed another—the main cluster of her mind's connection—to her bodies. And you all destroyed… many bodies… Damage was too great."

That made almost no sense. Minds weren't computers in a network… were they? Didn't matter. More questions, make her hold on. "You can do that? Sever *minds* from bodies?"

"I did to you… severing the squad from you… And as Cassandra did to Kael."

"As she…" Ellen faltered, and it was too much. She ended up on one knee, reeling under the weight and those words. Mo rushed back to her side to help her rise, taking part of the weight to move forward together. "As she *what*?"

"I did… what I could. But she severed… the connection. I tried—I fear—it was not enough—"

"Is he dead?" Ellen demanded.

"He's *not* dead," Jenny insisted. "You said he had a pulse."

"Just because his body is breathing doesn't make him *alive*, Jenny," she snapped, then immediately regretted it. "We're surrounded by 'live' bodies that aren't moving, dammit!"

"She watched me… unknit them…" Roya whispered. "There is a… chance."

"Who?" Ellen demanded.

"Is a… Is… a…"

"Roya!" Jenny's voice was raw.

Ellen was shaking now, and she did not think it was purely from the strain of carrying her love, which was mounting despite the technological assistance. She forced herself to take another step, then another.

"Wait! Roya! Hold on!" Jenny sprinted blindly ahead.

"Jenny, wait!" Mo cried, but having to carry Kael, neither she nor Ellen could try to catch her—or stop her.

You will not want to let me go. Wasn't that what Roya—as the empress, back then—had said the first time Ellen had spoken to her? That she would die someday, that she longed for it.

Shaking her head, Ellen pressed herself forward, one step, then another.

The asteroid shook around them, making Ellen stumble. If Mo hadn't been there, she might've ended up pinned to the wall. The suit wasn't meant for this, joints and servos starting to overheat. Together, though, they kept going. Ahead of them, Jenny was racing toward the next set of hatches that should take them back to the hangar.

The darkness and the quiet had only grown deeper, but now, she could hear something louder in the distance, a thundering rumble that could have been artillery—or the asteroid breaking apart. "Almost there, Kael. Hang on."

Whether he was actually alive enough to hear her, or if his eyes would be flat and blank as their zombie Udo Trynkei's—she wasn't going to think about that right now.

CHAPTER TWENTY

"HERE, IT'S RIGHT THROUGH HERE." Jenny waved them forward. "I can see the *Audacity*. Commander, you're, uh... gonna want to see this." Her low tone of voice said whatever she saw, it wasn't good.

"Going as fast as we can, Jen." Ellen and Mo dragged themselves forward, still carrying Kael between them.

The hangar had been littered with fuselage when she'd left it, and now, piles of unmoving Therokis had been added to the mix. Sleeping? Dead? The whole place was as dark as the chamber they'd just left, but a halo of light was coming from the hull of something new.

The *Everest*. The Union ship was docked in the hangar and not looking much worse for the wear. Although, it always looked pretty terrible, so it was hard to tell if it'd taken much damage.

The *Audacity*, though.

As soon as Ellen saw her, she knew. That ship couldn't fly, not without repairs anyway. The hangar was too dark to make out clearly what the damage was, but she could see a chunk of hull missing where the main reactor should be. More than anywhere else, Therokis were piled around it, as if they'd been on a suicide mission to destroy the thing.

And they'd succeeded.

All of the *Audacity* was dark. They were either running dark to hide… or unable to turn on the power.

"Let's try to get to the *Audacity* before the *Everest* lowers her ramp." No one had exited the *Everest* yet, but they had to be preparing to, any second now.

Wordlessly, they moved forward, picking their way silently through the rubble and bodies.

At the cargo hatch, Mo reached it first—and gasped. "Zhia!"

Zhia was lying still on the ramp. Alone.

"Let me look at her," Jenny whispered.

"I'm going in," Mo said. "Wait here."

Ellen leaned her and Kael's combined weight against the hull. This was her ship. Her cargo hold, where they'd met so many times. It stung for it to be hostile territory.

Mo reappeared. "All clear to sick bay. I can hear clanging in Engineering. Power seems out."

"Any sign of Levereaux?"

"No."

"To sick bay, then. Jenny can stay there with…" Ellen's voice faltered at the idea of the names she'd have to list off. "Jenny can stay there, then we help Bri."

MO HATED a lot of things about today, but seeing the *Audacity* so beat up… It was almost at the top of her list. The only thing she hated more was not knowing where Doug was, not being able to reach out to him. No matter how many times she'd tried to quietly mute herself and try to reach out to the ship—she'd gotten no response.

Now the hull was dark and silent, and hunkering down in sick bay felt like a fortified fox hole. Or maybe a trap.

She'd hurried to get everyone inside and quickly helped Jenny get a battery-powered medbot online so she could get to search the rest of the ship.

But she'd barely stepped out of sick bay—and Ellen was still inside the hatch behind her— when a voice stopped them.

"Hold it right there, and don't come any closer."

She froze, hands still on her rifle. The corridor might has well have been in the deep, it was so pitch black. The only light came from a few emergency indicators in sick bay, a few flashing strips along the edge of the corridor floor, and blue halos and tiny amber lights that winked at her from the end of the corridor.

The speaker was near the hatch to Engineering, but Mo couldn't see it in the darkness. The clangs inside had quieted. This speaker must have slid the hatch closed just before Mo had stepped into the corridor.

But that voice. Did she know it? It was robotic and vaguely familiar, but she couldn't place it.

"Identify yourself," she demanded. Why not? This was her home just as much as anyone else's.

"It is *you* who should identify yourself, foreign intruder—" the robot started.

"Wait—that's Mo!"

Her heart leapt. Now *that* was a voice she knew!

"Doug!" She rushed forward as soon as he appeared, gliding past the strange lights of the robot or whatever it was at the end of the corridor. She barely got her rifle pointed at the floor before his arms were around her.

In the darkness and her armor, she could barely see or feel anything, so it barely even felt like an embrace. But he was *there*. And unharmed. Alive. And so was she, mostly.

For now, that was more than enough.

"What happened here?" Ellen's voice behind her, and her boots on the metal grating, brought Mo even further back to reality.

"It's not good, Commander," Doug said.

"Commander!" Shirin rushed forward and threw her arms around Ellen. Through the visor, Mo could see her eyes widen. "Wait —where's my—" Shirin's sudden panic was palpable in the air.

"He's in sick bay," Ellen rushed to say. "He's alive."

"But he's hurt?"

"Sort of."

"Sort of? What does that mean—"

"I don't really understand it yet. Listen, we need to assess the ship first, okay? That's the best way to get you and your dad to safety."

"I don't want safety—I want to win—"

"We did. I think."

They all went quiet for long moment. "The Therokis seem incapacitated," she said slowly. "The *Alarus's* tank was thoroughly destroyed. The Starbird grid… well, it's powered down at least."

"The… what?" Doug said slowly. "Did you say what I think you just said?"

"I did. It's there, Doug. Built in life, in person. It was a real thing, *part* of the hive mind. Alien, human, computer—all merged into one entity."

"An entity bent on galactic murder and conquest," Mo muttered.

"Yes, that."

"I agree it is done," Isa said quietly. "There are… almost no telepathic energies in our vicinity."

"I don't like the sound of 'almost no' but I'm going to take your word on that."

Doug blew out a breath. "Well, if that's all true, I guess you better see this. Out of one fire, into another."

"I don't think that's the expression," Mo said quietly, giving him a small smile.

"I know, but I'm starving and I didn't want to think about eggs. And now I'm thinking about eggs. Great."

She snickered. "I bet there are powdered ones in sick bay."

He made a playful mock gagging noise as he palmed open the hatch to Engineering. At least, she *thought* it was playful.

Any of the lightness of her mood evaporated, though, once they were all inside. Mo hadn't been down here much in her time aboard the ship. Conversations between her and Bri petered out pretty quickly, almost like they were in a competition for who got to say least. But she did remember it usually was fairly bright, and the smell had definitely changed for the worse, although she wasn't mechanically inclined enough to home in on any of it. Her suit said the atmo was all still safe, so she retracted her helmet.

"Bri?" Ellen rushed past the others toward their chief of engineering.

At the far end of the cabin, Bri was on her knees next to a destroyed piece of equipment. "I got 'im, Commander, but... well, see for yourself. He got us."

"Cassandra's last laugh." Ellen shook her head. "He knew exactly where to hit."

Mo ran her eyes over the equipment, but in the dark, with all the charring, she was having a hard time placing what'd been destroyed. She didn't recall ever doing anything important in this corner of engineering before, except maintenance checklists on stuff that was literally never used.

"He got the backup parts printer," Doug quietly explained.

Ellen spread her hands. "With this destroyed, and the backup power connector, we can't repair any of the systems we need to repair the ship. And with this level of damage..."

"She's dead," Bri groaned. "We're adrift on this stupid rock!"

"No, we'll figure something out." Ellen bent down on one knee and put a hand on Bri's shoulder. "And stop beating yourself up. It doesn't help. Cassandra knew what she was doing."

"So do I. Or I thought I did."

"It's not your fault."

Bri scowled at Ellen, then shook her head. "It's my responsibility to keep this ship afloat. Period. Against crafty enemies and otherwise."

"And it continues to be your responsibility. And last I checked, wallowing in it doesn't help the ship's hull or any of its crew."

"Frag you, Ellen—"

"You think I've never screwed up? Try me."

The two of them glared at each other for a long moment, which

Mo sometimes felt was Bri's own version of a hug. Then finally Bri relented, glaring at the charred remains instead.

Ellen stood and looked at the others. "We stopped a terrible evil. That comes at a price sometimes. We are going to do what we can to fix what was destroyed and get us all home."

Ellen's eyes flicked to the side on those last few words. Mo didn't think she was saying everything she was thinking.

Jenny jogged up the hall, stopping at the hatch. "Commander, I got the backup batteries hooked up in sick bay. Holy moly, what happened here—"

"A very surgical attack," Mo said, sparing Bri from a second explanation.

"Where is everyone else?" Ellen asked.

"You should check the bridge," Doug said. "Adan and Levereaux were there last. Last I heard, Fern was in the gun turret."

Isa and Shirin exchanged frightened looks.

"What is it?" Mo was already moving toward the door.

"Our turret was stormed by Therokis. They were trying to break the glass."

Mo raised a hand. "Commander, I'll check on her."

"Yes, yes, go," Ellen replied.

"I'll take the bridge!" Jenny shouted.

"No, the two of you go together—turret, then bridge." Ellen shouted after them.

The sound of their boots pounding across the metal grating felt too loud, too exposed. Could it be heard outside the ship? Hard to believe with the damage outside and in Engineering that all the enemies were really neutralized. Mo wasn't getting off high alert just yet.

And the quiet growling she heard as she got closer to the turret didn't make her feel any better.

"Fern?" she called. She raised her helmet before she started to climb and set the voice channel to the external speaker.

The growl got louder. "Is that you, Mihio?" That was Fern's voice all right.

"Yes, ma'am. Jenny's here too."

"Good. Glad you're back. I'm going to need the both of you to get this idiot off of me."

The turret was in as bad a shape as Mo could imagine. Three Therokis had made it inside, and some kind of fight had gone down. It didn't even really matter anymore. Fern had defeated one, but he'd collapsed on top of her. And another was half on top of *him,* making their combined weight likely over a ton.

Mo and Jenny hauled the Therokis off Fern and shoved their attackers out the broken viewports so that at least they were out on the hull instead of lying inside.

Then they closed the blast door behind them as best they could without power and made their way down toward the bridge.

AS SOON AS Bridell had volunteered for team setting up a perimeter around the *Everest* in the hangar bay, Paul had known he'd have to follow him. It'd been far too long since he'd put on any kind of armor, but luckily the stuff was smart enough to do it itself, if he just held still.

Armor self-assembled, he glanced at himself in the mirror before he hurried down to the docking bay. He'd always been told he looked good armored up, and that hadn't changed. Yet, anyway. He should wear his armor more often. It was impressive.

He was feeling like a million credits by the time he reached the ramp leading out of the ship. As ordered, the team had set up a neat perimeter around the landing ramp. The electrical systems on the asteroid seemed to be out, so his crew were lining their perimeter and then the outer walls of the hangar with portable light sources, trying to chase away the darkness but only diminishing it very slightly so far.

Unfortunately, the small amount of light was still enough to reveal a macabre carpet of hundreds of armored forms collapsed and covering the ground.

He came to a stop beside Shu. She was still in her typical uniform, no armor, unlike most of the ground crew, but she wasn't straying more than a few meters from the ramp. "Are they… all dead?" he asked. "Wow. Did we do any of this?"

"No, sir, we didn't do any of this," she replied. "It was like this when we landed. And many of them appear to be unconscious or comatose, but uninjured. Only maybe a third of them are dead."

"Oh, goodness. Guess we're going to need a bigger brig."

Shu cracked a smile. "Yes, sir."

"See that the ones that are alive are taken prisoner." He scanned the scene around them. Ellen's ship, the *Audacity*, was on the other side of the hangar. It looked like hell, but it was still so dark, he could barely make out all the damage. "The *Audacity*…"

"Still has signs of life aboard, sir. Scans do not show any medical emergencies. Our plan is to secure the area first, then deal with the *Volga*, then the *Audacity*, most likely, sir."

"Good. Where's the gun array, are we getting it online?"

"There." She pointed nearby to an already well-lit area where ops was hard at work already. "The *Volga* won't know what hit it."

"Good, good. I'm glad they didn't use it on us." He pursed his lips, pausing. "Shu, uh… This might be a stupid question, but… why didn't they use it on us?"

"That's a good question, now that you mention it. I'd guess they hoped to capture our ships and turn us all into these guys." She waved a hand absently at the Therokis on the hangar floor, then adjusted her glasses. "Or maybe they were distracted by those that arrived before us. Or both."

"Speaking of getting distracted, I wanted to check in with everyone. I see Mertz, good. Where's Bridell?"

"I think he was helping them put the lights around." She pointed but continued to focus on her tablet.

"Oh, I see. All right, then. I'll just… give them a hand." And look for Bridell while he was at it.

Fortunately, Shu had been drawn in by something on her tablet and didn't notice him sliding away from her. He'd already confessed his suspicions to her, and she had pledged to scrutinize every argument Bridell put forward, but it wasn't her only job to babysit the other lieutenant. He briefly considered mentioning his concerns again, but he didn't want her thinking he was overly paranoid.

And he was feeling *very* paranoid at the moment, so if she thought he was, she might be right.

He skirted the outside of the perimeter until he reached a point where a crewman was cracking open light sticks and inserting them into the cubes that refracted the light in a large area. The crewman nodded to him. Casually, Paul grabbed the handle of one of the light cubes and kept walking, scanning for Bridell.

He caught sight of one light moving, faster than the others, away from the work area. As it skirted around the nose of the *Audacity,* he caught Bridell's image in profile. He looked alone and unarmored. Odd.

He strolled after his lieutenant, trusting his intuition on keeping his movements low key. He needed to do this himself.

No one seemed to notice him. He eased around the nose of the *Audacity* and then the next ship beyond it. He lost sight of him, but there was a dim light coming through a hatch on a far wall of the hangar.

He jogged up a set of stairs, going around a ridiculous amount of fuselage wreckage and armored bodies, before he reached the hatch. Inside, Bridell was sitting at a console, seemingly trying to power it on.

"What are you doing?" Paul said coldly, striding into the room behind him.

Bridell turned to look over his shoulder. "Just hurrying to get the guns activated against the *Volga,* sir. It'll be on us any second."

"This isn't the gun array. This is the security control room." Bridell was lying, so Paul would too. He had no idea what this room was for, security or otherwise.

Bridell's hands slowed on the controls, but then sped up again. He didn't stop. "Well, I thought we might need the power on. The security may be needed to let us access the guns, plus we need to get downloading whatever data they might—"

"That's Shu's duty. But you rushed straight in here. Without security. Or armor. Or adequate lighting."

"I thought one cube would be enough, but you were so kind to solve my lighting problem, sir. Progress."

A whirring sound kicked up. Paul's eyes shot to the hatch behind him, then the console. Where was that coming from?

Bridell seemed to have gotten something to turn on. Somehow, he was entering commands. Something wasn't right.

Paul stepped closer. "Be still, Lieutenant."

"Sir, I can't. Time is of the essence."

He pulled out his pistol and held it to the back of Bridell's head. "That's an order. Step away from the console. What's that sound?"

"Just the guns spinning up to take care of the *Volga*, sir, it should be ready any second—"

Liar. "Stand up, dammit, or I'll shoot."

He could feel Bridell's smirk, even though he couldn't see it. "No, you won't."

Paul faltered. "What?"

"You won't."

"Excuse me?" Was this really happening? He pushed the pistol's muzzle into Bridell's unarmored neck, forcing him forward in the seat. "Yes, I will."

Bridell just laughed softly. "Don't play the hero. You're a fragging coward who's never had a difficult choice in your life."

Paul tightened his grip on the pistol. "Who are you working for?"

"If anyone should desert the Union, it should be you. You cede to your subordinates on *everything*. Even something as stupid as getting onto this asteroid."

Paul said nothing. His hand was shaking, in spite of his attempts to steady it by jamming the pistol harder into Bridell's neck.

"You're not going to kill me now. You need me."

"Are you one of the Songbirds?" Paul demanded.

"Hell no."

"Then who? Turn it off. Now."

"There's nobody, sir." His voice went sarcastically imploring. "Sir, should I call Dr. Madsi? You're starting to sound a bit deranged, over the edge—"

The muzzle slid along the back of Bridell's neck from his hand's erratic shaking. Wait… there was something there. Something that hadn't been there before.

Frowning, Paul scraped the muzzle back and forth. Brownish makeup smeared away, revealing the barcoded stripes.

"Enhancer," he growled. Barcodes on their necks were tattoos given by the Enhancer cult to their members. How had he hidden it so well? "Traitor. This is your last warn—"

Bridell spun, reaching for Paul's arm, for the weapon.

Paul fired—and then he fell.

ELLEN WAS glad to have a break from making a list of all the damages—which she marked in soot with her finger on the wall. First, Fern sauntered her way in to say hello, then applied herself to adding to Ellen's quick-and-dirty wall-damage report.

Then, to her relief, Jenny came jogging back grinning, with Adan and Levereaux—and of course Mo—finally in tow.

"I'm so glad you're all back safely." Adan didn't stop his jog and ran all the way to Ellen, kissing both her cheeks. She blinked. She'd been on a lot of missions with him, but she'd never seen him do *that* before. "Hey, where's Kael?" Adan said, returning to Jenny to slide an arm around her armored waist. Which was harder than it looked. "Is he—" Seeing Ellen's face, he faltered.

"He's gonna be all right," Jenny cut in, but her tone was forced.

"He's in sick bay," Ellen said. "Unconscious."

"Oh, Ellen, I'm so sorry."

She held up a palm. She shook herself and set her jaw. She had to get a grip, or the emotion, the pain, would take her under. "I can't do this now. I'm in command. We have problems. We need to solve them as fast as we can."

"Yes." Adan sobered. "Of course."

"First and foremost, can this ship fly?" She looked to each of them, purposely not looking at the looming list of damage on the wall behind her.

They all looked at each other.

"Well. What do you think? Can the *Audacity* fly?"

"Without replacement parts?" Doug sighed. "No."

A tremor shook the ship around them, making Ellen grit her teeth. Didn't whatever was causing that shaking know they had *enough* problems to deal with?

"What do we do?" Jenny asked. "We can't just set up shop here."

"Do we know if the asteroid is stable?" Ellen asked.

Levereaux spoke for the first time, lifting up a tablet that lit her face with an eerie glow. "All scans I can currently do—which aren't many—indicate the asteroid is not stable, Commander. But I can't get a read on how long we have."

"Is the hull intact? If the atmospheric seal fails, are we all dead?"

"The hull's not intact—yet." Adan straightened. "But we can fix that much. Maybe. It'll be a lot harder without Xi and the bots. But theoretically, it is doable."

"Okay, there's our first order of business. Anybody who can, help with the hull. Let's get this thing sealed up. That way if this asteroid breaks in a trillion pieces or the atmo seal finally fails, we're not instantly dead."

"You got it, Commander." Adan was off at a jog without another word, Jenny trailing after him and motioning for Shirin to follow.

Ellen turned on her heel. The damage report was mostly complete—and extensive. If the asteroid broke apart, they might survive, but they'd drift forever in their current state. No propulsion. If they couldn't get the power back on, or some kind of reactor repair, they wouldn't last long before they froze.

They needed help.

She started toward the hatch.

"Where are you going, Commander? Sick bay?" Doug asked.

She stopped. If anyone else had asked, she'd have dodged the question. But she had to answer him. They'd been through too much. He'd brought her here, saved her in the first place.

She looked over her shoulder at him. "Doug, thank you for bringing me all this way. For helping me escape Arakovic, finding her, bringing her operation crashing down. I couldn't have done it without you."

"Whoa, whoa, whoa, what's going on? You're scaring me. All I asked was where you're going. Can I come?"

He was on to her. "I'm stopping briefly in sick bay. But then I'm going to get our spare parts. From the Union. And no, you can't come."

"Ellen—" Doug started.

"Hey, wait," Bri called after her.

She kept walking.

Inside sick bay, she pulled the hatch shut manually behind her. That must have been enough to slow them down. Or make them realize she wanted privacy.

"Would you like care for your wound, ma'am?" asked the bot Jenny had found the emergency batteries for.

"No, thank you, bot," she said quickly.

She stopped where Roya's small form lay on a table. She looked like she was just sleeping, blankets covering her. But the bot had removed the wires and tubes, and the display was blank. The centuries-old being was finally at rest.

"Thank you," she murmured, placing her hand for one brief moment on Roya's shoulder, then moving on before emotion could overcome her.

Where Zhia lay, the tubes were still connected, but the damage was severe. She'd given everything to try to keep them out of Engineering, Ellen was willing to bet. She gritted her teeth.

"Hang on, *jagiya*," she whispered. "I'll buy you a drink if you pull through."

Of course, that was somewhat a lie. She wouldn't be here to buy any drinks.

Lastly, she stopped at Kael's side. *His* health readouts were fairly good. Jenny had placed a new set of medkits and a splint on his leg, but he was all right overall. Except, obviously, he wasn't.

He wasn't coming back. She wasn't going to lie to herself. He was asleep now, forever, just like the rest of them, and it wasn't fragging fair.

But what in life was?

Blinking back hot tears, she bent down and pressed a kiss to his lips. The way he couldn't kiss her back was like a knife to the chest—and it said it all.

"Salaam, my love." She squeezed his hand one more time, with her good uninjured one. And then she strode for the door, listening until the corridor outside was empty. She had no energy for another argument or battle right now.

The corridor was silent. Everyone had busied themselves with repairs.

Time to do her part.

Outside the ship, she stopped at the first *Everest* crew member she found. "Where is Paul?"

His brow furrowed, and his mouth dropped open in lieu of a response.

"I mean, Captain Dealis. I mean, I'm here to turn myself in." She wasn't irritable. Not at all.

The crewman exchanged glances with two of his shipmates. "Your ship is right there, ma'am."

"We don't remember seeing you. Surely, ma'am. You did your duty to the Union. We don't hold it against you for running out when they pulled their slimy shit."

"We've heard the stories. We know what you did at SHR."

"I just did my job. I also made a promise and broke it. I've run from it long enough." She sighed. "Besides… my ship isn't going to fly in that condition. If the *Everest* isn't taking all of us in, I think we're stranded here on this rock."

Face pained, the crewman reached for his comm. "Lieutenant Shu, ma'am? There's someone here I think you'll want to see."

A sudden crack of gunfire made them all jump.

Ellen spun around. "What was that? Did anyone head that way?"

"I don't…"

"Didn't Captain Dealis go that way?" said an engineer as he cracked a light stick and slid it home. "I saw him wandering around the nose of your ship, ma'am. He didn't go on inside?"

Ellen caught her breath. Then she sprinted toward the sound.

"Ma'am! Wait, ma'am!"

"C'mon, you idiot, let's go help her!"

ELLEN TOOK the stairs two at a time to the control room—the exact same one Kael had barricaded himself in when those Therokis had dragged her away. There hadn't been another sound, but there was the faintest light coming through a viewport window.

The power was still out, but somehow, someone had powered something on in there.

The hatch stood open, and as she got closer, she realized there was something… a faint whirring. She couldn't place the sound, but her instincts were immediately on edge.

"Paul!" Even before she reached the hatch, she saw him. He was slumped against the back wall. "He's in here," she yelled to the others behind her.

She took another step and wondered belatedly if she should have stayed quiet. Slumped sideways in the chair was Lieutenant Bridell, a wound to the skull leaking blood and brain matter into a pool on the floor.

Paul groaned, and she moved toward him. His eyes flickered open as she knelt on one knee.

"You okay?" she asked. "What the frag happened?"

"Bridell—spy," he managed. "Enhancer." He gestured at Bridell's limp form, then winced and rubbed his head.

As a matter of fact, Ellen's head was starting to ache too. And the whirring was getting louder. "What is that sound?" she demanded.

The men from the *Everest* exchanged glances.

"Search the place," she ordered, hitting the helmet raise button on her armor. She reached for Paul's. What was he doing wandering around in dark hostile asteroids without even his stupid helmet on? "You, help me get the captain out of this area."

Her three companions immediately sprang into motion. The crewman she'd first spoken with bent to look under the console in front of Bridell while another shined a light up into an odd hole in the ceiling that had crates stacked near it, as though someone had used them as a ladder. The third helped her hoist Paul to his feet.

"There you go—" she started. He swayed and slumped on her comrade. "Er, maybe not—"

"Ma'am?" The young man near Bridell's feet held up a small device. The whirring grew louder as he lifted it. A timer on the outside of it was counting down in pale blue numbers. 06... 05... 04...

Oh, the irony.

"Knockout grenade—take cover!" Abandoning Paul, she lunged forward and grabbed it from his hand. Sliding out the door, she threw the grenade as hard as she could toward the blast doors she'd gone through to reach their inner sanctum. They still stood open, like a weird mouth still wishing it could eat them alive.

Then she dove back toward the open hatchway.

She winced inside her helmet as she realized she'd curled into a ball, her hands again naturally going to that cover-your-neck position that wouldn't really do much to help her. Apparently, they had always done that, and they always would. If only she had her *real* Foundation armor, because then she could've just held the thing and jogged off with it and not had to worry.

Figured the Enhancers would attack with the very thing the crew of the *Audacity* had gotten them with so many times. Probably wasn't a coincidence. The timed release, possibly in more than one wave—that was a special Enhancer touch to the usual tech.

As it was, as she got to her feet, the distance and the metal around them appeared to have been enough. The other Unionies were fine.

"Paul? Did that hit you?"

His eyes found hers, and after a second of him steadying himself, he nodded. "Not full blast, I don't think. A bit of a warning shot."

"Not like you gave him." She jerked a thumb at Bridell.

"I'll have you know, I gave him quite a few warnings to get off the console. He just wouldn't stop… whatever he was doing."

"Which was…"

They all looked at the console. A spinning progress indicator was still running.

"Argh, fragging, turn it off!" Paul tried to take a step forward, but Ellen had to catch him. The other three crowded around the console while Paul reached into his pocket and got out a comm. His voice was grim as he ordered for medical to come get Bridell.

"Got it, sir! I think we stopped the transfer… mostly."

Ellen winced. Well, whatever was done, had already been done. Maybe she could get Doug to hack in later to see what precisely had been stolen. It was the Enhancers that had kidnapped the *Alaruses*, bound them into human bodies, tried to "perfect" their forms, called them empresses, and overall, had been really big jerks about it, so it stood to reason Arakovic could have a lot of research of interest to them. At one point, she'd been a big client of the Enhancers.

The asteroid shook around them as med techs rushed in and started moving Bridell. One brought Paul a small vial. He lowered his helmet again and drank.

As his head cleared, he seemed to truly see her for the first time. "You're—you're alive. Alive! How did you not fall asleep on the bridge? What the hell happened? And what the frag are you doing here?"

She shrugged. "Long story. In short, it was a few things: technology; we got the bad lady; and my getaway vehicle is no longer vehicular."

His expression went from confused, to excited, to concerned. The asteroid shook again, harder this time. He grabbed for his comm. "Have you gotten access to that gun array yet or not? What's taking so long?"

"What's causing that shaking?" she murmured. Could it be the damage Jenny had done? Something else?

"Well, I don't know if it's the *only* cause, but one cause of the shaking is Colonel Tauber, trying to shake the damn asteroid apart around us."

Her eyes widened.

"Captain Dealis?" someone said from the comm.

"Yes?"

"The laser defense array is warming up, sir. We were delayed by the power loss but found a way to utilize the broken Theroki ship's reactor. But sir, I've got a hail from the *Lhotse*."

"The *Lhotse*. Captain Weyer?"

"Yes, sir."

"Put her through!"

"Dealis—what the ever-loving frag is going on? Did the plan work?"

He smiled. "Sort of, yes! The Songbird terrorists have been defeated, and this cell has been thoroughly destroyed."

"Excellent news. In other events, is Tauber trying to get you all killed? What the monkey gonads is he doing? You're *in* there, right?"

"He's definitely trying to get *me* killed. And probably a few others too." He glanced at Ellen, his look indicating he thought he was being sly not mentioning her name.

Yeah, he hadn't put two and two together how screwed she was.

Weyer cleared her throat. "Listen, my engineers—who are the best flipping engineers in the fleet, mind you—are telling me he's got maybe three or four more shots before you are in serious trouble."

Paul's face went green. "Our lasers are still warming. Electric was out."

"Then you are going to need my help, eh?"

Paul swallowed. "If… if you're willing."

She sighed. "Am I really doing this? They're gonna hang us, I think. Or put us away for a long time if your big bro's paperwork doesn't check out."

"I can't make that decision for you." He lifted his chin. "You are your own call, ma'am."

"As always." She cut the comm.

Paul's eyes widened as he met Ellen's. "What if she doesn't..."

"C'mon, let's check those lasers." She motioned him to follow. They dodged around Unionies setting up lights, tapping into the console, moving Bridell's body. The place was swarming now. Paul muttered commands into his comm as they ran. Far too many of the Union team were lightly suited up to be on ship, not in combat, only good for brief exposure to the deep...

For now, the atmo field still held. She gazed at the dim black form of the *Audacity*, still smoking in places and now lit dimly from beneath by Union light cubes. Beyond it, the endless blackness of the vacuum stretched out. She could see three smaller asteroids spinning and the wormhole gate far in the distance, but looming much closer was the *Volga*. Behind Tauber's ship, like a parrot on a pirate's shoulder, the *Lhotse* was coming closer. Both ships had taken more than a few hits. A dim whine rang out on the other side of the hangar.

The lasers.

Before they could fire, the *Volga* deployed its 5M torpedoes, four of them racing toward the asteroid.

"Incoming!" The cries went up all around her, people scrambling for cover and for the *Everest*'s ramp. Like they'd make it in time. Yeah, this was not something they'd trained for, that much was obvious.

She braced herself. God, did Doug have a suit on? Isa? Had they made *any* progress on the hull? There hadn't been enough time.

At the last moment, the lasers fired, targeting the 5Ms and popping them into little blasts of light like water balloons.

Simultaneously, the *Lhotse* fired—at the *Volga*.

Weyer had timed it perfectly for when the shields were down to fire the 5Ms, Ellen realized. At the distance and that angle, however, she couldn't make out the specific weapons system.

She didn't need to, though. Whatever it was did the job, rupturing the hull of the *Volga* enough that the interior oxygen ignited in a quick fireball. Light flashed around the *Volga,* and debris went spinning in every direction—its own kind of lethal projectile. Lights on the outside of the *Volga* went dark.

A cheer went up around her.

But Ellen wasn't done holding her breath yet. So maybe they'd taken out a critical system and stopped the *Volga*. The whole fragging spaceship was still careening toward them like an asteroid of its own. Or a planet.

"Ask Weyer to get her grab beam and stop that thing," she said to Paul, keeping her voice low. "Or we're still going to be the jelly in this sandwich."

"Uh, good point, yes. Obviously. I was just thinking that," he said as he lifted up the comm to his ear.

She glared at him, and he winked back at her.

"What? I was thinking about sandwiches. It's been a long day."

She snorted. "You can eat when we're not dead."

"A truer statement has never been uttered."

"Not on this asteroid anyway."

He spoke with Weyer for a few seconds, expressing his gratitude and also his deepest desires not to become a pancake or any other sort of food item resembling a human body thrust into the vacuum but also crushed between two much larger, very hard objects.

When he was done, he looked at her and tilted his head. "Why are you still here? Listen, you escaped fair and square. Do we really have to do this?"

She snorted. "What? You find it distasteful that your captive won't leave?"

"I can't say I'm thrilled about dragging you to face justice after all this. I will, but…" He looked away.

Sighing, she kicked at the deck. "I can't leave. They destroyed quite a bit of the *Audacity,* but most critically, the parts replacement printer and the energy hookups. We're fragged. We won't be spaceworthy without help."

"So you need spare parts."

"You can't possibly have that many spare parts."

"Have you seen the condition my ship is in? And the *Lhotse* is even worse."

"I did notice that."

"Which means we carry double the usual spares."

"And you probably need them. Look, I can't get out of this. I can't just zip away and keep hiding. You can't help me and also let me go. So I'm here. I'll go to my trial. Just help my friends not die on this asteroid, please."

It was his turn to sigh. "Fine. C'mon aboard. Let's see what we can do."

CHAPTER TWENTY-ONE

XI DRUMMED her fingers against the vid console's metal exterior. Judging by the video feeds, the threat had been neutralized.

For her part, she had shut down nearly all the electrical systems in the entire station, aside from her own personal access to the vid feeds and the one that maintained the atmospheric seal in the hangar. She could have toggled that one off, too, but it hadn't gotten *quite* that dire.

Although it had been close.

Xi wasn't sure what had caused the inexplicable sudden deactivation of about half of the Theroki force, but the rapid systemic failure had been clear. A few minutes later, the rest had gone down.

There appeared to be a few emergency subsystems she couldn't quite access, but the chaos of the darkness seemed to have been enough. It had also served a secondary purpose.

She looked out over the large chamber behind her. Rows and rows of clear cylinders stretched out in near blackness. Removing their electrical power had rebooted their security systems and switched them to backup batteries, which would eventually fail. And then, presumably, their occupants would be freed.

Xi wasn't quite sure if that would be a good thing or a bad thing, but for one particular cylinder, it was essential.

She strode quickly from the control booth to the fourth row, third cylinder. Leaning over, she saw the facial profile she'd been seeking, the swaths of blue hair that remained in spite of Cassandra's best efforts.

Xi began entering the deactivation sequence with her left hand without looking at the control pad. Her gaze stayed fixed on the woman inside, although she wasn't quite sure why. She wasn't looking for anything. She had no questions. But she couldn't stop herself from gazing through the clear sides of the medical chamber at the already familiar face.

Etrianala Kentt.

The fluid drained in 3.42 seconds, and the deactivation sequence took 5.68 seconds longer, which was infuriatingly inefficient. Strange that she could feel any fury toward such a mundane process that certainly maintained no will of its own, either good or bad.

The glass shell popped open, signifying it was finally complete.

Kentt's eyes fluttered open, the usual stunning blue a more ordinary color under the white medical light of the cylinder. "Xi... My knight in shining armor."

"I am not a knight," Xi said flatly.

"You are made of metal, though, aren't you?"

"Among other things."

Kentt smiled as she gingerly sat up. "Is it over?"

"I believe it is. I remained concealed and sabotaged their attempts to change your genetic code."

Her gaze dipped down to the floor for a moment, then back up. "Thank you for that. What now?"

"Our friends have arrived and sabotaged the systems. We can join them if you are able to walk?"

She tried to swing one leg over the side and winced. "I think that's a no."

"Then I could carry you if you wish. I can carry nearly 800 kilos without strain."

Kentt's smile widened. Xi was puzzled at why and made several notes for later analysis.

"Or you could crawl," Xi offered.

Kentt laughed softly. "I assure you, your strength is more than sufficient for me. I would very much appreciate your assistance."

Judging by Kentt's jump and her widening of her eyes, Xi surprised her by wasting no time scooping her up and marching quickly toward the hangar. While surprise hadn't been the intent, Xi gave herself a little pat on the back for a nearly 98.96 percent accurate chance that she'd correctly analyzed Kentt's emotional reaction at the moment.

The telepath sighed as her head slid to rest on Xi's shoulder. "Will you take us home, Xi?"

"I will take you to the *Audacity*. Capital cannot be reached yet. Will that suffice?" Xi stopped at the hatch leading from this chamber and pressed her knuckles into a palm pad. She'd removed all security settings on this door, so it *should* work, but she wasn't entirely certain until it actually did open.

"Yes. Yes. The *Audacity*. That's what I meant."

Xi wanted to ask what made a place home, as she started down the corridor, but Kentt's energy levels and vital signs were dangerously low. She recorded the question for later research. She settled for a simplified version. "The *Audacity* is your home now? For the moment?"

As usual, Kentt did not answer the question directly. "I've missed it. Haven't you?"

"I… I am not sure what that feels like." Did it feel like hovering in a metal supply cabinet for days, fixated on a particular cylinder and how one could sabotage or destroy it to free the victim inside, so that one day one might get to return to a place that was safe, that was… better in a way one couldn't quite articulate? "I believe I missed you," she said, as soon as she realized.

There was a soft hum from the back of Kentt's throat that Xi did not understand. Yet another thing to add to the unending list. "I missed you, too."

Xi found herself smiling as she reached the last hatchway before the hangar. She stopped at the command pad nearby, checked the atmo levels in the hangar—still adequate to support one particular telepathic human life.

She found herself taking an entirely unnecessary deep breath as she ordered the hatchway to open. Let the *Audacity* still be there to carry them *both* away from this mess.

Home.

ELLEN HURRIED after Paul through the rusting, dripping corridors that hadn't improved during her time away from the ship. It didn't really make sense that such a precious resource as water would constantly be running rampant around this ship, degrading wherever it happened to slide, but sometimes, life didn't make sense.

They'd taken down Cassandra, only to have the *Audacity* dead in the deep as well. She couldn't count how many Therokis had been defeated, or even understand if they were still alive or dead, but did it even matter? If she'd lost Kael in the process… or Zhia or Roya or any of them…

Had anything truly been worth that price? She should've thought of another way. A way that didn't get so many of them hurt or killed or put in danger…

She'd won. And yet, she'd lost everything that mattered.

Paul stopped abruptly, and she was so lost in her thoughts, she almost ran into his back. "Shu, there you are. You said you had someone who needs to speak with me?"

"Yes, sir."

"Are we sure the asteroid will not break in half while we're speaking?"

"We're about seventy-six percent sure, sir."

"Is that a yes?"

"I'm not sure, sir."

"That does not make me feel better. Listen, the *Audacity* needs urgent assistance from us."

"Hey, I can just go to the brig. If you could send someone from Engineering, I can give them details." Right now, just staring at the steel ceiling was about all she had the energy for. "Oh, and a medic. I have a hole in my hand. There… might be some digit loss."

"You *what*?" Paul's eyes widened.

"Wait, Ryu will want to hear this, too, sir."

She frowned. "I will?"

"All right, but first—send word to Engineering to help the *Audacity* with their spare parts problem, please. Immediately. At the very *least*, get them what they need to repair their parts printer and start making parts on their own. If we have the right things, that ship's probably a decade younger than the *Everest*—maybe we can make some fortuitous trades and get everybody a smoother ride."

"Yes, sir. Sending a message now." She scribbled into her tablet. Then she spoke into her comm to sick bay, summoning a medic to a nondescript cabin. "Please, right through here."

They all sat together at the table. "Okay, put the call through," said Paul.

The wall display flickered to life. Ellen raised her eyebrows.

Paul shot to his feet. "Jim! You're alive!"

"Nice to see you, too, Paulie. Indeed I am, but not for the enemy's lack of trying. You didn't think I'd go down that easily, did you?"

Paul sat slowly, his face stern. "No offense meant. We faced quite the formidable force here… I'm not quite sure how *I'm* alive, to be honest with you."

"We managed to root out a Songbird cell here… eventually. And I only had to almost die six times to do it."

"Eight times, sir," someone muttered off screen.

"The one in the bakery doesn't count."

"Pardon?" Paul leaned forward.

"Nothing, nothing. That's not the point of this call. I have some news that is relevant to your captive, Captain Dealis."

"Oh?" Paul glanced at her. "Considering she wasn't my captive an hour ago, that's news to me…" he muttered.

"Pardon?

"Nothing, nothing. Carry on."

Jim smiled. "I received some very surprising reports from two of your subordinates, Captain Dealis."

"Oh?"

Ellen's gut twisted. She didn't like the sound of that.

"Yes, Lieutenant Shu and Ensign Mertz had some very interesting things to point out—both with respect to the law and Union operations—on this one."

"The law?" Oh no. So much of everything that had just happened probably couldn't have if Paul hadn't known the right people in the right places at the right time… There were reasonable accusations of nepotism that would likely be made. And surely, some would object to how he put his crew's life in danger on a whim that *could* have turned out to be a lie or a trap or a wild goose chase. It hadn't been, but…

"Ensign Mertz, you were the one that pointed this out to me. Would you care to illuminate the issue for us?"

She braced herself.

Blushing, Mertz ran a hand through his maroon hair before he spoke. "It is really due to Lieutenant Shu's astute observations that I noticed anything. She repeatedly pointed out the extraordinary nature of our difficulty to get ahold of the facts around this case. I noted that all that red tape was, in and of itself, suspicious. When we were able to obtain some of the information through… extraordinary means…" He cleared his throat, glancing at the ceiling like he was trying to avoid glancing at her. "We were then able to externally validate its accuracy. Then we sent the highly unethical and unusual details of the situation to Senator Dealis."

"Why didn't you come to me?" Paul demanded.

"We wanted no potential conflict of interest, sir," said Shu. "And you were busy."

Paul opened his mouth, his face reddening slightly, then seemed to rethink his objections and shook his head. "Proceed."

"The problem they reported to me," Jim continued, "was that the Songbird Project violated the Union's own laws, specifically the Heroes Rights Act for Soldiers and Sailors of 2284. In particular, that act forbids any military branch from experimenting on its members without their knowledge and informed consent."

"Which this project clearly did not have," Mertz cut in.

"It is common for general research projects to be periodically checked for compliance here," Shu said, "and it is also common that compliance officers don't have the levels of clearance needed to verify the behavior of the most top-secret research projects. Further, they often aren't informed the projects even exist. If a top-secret project is known to only a few, compliance officers must rely on those running the project to follow the rules willingly—or inform them of their existence. And if they don't..."

Mertz pressed his lips together. "Nobody can do a thing about it. Unless word gets out."

As they'd been speaking, another few officers strode in. One of them had a captain's insignia, and her uniform read WEYER. Huh, had the *Lhotse* docked on the asteroid as well? Maybe they knew the asteroid was stable.

Or maybe the *Lhotse* was in bad shape too. Whatever the case, Weyer and her staff didn't speak, just settled in beside them. Paul greeted them with a nod.

Jim smiled, catlike, almost predatory. "Yes, in fact, when I was able to unseal the records by showing up at Rios III myself, they even included clear documentation of how each person was entered into the program and how many of them were entered into the project due to being in reconstructive hibernation for an extended period. In other words, unconscious and unable to consent."

Ellen cleared her throat. "I'm glad you uncovered the truth of this project. Maybe you can add this to Tauber's posthumous trial. But it doesn't change anything. The past is in the past."

"Oh but it does change things, Ms. Ryu." Senator Dealis adjusted the uneven lapels of his suit and straightened. "I have the pleasure to present to you, if only in digital form at the moment, this certificate of honorable discharge."

She blinked. "What?"

The senator smiled. "In the eyes of the laws and courts of the Union, including a ruling by General Koia Sectera, you are no longer a deserter or wanted for any crime in the eyes of the Union. At least, at the current moment."

She caught her breath. "You—what—you've got to be kidding."

"Do I look like I'm joking, Ms. Ryu? Additionally, if and when it suits you, I would like to welcome you to the Inner Planets for a formal retirement ceremony."

"That's not necessary—" she started.

"No, it's not," he added. "But I'd like you to consider it anyway. And please also consider bringing along Lieutenant Shu and Ensign Mertz who deserve to be recognized for their dedication to the truth, law, and human rights on this issue. They've done their part to stamp out corruption in our great Union. My high recommendation has also been added to their personnel file."

Shu was blushing now, and Mertz had covered his mouth with his hand, as if trying to hold in some excited exclamation.

Senate recommendations would advance their careers substantially. And a big award ceremony full of pomp and circumstance? They'd be much talked about for a time, if not a bit famous. Shu might even get a ship of her own out of it, eventually. And the senator would be in all the pictures, smiling for the camera.

That was the game Dealis was playing—she should have known. Not so different from his brother. It was a win-win, she supposed. Dealis would link himself to positive causes—and these noble young officers, and her war record, and a recent victory, if they told of what had happened today. Victories were all too hard to come by.

And why not lift up these officers and his own brother, who had the intrepid spirit to actually track down the elusive deserter—but also the wherewithal to clear her name? A campaign story easily spun. She could see it now.

Getting paraded around on the arm of not one Dealis but two sounded like torture, but at the very least, she owed it to Mertz and Shu to consider tolerating it.

But if Kael were still… like he was now… she couldn't ever leave him for that. Heat pricked at the corners of her eyes. She blinked hard, looking up toward the ceiling.

It took a long moment before she could speak again. All of them staring at her didn't help.

"Of course I'll consider it," she said. "We can discuss—at a later time. I, uh, still have a hole in my hand, though. I think the medkit may be running out of battery." Or her painkillers were wearing off. Or the adrenaline, or both.

"You—what? Ma'am!"

Lieutenant Shu swore and attacked her tablet. "Where is that medic?"

"It also means," the senator said, surprising her, "that Colonel Tauber violated the human rights of over seventy-six soldiers, sailors, and marines that we know of. Captain Dealis and Captain Weyer, I order you to put the colonel under arrest and transfer him immediately to the Inner Planets for trial."

Weyer pursed her lips and looked at the table. "I, uh… Well, sir. That's going to be difficult."

Jim frowned. "What is it?"

"It's my fault," Paul said quickly. "We blew up his ship, Jim."

"You *what*?"

"He's pretty dead," Weyer added.

Paul waved a hand in the air. "He was trying to kill us all!"

Jim's frown deepened. "But there were innocent people on the *Volga*."

"Actually, I'm not sure there were, sir," said Weyer. "I took a shuttle over here. Meanwhile, my crew has been boarding what remains of the *Volga* to see if we find any survivors. But they haven't found anybody alive. In fact, the whole place looks like it was torched a while ago. Before we got there. Some real weird stuff in that ship, Senator. I don't want to know. I don't think you do either."

"Dammit." Jim sighed. "It's been that kind of week. All right, all right, well... I can still have the trial posthumously. Screw it! I do want to know. I want every *shred* of evidence you can get from that ship. I want you to tractor the entire carcass back here. Maybe it will help us root out these traitors."

"Absolutely, sir." Weyer nodded. "Will do."

"I'm not letting his death sweep this abuse of power under the rug. I want an example made of this to keep it from ever happening again. Corruption must be made an example of. Now, I do need to get to my next meeting, so—"

"Wait, sir, there's something else." Ellen looked at the others. "There's another Alarus. Headed toward the Puritans right now. Tell him."

"I beg your pardon?" Jim asked.

"What the hell..." Weyer muttered.

Shu spoke up. "We need to get Admiral Sectera on the line. If you think we can trust her."

"I'm certain we can." Jim nodded. "She already had the chance to kill me."

"Twice," someone off-screen muttered.

Jim waved at whoever said it, glaring a little, then turned back to face the video camera, smiling.

"Even if we can trust Sectera," said Paul, "we should contact several admirals. It's easier to be sure they hold each other accountable. Mertz, get in touch with the staff of Sectera and Iosadar and Kedar as well."

"Yes, sir."

"We can brief the admirals, Senator," said Shu. "Long story short, there is a significant Songbird presence in the ships headed to the Puritan front line. It must be promptly eliminated."

The senator's eyebrows rose. "I'll trust you all to handle that. I've interfered enough. I'm lucky they'll still talk to me after I circumvented the chain of command. Now, do let me know if you run into any suspicious resistance. We *will* root these traitors out. Anything else, Captains?"

"No," Captain Weyer said quickly. "Thank you, sir, for putting us on the side of right in the end here. Your brother sure had me worried for a minute or two."

"He worries all of us in the family, all the time, so you're in good company."

Paul rolled his eyes. "Nothing further, Jim. I mean, Senator."

"Excellent. Ms. Ryu, please be in touch. And welcome to no longer being a fugitive. From the Union, anyway."

"Thank you, Senator," she replied. "I'm deeply grateful. I will contact your office soon. Maybe."

"Have a good evening, all of you." And then the elder Dealis was gone.

"He's handsome," put in Captain Weyer. "And he knows how much nonsense you get into, Dealis. So he must be smart. Is he married?"

Paul rolled his eyes. "He ate his boogers as a kid, I'll have you know."

"And you didn't?"

He made a disgusted noise.

"Yeah, right."

"No, he's not married. Now don't you have a piece of hull plating drifting into a gravitational field to take care of?"

Weyer snorted, grinned, and spun to walk away. "Probably do, yeah, but when I'm done…" She winked over her shoulder at him.

"That woman…" He shook his head as the door slid shut behind her.

"Is quite unique," Ellen offered.

"Is one of the best captains I've ever worked with, but definitely don't tell her I said that."

As if she'd actually heard him, Weyer suddenly turned and marched back. "Hey, while we're granting amnesty here or whatever, my prisoner's missing from my brig." She narrowed her eyes at Ellen. "You wouldn't have any idea how that happened would you?"

"I didn't make the giant hole I saw," Ellen said flatly, "if that's what you're implying. Holes, I guess. The Therokis were wrecking the place."

Weyer snorted. "Look, at this point, I don't give a shit. Dealis—the war hero here got her fancy certificate. Does that mean her boy toy is off the hook with us too?"

"He's not my—" The pain in Ellen's chest made it hard to object, but the words stammered out on their own.

"He's off the hook," Dealis said quickly. "Where is he, anyway?"

Ellen's mouth fell open slightly. Her face must have said it all, because their faces certainly did. All the mirth suddenly drained from them.

She tried to swallow the tightness in her throat so she could answer them. It only partly worked. "He's, uh… he's not dead. Yet. At least I don't think. He's in our sick bay. He's unconscious. I'm rambling. He might live. Maybe not, though."

"I'm sorry to hear he was injured," Weyer said carefully. "He is a brave and fierce soul. I hope he recovers."

"Me too." Her response was barely a whisper.

"Speaking of injured," Shu said sternly, "the medics never showed. We need to get this one to sick bay."

"Wait." Paul stood. "Before you go. I have something to say. The people who did this are never going to apologize. The Union will never apologize. But let me apologize. I'm sorry this ever happened to you, Ellen."

Their eyes were locked a long time. "It's okay," she said. "I forgive you."

His brow twitched slightly.

"For all of it." She swallowed. "We all make mistakes."

He snorted. "Not you."

"Even me."

His lip quivered.

"If you really want to make amends, stop that crazy operation before too many people are killed—Union *or* Puritan."

"We will stop it. I swear it to you."

She looked at the table, then back up at him. "And if you can't stop it, promise me you'll forgive yourself?"

"Now you're asking for a lot." A smile twitched up the corner of his mouth.

She turned toward the others. "Thank you, Shu, Mertz. I didn't think my situation really mattered to me, but… maybe it mattered more than I realized. It's more than just 'one less target on my back.' "

Mertz grinned. "We know."

Shu was stoic as always but nodded once, crisply. " 'Injustice to one of us is an injustice to all of us.' We couldn't just ignore it."

"Still. Thanks." Ellen blew out a breath. "Does that mean I can go?"

"Yes, ma'am, it does. To sick bay for your hand."

She nodded. And then she would go home. And maybe, just maybe, *Audacity* would even be able to fly.

CHAPTER TWENTY-TWO

ELLEN WASN'T sure she'd ever seen quite such a welcome sight as that of Arakovic's stupid asteroid drifting away on the view screen. Kael's fingers were cold in her hand. Her normal right hand.

The left one was still encased in medkits and splints, recovering from Dr. Dremer's augmentation surgeries. Her smallest two fingers had been casualties, as well a large part of her palm. When her healing was complete, the fingers would look ordinary, but yet another part of her had gone cybernetic. Maybe if she lived long enough, she'd be able to compete with Kael.

Audacity hummed quietly around her, not perfectly mended. But mended enough. Perfection was illusion anyway.

She was grateful to be safe. Grateful to be alive.

She squeezed his fingers and hoped that he'd squeeze back , if even just once. Zhia's unit beeped quietly beside them.

Watching the asteroid fade away gave her a flash of anger. Why did people always think they knew what was best for other people? Why couldn't they just leave well enough alone? If it weren't for Arakovic and her misguided pursuit of peace, maybe she and Kael would be having dinner somewhere a hell of a lot nicer than this ass end of a galaxy's asteroid-filled backwater.

Then again… If it hadn't been for Arakovic, she'd never have met Kael. Or Zhia, Doug, Dremer, or any of the people she most cared about in the world at this point. The deaths, the corruption, the cost —nothing would ever be worth those. But could she really say she'd go back and change anything?

She rubbed her face with her good hand, then curled her fingers around his again. She needed sleep. It'd been hours that she'd been sitting here while they ran diagnostics and prepped for liftoff. She wasn't thinking straight. The past couldn't be changed, so what did it matter what she wished about it?

It had all happened, for good or ill. Wishes for the future wouldn't amount to much more than a hill of beans either. All she could do was be here, in a somewhat unfounded optimistic hope that maybe her presence mattered to one or both of them.

Their John Doe, Udo Trynkei, had never woken up, though. She really had no illusions about the direness of her situation. Kael wasn't going to wake up either. But, at the moment, she couldn't seem to bring herself to accept that. What if she was wrong, and he did wake up, and she'd given up too soon? Ugh, this was horrible.

"I hate being helpless," she murmured.

"I concur, Commander," Xi said, interrupting her thoughts.

"Hmm? Oh." She hadn't quite realized she'd said it aloud. "Sorry, I'm tired. When will we reach the home world, Xi?"

"The *Alarus Octendi* home world is about three days' transit time."

"Thanks." Three long days of this. It sounded like pure torture.

She leaned back in the chair she'd dragged into sick bay for this purpose. Well, she didn't know what the purpose was exactly. She doubted her presence did anything. But she couldn't really bring herself to be somewhere else unless she was urgently needed.

"You better wake up, you brute," she whispered. "You should be the one to scatter Roya's ashes. You started all this, waltzing onto my ship with that capsule."

His breath was slow and even, and although she scrutinized

every crevice of his face for a twitch or any slight reaction, she saw nothing she hadn't seen five minutes ago.

Yeah, ordering him to wake up wasn't going to make it happen, or she'd have done it a thousand times. Still, she squeezed his hand again.

"You were never great at following orders," she muttered. "And I fell in love with you anyway. Can you believe that?" She shook her head. Her vision blurred. Certainly not from tears. She'd never been a crier, and she certainly hadn't cried like her heart was bleeding in the last day or two that they'd repaired the ship. Not that she really knew how many hours had passed. Not that she cared.

"How am I ever going to care about anything ever again?"

No one answered her. It was nice that none of her friends, not even Xi, were quick to lie to her, but in this case… she'd have appreciated any answer, any hope that there was some way this pain might someday go away.

She'd been happy as hell to fight or die trying. But sometimes, surviving was worse.

ELLEN HEARD footsteps coming up the hall toward sick bay.

"How is he?" Zhia leaned against the hatch and smiled at them. Mo leaned against the doorway, greeting Zhia with a nod.

"Glad to see you're feeling better," Ellen managed. "Up and about."

"Miracles of morphine and cybernetic hip replacements. But enough about me. How's our trooper?"

"Biologically, the machines say he's fine," said Jenny, checking some cables feeding into Kael's arm. "He's… deeply asleep."

Ellen ran her fingers over the back of his hand. "He never slept this deeply, as long as I knew him. Not… most of the time anyway."

"I'm sure he'll snap out of it. That was a hard battle. We don't know what it took to match wits with Cassandra," said Jenny.

Ellen didn't want to think about it.

Jenny took off a glove and started entering something into the nearby console. A band circled one finger, the shine catching Ellen's eye. "Hey, what's that?" She pointed.

Zhia grinned. "The commander hasn't seen the ring!"

Now it was Jenny's turn to blush. "I know it's not strictly by the book, safety-wise… but with all our injuries and this crazy mission, I thought we needed all the luck we could get. And... then I just never took it off."

Ellen waved at the air. Their "mostly military" rules of decorum still applied and always would. "Is that strictly decorative or…?"

"Or does it have a certain meaning?" Zhia finished.

Even Mo was smiling now. "She showed it to us when she got it, Commander, but I didn't have you two to do all this drilling for me."

Jenny looked at each of them in turn, like a mouse trapped in a corner. If she could've run or climbed out the ceiling, Ellen was sure she would have. "Adan got it for me."

Ellen raised an eyebrow. "So you're going to have little climbing bionic babies together and stuff? That's great, Jen."

"We don't know what it means exactly yet." Jenny's face was red as a pepper now. "Just that it means something. I don't know. Hard to make plans when you're flying toward your possible death and all. Felt a little delusional."

"We're all delusional in love," Zhia said simply.

Ellen cleared her throat. "Look at me. I've been sitting here for like three weeks."

None of them said anything, the look of concern and sympathy on their faces *not* helping her feel better.

"I was trying to make a joke. Bad one. Sorry." Ellen forced a smile. "Something is enough. Sometimes you just know, something is different, and it will never be the same." She looked to his face and curled her fingers tighter around his.

"You never know," Jenny said gently. "Hang in there. We're almost to Tarkos. Isa thinks maybe… with help…"

She waved at the air again. "Don't. Like you said. I don't need delusions about the future. I don't need hope—"

"We all need hope." Jenny's frown was deep.

"Hope should be based on something," she snapped. "It should be rational."

Zhia cocked her head to the side. "Should it? Is it *ever* really?"

"Lots of people have done the impossible," Mo said. "All *he* has to do is wake up. Lazy Theroki."

The air was tense for a long moment, the silence pregnant, before all of them burst into laughter, tinged with sadness.

"Keep calling him that," Ellen said, wiping wetness from her eyes that was certainly from mirth and not pure agony, or a mixture of the two. "Maybe that'll get through that metal skull."

They chatted for a while longer. First Zhia retired, still weak from her surgeries and wounds and needing to rest. Mo listened in silence most of the time before finally drifting away with a quiet nod.

She and Jenny talked a while longer, about what to do next, about the stars, about the past, about the future. Before Jenny turned in for the night, she ran a hand over Kael's forehead.

"Wake up, silly Theroki. We have work to do. Good night, Ellen. You get some rest too."

Ellen nodded. But she woke, who knew how much later, when Dr. Levereaux found her, asleep in the chair, her head against Kael's hands.

"Go to bed," Levereaux said gently. "I'll sit with him. That hand will heal faster if you actually sleep."

Ellen followed the doctor's orders. But when she lay in the bed that the two of them had shared, it took a very long time for sleep to come. She thought about Yamamoto and the ten members of the squad and all the others who, like Kael, were lost to her after that blasted asteroid. She turned on the wall display and stared at the pictures of nature that Kael had once watched, not sure if she was searching for peace or just some scrap of him to hold on to.

It would be the first of many nights like that. And when they reached Tarkos, and she sat listening to the ocean, she only thought of him, the time they'd sat together on the beach the first time he'd seen the ocean.

Sleep was a stranger. There was only pain and loss.

QUIET. Everything was quiet, and it had been for such a long time.

Nobody could get to him here. He'd often hidden like this as a child, from attackers, from sandstorms, from hungry dogs. He always had to leave eventually, when he got too hungry or thirsty, but strangely, that hadn't happened yet. It had been a very long time.

But if he didn't need to leave to survive... Staying hidden, staying safe—that was the wise option.

Outside of his hiding place, he heard voices.

"Whoa. What happened to him?" He was sure he didn't know the voice. He kept absolutely still. Were they talking about him?

"That's Cassandra's last victim." A different voice. Both feminine, but not his mother. Where were they? Could they see him?

His heart pounded against his ribs, but he kept his breathing slow. Whoever this Cassandra was, it didn't sound like he wanted to know or get mixed up with her. It was best to lie low, stay hidden.

He closed his eyes, like not seeing would make *them* not see *him*. It seemed to work. In the ensuing quiet, he drifted off to sleep.

"It's not without risk." A new voice woke him from his slumber. Perhaps he'd taken the quiet for granted. "What if she's still in there?"

"What if *he's* still in there?" This was another feminine voice, but younger. The passion in her voice was surprising for some reason.

"Isa, the risk is real." The speaker was pained. The name twisted something in his gut, but he couldn't place it.

"Better to die trying than to lie down dead, Kentt."

"Did you steal that from his memories?"

He caught his breath. Something about those words... they felt powerful. Powerfully familiar, too, like something he'd had tattooed on his heart. He looked down at his skin for the words, but then shook his head.

He was being silly. He was just a kid. He didn't have any tattoos, and he didn't know any girls named Isa, and if he just stayed here in this hole, he'd be okay.

For a while, the silence returned.

He was dozing off later when a glare abruptly woke him. Above him, a triangle of light cut into his world, slicing into the dark rectangle of his cement sanctuary.

What—or who—was this? Maybe he would need to leave after all.

Kael?

Who could it be that knew his name? So few knew his name.

Especially after his mother had died. That was the first time he'd holed up here. His chest ached at the memory.

Kael?

It was a woman's voice. But it couldn't be his mother's. Technically, he couldn't remember the sound of her voice, so he couldn't say for sure, but she was gone. Dead. Who could it be? Unlikely to be someone he could trust—that was no one.

Something about the thought rang untrue. No, there was another. A woman.

An image flashed through his mind. Brown eyes, a smile somewhere between feral and amused.

The image fled, and he was alone again. He squeezed his eyes shut, but the light still glared down at him. He wanted to sigh, but he was too exhausted to even bother. Who had to come here and bother him? He'd been safe, this had been easy.

Now, he'd have to run again. And defend himself from whoever was poking his pathetic excuse for a home with their stick. And do it all alone. Always alone.

The sense of wrongness tugged at him again, the image of the woman nudging at him like an ocean wave that had gone out and was rolling back in again. Charcoal hair. Striding around her desk to rest one hip on the corner. Folding her arms and frowning at him. Sexy as hell.

Kael? A hand reached down into the tunnel, into the darkness.

Ellen.

The enormity of it crashed over him, years' worth of memories, years' worth of pain. The final moments. Cassandra. Roya. Ellen.

Oh, God, was she dead? Had she made it out alive?

Had *he*?

He lunged toward the hand, reaching out to grasp it, jumping with every bit of strength he had left—into the light.

CHAPTER TWENTY-THREE

ELLEN SAT ON THE BALCONY, looking out at the waves. Clouds covered the heavens in a cottony blanket of white, the air warm and humid around her. Her green tea had steeped a little too long. It was bitter and cooling in her hands, the steam wafting across her skin as the ocean waves crashed against the beach below. The wind had a pang to it, a warning of a storm on the horizon.

Six months.

It was a little embarrassing, but in the six months since… everything had happened… Ellen had become a creature of persistent, robotic habit.

At first, she'd stayed in sick bay all the time. All the time they'd let her, anyway, which was most of it. There'd been breaks, of course. When they'd landed to scatter Roya's ashes in the vast ocean deep, she'd gone. But as soon as she'd stepped back aboard the *Audacity*, she'd been back at Kael's side.

Eventually, though, it became clear that she couldn't just sit in sick bay forever. And when days turned to weeks, she'd had to face the inevitability of it. The terrible, overwhelming, oppressive certainty that this might just be her life now.

He might never wake up.

And as much as she might have liked to never leave him, in practice, it was making her physically sore, sitting so long. Emotionally sore, from staring down the pain all day. And bored. Oh, so, bored.

Alternating between searing torture and boredom—a sure way to off herself, if that was what she'd wanted. And the thought did occasionally cross her mind. She could see why it had crossed Paul's.

But Kael wouldn't have wanted that.

Still, living no longer made sense the way it had before. It felt… bizarre. Pointless. Why bother?

So she'd approached it mechanically. With a plan, a strategy. She'd even written it out in her tablet. Things that were necessary for life—what were they again?

Eating. Sleeping. Water. Exercise. Work. Repeat.

She designated a time for them and proceeded to do them robotically, without passion, because he would have wanted her to.

The green tea on the balcony was part of that. She moved her hand from her lap to her mouth, the requisite motion required to consume the antioxidants and hydration. Staring at the ocean, too, that was supposed to help.

Sometimes, she let herself remember things: sitting by the ocean, the day she'd bought him his first Foundation suit of armor, the first time he'd seen the waves. Sometimes, she remembered how he'd watch the nature scenes, part of Taylor's assignments for him, ocean included.

Sometimes, she didn't let herself think at all. Hand to mouth. Too weak, too bitter, too hot, too cold. And then she'd go inside and begin at least one hour of attempting to work.

It didn't always "work" to try to work. It didn't help that her "work" was suddenly unmoored as well.

Every single one of them needed a break. She hadn't wanted one, but they'd insisted. Dr. Levereaux had suggested settling down for a bit, helping out with the rehabilitation of the environment on Tarkos. And the Simmonses had been happy to purchase as many closed-down resorts as anyone's heart had desired now that their finances were back under their control.

Ellen hadn't taken part in the discussion, but apparently, they'd settled on three in a row, connecting a gorgeous stretch of beach.

So now, her work was supposed to be to think about what to do next and occasionally help the scientists with executing their elaborate plans for fixing the planet. Earth had been a lot farther gone than Tarkos when they'd arrived, and Earth had been rehabilitated, so the scientists were pretty sure Tarkos could be saved.

She, personally, hadn't been so sure. She still wasn't. It didn't make her want to hurry to finish her tea or stop staring at the ocean to go look at what the day would bring.

Nothing about the future seemed certain. Certainty seemed impossible. How was she supposed to make a plan? Everything was different now. Nothing would ever be the same.

The mission that had consumed her life for so long was complete. Her one most important companion, the one she'd wanted to be with forever, was no longer at her side, not really.

Had she ever told him that? About forever? She couldn't remember, and that hurt almost as much as not having him there.

How could she possibly think about a future coming out of a present that was so unexpected, so confusing, so… unmoored? Every time she tried to think, to plan further than her little robotic routine, all she got was question mark after question mark. What if she made a plan without him, and the next day he woke up? What if she kept waiting and just withered away to nothing on a balcony until her dust blew away in the wind?

Her tendency was to lean toward the latter. But if she really thought about it, what would he have preferred?

Certainly, he would have wanted her to live her life. But what *was* her life without him in it? She had nothing she wanted anymore. Even guilting herself that he wouldn't have wanted her to feel this way didn't work.

If he wanted her to live her life, then he'd have to wake up and make her, because as far as she could tell, she'd become an automaton, miming her way through the motions. Pretending at life.

Darker clouds were rolling in over the ocean. The storm approached.

Her mood dark, she finished the last of her tea and dutifully, according to her habit and plan, sat down at the desk. She opened her files.

The agenda for the day was the one changeable thing. Sometimes, scientists needed supply runs, security oversight, had questions. She was perhaps turning into some kind of weird resort slash lab administrator, but she tried not to think about it.

Today, her agenda had a generically labeled meeting just downstairs, at the conference room by the hibiscus flowers. In fifteen minutes.

She sighed. What she really wanted to do was climb back into bed. But she was nearly through her plan—food had been consumed, water and tea imbibed, and she'd assaulted her punching bag with less fury than she had in the past. But she'd mustered a little energy, letting herself think about her situation and all that she'd lost.

Hygiene, then—check. Now work. One hour, minimum.

Then fall apart. No sooner.

She fiddled with the files, trying to answer Doug's big question of what came next. But nothing would come.

She forced herself to read over what intel she could find about the shreds of Enhancer cells that remained. There was only evidence of a single one remaining. However, she kinda felt like all they needed was one to regrow, respread again, like some kind of invasive plant, one seed remaining, and all hell could break loose.

There were Puritan pirates marauding on Union frontier planets. There were bounties for bad actors that could be researched and considered. They could spend years just finding and rehabilitating all the facilities and planets the Songbirds had poisoned and destroyed.

They could… They could… They could… stare at the ocean and take a nap.

Perhaps they were right about the break. Perhaps she just hadn't really let herself take one. Maybe if she actually did, someday, the real her would come back.

She was pretty sure that woman had died next to Kael, though.

She checked the time. Five minutes till her meeting. She might as well head on over and be early.

"ELLEN?" He sat up abruptly, panting, like waking up from a nightmare.

The world around him was blurry and over bright. He blinked a million times, trying to bring it into focus.

For a second, he saw a medical-type room, a care unit he was lying on, and a dozen figures crowded around him, mostly wearing blues and blacks. The blurriness persisted, but he thought he saw Dr. Dremer's face. Maybe Isa's?

"What is your name?" That was *definitely* Dremer's voice.

"Dr. Dremer?"

"Your name is Dr. Dremer?"

"No, uh—" He rubbed his face. "Excuse me? What?"

"Yes, it's me. I asked, what is your name?" she repeated patiently.

He shook his head, trying to clear it. "Is this some kind of joke?"

"No, but we understand your confusion. When you're ready, please answer the question. Your name, please."

He groped for an answer. Sidassian? Disassian? Asidian? Rhee? Who was he even talking to, to remember what he was supposed to say? "Kael," he said finally.

The figures around him shifted uneasily. What? That was his name. He'd just left out the surname, so what? These were strange questions.

"How many fingers am I holding up?" That voice was Levereaux's. He could sort of make her out now that he knew from the voice.

He tried to focus on her fingers. "Four? It's real blurry. What is going on?"

"Where were you born?" Dremer asked now.

He scowled. He was way too out of it to gauge who he was talking to and, therefore, what he was supposed to say. Dremer was supposed to be on his side, right? "You want the real story or the cover one?"

She snorted. "Real."

"Faros. Somewhere in the tunnels."

Levereaux's blurry form looked down at her tablet—or maybe it was a clipboard. Then she looked back at him, and he could almost make out her typical dissatisfied expression, as if he were a specimen pinned to a board that didn't quite measure up. "How many brains does an Earth-native octopus have?" she asked.

"Ten, distributed through the tentacles," he answered easily. Then he frowned. Wait. How… how did he know that?

"And how many does an *Alarus Octendi* have?" Levereaux continued.

"Twelve…" he said grudgingly, because the knowledge was there, on the tip of his tongue. "It's similar to an Earth octopus, but it has three in its bulb. That's weird. How do I know that? Is Ellen here? Is she okay?"

Dr. Dremer didn't immediately answer. The room felt colder all of a sudden. "What are the coordinates for the planet the *Alarus Octendi* originated on?"

Slowly, gritting his teeth, he rattled them off. "What's going on?"

The scientists shifted again, subtly moving away from him.

"Who is this?" Dremer said.

A girl stepped out from behind her, eased closer, and gave a tentative wave. He squinted. "My eyes aren't really—Shirin!"

She rushed forward. "You *did* come back for me."

He hugged her hard, even though it made his head swim. "I heard you were there, on the ship."

"She was quite heroic," said Isa.

Shirin waved at the air. "I didn't do anything special."

"Other than patch the hull in a dozen places and save our lives at least once." Isa was smiling, he could tell from her tone. She smiled so rarely. "Nothing special."

He squeezed her tighter. "Are we done here? I have my own questions. Is Ellen okay?"

"Not quite," said Dremer. "Sorry. But yes, Ellen is safe."

"I have a few more questions." Levereaux paused. She did not sound sorry. "What is peace?" Apparently, that was the next question Levereaux had on her notebook.

He hesitated. Peace… peace is death, Roya had argued. Cassandra? Her ideal peace had been a living oblivion, subtly different but also in some ways the same. But he knew better, didn't he.

"*Salaam*," he said, bowing his head. "Peace is the absence of fighting. Not that I've ever known it. Maybe it's just a dream." His head was starting to spin. He flopped back down on the gurney. Maybe his adrenaline was running out.

"You hesitated there," Dremer said slowly. Maybe he'd passed their test. Or maybe she was just out of questions. "Tell us what's going through your mind, Kael."

"I'm wondering what the frag is going on. Why can't I see?"

"What were you thinking about with respect to the question?"

He sighed. "I was considering what Roya and Cassandra had argued were peace—but I know that's not what it is."

"It's not just the absence of war, my friend," Dremer murmured. "It's a positive state of justice. A wise man once taught us that."

"But the octopus brains and the coordinates… How do I know that stuff?" He brought one hand up to knead his forehead, a growing pressure behind his eyes. The other arm he kept around Shirin, who seemed to appreciate it.

"Do you feel any different?" Levereaux asked.

"Well, I can't see any of you for shit. My eyes won't clear, and I'm dizzy as hell."

"That's the drugs."

"What? Oh. Why…" His voice trailed off. They were worried he was dangerous, weren't they? He knew the answer. "Well, then, all things considered, I feel pretty good. Those random facts sprinkled in are making me a bit nervous though."

"No urges to kill all of humanity?"

He snorted, then he regretted it. He couldn't tell if Levereaux was joking or being absolutely serious. "Um, let me check." He paused for dramatic effect. "Of course not! Jeez, Levereaux, is that something you like to think about?"

"Isa?" Dremer moved toward his feet. "What is your analysis? Kentt? Pria?"

"What is going on? Who is Pria?"

"He is himself," said Isa.

"I concur." That was Kentt now. Blinking around, he could just make out her extra-bright eyes to his right. "Cassandra is dead."

"But… there is a little left." Isa's tone was sad.

"Can someone *please* fill me in here?" he pleaded. "Why isn't Ellen here?"

Dremer cleared her throat. "You've been in a coma. For a while. Isa, Kentt, and Pria used some tricks Isa learned from Roya to… bring you out of it."

"We reconnected your mind to your body," said Isa, pride in her voice.

"Okay, so why all the extra stuff, then?" he asked.

"We only have theories," Dremer replied. "We think that your mind was disconnected from your body while it was still connected to Cassandra. And when you were finally physically disconnected—"

"No, Cassandra was dead by then," he said.

"Good," said Isa, picking up the explanation. "But Starbird survived much of Cassandra and Roya too. The network was still intact until the nuke programs Ryu installed were able to gradually destroy it. There was a period you were connected to it."

He frowned, remembering all of Ellen's dreams. "So some of Starbird crawled into my head to stay?"

"Basically. You said Roya was there too?"

"For some period, yes. I'm not sure how long. She advised I hide to survive."

"You hid well," said Isa. "Almost too well."

"How long has it been? I feel weak. Exhausted. And why isn't Ellen here?"

"It's been six months."

He lost his breath for a moment, then shook himself. "Ellen. Can I see her? And can I get rid of these drugs too? This is like being seasick in a freefall."

They all exchanged looks.

"Kentt? Pria?"

"Who is Pria?"

"I agree with Isa's assessment. He appears to be himself with a little added… book knowledge, I suppose you could say."

"All right. Then let's get Ellen. We didn't want her here if you were… dramatically not yourself."

Oh. That hadn't even occurred to him.

"I'll turn down the drip," someone said.

"Is that you, Jenny?" he asked.

"Yep, alive and kicking. You should be able to see straight pretty quick."

He let out a sigh as he started to steady. Shirin's face came into focus.

She squeezed his arm. "We'll talk later, Dad."

He frowned. "Those are some awesome shoes. Where did you—"

"Why, thank you, Master Sidassian," Rich piped up, "I am so glad someone noticed!"

He shook his head, which he regretted because he instantly felt nauseated again. He ran a hand down his face. "Good to be back, Rich, Dremer—everyone."

ELLEN HADN'T THOUGHT it was possible for her mood to darken even further, but the storm seemed in sync with her soul and her torment, dumping down sheets of water just as it was time to walk to her meeting.

She didn't resent the change in the weather, though. She felt a weird connection to nature now that she'd rarely felt in her life, living mostly on steel ships in the deep. One might feel connected to a ship, but it wasn't the same. Metal boxes did not have weather and they did not shift and reflect or defy your moods.

Her hair was dripping wet when she made it inside the conference room. Many members of her team were clumped around the meeting table. Except, it didn't look like an ordinary meeting table. She stopped in the doorway, trying to make sense of the scene.

A beep cut through her confusion. She knew that sound, knew it all too precisely—the heartbeat of the monitoring machines in sick bay. But they weren't in sick bay.

Dremer turned toward her, smiling. "Ellen! How are you this morning?"

She didn't answer. You could only say "devastatingly horrible" so many times before it felt like you were being rude rather than simply answering honestly. She gestured at the crowd instead. "What's going on here?"

The bodies parted. The table wasn't a table but a grav stretcher, and on it—on it—he was—it was—he was sitting up.

Looking at her. Blinking.

"Kael?" The word exploded from her without trying. Her body felt somehow cold from the rain and as insubstantial as mist.

He swung his legs around and stood—only a little unsteadily—and rushed to her.

And picked her up off her feet.

"Kael, you're—Kael—you're—"

He smiled.

"He woke up," Dremer said simply, behind him.

"We helped him a little," said Isa quietly.

"Kael, you're—" Her brain seemed to be stuck in some kind of shocked loop, trying to kickstart itself after so long in persistent vegetative hibernation.

"You're all right. You're all right." He laughed with relief.

"I am. Except that I'm in the air. Where are we going? Put me the frag down."

"I can't. Not yet."

"You're awake." Her tone was still utterly amazed.

"I am. What is this place?"

"It's… complicated."

He looked out the door behind her. "Is this a resort? Is that a *snake*?"

"That's a hibiscus bush. And a palm tree. Oh that, that's a lizard, not a snake. But there *are* snakes here."

"Why are you two talking about snakes?" Shirin folded her arms across her chest, scowling almost like a mom finding her two children playing with snakes instead of two adults being idiots about them.

"Long story," Kael said quickly. "I'll be going now."

"Wait—what—"

But before she could protest any further, he was marching with her in his arms out into the rain. She could hear them all laughing behind her, someone calling out, "Have fun, you two."

"What are you doing?" she demanded. The rain hit them both hard now, immediately soaking them through.

"Losing the crowd. Tell me where to go."

"That way." Overhead, thunder rumbled, and for some reason, it made her grin.

"Is that the way to the snakes?"

"It's the way to my bed."

"Even better. We have some work to do."

"Work? You just woke up, and my work was supposed to be that meeting—"

"I have some work to do… on you."

"Oh. Oh. Very well, then. Proceed."

"You're all right." He still sounded shocked.

"I should be saying that to *you*. You've been in a coma for six months. You jerk, I thought you were never waking up."

"I'm sorry, Elle. I really am. I didn't know—"

"Don't apologize. It wasn't your idea. Jeez. I'm just happy you're awake now."

"How did we get away from the Union?"

"We just flew away. Shu and Mertz found a legal process for an honorable discharge because the original Songbird program should never have been authorized under Union law. I'm not a deserter anymore."

"Well, that must be so disappointing." He held her closer for a moment. "Which way?"

"Up that path. Yeah, now I'm just an ordinary old ex-soldier."

"Ordinary? Really, Elle."

"That way is my villa."

"We have villas? Do all ordinary ex-soldiers get villas?"

She snorted. "Levereaux wanted to help rebuild Tarkos. Resorts were abandoned, so… Doug bought a few."

He kicked at the door, and it swung open. "I hope that thing has a lock. I do not want visitors."

"There's a bolt—if you didn't bust it with that kick. Put me down, you brute, and I'll slide it—"

He managed to swing the bolt home with one knuckle and headed straight for the bed. The wide bed, with its white linens, sat next to some huge indoor plants and wide two-story windows that looked out over the ocean. Through the glass, she could also see the balcony where she'd sat that morning. A snake curled around the railing, making its way off of one tree and toward the branch of another.

Their eyes met, his twinkling. "Ellen Ryu, you have a mighty strange taste in vacations."

"I might say that reflects more on you and your highly strange taste in women than it does on me."

He snorted and laid her on the bed, sliding beside her. "I'm not going anywhere. For a long time."

"Me neither."

They were both quiet for a moment, listening to the crashing of the waves and the rain hitting the water.

"I mean," she said softly, "you can only have so many lucky hands. Sometimes, you have to cash in the chips while you're ahead." Her smile was crooked.

"That's what you say now. Wait until the next disaster strikes."

She snorted. "No, no. We've earned this. Rest. Retirement, maybe."

"Aren't you a little young for retirement?" He kissed her cheek.

"Yeah, but you're practically an old man, so…"

He chuckled. "You talk a big talk. But I know you. Eventually, something's gonna happen. And we will want to help. Try to save somebody. Even if it's hopeless."

She shrugged the shoulder that wasn't tucked against him, staring up at the ceiling, just breathing in him being beside her. His words… That had been who she was, before everything had happened. Before she'd thought she might have lost him forever. It seemed like the memory of another person, someone she'd only read about or a different life. Had she really been so passionate once, so devoted to making the world a better place?

Could that spark of fire ever really come back?

And yet, even his few words had stirred something in her. She wasn't sure if it was a memory of what once was or some new fire… and it didn't particularly matter.

She tore her eyes from the ceiling and met his. They were the same chocolate brown, filled with the same earnest laughter. "Well, what else do you want to do, lie down dead?"

"I think I nearly did."

"Good thing that you didn't."

Grinning, he crushed her hard enough against him that she squirmed until he loosened his grip. "Better to die fighting."

"Also glad neither of us did that. But first, we need rest. Quiet. The ocean. And, um—something a lot better."

"Cookies?" His eyes told her he knew exactly what she meant.

"Mmm. Definitely." She pressed her lips against his and shut her eyes. "Later."

WANT MORE?

WHAT COULD MAKE a loyal soldier break her word? Find out where the saga began, before Ellen ever set foot on the *Audacity*, in the free prequel *Deserter*.

AFTERWORD

Thank you so much for reading! This series was my longest yet, and it's hard to believe all that has changed since when I started writing about the *Audacity* in the winter of 2017.

Special thanks to Shelley, my editor, for prevailing on getting the last few edits done on this book in spite of personal upheaval and a fragging hurricane. Truly pulled through on your "oath of duty" there. Many, many thanks!

I have no further books planned in this world, but I may have some short stories. I'll certainly miss writing about Ellen, Kael, and crew. If you'd love more, reach out and let me know on my website: www.rkthorne.com. Or tell a friend about my work to support future books.

For news about my upcoming book releases, sign up for my newsletter: www.rkthorne.com/get-updates/

Most of all, may you have pleasant travels and never lose hope that together we can make the world a better place.

ALSO BY R. K. THORNE

The Enslaved Chronicles

Mage Slave

Mage Strike

Star Mage

"Takar at Night" (FREE Bonus Epilogue)

The Audacity Saga

The Empress Capsule

Capital Games

Child of Wrath

Songbird Rising

Oath of Duty

Deserter: An Audacity Prequel (FREE Bonus Novella)

The Legends of the Clanblades Series

Dagger of Bone

Blade of the Moon

Untitled (Forthcoming)

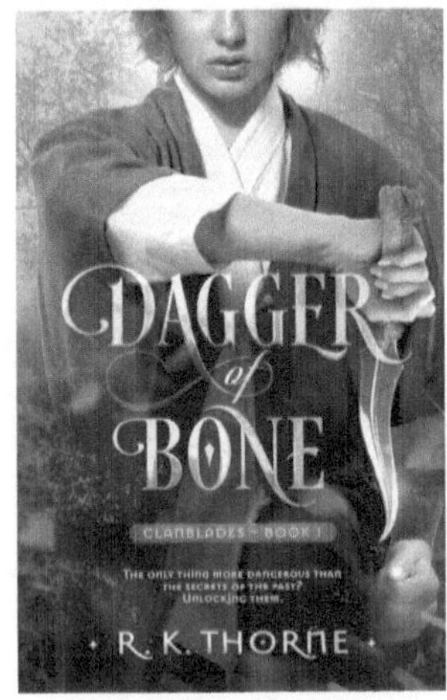

ABOUT THE AUTHOR

R. K. Thorne writes romantic epic fantasy and space opera that bubble over with action, humor, and hope.

A long-time gamer and dungeon master, she's fueled by her addiction to notebooks and yoga.

Too much coffee, RPGs, and really good books all keep her awake.

For more information:
rkthorne.com

www.ingramcontent.com/pod-product-compliance
Lightning Source LLC
Chambersburg PA
CBHW030541310726
48979CB00010B/1986/J
9781950993093